Buried in Secrets

Books by Denise Grover Swank

Buried in Secrets

Carly Moore Book Four

Denise Grover Swank

Chapter
One

Carly, you're going to be late again."

I glanced up from my computer screen and blinked at Carnita, the town librarian who had become my friend over the past seven months. She sat at her own desk about six feet away, perpendicular to the row of three computers for library patrons.

"Thanks." It wasn't uncommon for me to lose track of time, and if not for her, I'd never get to work on schedule.

"You must have found something fascinating to hold your attention that long."

I jotted one last piece of information down in my notebook and closed out the tab. "Yeah, well…"

"You must have enough information about the history of Drum to write a book," Carnita said, sounding excited. "Just imagine. A book to memorialize Drum!"

From what I'd learned about the history of Drum, it would be more like an exposé.

I laughed. "I'm no author, and even if I was, I'd stick to fiction. Did you happen to get those new Shannon Mayer books?" Before moving to Drum, I'd read almost exclusively e-books, but Drum, Tennessee was a rural town in the Smoky Mountains and internet access was sparse. While I could connect to the internet to download a book the library and Max's Tavern, my phone was a plain, pay-as-you-go model that struggled to find reception and didn't have internet access, and I didn't have a tablet.

She laughed. "Since you're one of the few people around here who requests books, I was able to order three. They should be here in a few days."

"And the new copies of the Baby-Sitters Club? I had a couple of girls at Tutoring Club ask about them."

"They're supposed to arrive next week, but I'll be sure to let you know when they show up." She smiled. "I appreciate you encouraging them to come in here and check out books."

"Who knows," I said, "maybe some of them will go to college one day. They need to learn librarians are their friends."

"If I didn't know any better, I'd think you'd been a librarian yourself," Carnita said warmly.

"Nah," I said. "I've just spent a lot of time in them." I grabbed my oversized purse off the floor and stuffed my notebook inside. "Thanks for taking my requests, Carnita. You're the best."

She beamed. "Girl, if you keep encouraging people to come in and borrow books instead of DVDs, I'll fill as many of your requests as I can!" Since most of Drum and the surrounding area didn't have cable TV either, the library had about three times as many DVDs as they did books.

"We both know the kids in Tutoring Club need to read, period, but the adults are a harder sell. I'm trying to get enough people together to start a book club," I said. "But they have to realize they like to read first."

"Keep it up, and I'll give you a permanent spot on the computer waiting list."

I laughed. "That sounds like a deal." I usually had to sign up for computer time a week or more in advance.

I headed out the door and down the block and a half to Max's Tavern to start my shift. Carnita thought I was researching the history of Drum, and she wasn't wrong. I'd just narrowed my focus to any seemingly motiveless crimes committed in the area over the last forty years. It had taken me months, but I'd come up with over two dozen. My goal was to tie them all back to Bart Drummond, the town patriarch who ruled with his wealth and his not-so-secret favor system. People came to Bart and asked for help—a multiple month extension on a late mortgage. Getting out of a DUI. Landing a job. Bart was often more than happy to play Santa, but his gifts came with a price: at some point, he would ask for a favor in return, and they would have to do it. No questions asked.

I was sure a few of those favors had ended in murder.

Part of Bart's power came from his family history. The Drummonds had helped found the town nearly two centuries ago. It was named after them, which only seemed appropriate since they'd run it since its inception—first with their moonshine business, and later, lumber profits. But moonshine was now legal, and the lumber business had shut down. The Drummonds didn't have the power they once had, but they hadn't been stomped to the ground either.

But I planned to put on a pair of heavy boots and finish the job.

I walked through the back door of the tavern, changed into my T-shirt, then headed out to the dining room.

Ruth was waiting on a table, but she shot me a quick glance that let me know she wasn't happy.

I sighed, wondering what was wrong. Ruth was the unofficial manager of Max's Tavern, mostly because Max, the owner, preferred for someone else to make the tough calls.

Although I counted her a friend, there was no denying she was temperamental, and she'd been extra moody lately. No one knew what she was so upset about, and we all knew better than to ask, but when in doubt, it was always safe to presume Molly was to blame.

Max was behind the bar, wiping down the counter where he kept the liquor bottles. They tended to get dusty since most customers kept to the basics in Drum—draft beer and whiskey. It was rare we got an order for a cocktail, and it usually came from a sporadic out-of-towner.

"Need any help?" I asked as I walked behind the bar. There were only two tables with customers and they both belonged to Ruth, leaving me with nothing to do.

"You want to clean?" he asked with a laugh. "You must have caught wind that Ruth's in a mood."

"All it took was a glance," I said. "What happened?"

"One word: Molly."

I resisted the urge to groan. Molly's sister, May, had been married to Franklin, aka Tater, who'd left her for Ruth. To say there was bad blood between the two women was an understatement. They were like gasoline and a lit match.

Max never should have hired Molly in the first place, but he often did things he shouldn't, and he refused to fire either one of them. Of course, he knew better than to try firing Ruth— she'd worked there longer than he had. Besides, he probably knew I'd walk out in solidarity. Moody or not, Ruth was my friend, and she wasn't two-faced. You always knew where you stood with her, and here in Drum, that stood for something. Molly, on the other hand, had made nice with Ginger, the other lunch waitress, only to paint her (and Ruth and me, of course) in a bad light to Max.

"You need to stop having them work a shift together," I said under my breath, so Ruth wouldn't hear. "You know it causes problems."

"I *didn't*. But I guess Molly left Ruth a note telling her she'd left the bathroom dirty last night."

I sucked in a deep breath, telling myself that I really needed to learn how to meditate. "*I* cleaned the bathroom before I left at ten last night, and only a handful of guys were left at the bar. So unless some drunk went in and peed or pooped everywhere, I'm sure it was fine." I gave him a look. "Did you check it?"

"Hell," he said in exasperation. "I didn't even know it was an issue until Ruth marched in the dining room an hour ago and shoved the note in my face."

"You know Molly's just stirring up trouble," I said.

"Well, I do *now*."

But that wasn't true. He'd known for a while, and in typical Max fashion, he'd buried his head in the sand and ignored it.

If he wasn't going to deal with this, then I was. "You *have* to fire her, Max. You don't need to wait until you find a replacement. Ruth and I can take on more lunch shifts, and Ginger might be able to pull a dinner shift every now and then if one of us needs a day off."

He frowned as he wiped down a bottle of brandy. Based on the yellowed label, it had to be a couple of decades old.

"When you find a replacement, the person should be part-time," I continued. "It's been hard to get enough hours for three full-time waitresses."

He should have fired her two months ago. Less than a week into her employment, it had become obvious it wasn't going to work. But Max hated conflict, and truth be told, he didn't like change. It was like pulling teeth to get him to do something that wasn't part of his routine.

"How about I take charge of looking for someone?" I suggested.

"I don't know," he said, his mouth twisting to the side. "I doubt Ruth will go for that."

"We both know something's going on with Ruth, so I'm not sure we should dump this on her. How about I tell her you've given us the green light to hire someone else. Maybe she and I can do it together."

"But I haven't even fired Molly yet."

"You need to do that tomorrow. First thing when she shows up. I'll cover her lunch shift. I'm coming in early for Tutoring Club anyway."

He gave me a sideways look. "So you're the one runnin' things now?"

I laughed. "Me and Ruth. Glad you noticed."

He grunted and turned back to his task.

I headed over to intercept Ruth, hoping the news that Molly would soon be history would cheer her up.

"You're never gonna believe what that bitch did now," she snapped, her eyes blazing.

I put a hand on my hip and shook my head. "Max already told me. He also told me that you're right. She's got to go." I knew better than to admit that I'd been the one to convince him. She'd be madder than a wet hornet that he'd listened to me and not her.

"Finally," she said with plenty of sass, but I could see the relief in her eyes.

"I told him that you and I are going to take charge of hiring her replacement. A *part-time* replacement."

She lifted her hands. "Praise the Lord."

"How do you want to go about this?" I asked. "Put an ad in the Ewing paper?"

"Maybe," she said. "I might know someone."

I wasn't sure what to make of that. She hadn't mentioned this mysterious "someone" two months ago, before Molly was hired, and even though we'd gotten more time off lately, neither one of us had much of a social life.

"Want to give me a hint who?" I asked.

"You don't know her. I'll give her a call and ask."

"Max hasn't fired Molly yet, so we need to be discreet until he does."

She rolled her eyes but nodded. Her mood hadn't lifted as much as I'd thought it would, which suggested something other than Molly was weighing on her.

A family of regulars walked through the door and settled down at a table in my section. The boy was part of my tutoring club, which Max and Wyatt had encouraged me to start back in April after I'd helped a couple of kids with their math homework. My cover story was that I'd tutored students as a second job, but the truth was I used to be a third-grade schoolteacher in my old life in Dallas. Back when I was Caroline Blakely, oil heiress, engaged to a man who'd conspired with my father to kill me.

"Miss Carly," the little boy called out as I approached their table. "I read part of that book about the guy in the underpants! Two whole chapters!"

"You did? That's great, Dustin!" I rubbed his head.

He beamed with pride. Reading had been a struggle for him, but after our first sit-down talk at Tutoring Club, I had concluded he just hadn't found anything he loved yet. I'd ordered some books of my own to hand out to the kids, and when they really loved a book, I let them keep it. The fact that he'd read two chapters since the day before, during summer break no less, was amazing.

His parents looked equally pleased. Thank goodness. His father had been resistant to his son spending part of his summer "learning."

I took their drink orders and then waited on a group of construction workers who looked beat from working outside all day. It was cooler at our altitude, but it was still hot working in the sun.

More construction guys came in soon after. There wasn't a ready supply of skilled labor on the mountain, so Bart had to bring them in from out of town to build his resort. Some of them stayed in the fleabag motel Max's father owned across the street, but the rest were holed up in Ewing, much to Bart Drummond's chagrin. Or so I'd heard. I hadn't seen the man for nearly three months. The last time I'd seen him, we'd stood side by side, studying the hole where his oldest son's girlfriend's body had been discovered.

The excavation and foundation guys had left, replaced by construction workers, electricians, and plumbers. The only continual workers were the construction manager, a few of his underlings, and my friend Jerry, an older man who was a permanent resident at the motel across the street.

Jerry was well into his sixties and had been down on his luck for as long as I'd known him, but it hadn't been difficult for him to land this job. The contractor had approached him in the tavern and offered him a full-time gofer gig on the spot. It stank of week-old fish, but I hadn't had the heart to destroy Jerry's happiness by saying Bart Drummond might be using him. Nearly three months had passed, and I hadn't caught wind that they were using him for anything nefarious. Then again, Bart Drummond loved to play the long game.

A little after seven, Wyatt Drummond walked through the door. He was Max's older brother and my former, sort-of boyfriend. If you could call seeing someone off and on for three weeks a boyfriend. I knew he preferred that term, and if he had his way, I'd be calling him that still. But Wyatt was the kind of man who collected secrets and wasn't generous in doling them out. Even though he knew the truth of who I was—who I'd been—I knew next to nothing about him, and he wasn't inclined to share. Worse, he'd pretended differently to keep me on the hook. In the beginning, he'd convinced me we could work together to take down our corrupt fathers. I was working alone now, but I fully intended to make both men pay their comeuppance. Because Bart Drummond knew who I was too, and he'd threatened my landlord Hank, which made this very personal.

Wyatt often worked the bar with Max on the weekends, but he rarely came in on a weeknight unless Max needed the night off for a rare date, or we were busier than usual. We weren't crazy busy, so I had no idea why he was here.

He made a beeline to the bar, straight for his brother. They talked for a few seconds, then Max glanced around the room and the two men headed for Max's office.

"What was that about?" Ruth asked, sounding more perplexed than upset that Max had left the bar unmanned.

"I have no idea. Are you good on drinks?" I asked. "My section's caught up if you want me to fill any orders."

"I'm good." She headed off to one of her tables, and I studied the entrance to the back. In the seven months I'd been around, I'd only seen the two of them hole up in Max's office twice. The first time was when Max was hiding Lula, their half sister, and it had happened again when Wyatt was about to be arrested for murder after his ex's body was found. Whatever they were discussing wasn't good news.

I considered going back and trying to eavesdrop, but a couple of customers walked in and sat at one of my tables.

About five minutes later, Wyatt walked out and headed for the front door. When he saw me, he gave me a long, unreadable look before he left.

"And what was *that* about?" Ruth asked behind me.

Max walked out of the backroom next with a haunted look in his eyes.

"I don't have a clue." But I intended to find out.

Chapter Two

I woke up the next morning, stretching in my bed and wishing for the umpteenth time that Drum had a gym. While I tried to make healthy meals for Hank and me, my hours at the tavern weren't conducive to exercise. Marco and I sometimes ran together, but I hadn't seen him in nearly a week…which was starting to worry me. We'd had a discussion that hadn't ended well, and now I wondered if he was giving himself space to figure out where to go from here.

Marco had been my best friend for most of the seven months I'd spent in this town, but a couple of months ago, I'd begun to realize I had more than friendly feelings for him. He'd made it obvious he had feelings for me too, but we both knew I had major trust issues.

Finding out your fiancé wanted to have you murdered tended to do that to a woman, and I'd followed up that disaster by dating Wyatt, whose secrets had nearly gotten me killed. After all of that, I'd resigned myself to possibly entering a nunnery.

So Marco and I both pretended we were just friends. Still, after our last conversation, it was clear our pretending wasn't going to work much longer.

I suspected he was already tired of our dance.

A soft mewl caught my attention, and I smiled as my nearly four-month-old gray kitten pawed at my hair.

"Hey, Letty. Good morning to you too." Maybe it was strange to name a cat after a person, but my kitten Violet was feisty and fearless and liked to do things on her own terms, just like my friend who had lost her life to cancer.

Scooping her into my arms, I snuggled her for a moment before she decided she'd had enough and jumped out of the bed, pawing at the bedroom door.

I followed her, heading into the kitchen to pour myself a cup of coffee. I was much too reliant on the stuff to keep me going. It was borderline unhealthy, but it was necessary since I got so little sleep. Maybe it was time to consider finding another job.

I nearly snort-laughed at the thought. I'd been lucky to get my job at the tavern. A good portion of the people in and around Drum were unemployed. I made decent money, and if I were being honest, I had nothing going on in my life other than work, hanging out with Hank and our two kittens, and the time I spent with Marco. And of course my tutoring club, but I couldn't run it if I didn't work at the tavern.

I took my coffee and opened the front door. Letty shot outside, running straight for Hank's bird feeder. Birds squawked and flew into the air in protest.

Hank, who was sitting in his chair on the porch, shot me a scowl. His crutch was leaning against the house and his kitten, Smoky, was curled up on his lap while he stroked the back of her head. Although we'd taken the cats in as a pair, Smoky had claimed him, and Letty had claimed me.

"Sorry." I set my full mug down on the table between the chairs. "Want some fresh coffee?"

He held out his nearly empty mug, and I went back into the kitchen and refilled his cup before returning to the porch. I handed his mug off to him, watching as Letty slunk around the bird feeder, probably hoping the birds would come back.

"I think we got the wrong cats," I said with a grin as I sat in the empty chair.

"You think I should've gotten the murderous cat?" he asked with a dark look.

I gave him a sideways look before I took a sip of my coffee. "I was thinking she stirs up trouble, but if that's your takeaway…"

Any sixty-seven-year-old man had a past, but Hank's was more colorful than most. Over the course of the past seven months, I'd discovered that Hank used to run the largest marijuana distribution outfit in eastern Tennessee, as well as some other illegal drugs. I still hadn't pinned down when he'd "retired" but my best guess was around a decade ago. Hank didn't like to talk about his past, and I usually didn't press him on it. I'd seen him kill a man without hesitation, then calmly tell me how to go about destroying the evidence. He'd shot the man to save my life, but the way he went about it told me it wasn't the first time he'd killed someone, and he'd pretty much told me that he suspected it wouldn't be the last. Drum, Tennessee wasn't exactly a sweet and cozy town, but it wasn't the town activities that had elicited the statement. He'd told me if my father or any of his men came looking for me, he'd kill them on the spot.

I believed him.

He laughed. "Girlie, you think you don't do your fair share of stirrin' the pot?"

I grinned. "Gotta keep things from getting dull."

Releasing a contented sigh, he leaned back in his seat and sipped his coffee. "You thinkin' about changin' your hair color?"

I reached for the ends of my shoulder-length hair. I was a natural blonde, but I'd been dying it auburn since I'd changed my name last November. "What makes you ask that?"

"The box of hair dye in the bathroom."

I gave him a puzzled look, then it dawned on me what he was talking about. "Ginger wants me to go strawberry blonde. She must have left it when she cleaned the house yesterday afternoon."

"That's too close to your natural color, ain't it?"

"Yeah," I said. It felt like a lifetime ago that I was blonde. "And no, I'm not going that light, although I'm kind of tired of being red." Poor Hank. Since my dye job was so much darker than my normal color, I was constantly touching up my roots. It seemed like the house was always full of dye fumes.

"It'd be easier to get a wig," he said.

I laughed. "You ever wear a wig, Hank?" I asked, then took a sip of my coffee. "They're itchy and hot." Then I added with a smirk, "And no. I'm not shaving my head."

"You can't spend the rest of your life dyin' your hair to stay hidden."

"Why not? Plenty of women dye their hair so often they don't even remember their natural color."

"That part's easy enough to figure out," he said with a snort. "They only have to look at their bush."

"Hank!" I protested with a laugh. "Gross. And most women wax down there now."

His eyebrows shot up. "They what?" Then his eyes narrowed. "Do…" He shook his head. "Never mind."

"Let me just say that the women in Drum seem to have other concerns, and I live in Drum."

He shuddered and grimaced.

We were silent for a moment, and I figured his thoughts had moved past the pubic hair (or possible lack thereof) of the women in Drum, but what he said still surprised me.

"I think we're goin' about this all wrong." He cast a glance in my direction. "Instead of keepin' you hidden for the rest of your life, we need to figure out how to bring the bastard down."

The bastard meaning my father.

My jaw dropped and I stared at him like he'd announced he was thinking about running through town naked. While I fully intended to do something about my father—after I got Bart out of the way—Hank had always been after me not to borrow trouble. "Have you lost your mind?"

"You're tellin' me that you intend to spend the rest of your life in Drum? That would be an absolute waste."

"And you're telling me you'd *leave* Drum?" I asked. "Because we're family now, Hank, and I'm not leaving without you."

"I was born on this mountain, and I'll die here. I ain't goin' nowhere. You, on the other hand, dropped in outta nowhere, and you can leave just as easily. But not until I know you're safe. I've been given' some thought on how to deal with your father."

I shook my head, staring at him in horror. "Hank, you need to stay *far away* from my father. He's no one to mess around with."

"You see a one-legged old man in this chair," he said with a look of defiance. "But I assure you, I was once a man to be feared."

"I know you were." My mind was working overtime, trying to figure out how to defuse this situation. "But one bad guy at a time, okay?"

"Why are you so damn set on bringin' down Bart Drummond?" he asked in contempt. "His history has nothing to do with you."

Because he threatened to release information to have you arrested. But I couldn't tell him that because he'd likely go confess rather than let that asshole think he was controlling me.

"You know I blame him for Seth's murder. I vowed to hold the people responsible for his death accountable."

"And you did," he said. "You killed Carson Purdy. And Carson and Bingham took care of the rest."

My first night in town, I'd see three men drag Hank's seventeen-year-old grandson out of a motel room several doors down from mine. They'd killed him in cold blood. Carson Purdy, Bart Drummond's ranch overseer, had been behind it. It wasn't much of a stretch to think Bart might have been involved too. Even if the authorities had claimed otherwise.

"We don't talk about your past much," I said. "But I need to know more. I need to know how bad it was."

"The past is the past," he said with a sigh, then his voice took on a hard edge. "I ain't that man anymore, but I can drag him out of the closet if need be."

"You can't take on my father, Hank," I said. "He's bigger and badder than Bart Drummond."

"Don't underestimate me, girlie," he said, stroking the back of the kitten's head. "I'm capable of more than you think."

That was exactly what I was afraid of.

Chapter Three

Molly's car was in the parking lot when I pulled in at five minutes before noon. I usually showed up earlier when I worked the lunch shift, but I had purposely arrived as late as possible, hoping to avoid the fallout of Molly being fired. I could hide out in my car and wait for her to leave, or I could go in and go over the lunch specials with the cook, Tiny.

I was done hiding from my problems, so I got out of the car.

Tiny was in the kitchen with his newest cook, Pickle, the fourth assistant cook since I'd started. The first had been murdered and the other two fired. So far, Pickle (the nickname Tiny had given him; Max had told me his real name was Fred) was working out better than the last two.

Tiny cast me a dark look when I stood in the doorway to the kitchen. "Don't you *think* about crossing that line."

Tiny didn't have many rules, but he wouldn't stand for anyone setting foot in his kitchen.

"Is Max talking to Molly?" I asked.

He cast a glance out through the server window, then grimaced. "Yeah, and it don't look pretty."

"Then I'm a refugee seeking asylum."

He laughed at that, then motioned me in. "I like you, kid."

I walked in and peered through the window myself. Max and Molly were standing next to the bar, and even though they weren't raising their voices, their body language made it obvious their talk wasn't going well.

I perched on a stool in the corner, out of sight from the front. "How long has that been going on?"

"Five minutes or so. Ginger walked in and heard 'em, then walked right back out."

"To be fair," Pickle said, "they were a lot louder when she walked in. Max started talkin' to her, which only pissed Molly off more."

I nodded. I suspected Ginger had headed over to Wyatt's garage to hang out with her husband until the coast was clear. "What's the lunch special?"

"Tuna melt," Tiny said with a look that dared me to protest. He knew I hated tuna melts.

"Good thing I had time to prep the dining room last night," I said. "We're gonna be lucky to open on time as it is." I leaned forward and got another glance at the two of them. Molly was pointing her finger at Max, jabbing it like she was trying to make a point. Thankfully, Max didn't look like he was about to cave.

Then Molly turned abruptly, and her gaze landed on me through the window.

I froze, wide-eyed, then sat back on the stool. "Shit."

A few seconds later, Molly showed up in the doorway to the kitchen. "Happy now, bitch?"

Tiny took a step forward and pointed to the back door. "You need to be leavin'. *Now.*"

Molly shot him a feral glare, released a frustrated growl, and threw the back door open so hard it bounced off the outer brick wall. She stomped out, then banged it shut behind her.

"That's the most excitement I've seen since I got here," Pickle said, his eyes shining.

"Stick around long enough and you'll see plenty more," Tiny said, then he looked at me with raised eyebrows, but his tone gentled. "The coast is clear now. You scoot."

I walked over to him and kissed him on the cheek. "Love you too, Tiny."

"Awww…" Pickle said with a grin.

Tiny's face reddened, the first time I'd ever seen him blush. I pulled my dinner out of my purse and put it in Tiny's refrigerator.

"My cookin' not good enough for you?" he asked as I shut the door.

"On the contrary," I said with a laugh. "It's too good. My jeans were getting tight." I stuck my thumb under the waist of my jeans to demonstrate.

He rolled his eyes, and I shot him a grin as I walked off to stow my purse in my locker in the backroom. Max was behind the bar when I walked into the dining room, his hands on the counter, his head hanging between his arms.

"You okay?" I asked softly as I approached him.

He stood up and released a sigh. "I fuckin' hate that part."

"I know," I said. "But if it makes you feel any better, everyone thinks you did the right thing. Even Tiny."

He nodded, but he didn't look any happier. "Someone needs to call Ginger and tell her it's safe to come back."

He seemed like the logical person to do it, but I guess he felt he'd done enough for the day. I sucked it up and called Drummond Garage, cringing when Wyatt answered and not Junior.

"Drummond Garage."

"Tell Ginger it's safe to come back," I said without introduction.

"Carly?" he asked in surprise.

"Yeah. Just tell Ginger that Molly's gone."

He was silent for a moment, then said, "Everything okay over there?"

"Yeah. Peachy." I hung up, feeling guilty although I had no idea why. I sure didn't regret getting Molly fired, and I had no idea why I'd feel guilty over Wyatt. He might still think we belonged together, but that didn't make it so. He'd made his bed of distrust and deceit, and now he could lie in it. I didn't owe him a damn thing.

I went and unlocked the front door. It was several minutes after noon, and I found myself facing down some angry customers. Not that I blamed them. They were construction workers who only got an hour for lunch, and at least twenty minutes was spent on the drive from the construction site and back. We'd just stolen part of their time.

I apologized as I let them in, telling them their drinks would be on the house, and shot a dark look at the bar, daring Max to contradict me.

I started taking orders and Ginger showed up about five minutes later. She looked worried, but it was too busy for me to fill her in about Molly. We'd just gotten things under control when two middle-aged women walked in. Even though I'd mostly worked nights and weekends the past few months, I'd done enough lunch shifts to know the regulars, and Diane and Martha were part of a small group of women who always showed up on Fridays for lunch. Today was Tuesday.

"Good afternoon, ladies," I said good-naturedly when they took a seat in my section. "What a surprise seeing you today."

Diane gave me a pointed look. "Emergency meeting. Sandy will be joining us." Which meant they were one short of their usual number. The fourth member of their cohort was a woman named Pam. But if it was an emergency meeting, it stood to reason at least one of them would be a no-show.

"Okay," I said, surprised by her serious tone. One of the reasons I loved them was because they liked to order frozen margaritas with their lunch—an unusual request at Max's—and they always seem to have fun.

"You haven't been here for about a month or so," Martha said, looking me up and down. "Did you take a vacation?"

"One of our lunch shift waitresses isn't with us anymore, so I'm covering her shift." Then I smirked. "Does *anyone* around here go on vacation?"

"We used to go to Dollywood," Martha said. "When the kids were little."

Diane snorted. "That's not a vacation. A vacation is gettin' away somewhere far enough away that you can't come home for a potty break."

"Not all of us can hold it forever," Martha said in disgust. "Some of us had bladders that were wrecked in childbirth. All three times."

That was my cue to take my leave, but first I needed to get their order. "You want your usual frozen margarita pitcher? And an extra glass for when Sandy joins you?"

"Yes," Martha said a little too exuberantly.

"Most definitely not," Diane said with a stern look. "We need all our wits about us today." I'd figured out months ago that Diane was the unofficial leader of the group. Sandy, the woman they were waiting on, gave her trouble from time to time, but Martha and Pam usually went with the flow.

Against my better judgment, I said, "This sounds serious."

Martha's mouth pinched. "Pam was arrested last night."

My eyebrows shot up. While the group of four friends could be a little on the rowdy side, they weren't criminals by any stretch of the imagination. Pam must have been arrested for unpaid parking tickets or something of the sort, although no one got parking tickets around here. Most people were arrested for drug possession or DUIs.

"Martha!" Diane admonished.

"What?" Martha shot back, getting irritated. "It's not like I'm saying anything she couldn't find out from the *Ewing Gazette.*"

"Does she look like the kind of woman who reads the *Ewing Gazette*?" Diane asked.

I gasped in surprise. I wasn't a subscriber, but I read the *Ewing Gazette* religiously at the library.

Diane must have realized I was offended, because she rolled her eyes. "Sorry, Carly. I completely forgot you're not from around here."

"Or that she's the one who started the kids' tutorin' club and literacy initiative," Martha grumbled, her arms crossed over her chest.

I waved off her words. I wasn't looking for accolades, and flying under the radar had its merits. "Don't worry about it. And Martha's right. If it's in the paper, I'll find out eventually. Save me some time and tell me what she was arrested for."

"Murder," Martha whispered.

My eyes shot wide. Pam was meek and mousy and the last person I'd suspect of murder. "Oh, my word. There has to be some kind of mistake."

"Sadly, *no*," Diane said with disgust. "There's no doubt she killed him. There were multiple witnesses."

It sounded too crazy to be true. "Then I'm sure it was justified, and she'll get off in no time." My mind was racing, trying to fill in the blanks. Was she a victim of domestic violence? I just couldn't see Pam committing cold-blooded murder.

"I don't know," Martha said with tears in her eyes. "It's not lookin' so good."

"I'm sorry I'm late!" Sandy called out as she slid into the chair between the two women. She was wearing a pair of shorts and a dirt-smudged T-shirt. Most people didn't dress up around Drum, especially when they came to Max's Tavern, but these women had always made an effort to wear makeup and choose nice blouses. Not today. Sandy had dirt smudged on her cheek.

Diane gave her a disapproving look. "*Really,* Sandy. Did you roll around on the ground then hop up and get in your car to come to town?"

"I've caught a mole eatin' my potatoes," she said, as though it was explanation enough. She glanced up at me. "We're gonna need our usual margaritas. Stat."

"We've decided margaritas are crass given what's goin' on," Diane said with an upturned chin.

"Now is not the time to have a bee up your tight ass, Diane," Sandy said matter-of-factly, then her face softened as she looked up at me. "Good to see you, Carly. We've missed your happy face. Now run along and get that pitcher."

Effectively dismissed, I went to the bar to place their order, but Max was already mixing it up.

"Something's goin' on with the ladies club," I whisper-shouted, using the name we'd unofficially given them. "They said Pam was arrested for murder!"

He gave me a look but didn't say anything.

"You already knew?" I asked in surprise.

He turned on the blender, blocking any further conversation in a way that felt intentional. Taking the hint, I checked on the orders for my other tables, carrying out more tuna melts than I ever wanted to see again in my lifetime.

But I couldn't get my mind off the fact that mild-mannered Pam had supposedly committed murder, and Max already knew about it. But how?

Then it hit me like a black iron skillet to the head.

What if Pam had fulfilled one of Bart Drummond's favors?

Chapter Four

I checked on a couple of other tables, then delivered the margarita pitcher and glasses to the ladies club.

"What's the special?" Sandy asked as she took the pitcher out of my hands.

I set the glasses on the table and tried not to make a face. "Tuna melt."

She gave me a look of disgust. "Then I'll have a burger."

"Sandy," Diane admonished sternly. "Have you no decency?"

"You want to talk about decency?" Sandy asked, her brows practically shooting up to her hairline. "Serving tuna melts is the epitome of indeceny. In fact, I'd appreciate it if none of you ordered one either. I'd rather not sit at a table with that fish smell."

"I'm not talking about the special. I'm talking about your concern over eating and"—she lifted her nose—"*drinking*."

"People still gotta eat, Diane," Sandy said with a sigh as she poured herself a drink. "Now order, Martha."

Martha's mouth rounded as she glanced from Diane to Sandy, then back to me. Her expression turned apologetic. "Since I can't have the tuna melt, I'll take a club sandwich."

I turned my attention to Diane.

Her jaw set and she gave me a defiant glare. "The tuna melt." She turned her glare on Sandy. "Now what are we gonna do about Pam?"

"We can organize some meals for Rob and the kids," Martha said, worry filling her eyes.

"That's a good idea," Diane said, pulling out a notebook from her purse. "I'll create a list of people who might want to participate, and I'll start making calls after lunch. Those boys still gotta eat."

Sandy snorted. "Meals? She needs a good lawyer. She needs bail money."

"Has she been arraigned?" I asked.

Diane shot me a dark look to let me know my input wasn't appreciated.

"We don't know." Sandy took a big gulp of her drink, then shuddered. "Maybe we should have gotten a pitcher on the rocks." She glanced at Martha. "Brain freeze."

Diane's glare now suggested she thought I'd made the drink extra cold to interrupt their meeting.

I got the hint. I wasn't welcome, not to mention I had other customers who needed my attention. Besides, it could be pure coincidence that Pam had killed someone within a few hours of Max and Wyatt's closed-door meeting the night before. I needed to know what had happened before I could jump to any conclusions.

While I wanted to stalk their table, my other customers kept me busy, so I didn't get back to the ladies club's table until I brought out their food. (I'd changed poor Martha's club sandwich to the tuna melt she'd originally wanted.) They were talking about Pam's kids—two high schoolers and a daughter who was married with a baby—and the support they were going to need since their father was worthless.

I set the plates on the table and asked if they needed anything else, but Diane sent me on my way. She made it obvious they wanted privacy, so I stayed away until they'd finished eating, then came back and asked if anyone wanted dessert. Sandy ordered strawberry pie, and Martha looked like she wanted something, but Diane's look of admonishment stopped her.

"We'll take our checks," Diane said flatly, giving Sandy a look that didn't seem to faze her one bit.

The lunch crowd had thinned, and Ginger was busing a table, so I went over to help her. "What do you know about the ladies club?"

Her gaze shifted to the group of women, then back to me. "You mean Diane's clique?"

I picked up a couple of empty sugar packets off the table and put them on a plate. "Is that what they are?"

She shrugged as she grabbed a handful of dirty silverware and placed it on top of a plate with a half-eaten sandwich that reeked of fish. "They've been meeting for over twenty years, and they never invite anyone else."

"I thought they were just a group of friends who met for lunch every couple of weeks."

"They are, but it started back in high school. They sat together at lunch every day and kept meeting after they graduated."

My brow furrowed. "How do you know so much about them?"

She shot a glare in their direction. "My mom went to school with them."

Their kids were several years younger than Ginger, so her statement caught me by surprise. A quick bit of mental math suggested her mother had had her as a teenager. Judging by Ginger's contempt for the ladies club, I suspected they had not treated her mother kindly. "What do you know about Pam?"

We carried the plates and glasses to the tub Tiny kept outside the kitchen.

"Pam Crimshaw? There's not much to tell."

"I know she's married and has three kids. Does she have a job?"

"Nope. Her husband works at a hardware store in Ewing, but she stays home. Used to run a daycare out of her house when her kids were small, but I don't think she's done that for a while." She propped a hand on her hip. "Why are you suddenly so interested in her?"

"She was arrested for murder yesterday."

Shock washed over her face. "*Murder?* Are you sure it was Pam?"

"That's why the women are meeting today. To discuss her arrest. They say there were witnesses."

"Did she kill her *husband?*"

"I don't think so. They're organizing meals for him and the kids."

She shook her head. "I don't believe it. She's the last person I'd expect to do something like that. Do you know who she supposedly killed?"

"No, but why did you ask if it was her husband?"

"Rob Crimshaw is *not* a nice man. I figured she'd probably had enough."

If she hadn't killed her allegedly mean husband, who had she killed? I needed to get my hands on that paper.

Pursing her lips, Ginger said, "You never suspect the quiet ones."

There was probably some truth to that.

I came back to the ladies' table to bring Sandy her pie and deliver their checks, but all conversation ceased as I approached them. I considered asking Sandy if I could contact her with more questions later, but Diane had made it clear no further questions would be welcome.

With a thin window of opportunity between the end of lunch and the start of Tutoring Club at three-thirty, I asked Ginger if she could cover for me while I made a quick run to the library. Everyone was used to me hanging out over there by now, and she agreed without asking any follow-up questions. Max had gone back to his office, but I decided not to bother him. I knew he wouldn't care if I left, and Ginger could call him out to help if she needed it. Before I headed out, I went behind the bar and used the phone under the counter to try calling Marco's cell phone. With the limited cell coverage in the county, the chances of reaching him were slim, but he always checked his phone when he was within range of a cell tower, and if I left him a message, he'd call me back as soon as he got a chance.

Sure enough, the call went straight to voicemail. I tried to squelch my disappointment. I really wanted to hear his voice. I needed to know that we were okay. "Hey, Marco. I have a question about a murder arrest yesterday. Call me back at the tavern when you get a chance." Then, because I hadn't seen him in several days, I added, "I miss you."

Since I figured he wouldn't call me back immediately, I hurried to the library to check out the *Ewing Gazette*.

Carnita greeted me with a warm smile, but then she frowned and cast a glance at the occupied computers. "I had no idea you were coming in today," she said. "I don't have you down for one of the screens."

"I'm not here to use a computer," I said. "I need to see this morning's newspaper."

She gestured to a table in the book section. "I think Mr. Blimey left it on the table." She shook her head and clucked. "I keep tellin' him to put it away when he finishes readin' it, but he never does."

"Makes it easier to find," I said, hurrying over to the table and picking up the paper. There on the front page was the headline "Drum Woman Allegedly Murders Ewing Man." Underneath the headline was a photo of an Ewing police car in a parking lot surrounded by crime scene tape. A small photo of Pam's mug shot was embedded in the lower right corner.

I sat down in the chair, letting out a little gasp. Somehow I'd hoped her friends were wrong.

I started reading the article, my stomach churning. It said Pam had pulled into the parking lot of Jim Palmer Insurance, walked into his office and, without saying a word, shot him in the chest multiple times in front of two staff members and a customer. The police had found her sitting in her parked car at the Sonic restaurant down the street. She'd provided no reason for shooting him, and Palmer had died on the way to the hospital. Pam was currently being held without bail at the Hensen County jail.

I put the paper down and sat back in my chair. This wasn't necessarily a Bart favor. Maybe she'd been pissed about her insurance rates, or maybe she and Jim Palmer had carried on a secret affair and he'd tried to end things. Just because a seemingly innocuous woman had walked into someone's office and shot him in cold blood didn't mean Bart Drummond had sent her there.

"You readin' about Pam Crimshaw?" Carnita asked.

It took me a second to register that she was talking to me. "Yeah," I said shaking off my stupor. "Her friends came into the tavern today, and they told me a little about what happened. I guess I had to see it for myself."

"Talk about the shock of the century." Carnita shook her head slightly. "No one could have seen that one comin'."

I got up and walked over to her. "Did you know her?"

"Of course," Carnita said. "I know most everyone around these parts. They might not be readers, but they like to watch movies." She gestured to the rows of DVDs. "Pam used to get a lot of kid movies when she was running her daycare, but she stopped once her boys got older. Now she gets copies of Hallmark movies and such."

"She seemed really nice," I said, unable to shake my shock. "I just can't believe she'd do something like that." Pam had always been kind to me. One afternoon back in April, Molly had been stirring up even more nonsense than usual, and Pam had pulled me aside and encouraged me to continue being my sweet, kind self and not get caught up in her drama. In that moment she'd reminded me of my mother, who'd given me that same advice after I came home from school one day, upset that a girl in my class hadn't invited me to her birthday party. I struggled to see that kind-hearted woman as a cold-blooded murderer.

"I can't either," Carnita said. "Makes you wonder if she started doin' drugs."

It definitely wasn't unprecedented. Ruth's mother had started using when Ruth was in her late twenties, and Hank's adult daughter had died from an overdose from a bad batch of drugs nearly two years ago.

"Where would she have gotten them?" I asked.

Carnita held up her hands. "I'm not part of any of that."

"Yeah, sorry," I said absently. If I wanted to know whether Pam was a user, the person to ask was Todd Bingham, the local drug lord.

"I feel bad for her kids, though," Carnita said. "Ashlynn's got a baby due in a few months, and Ricky'll be startin' his senior year in August. Poor Thad just finished his freshman year and got into a bit of trouble at school last year. He really needs his mother, and Rob isn't the nurturing type."

"Do you know much about her husband?"

"He's stoic and on the gruff side. Not very affectionate, and as far as I can tell, he's never really been part of those kids' lives."

"Do you know if Pam knew Jim Palmer?"

Carnita shook her head. "I have no idea."

"Is the copy machine working?" I asked. "I'd like to make a copy of the article."

"What on earth for?" Carnita asked.

What excuse could I give that wouldn't sound suspicious? "History," I said a little too quickly. "To add to my notes."

"I can't wait to read this book of yours."

"I'm not writing a book, Carnita."

"Whatever you say," she said with a wink, then waved. "Just take it, you and Mr. Blimey are the only ones who read it, and he's finished with it."

I grabbed it off the table and folded it in half. "You're the best."

"I can beta read your book for you," she said, her eyes shining brightly.

"Carnita," I said, "even if I were writing a book, I'm still in the note-collecting stage. I'm not sure it will ever make it past that. I'm just learning about the town."

She gave me a knowing look that suggested she didn't believe me for a minute.

"I've got to head back to the tavern," I said, tucking the paper under my arm. "Thanks again, Carnita."

Her forehead furrowed. "We really should do something for Pam's kids."

"Her lunch friends are starting a meal drive," I said. "You could call one of them and sign up for a night. Diane Lassiter seemed to be in charge of it."

"I was hoping to do something more helpful, but for the life of me, I don't know what."

"Me too," I said, then walked to the door. What Pam needed was a good lawyer, and I knew they didn't come cheap.

Chapter
Five

When I got back to the tavern, I stuffed the newspaper in my purse in the locker, locked my padlock, then headed out to the dining room. Max was back behind the bar, and Ginger was busing a dirty table while a couple of older men lingered with cups of coffee.

I slid behind the bar and leaned against the counter. "Did Marco call while I was gone?"

"No," he said, glancing up at me. "I haven't seen him in nearly a week. Is everything okay with you two?"

"Of course," I said, straightening my back. "Why wouldn't everything be okay?" It came out too quickly, my tone a bit brittle.

"This the longest I've gone without seein' him," Max said. "I figured you'd know if something was up."

"You could call him yourself, you know," I said. "You don't have to wait for him to drop by."

His eyes widened. "Did he say something?"

I laughed. "No. But I *do* know that he's workin' more hours starting last week, so it's probably keeping him busy."

"So busy he hasn't been in for nearly a week?" he asked skeptically.

He had a point. While Marco didn't come in every night, he usually came in every two or three. I hadn't heard from him at all since our last conversation.

My face must have given away my confusion, because he asked, "Did something happen between you two?"

"What? Why would you ask that?"

"Because you two are pretty close lately, and if you had a fight…"

"No. We haven't had a fight. I'm sure he's just busy." Which was partially true. Our discussion hadn't been a fight, but I knew it had upset him.

He leaned an elbow on the counter. "Then why are you expecting a call from him? He hardly ever calls here."

While I knew he and his brother were at odds with their father, I still didn't totally trust them when it came to Bart Drummond. I wasn't ready to share my working theory about why Pam might have shot Jim Palmer. Still, maybe I could switch this conversation around to my advantage. "Is everything okay with Wyatt?" I asked, then added, "You two went into the back to talk last night. I haven't seen you do that since he was a person of interest in his ex-girlfriend's murder." I lowered my voice and asked, "Is he in some kind of trouble?"

He gave me a surprised look. "No. Everything's fine." His gaze narrowed. "I thought you weren't interested in my brother."

I should have expected that. "I'm not interested in getting back together with him, if that's what you're insinuating. But I still care about his well-being. I *did* try to clear his name when the sheriff deputies put out a warrant for his arrest."

He lowered his head closer to mine. "Look, the last thing I want to do is get in the middle of your love life—"

I pointed a finger at him. "You can stop right there, because I know whatever you say next is bound to get one of us into trouble."

His mouth twisted, and then he blurted out, "What's goin' on with you and Marco?"

"I told you, nothing. He's workin' a lot." My jaw tightened. "And I find it insulting that you persist in thinking Marco and I are romantically involved when we've told you a million times we're not…not to mention that you seem to think I'd jump from him back to Wyatt before the sheets were even cold."

A smug look filled his eyes. "I find it interesting you mentioned sheets."

I groaned. "I was trying to prove a *point*, Max."

"And I was tryin' to pick up on it." But then he sobered. "Why hasn't Marco been in? For real?"

I pushed out a sigh. "Shouldn't you be asking Marco that question? He *is* your best friend."

"Not anymore," he said without any hint of anger. "You claim that title now."

Ouch, but he wasn't wrong. We definitely spent more time together than the two of them did. "Max…"

"Hey," he said, "I know full well I brought it on myself, but that's a discussion for another day. Still, I've never known the man to claim a woman for a friend and not be sleepin' with her, so color me all kinds of confused. Especially if he's playin' the long game. Half a year is one hell of a long game."

"Maybe Marco hadn't been friends with a woman before, but he'd never been shot before either. Staring down the barrel of Carson Purdy's gun changed us both. I'm not sure we ever would have been friends if we hadn't gone through it together, but the experience bonded us."

"Jerry went through it too, and I don't see you spendin' all your time with him."

I released a sigh. "You know why we really bonded, Max. I don't think either of us wants to get into that." Our friendship had deepened during our search for Lula, which would have ended the day it began if Max had been honest with us.

He nodded but didn't say anything. He'd confessed before that he was fully aware he'd screwed up, but it still wasn't something either of us openly discussed.

"Look, Max, I know he still considers you a close friend, so maybe—"

"I'm your friend too, Carly. At least I'd like to think we're friends."

"Of course we are," I said, meaning every word. You couldn't work with someone for fifty plus hours a week and not be friends, Molly being the exception. But my connection with Max went deeper. He'd taken me in when I was in a desperate place, stood by me when things were rough, and offered me protection when he barely knew me. He'd been there for me before anyone else, Marco and Wyatt included. I couldn't forget that. But I also couldn't forget he'd put Marco and me in danger. "I owe you more than I can ever repay you, Max."

"I ain't lookin' for repayment, Carly," he said, sounding hurt.

"I didn't mean it that way," I said with a frustrated sigh. I reached over the bar and covered his hand with mine. "We're friends, Max. I've found that true friends are hard to come by. So thank you."

But even as I said the words, I wondered if they were true. Max was a confusing conundrum. One minute he was vowing to protect me against outside forces because his employees were family, and the next he was full of secrets, some of which I worried would end up hurting me. Still, I reminded myself that he was a different case from Wyatt. He didn't know all of *my* secrets. What made me feel entitled to *his*?

He nodded, glancing away.

"So why *did* Wyatt stop by?" I asked, deciding to press the issue.

He hesitated, then pulled his hand away. "Just some work stuff." He headed to the back, ending the conversation.

I didn't believe it for a minute.

The afternoon was slow until Ruth showed up at three. She headed straight for me as soon as she emerged from the back, still tying her apron.

"Did he do it?"

It took me a second to figure out what she was talking about. "Oh, you mean Molly. Yeah. He did it."

Confusion filled her eyes. "What did you *think* I was talking about?"

Releasing a sigh, I said, "The talk of the town is that Pam Crimshaw killed a man in Ewing yesterday."

Her mouth dropped open. "*Pam* Crimshaw? Are they sure it wasn't *Rob*?"

"Yup. She walked into an insurance office and shot an insurance agent in cold blood, in front of his office staff and a customer. At least that's the story. No reason was given."

She put a hand on her chest. "I can't believe it."

"I know," I said. "She seems so sweet. I've never even heard her raise her voice or take a tone. Which is saying something considering how bossy Diane can get."

"She went through a rough patch with Thad, but even then she seemed sweet as pie."

I shook my head. "Carnita mentioned something about Thad getting into trouble. Do you know any details?"

"Just that alcohol was involved and he totaled Pam's car. Everybody lived, thank goodness." She paused. "I can't believe she'd kill anyone."

She started to head off, but I grabbed her arm and lowered my voice. "Did you talk to the person you were considering for Molly's job?"

"No. I decided to wait until I found out Max had actually done the deed. Honestly, I was sure he'd chicken out. Did you prod him to do it?"

"No, he was in the process when I showed up. In fact, it must have gotten heated because Ginger fled to the garage."

She lifted her chin. "Well, I'm proud of him. I'm gonna go tell him so." She turned toward the bar, then said, "And I'll cover Molly's lunch shift tomorrow. You come in at five."

"Thanks."

She went to congratulate Max for firing her nemesis, but he didn't look grateful for her praise.

Kids started arriving for Tutoring Club at three-thirty. Most were elementary aged, but I also had a couple of reluctant middle schoolers. I had the older kids practice some math problems on mini-white boards I'd picked up at the Target in Greenville, and the younger ones worked on addition and multiplication worksheets. When the younger kids finished, we discussed which book we should read for the next book club meeting. (Captain Underpants for the win. I knew Carnita had three copies and I had two. Hopefully, I'd be able to pick up a couple of other books in the series by next week.) I let the two middle-school students pick their own books—*Hatchet* for the seventh-grade boy and a copy of a Baby-Sitters Club book for the sixth-grade girl. Both students struggled with reading, enough so that I'd suggested to their mothers that we set up some one-on-one sessions every other Monday, a half hour before the start of Tutoring Club. I wasn't a reading specialist, but I planned to do some research on working with middle-school students. Helping these kids was giving me a sense of purpose I hadn't felt in a long time.

While the kids were working, I could hear the mothers whispering about Pam. I tried my best to eavesdrop, but the kids needed too much help. I wasn't sure what was going on in Drum Elementary, but it didn't seem to involve a whole lot of teaching. Of course, I was sure they didn't have many resources, but so many students were behind it seemed like the school itself was offering insufficient instruction. In any case, I didn't hear anything of use.

My next hope was the evening dinner crowd…which proved just about as useless. People were discussing the murder—gossiping was a huge form of entertainment in Drum—but I didn't hear anything I hadn't already learned. Pam had killed Jim Palmer. No one knew why. Diane Lassiter was organizing a meal train. There was plenty of speculation that Pam and Jim had been carrying on an affair, but no one had ever seen them together.

Jerry showed up at around seven, looking tanned, dirty, and tired. I headed over to take his order as he plopped down on a barstool at the counter.

"Hey, Carly," he said, beaming. "How're you doin'?"

"I'm about as tired as you look. How's the new job goin'?"

"Great," he said with a soft groan as he settled onto the stool. "In fact, I just got a promotion."

"Wow! That's wonderful!" I meant every word of it. His job at the construction site had given him a new sense of purpose. He felt needed and productive, and for the first time in a long time, he actually had some money. "What will you be doing now?"

"I'm workin' for Bart Drummond himself."

The blood rushed from my head. I felt like I was going to pass out.

"You don't look so good," he said with worry in his eyes. "Maybe you should sit down."

While part of me really wanted to, I'd draw all sorts of attention. Instead, I leaned against the counter, trying to look as nonchalant as I could manage. "I'm okay," I said with a dismissive wave. "What sort of things will you be doing?"

He hesitated. "Things on his land. Stuff Carson Purdy used to do."

"Wow…" I forced myself to smile, but it felt a little wobbly. "How'd that come about?"

"Well," he said slowly, as though he was having second thoughts about telling me.

I widened my smile to encourage him, but the look in his eyes suggested that I looked like a makeup-less Joker. "I'm sorry, Jerry. You just caught me by surprise. You must be doing an amazing job at the worksite if you're workin' for the man himself."

"Mr. Drummond invited me up to the big house for lunch—me and my foreman—and he asked us both about the job and how things were goin'. Mr. Drummond told me he'd heard I was doin' good work, and he thought good work should be rewarded. Then he asked me if I wanted a promotion."

"Wow…"

"It even comes with a house, Carly," he said, warming to the topic again despite my lack of enthusiasm. "On the Drummond property so I can be there to oversee things."

I swallowed my rising bile. "Jerry… It's Bart Drummond."

Uncertainty wavered in his eyes. "He told me he knew about my involvement in the Carson Purdy mess. He said if nothing else, he owed me a job for savin' his son."

"But Jerry…"

"I know what people say about him, Carly," he said softly. "But he believes in me. He was the one who got the foreman to give me a job in the first place. He wanted to see how I handled the responsibility." The pride in his eyes was nearly my undoing.

"I've always believed in you, Jerry," I said, past the lump in my throat. With every fiber of my being, I believed Bart Drummond was using him—possibly so he could use him against me at some point—but I couldn't take this victory from him.

Leaning over the bar counter, I called Max over. He headed toward us, giving me a worried look as he took in my expression.

"Everything okay?" he asked, wiping his hands on a bar towel.

"Jerry needs a drink on the house," I said, forcing cheerfulness into my voice as I held Max's gaze. "He just got a promotion. He's taking over Carson Purdy's job."

Max's eyes flared, and then he cast a glance at Jerry, forcing a smile of his own. "Well, now, that *is* news. How'd that come about?"

Jerry told him about his lunch with Max's father, adding more details than he'd shared with me—he'd served steak and baked potatoes!—and Max didn't look any less horrified than I felt.

"Why ain't you two more happy for me?" Jerry asked, sounding hurt.

I leaned closer and lowered my voice. "Jerry, it's Bart Drummond."

"You already said that."

I turned to Max for help, and he stared at me like a deer in headlights for a solid ten seconds before he forced a grin. "You're right, Carly. This calls for a drink on the house." Then he headed down the bar to pull a draft.

"I know it's Bart," Jerry said with a serious expression. "But I need this job. Okay?"

My lip quivered and tears flooded my eyes. "If you're hurtin' for money, we'll figure something out, okay?"

"No," he said solemnly. "I want this. I need you to be happy for me, okay?"

I nodded and hugged him, ignoring the fact that he smelled like sweat and damp earth. I couldn't imagine Bart Drummond letting him into that fancy house on the side of the mountain, full of expensive furniture. Not smelling like this. The asshole had probably made him eat outside.

Jerry kissed my cheek, then pulled away from me. "I know you're upset because you'll be seein' less of me, but I'll still come see you."

I nodded, swiping a stray tear from my cheek. "You better." I sniffed, trying to collect myself. "What can I get you for dinner?"

He ordered meatloaf and mashed potatoes. Resisting the urge to suggest a side salad instead of the starch, I headed to the food counter with his order.

"What's goin' on with Jerry?" Ruth asked as she came back to pick up an order.

"He's not going to be coming around as often. He got a promotion."

"At the jobsite?" she asked in disbelief. "What's that got to do with him comin' in or not?"

"Because he's going to be working for Bart Drummond himself. He's giving Jerry the overseer job."

"You're kiddin' me," she said in a flat voice.

"I wish I were."

She sucked in a breath as she studied Jerry from across the room. "What's that old man up to?"

"You think he's up to something too?" I asked.

She wrinkled her brow. "Of course he is. There's no way Jerry's qualified for that job."

Was that Drummond's plan? Put Jerry in a position that was over his head and make him feel like a failure? Use him to mess with me? Hurt him in retaliation for killing Carson?

Could I stand by and let any of that happen?

I really needed to speak to Marco.

We were busy for another hour, and I didn't get a chance to talk to Max until after Jerry had eaten his meal and left.

"Did Jerry say when he was moving out?" I asked him when I finally got a chance. It stood to reason that Jerry would have to give him notice since Max ran the motel.

"Tomorrow."

I gasped.

"Now we don't know that my father's up to anything sinister," Max said with a sigh as he leaned his hand against the counter. "He often *does* hire people based on their work ethic." The conflict in his eyes told me how much he was trying to convince himself.

"And do you truly believe that's the case now?"

He swallowed and didn't answer.

"We'll never see him," I said, my stomach churning.

"He said he'd drop by from time to time, but he seemed to think he'd be too busy to leave the property much."

"You have to stop this, Max."

He turned to me in surprise. "I can't."

"Then tell me why he's doing this."

"Because it's a promotion," he said in exasperation. "It's more money than he's ever made in his life, and he thinks he'll be respected."

I heard the doubt in his voice, and while I shared it, he'd misunderstood the question. "Not Jerry, Max. Your father."

But he didn't have an answer either.

Chapter Six

When I still hadn't heard from Marco by ten, I started to get worried. I tallied up my tips and left Tiny's share in Max's office, then headed out the back door to my car, my pepper spray firmly in hand. I never went out the back door at night without it. I'd been caught off guard on a few occasions, and it wasn't happening again. For a split second, my heart skipped a beat when I saw a figure leaning against the trunk of my car, his arms crossed over his chest, but then I saw Marco's Explorer parked next to it.

Marco didn't move when he saw me, just watched as I came closer. He always looked good in whatever he wore, whether it was his sheriff's deputy uniform or the jeans and light gray T-shirt he had on now. His blond hair had been trimmed since we last saw each other, which made the separation feel longer. I hadn't even realized he'd had an appointment. His eyes were glued on me and held a heat that had nothing to do with the summer evening.

I flushed with a heat of my own.

My heart skipped a beat for an entirely different reason this time. I'd missed this man more than I'd ever missed anyone besides my mother, and we'd only been apart less than a week. How long could we keep pretending we were just friends? It had worked for a few months, but it was getting harder and harder. The fact I hadn't seen him made me wonder if Marco had finally hit a wall.

"Hey," I said, as I approached him. I was yearning to reach out and touch him, but I kept my hands at my sides.

He shifted his weight, dropping his arms. The heat in his eyes dimmed, replaced with determination.

"Is everything okay? Why didn't you come inside?" I asked, suddenly afraid to hear the answer. Had he grown tired of waiting for me to change my mind? Was he cutting me off out of self-preservation?

"I got off work late, so I decided I'd take a chance and drop by. Figured you'd get off at ten, so I just waited outside."

A chill ran down my back. We hadn't talked in days, and he had no idea the whole Molly debacle had finally come to a head.

"How'd you know I'd be getting off early?" I asked, then instantly regretted it. What was I doing? I was suspicious of practically everything—with just cause—but this was *Marco*. Would I ever be able to *truly* trust him? Was it fair to give in to my feelings if I didn't?

He realized my concern and sat up straighter. "I saw your car in the parking lot during the lunch shift. You usually get off at ten when you work lunch." His eyes narrowed. "Why were you working over lunch?"

I shook my head, still agitated, but mostly because I was disappointed in myself. "It doesn't matter. Why didn't you come in?"

"I needed to see *you*."

That sounded ominous.

He cast a glance at the second floor above the tavern—Max's apartment—which seemed to confirm my suspicions. "I thought about waiting for you at Hank's, but I figured you could come over to my house so we could talk."

Which meant he didn't want Hank to hear either. Even more ominous. Did he have information to share with me about Pam?

"Yeah," I said, running a hand over my head. I was tired, and while I kept clothes at Marco's, I hadn't told Hank I was staying over, which meant I'd need to head home after our chat. But I'd missed him so much, I'd drink five cups of coffee to wake up if need be. "It would be super helpful if this town had functional cell towers."

He grimaced. "Be careful what you wish for." I knew he was talking about the cell tower that was supposedly being installed at Bart's resort, which would provide that section of the mountain with cell service. But it also ran the risk of putting my face on the internet, which meant my father might be able to find me. "You look tired. Do you want to do this tomorrow?"

His distance was scaring me, and I considered telling him I wanted to wait so I could buy time to prepare for whatever he might be about to tell me. But that was what Caroline Blakely would have done, and I wasn't that coward anymore. "No. I'm good. Let's go."

He gave me a grim smile. "I'll follow you."

I was anxious the entire ten-minute drive to his house, but I felt some of my taut nerves ease as I pulled up to his small two-bedroom house in the woods. I loved his house and the peace I found there. It was tucked in the woods several hundred feet from a two-lane county road. A sliver-sized view of the valley was visible from his front porch, one of my favorite places at his house. Still, I wasn't a total fool. I knew a large part of the peace I found there was because of the man who owned the house.

We both got out of our vehicles, and I met Marco at the base of the short path to his house. He gestured for me to take a seat in my usual chair. Warmth coursed through me. He'd prepared. An afghan was thrown over one arm, and a thermos, presumably filled with the hot tea he knew I loved, sat on the table between us. It was June, but it got cool at night at this altitude.

"I haven't seen you much over the last week," I said instead of asking him what news he had to share. At the moment, I was more worried about him…about us. I'd been scared all week. Not talking to him for five days was not the norm for us. No matter how busy we were.

"I've been tied up with a case."

That offered some relief. Marco wanted to become a detective, but his law-abiding ways hadn't suited the people in power. It was no small miracle he'd kept his job as long as he had, something I suspected he'd managed by keeping a low profile.

But everything had changed back in March, when Marco and I had discovered one of the corrupt deputies, Paul Conrad, was guilty of a whole battery of crimes, from covering up the death of Wyatt's ex-girlfriend to using his badge to sexually harass and blackmail women. Paul had almost murdered Wyatt and me, but Marco had cornered him. Rather than go in for questioning, Paul had killed himself, taking whatever knowledge he had of the other corrupt members of the department with him. Nevertheless, the entire sheriff's department had been under investigation by the Tennessee Bureau of Investigation. Several deputies had been relieved of duty, and Marco had been given more responsibility.

We hoped they'd weeded out the worst of the corruption, although neither of us was naïve enough to think they'd gotten it all. I could see him fighting a smile.

I sat up straighter and reached for the thermos. "As a *detective*?"

"I'm not in charge of a case, but I'm working with the lead detective—Marta White. And she set me loose to investigate a robbery while she works another case."

"Marco, that's great!" I gushed. "It's about time they start taking you seriously." I knew from experience he had a knack for detective work. He and I had questioned plenty of people while investigating our own cases, but the sheriff's department had kept him doing scut work.

"Thanks," he said with a grin.

"Is Detective White working on Jim Palmer's murder?" I asked, my stomach flip-flopping. Dare I hope that Marco might be that close to information?

"No," he said with a frown. "There's plenty of speculatin' goin' on in the sheriff's department, but unfortunately, the investigators don't know much other than the few details the witnesses have told them."

"That she walked in and shot him in cold blood?"

"Pretty much." He grimaced. "That information is obviously public knowledge."

I took a sip of the hot tea, letting it warm my insides. The air wasn't cold, but I'd forgotten my jacket and I was wearing short sleeves. I tugged the afghan over my shoulders. "Do you think Pam Crimshaw killed Jim Palmer as one of Bart's favors?"

He pressed his lips together then frowned. "That's why I wanted to talk to you. I think maybe she did, but the guys workin' the case are part of the old guard. I don't have any proof, but I wouldn't be surprised if they're on Drummond's payroll. They likely won't dig very deep."

"So we do the digging instead."

He paused. "This is a high-profile case, and if it really is tied to Bart, he's gonna be watchin'. You won't be able to fly under the radar, Carly, and I can't take part in any digging you do."

"So you think we should just let this go?" I asked, incredulous.

"I'm not sayin' that," he said calmly. "But we don't even know if it's tied to him. We could waste a lot of time lookin' into it and find out it's all for nothing. Pam Crimshaw's husband is one mean son-of-a-bitch. Maybe she put up with one berating too many and then just snapped. Who knows. Maybe she found out her car insurance rates went up from Thad's DUI, so she went gunning for her insurance agent."

"Jim Palmer was her agent? No one I've talked to seems to know."

"He wasn't at the time of his death, but I don't know about before that. Maybe he was a year ago. He could have dropped them because of Thad's incident."

"Everyone keeps mentioning that her son Thad got into trouble. What happened?" Ruth had given me the basic story, but I figured Marco would have more details.

"A couple of years ago, Thad and his friend got drunk and took Pam's car on a joy ride."

"He had to have been, what? Fourteen?"

"Thirteen. Thad hit another car head on. Thank God no one died, but the boys and the driver of the other car were seriously injured."

I sucked in a breath. "I take it they didn't charge him as an adult."

He grimaced. "No. Thad got off with community service, but the driver wasn't too happy about it."

"Is that type of punishment typical?"

He shrugged. "It's all up to the judge."

I gave him a long look. "So it's not outside the realm of possibility that Pam or her husband went to Bart for a favor to help get him off?"

Something flashed in his eyes, and I knew he'd already considered the connection. "It's definitely possible."

We both sat in silence for a moment.

"And you don't think this will come out in the investigation?" I asked. "I thought TBI was rooting out the corruption in the sheriff's department."

"They are, but Detectives Vaughn and Temple are both well-respected veterans. They're above suspicion, and if Bart's lining their pockets, they're smart enough to cover their tracks." He lowered his voice. "This isn't my investigation, and even if it was, I wouldn't be able to share confidential information. But there's gonna be a press conference tomorrow, so I'll tell you this much: Pam confessed. She said she felt like killing someone and chose the victim at random. Detective Vaughn's buyin' it hook, line, and sinker. Either he's on Bart's payroll or he's doin' it out of pure laziness. You won't find many detectives who'll question a full confession."

"I'd bet money there's a link to Bart," I said. "Wyatt came into the tavern last night. He said something to Max, and the two of them disappeared into Max's office for a few minutes before Wyatt up and left. I haven't seen them go to Max's office like that since Wyatt was under investigation for Heather's murder. They know something."

"What time did he show up?" he asked, straightening in his chair.

"A little after seven."

He pressed his lips together as he stared off into the woods next to the cabin. "That was a couple hours after she was arrested, so the timing's right." He shifted his weight. "It would be great if I could just go ask Max what he knows, but we both know he won't tell me." A quiet anger simmered below the surface.

"Does that really surprise you?"

He turned to look at me, pain filling his eyes. "Yeah. It does. Before he came back to Drum to be his father's bitch, he would have told me in a heartbeat."

"But you have to wonder how much they know about their father's business given Wyatt came in two hours after all of this went down."

"That or they're on the alert for anything that might be tied to their father."

"Less than two hours later? I've been researching Bart's favors for months, and I still didn't find out until the next day. That means they've likely got a source in the department or in Ewing. And that source wasn't you."

He groaned. "Shit."

We sat in an uncomfortable silence for several moments, which wasn't the norm for us. One of the things I loved about our friendship was that neither of us felt the need to fill the quiet. Maybe it was time to address my fears.

"I've missed you, Marco," I said softly. "A lot."

"I've missed you too."

"Are you sure it's just your job that's kept you away?"

He turned to me in surprise. "You think I'm mad at you?"

"No...I don't know. It's just that we've never gone that long without talking, and then I called and left you a message and you never called back."

He gave me an apologetic smile. "I didn't call you because I planned to come see you. Plus, I got tied up with my case, and it was after eight by the time I wrapped things up. I figured I'd just wait for you to get off work. I would have called, but I honestly didn't want Max to know about any of this."

I cringed. "I told him I was expecting a call from you. Now he thinks we're having a fight."

"Sorry."

"I think he misses you," I said softly.

He was silent for a long moment. "He made his choice," he said, his voice rough.

"Did he though?" I whispered. "Maybe he feels caught."

"For the longest time, it was me and Max against his father," he said, sounding weary. "Then it all changed when he left college to come back and run the bar. I hung in there anyway, believin' there was a reason for it, but he still refuses to tell me what it is. After the whole Lula situation, I went to see him. I asked what his mother had said to convince him to come back to Drum. He said she'd reminded him that family helps family. That he came back for her, not his dad."

"Do you believe him?"

"Yeah," he said. "I do, but he still has plenty of secrets, and one way or another, he's still doin' Bart's bidding. I told him we were at cross purposes. We haven't been the same since."

I didn't say anything. I wasn't sure what to say. My own lifelong friend had betrayed me so thoroughly it was easy to paint him as a villain. The situation between Max and Marco wasn't as clear-cut.

"I can't help thinking maybe I never really knew him," Marco said. "Maybe he was only against his father because he was on the outside lookin' in. And when his father finally changed his mind, he came runnin' and became his daddy's lap dog."

"Do you really believe that? He hasn't gotten along with him since the whole Lula incident."

"He's still runnin' the motel," Marco said. "He's still under his father's thumb."

"But you just said he came back for his mother," I said. "And we can't forget that he and Wyatt were hiding Lula from their father. It sounds like a complicated mess."

"Now you're defendin' him?" he asked in surprise.

"I'm just sayin' that everything's not always cut and dry. Obviously Max feels like he has good reasons for what he's doin'. And if it's on the illegal side, you're a deputy sheriff. An honest one. Maybe he became privy to the family secrets, and now he feels bound to protect them."

"Makin' him an accessory."

"It's not easy to turn your back on family. I'm the perfect example of that. My father treated me like crap. I tried to cut him out of my life, but truth is, I didn't fight too hard when Jake sucked me back in. Maybe the same thing happened to Max, only it was his mother who reeled him in."

"And yet he won't tell me any of it."

"Again, you're a deputy sheriff. He knows if he was part of something truly heinous, you'd turn him in. He saw proof of that when you questioned him about Lula."

He didn't respond.

"Maybe you should go to him as a friend, tell him you left the badge at home and everything he tells you has impunity."

He leaned his head against the back of his chair and released a heavy sigh, making me think he'd given this plenty of consideration. "The badge doesn't work that way, Carly."

"Then maybe you need to decide what's more important—the badge or your friend." He started to say something, but I held up my hand. "I'm not saying you condone anything truly bad, but maybe he feels trapped and the one person he always thought he could turn to is no longer available."

"It's not that simple, Carly."

"I know." Nothing was simple. I'd learned that lesson long ago.

Chapter Seven

There's something else I need to talk to you about," I said. "Something that has me worried."

"Okay…"

"Bart offered Carson Purdy's job to Jerry."

He bolted upright. "He *what?*"

I relayed everything Jerry had told me and also Max's reaction.

"So Max isn't happy about it either?"

"No."

"Maybe that's my in to talk to him," Marco said as he ran a hand over the top of his head leaving his hair ruffled.

I found myself wanting to smooth it out. Wanting to touch him.

Marco continued, unaware of my inner struggle. "I'll tell him I heard about Jerry and ask him what he thinks."

Focus, Carly. This was why I needed for us to remain friends. Starting something with Marco would only distract me. "You think he'll give you an honest answer?"

"It'll give me a better in than anything else we've discussed."

He was probably right. "When do you plan to talk to him?"

He glanced at his watch, then back up at me. "I'm thinkin' about goin' tonight."

"You should probably talk to him without me around."

Pushing out a sigh, he said, "Agreed."

I started to get to my feet. "Then I'll head home so you can do that."

He leaned over, reaching for my arm and tugging me back down. "I'll wait until after closing. I want to have his undivided attention and I don't want anyone else around." He hesitated. "Why don't you stay here while I'm gone, and then I can tell you what he says when I get back? You were plannin' to stay anyway, weren't you?"

I felt torn. "I don't think I should tonight. I didn't warn Hank, and it's too late to call him. He'll worry if he gets up and my car's not out front."

"I should have called you earlier," he said, his voice heavy with regret.

A week ago he probably would have, which only reminded me that we still hadn't addressed the elephant in the room.

"Marco, there's something goin' on between us. Not seeing or talking to each other for five days just isn't like us, and I think we need to talk about it."

"What's there to talk about?" he asked, but he sounded slightly defensive.

So I was right, not that it made me feel any better. Actually, it filled me with dread.

"I think I'd like to know what answer you were looking for when we had that discussion about marriage," I said carefully.

Marco had invited me to a friend's wedding in Atlanta, which had led to an awkward conversation. He'd mentioned he wanted to get married someday, and given his parents' difficult relationship and his preference for serial dating, I'd reacted with surprise. He'd quickly changed the subject.

It had felt like nothing at the time, but as the week had gone on without any word from him, it had become apparent it was a bigger deal than I'd thought.

He shifted in his seat. "There's nothing wrong with sayin' that I've done a lot of thinkin' and decided I do see marriage in my future." He cast a glance at me, then turned away. "It's actually pretty *normal*." He added softly, "Even for a guy like me."

"Of course it's normal," I said, close to tears. I had a feeling this discussion could change things irrevocably between us, and I couldn't bear to lose him. "And what's that *even for a guy like me* nonsense? Plenty of guys sow their wild oats before they settle down. Of course you can get married and start a family…someday."

There'd been no mention of a family in our previous conversation, but the few times Marco had helped with my tutoring club, he'd been amazing with the kids. Wanting a family seemed like a natural part of his happily-ever-after package.

His lips twitched with a grin. "Sow my wild oats? I can tell you've spent too much time with Hank."

"Who else was I going to hang out with while I was missing my best friend?" My voice cracked partway through, giving me away, not that I needed any help. He knew me well enough to read me.

He didn't say anything for a moment, just studied me with those blue-green eyes. When he did speak, it blew apart my world. "Maybe it's time we both put our cards on the table."

Fear washed through me, and everything in me screamed to tell him no. I wasn't ready to face this now, but then again, I wasn't sure I'd ever be ready. "Okay."

He scooted his chair so that we were nearly face to face.

"Carly, I know you're still in no place for a relationship. I value our friendship, more than you probably realize, but I've made no secret I'd like for us to be more than friends."

"I know," I whispered.

"I'm not pressuring you," he said, emphatically. "It's important you know that."

"I know," I repeated.

"But I need to know if I'm wanting something that's never going to happen." He swallowed. "I need to know if I should let this…go."

I leaned forward and took his hand, linking our fingers. "I can't promise you anything, Marco. I'm super messed up. I've spent all week wondering if you'd decided I was too much of a mess to deal with, and then you showed up outside the tavern, and I was so happy to see you. But it rattled me when you said you expected me to get off at ten. My mind went to sinister thoughts." Then I added in shame, "About you."

Hurt filled his eyes. "You think I'd do something to hurt you?"

"No," I said insistently, squeezing his hand. "That's just it. I don't. And I immediately chastised myself for it. But it's instinct now—my first reaction is to question everyone and everything. Because I didn't see it coming with Jake either." My voice broke. "And trust me, I know how unfair it is to compare you to him. You're a good man, and he's a snake. You deserve better than that from me."

He slowly shook his head. "*No.* He spent your entire friendship manipulating you, spying on you for your father. Calling off the men in your life. That would mess anyone up." He shook his head. "Carly, I *know* it's hard for you to trust. I'm doin' everything in my power to prove that you can trust me."

"I know," I said, a tear slipping down my cheek. "Do you have any idea how guilty that makes me feel?"

He shook his head again. "You haven't done anything *wrong*. You have absolutely nothing to feel guilty about." He gave me a soft smile. "I'm your friend, no matter what. If you tell me that you'll never have romantic feelings for me, I'll find a way to accept it and be your friend from now until eternity. But if there's a chance…"

His face was passive, yet I knew he was scared too. He had to be wondering if rocking the boat of our fragile feelings would capsize us.

"I can't promise you anything, Marco. And I definitely can't tell you that I can give you a family someday." A lump burned in my throat as I let down the wall that had held back my fears. "I can't risk having kids with my father out there, trying to find and kill me." A sob broke loose and my eyes flooded with tears. "How selfish would it be to bring children into that situation?"

A soft smile covered his face and tenderness filled his eyes. "I'm gonna help you bring him down."

My back stiffened. "Wyatt promised me the same thing and he got stalled on part one—dealing with his father."

His body stiffened. "You're comparin' me to Wyatt Drummond now?"

"No!" I got up and walked to the porch railing, staring into the dark woods. Trying to pull myself together. "I'm sorry. That was uncalled for."

When he didn't say anything, I spun around to face him, my butt leaning against the railing. "I had hopes and dreams too," I said with a wry laugh as I wiped the tears from my face with my fingertips. "I wanted to marry a man that I loved and who loved me—*really* loved me. I wanted kids and a happy home." Another sob broke loose. "I've never wanted much, Marco. I just want to be loved."

He remained in his seat staring at me with a tenderness that stole my breath.

"Am I that unlovable that men have to have a reason to care about me? Jake. Wyatt. My dad."

"No, Carly," he said softly, getting to his feet but keeping his distance. "I can assure you that you're not. People love you for just being you. Hank treats you like his own daughter and doesn't want a thing from you. Those kids at the tutorin' club adore you. And sure, you're givin' them something, but no kid that age is excited to come learn. They're eager to see *you*."

I nodded. Hank was more of a father to me than Randall Blakely ever had been. Then again, I was pretty sure Randall Blakely didn't consider me his real daughter. And those kids…they gave me a sense of purpose I hadn't had in over a year. But they were also a sharp reminder of what I'd lost. What I'd probably never have again.

"And they're not the only ones who love you, Carly," he said, taking a step closer.

My heart raced, because our conversation had circled back to square one.

His shoulders lifted. "You want to neutralize Bart Drummond before we go after your father. So we need to step up our efforts to make that happen. We're going to look for the chink in his armor, and Pam Crimshaw just might be it."

Tears streamed down my face, because I knew what he was doing. I'd learned long ago that talk was cheap. Actions were what mattered, and he was ready to step up and do his part.

"You could get in trouble," I said. "It's an active investigation and you can't be part of it."

He closed the distance between us, pulling me into a fierce hug. I wrapped my arms around him and buried my face in his chest. While part of me ached for more, the part that had missed him so deeply soaked in his nearness. "Don't you worry about that. I have other avenues. How about you focus on talking to Pam's friends and kids? Find out what state of mind she was in after Thad had his accident a couple of years ago. We'll figure out where to go from there. And maybe it's time to dust off some of the other cases you've been lookin' into. We'll figure out a way to ask questions without lookin' nosy."

I nodded against his chest, starting to feel foolish for breaking down. "Sorry I lost it like that."

"No," he said, squeezing me tighter. "You keep it all bottled up. It's okay to break down from time to time." He lifted his hand to my cheek and tilted my head back to stare up at him. "Thank you for trusting me enough to do it in front of me."

I nodded, not feeling steady enough to speak.

"How about I come over to Hank's tomorrow morning before I head to work? I'll tell you what I found out from Max, and we can narrow down the cases you've collected and figure out which ones to focus on."

"Okay," I said. "I'll make you breakfast."

A mischievous grin lit up his eyes. "It's not going to be some of that healthy shit you feed Hank, now is it?"

I laughed, and it felt good. "If you want real bacon, you'll have to bring your own. But I'll make sure the pancakes and eggs are as *real* as they can be."

"Deal," he said, relief filling his eyes. "It'll be kind of early. Seven?"

"I can be up," I said. "Which means I better go home and get to bed."

He started to say something, then stopped. "Yeah. Good idea."

I started for my car, and he fell in step beside me. When we reached the driver's door, I glanced up at him, my heart skipping a beat. He was such a good-looking man, and more importantly, he was a *good* man. Why was I taking my time with this?

Especially since I was finding it harder and harder to ignore the pull I felt toward him. Why didn't I just give in? We both wanted this. But I couldn't do it.

Not yet.

"Marco, I didn't answer your question about a future, and you definitely deserve one. It's not fair to leave you hanging, wondering if your feelings will ever be reciprocated."

He watched me, not saying a word.

"The answer is yes," I whispered. "I feel everything I think you feel, but I need more time. I've been hurt…"

He put his finger on my lips. "I know, Carly. No explanation needed."

My lips tingled at his touch, and I felt the strongest urge to kiss him, but he pulled his hand away and reached for the car door. "Call me when you get home. With Pam and our plan to start diggin'…I think we'll need to do more frequent check-ins."

"Agreed."

I got in and backed up to turn around and head down his long driveway. When I stopped, I gave him a wave and he waved back with one hand, the other in his pocket. He looked so inviting standing there, so welcoming, and I wondered what it would feel like to go home to this man every night and let him envelop me in his arms. To fill a home with children. Did I dare let myself entertain that daydream?

As I drove home, I realized that for the first time in a long time, I felt a spark of hope. It wasn't lost on me that Marco had put it there.

Chapter Eight

I emerged from my room at six-thirty, my kitten at my feet. I'd stayed up late. Again. But I had something to show for it this time—I'd stumbled upon something promising while making a timeline of the events I'd been researching. I was eager to show Marco when he got here.

After a quick stop in the bathroom, I found Hank in the kitchen, scooping coffee grounds into the coffee maker. He glanced up in surprise. "What are you doin' up?" His eyes widened. "And dressed."

"Marco's comin' over for breakfast before he heads into work. I'm making pancakes and eggs."

He gave me a blank look. "You're makin' him breakfast at the crack of dawn? What'd you do?"

I jutted my head back. "What are you talking about?"

"I can't think of any reason *you'd* get up before seven to make breakfast unless you had a fight and you were in the wrong."

I grimaced. "No fight. We need to discuss some things."

"That's called makin' up after a fight, but in a real relationship, sex is usually involved."

"Hank!"

He gave me a knowing look. "I speak the truth, and there's no harm in findin' a man to scratch an itch."

My face flushed. "*Hank!*"

"Just sayin'."

"I don't see you lookin' for a girlfriend," I countered.

"When you've been blessed with the love of your life, everyone else pales in comparison." He headed for the doorway. "Since you're already up, I'm headed out to the porch. Bring me a cup of coffee when it's done. And don't let your hellcat out. I don't want her scarin' off the birds."

I grinned at his description of Letty. "Yeah, of course."

He went outside, but his statement stayed with me while I pulled out the ingredients for pancakes. He'd lost his wife Mary to breast cancer a few years before. I knew he'd loved her, but this was the first time I'd heard him refer to her as the love of his life. There wasn't much around the house to suggest she'd lived here, even though he'd owned the house for years. In fact, I'd often thought it strange that he lived in this small, run-down house when he'd supposedly been the drug kingpin of eastern Tennessee. Any money he'd earned was clearly long gone. *My* running theory was that he'd spent it on Mary's medical bills—I knew from taking care of Violet during her last month that medical care wasn't cheap—but a lot of townsfolk thought he'd buried it.

After I made the pancake batter and put a cookie sheet with turkey bacon in the oven, I poured two cups of coffee and walked out to the front porch, making sure to keep Letty inside. Hank was sitting in his chair, his kitten on his lap. I handed him a mug as Marco's Explorer pulled into the drive.

"Want me to bring your breakfast out here or would you rather eat it later?"

"Didn't have a fight, eh?" he asked with a smirk.

I rolled my eyes. "So you want to come in and eat with us? I can set you a place at the table."

"No," he grumped. "I'll stay out here."

Marco's SUV came to a stop and he got out. He was wearing his uniform and his hair was still damp, and the image of him in the shower flashed through my head. I sucked in a sharp inhale, and Hank shot me a grin that suggested he knew he was right about me having an itch.

Marco gave me a tentative smile. When I smiled back, relief flashed through his eyes, and he lifted a hand to Hank. "Good morning, sir."

"I heard you were droppin' in for breakfast," Hank said as he stroked the back of Smoky's head.

Marco nodded as he approached the house. "That and Carly's good company."

Hank shot me a mischievous grin and started to say something, but I smacked his arm, making the coffee slosh in his cup.

"Come inside and I'll start the pancakes," I said.

"Don't let her feed you that turkey bacon shit," Hank said as Marco climbed the steps. "*I* may be stuck eatin' it, but that don't mean you have to."

"Trust me," Marco said with a chuckle. "She's tried to trick me into eatin' that stuff before. I know better than to fall for it."

"You two are terrible," I grumbled, then turned on my heels and went back into the house. "Don't let Letty out. She'll scare Hank's birds away," I called over my shoulder. "Or on second thought, go ahead."

Hank let out a burst of laughter and Marco joined him.

I headed to my room to get my notebook, then found Marco in the kitchen grabbing a mug out of the cabinet. Letty was rubbing herself against his leg and releasing a soft purr.

The thought of Marco's hands making *me* purr flashed into my head, catching me off guard. If I was avoiding a relationship with him to keep from being distracted, I was epically failing.

"How'd it go last night with Max?" I asked as I leaned against the door jamb.

"You look exhausted," he said, shooting me a glance before he poured himself some coffee. "I feel bad that I made you get up early."

"I was the one who invited you, so quit stalling. It must not have gone well since you're changing the subject."

"Long story short, I didn't get anything of use."

"What's the long version?" I asked, walking past him to turn the stove burner on.

"I showed up a little before closing and told him I felt like hanging out…like old times. So after he closed, we sat at a table and talked for a while. The conversation worked its way to Jerry."

"Did you bring it up or did he?"

"Me, but it happened organically. He told me that Jerry was moving out, and I asked why. He told me about the job, and I said I didn't trust his father. He admitted he didn't either, but he doesn't know what to do about it."

"He won't try to talk Jerry out of it?"

"No. We discussed whether he should, and in the end we both agreed we needed to let Jerry be the one to make this call."

I started to protest, then reluctantly decided he was right. Jerry was a grown man. I'd shared my reservations about the whole thing. He might be insulted if I continued trying to dissuade him. "I don't want to see him get hurt. And I'm not just talking about his feelings, Marco."

"I know, but for now, we're stuck."

I nodded, even if it didn't feel right.

"Can I help with breakfast?"

"No," I said, handing him the notebook. "Why don't you look over my notes? We can talk through them while I cook." I'd already come to a few conclusions, but I wanted his opinion before I mentioned them.

He sat down at the table, and as I cooked the pancakes, we discussed the cases I'd identified as possible Bart favors (all based on supposition and reading between the lines—he was good enough not to be obvious). This wasn't the first time he'd heard about the majority of them, but this was the first time we'd looked at them together with a critical eye, trying to determine which leads were most promising.

"Hey," Marco said, sitting up. "This one's new."

I glanced over my shoulder. "Which one?"

"The Drummond lumber yard employee whose house exploded from a gas leak twelve years ago." His gaze lifted. "It looks like it was considered an accident."

"It was," I said as I cracked several eggs into the skillet. "But a family of five died in the explosion."

"You don't think it was an accident?"

"I wasn't sure at first, but then I discovered that about a week after the funeral, a man crashed his car into a tree on Highway 107."

His eyes widened slightly. "Go on."

"The article says that there were no signs of skid marks. There were no other cars. No alcohol or drugs involved. He just hit a tree."

"Are you suggesting it was attempted suicide?"

"I'd bet money on it," I said, turning around to face him. "He tried three more times over the years in various other ways. If you flip forward several pages, you'll see them all. His name is Ted Butcher."

"Was he ever successful?"

"I didn't find an obituary on him. His last two attempts were drug overdoses, and I suspect they only made the paper because he was found in public locations. The Ewing city park and the grocery store parking lot. The last one happened two years ago."

He cocked his head, studying me. "Why isn't it next to the explosion?"

"Because I didn't connect him to it until last night. After I came home from your place, I started looking them over."

"I thought we were going to work on it together."

"We are," I said, flipping the eggs. "But my notes were in my purse, just begging to be looked over again. Ted Butcher and the explosion weren't even on my most promising list before last night." I took a deep breath. "Look. I don't know that all of these cases have anything to do with Bart. I don't know that *any* of them do. I just searched out weird, unexplained accidents and deaths. Ted caught my attention because he tried to kill himself so many times, in different ways. It wasn't until I put together the timeline that I realized his first attempt was two weeks after the family died." I pointed to the book. "The timeline's at the back."

He started flipping pages, then stopped on a page and began to read. After a few seconds, his gaze lifted. "I think you might be on to something, Carly."

"So I need to talk to Ted Butcher."

He made a face. "If his last two dances with death were drug overdoses, it sounds like he's a habitual user." When I gave him a blank look, he added, "He loses credibility."

"So you're saying if I can get Ted Butcher to confess to doing Bart Drummond's bidding, it might not help me one bit."

"Help *us* one bit," Marco said. "And yeah. That's exactly what I'm sayin'…unless he has evidence tying him and the deed to Bart."

"How likely is that?"

"Not very."

I pulled the cookie sheet with turkey bacon out of the oven, and Marco made another face. "I'm not eatin' that, Carly."

"Good. More for me and Hank."

"Your reluctant prisoner."

"Hey!" I protested, turning to face him with a pair of tongs in my hand. "I'm only trying to prolong his life. And he doesn't protest. Much."

He grinned. "I was teasing. But I'm still not eating turkey bacon."

I dished up a plate for Hank and cut his pancake into pieces before pouring a small amount of maple syrup on them. Then I grabbed the coffee pot to give him a refill and carried it and the plate out to the porch. When I came back, Marco was patiently waiting, his forearms on the table, but he gave me a weird look.

"What?"

"Do you cut up his meat for him too?"

It took me a second to realize what he was saying, and it didn't set right. "Are you serious?"

"I know your job is to help him in exchange for free rent, but he's not feeble."

"The man is eating on his front porch so we can have privacy," I said in a low tone, internally acknowledging that Hank was on the front porch because that was where he chose to be, but even so. "He's got a kitten in his lap. How's he going to balance a plate and a kitten while he's cutting up his pancakes?"

Marco held up his hands up in self-defense. "Okay, you're right. I'm sorry. I hadn't thought of that."

I stared down at him, my all-too-familiar fears bubbling up. "I don't know whether to believe you or question if you said that just to shut me up."

His eyes widened in surprise, but then he said, "Honestly? Maybe a little of both, and I'm sorry for that." His mouth pulled into a pained grin. "You make me a more honest man."

I knew he hadn't meant anything malicious, yet the hairs on the back of my neck still stood on end.

"Sit down," he said, gesturing to the chair on the other side of the table. "Let's figure out a game plan."

I put a plate of bacon and eggs on the table and sat down, watching him for a second while I nursed my coffee. I hated that doubts about him were swirling in my head. He thought I babied Hank too much. There wasn't anything sinister in saying so. Yet my fragile psyche reminded me that I'd let men control me for most of my life, and that I'd always made excuses when I saw warning signs. I didn't want that to happen with Marco too.

"Do you want to talk about Hank?" he asked evenly as he picked up his silverware.

"No. I do *not* want to talk about Hank," I snapped.

"I was wrong to say that," he said. "But he used to be a very powerful man. Just tread lightly."

Squinting, I shook my head. "What exactly are you suggesting? That he'd hurt me if I make a wrong move?"

"No," he said patiently. "Just the opposite. He cares about you enough to let you do things he'd normally do himself, just to make *you* happy. I'm sayin' don't take too much of his independence from him. That's all."

I didn't think we were in danger of that happening, but it was something to consider, so I nodded. Then I picked up my fork, eager to change the subject. "So I need to track down Ted Butcher."

"You're gonna need an address. I can come up with that, but I don't want you goin' there alone. I'll go with you. Who knows how dangerous he might be?" He frowned. "I'll look up his priors while I'm at it."

"Okay," I said, slicing off a piece of pancake. "Sounds good. I'm also going to find Sandy Steadman and talk to her."

He gave me a blank look.

"She's one of the ladies lunch club members, and she seems the most likely to talk. Plus, she's not dangerous. I'll ask her about Pam's son and see if I can get more information about his arrest. The personal stuff Pam went through, not the legal details."

"That's a good idea. I'd feel better if you stick to the people least likely to hurt you, but don't take any chances. No one thought Pam was dangerous either. If you're worried about your safety at all, walk away or find a way to contact me. I'll come straight away."

I nodded. "I thought I might talk to Pam's daughter too. Take her a casserole and see what she says."

He took another bite, his expression thoughtful. "Yeah, that could be good. Try not to make it look like questioning. You're just expressing your concern and checking on Pam's well-being." He looked up at me. "What time are you going into work today?"

"Five."

"So you have all day." His lips twisted. "Are you wanting to fill it with this stuff or do you have something else you need to do?"

"This is it."

"Then let's pick another old case to look into as well. If Bart catches wind we're tryin' to pin him to the wall, he's gonna pull out all the stops. We need to make sure we've got enough evidence to arrest him...and keep him in custody."

"Don't you think he's more likely to figure out what we're up to if we poke into several of his favors?"

He was silent for a moment. "We don't have to go balls to the walls with more than two cases. You stick to gatherin' information about Pam, and I'll see what I can dig up on Ted Butcher. Then we'll meet later to discuss what we've learned."

"I'm workin' until midnight."

"Tell Hank you're stayin' with me tonight. I have some interviews this morning, but I'll come by the tavern to check on you after I get off my shift."

I smiled at him. "Look at you. All grown up and doing big boy stuff."

He laughed. "I could take great offense to that, but I'm so grateful to have the opportunity—" his grin spread "—I have to agree with you."

I lifted my coffee mug. "To a successful investigation."

He touched his mug to mine. "All of them."

Chapter Nine

W e came up with a short list of people for me to talk to before I went to work, deciding that I should stick to visits I could call social visits, so I didn't attract the attention of the sheriff's department or Bart Drummond himself…if he was involved.

"Why isn't the Ewing police department handling the murder investigation?" I asked as I pushed my empty plate away. "It happened within the city limits."

"Because the sheriff's department would end up handling all the forensics anyway," he said. "We usually claim jurisdiction over murder cases. In some cases, the Tennessee Bureau of Investigation comes in and takes it over from both of us."

"Do you think the state will take over in this instance?"

"No. It's pretty cut and dry. Pam Crimshaw shot Jim Palmer at close range with a handgun in front of three witnesses—two employees and a customer. There's no doubt she did it *and* she confessed. Her motive doesn't really matter in terms of the case."

"Even if we prove Bart was behind it, Pam's still going to prison, isn't she?"

He gave me a long look. "She killed a man, Carly. A man with a wife and two kids. She stole him from the people who care about him."

I nodded, knowing he was right, but Pam was so quiet and meek. I suspected it would have taken a lot to make her shoot someone.

"Too bad I can't talk to the victim's family," I said. "If she killed him as a form of repayment to Bart, then he must have gotten himself into trouble. Maybe he even asked for a favor himself."

"There's always the funeral or the wake," Marco said. "I can come with you. The body's in Knoxville for an autopsy, so the funeral will probably be in a few days."

"That would be tasteless to ask questions there," I said, feeling slimy.

He pushed out a sigh. "I can figure out a legitimate excuse for us to go."

Still, it felt smarmy. We would be questioning the character of a murdered man. Then again, I had no intention of approaching anyone in his family, and it would be a good opportunity to learn more about him.

"I've been thinkin' about Jerry," he said slowly, as though he anticipated my reaction and was preparing himself for it.

"And?"

"Him workin' on Drummond's land might be a good thing."

My mouth fell open. "You've got to be kidding me."

He held up a hand. "Now hear me out."

I gave him a dark look.

"Jerry might be a little slow at times, but he isn't stupid. What if he has his own reason for workin' for Drummond?"

"And what would that be?" In my mind's eye, I saw Bart Drummond. Then a new fear struck me. "Oh my God. Do you think Bart considers this a favor?"

His eyes widened. "*What?* No. Jerry didn't ask him for a job. He said Bart offered it."

"So why do you think Jerry took it?" I asked.

"What if Jerry means to spy on him?"

"Jerry? Spy?" I asked in shock, but after a moment's consideration, I realized it wasn't such a shocking suggestion after all. Jerry had shot Carson Purdy, saving our lives. He was tougher than he seemed. And yet... "He has no reason to. He has no idea we're digging up dirt on Bart, and I've never heard anything about him having a personal vendetta against the Drummonds. His wife died of cancer, which not even Bart Drummond could have pulled off. It seems unlikely."

"Maybe so, but we could try to use him."

"First, listen to what you just said," I said, getting irritated. "*Use Jerry?* The man who saved our lives?" I shook my head. "No. We will not be *using* Jerry."

He reached across the table and placed his hand over mine. Tingles shot up my arm and I ached to turn my hand over and link our fingers. To prolong the moment. Which irritated me given the fact I was pissed. It made me question my judgment. Again.

"Carly, that's not what I meant," he said, squeezing my hand, obviously oblivious to my reaction. "It was a poor choice of words, so just hear me out. That man thinks the world of you. He'd keep an eye out for things if you asked."

"I'm already worried about him working for the devil himself. The last thing he needs is to put himself at further risk." I shook my head again, forcing myself to pull my hand out from underneath his. "No. Absolutely not."

"Okay," he said, sitting back in his seat. "We'll leave it be."

Maybe so, but I couldn't help thinking that he only intended to leave it be for *now*.

Standing, he picked up his plate and walked over to the sink. "Let's agree to check in with each other at some point today. Where are you going to get started?"

I stood too, pursing my lips. "Ewing. I'm thinking I might go see Thelma at the nursing home. She knows a lot about Bart's favors. I think I found the house fire she mentioned in my research. A lot of innocent people died. If we can link Bart to that one, we might have something. Maybe she'll tell me more this time because I have names and dates."

Thelma was my friend Greta's grandmother, and she'd proven a wealth of information about all things Drum related. Particularly the Drummonds.

"Just be careful what you allude to." Since Hank didn't have a dishwasher, Marco plugged the sink and filled it with soap and water. "We don't want to tip anyone off to what you're up to."

"Thelma won't tell anyone."

"Probably not, but there's a chance other people might be listening." He held out his hand, reaching for my plate.

"You sound paranoid," I said, handing it to him with a weak smile. "But so am I. I'll be careful."

He washed a plate and handed it to me to dry, I took it without even thinking. We'd spent enough time together to have a comfortable routine when we were at Hank's—he preferred washing and I liked to put the dishes away.

"If you're planning on bringing Pam's daughter a casserole today," he said, scrubbing the next plate, "you might want to run to the Dollar General to pick up some ingredients that are more Drum friendly."

I laughed. "You think the good people of Drum won't like cauliflower rice?"

He shot me a grin over his shoulder. "Not likely. I love you, and even I won't eat it." He froze for a second before turning back to the sink. "You know what I meant."

Still, some of the awkwardness from the night before had leaked back in. My heart stuttered. Marco's affection for me went deeper than friendship, and however reluctant I was to admit it, I knew the same was true of my feelings for him. But if we brought it out into the open, we'd have to *do* something about it, and I still wasn't ready. So I ignored his profession, even as it burned inside of me.

"Message received," I said in a teasing tone. "No casseroles with cauliflower rice for you *or* the citizens of Drum."

He handed me a plate, his ornery grin back. "Trust me. We *all* thank you."

We finished up the dirty dishes, and he helped me decide on what to bring Pam's daughter and Sandy from the ladies club. Chicken and rice casserole for Ashlynn, and brownies for Sandy. I had all the ingredients for both and wouldn't have to run into town to get anything.

Marco pulled the drain stopper and let the water out of the sink, then cast a glance at the clock on the wall. "I need to get going, but if you're still in Ewing this afternoon, give me a call. I have an interview there at one." He hesitated, sounding unsure of himself. "Maybe we can do a late lunch."

"I'd like that," I said, hating that we were suddenly tiptoeing around each other. A week ago we would have just planned it and been done with it.

He dried his hands with a towel, his biceps reacting to the simple movement in a way that attracted my eyes. Then he turned to me, putting his hands on my upper arms as he held my gaze with a serious expression. "Be careful, Carly. Very careful. Try not to look too suspicious."

"Okay."

He hesitated again, acting like he wanted to give me a hug, but instead he dropped his hold and headed for the front door.

I followed, my heart heavy. Hank was in his chair, still petting his kitten. I realized too late I hadn't been careful about letting Letty out. She bolted over the threshold, straight for the bird feeder. Birds went flying, some squawking in protest.

"Look what you did," Hank grumbled, then pushed out a sigh.

"She's a hellcat, Hank," Marco said with a grin as he opened his car door.

"I thought gettin' that cat fixed would settle her down," Hank said.

Marco laughed. "I was talkin' about her owner."

I snorted and rolled my eyes, but I grinned back. "Better that than a pushover."

Hank grumbled something about being stuck with *two* hellcats, and at least Smoky was sweeter than pie, but he gave me a soft look. I'd been a pushover, and now I wasn't. He knew it and was as proud of me as I was of myself.

We watched Marco pull away in silence while Letty skulked around the yard, trying to find more birds to torment.

"You two okay?" Hank asked.

I started to tell him we were fine, but I was done lying to him. I might keep things from him—sometimes because he insisted he didn't want to know all of my secrets—but I refused to lie. "Honestly, I don't know."

"That boy loves you, you know."

Tears stung my eyes. "I've suspected."

"You love him too."

I shrugged. My feelings were complicated, mostly because I didn't know how to trust them. "Maybe."

He kept his gaze on Letty, who was still as a tree stump, watching the bird feeder. "I've been in love a few times. Only found one woman I loved more than I loved myself. That's a sign of true love, girl. If you love someone else enough to give up part of yourself to make them happy."

The pancakes began to churn in my stomach. I wasn't sure I would ever love anyone enough to give up part of myself. Not anymore. "I gave up part of myself for a man before, Hank. That's why I'm standing here now."

"You picked the wrong man, girlie. Ya *both* gotta be willing to sacrifice yourselves, or it ain't gonna work. That's why Wyatt was never gonna be the one for you. He wasn't willing to give you what you needed." He pointed toward the road. "*That* man would take a bullet for you without even blinkin'. He'd move to Timbuktu if you asked. He'd give you babies if you want 'em, and not if you don't. But you gotta love him the same way, or it won't work any better than bein' with Wyatt."

His words beat into me. They had the feeling of truth. But even though I knew Marco would run with me if I asked, I doubted he'd be happy about that decision. And I couldn't think of a single thing I was willing to give up for him. I wasn't sure if that was a sign I didn't love him enough or if it just made me a bitch. Part of me felt like I had nothing left to give up.

"Don't look so troubled," Hank said with a sad smile. "You don't trust easy, as you shouldn't, but you trust Marco more than anyone else in this God-forsaken town. That has to mean something."

"What if it takes me too long to figure out how I really feel?" I asked. "What if he gets tired of waiting?"

Hank reached over and took my hand. "Then it wasn't meant to be. There ain't no rule book that says we get a great love. And there ain't no rule that says we won't get several. But I truly believe the Almighty has a plan for us. That He takes the shit life throws at us and turns it into fertilizer for new things."

I gave him a skeptical look. "Since when did you become a philosopher?"

"Sittin' on the porch has given me plenty of time to think, but you know I ain't wrong. If that fiancé of yours hadn't screwed you over, you wouldn't be standing here now."

I put my hand on my hip. "You're pretty wise for a cranky old fart."

He belly-laughed. "Some would disagree with that."

"Not about the cranky part," I said, picking up his empty plate. "Since you're so contemplative, I'll let you have one of the brownies I'm about to make for Sandy Steadman."

His eyes narrowed. "Since when were you friends with Sandy Steadman?"

"We're not exactly friends. She's a customer at the restaurant."

"Why are you bringin' a customer brownies?"

While I suspected Hank didn't know anything about Pam, it wouldn't hurt to ask him. I sat down in the chair next to him. "A woman killed a man in Ewing a couple of days ago."

"And that has something to do with Sandy Steadman?"

"Yeah, sort of. Sandy's one of Pam's best friends. They had lunch together every other week or so at the tavern." I paused. "I'm taking her brownies because I hope to get information from her."

"Am I going to regret asking why?"

"Probably," I said with a small smile. "Pam Crimshaw shot a man in cold blood in his insurance office, then drove to Sonic and waited for the police to come arrest her."

His startled look slipped into a frown. "Why'd she do that?"

"She didn't give a reason. She said she just felt like it."

"She just felt like shooting a man in his office?" he asked in disbelief.

"Pretty unbelievable, right? Marco doesn't think the detectives on the case will dig any deeper, but it sounds awfully fishy to me. To both of us."

He was silent for a couple of seconds. "You think it's a Bart Drummond favor."

"Yes." When he didn't say anything, I asked, "Do you know anything about Pam? Her husband's name is Rob."

He frowned again, then shook his head. "Not much, but I knew a Stewie Crimshaw. He had a couple of sons. They'd be in their forties about now."

"That would fit. Anything you remember about him that might help?"

"Just that he was a mean son of a bitch. He beat his wife and kids."

"I hear Rob's not so nice himself."

"The apple doesn't usually fall far from the tree," he said.

That wasn't something I could ask Pam's daughter, Ashlynn. *Did your father beat you?* wasn't exactly a good conversation opener. In fact, the more I thought about it, the more I wondered if I should talk to her at all, but I decided to take her the casserole anyway. I lived in Drum. I was part of the community, and I needed to act like it. I'd take it from Hank and me.

"You could be gettin' yourself into trouble with this one," he said gruffly. "While I suspect a lot of the things that have been blamed on Drummond over the years had nothin' to do with the man, the favors are real, and he holds people accountable." He gave me a look that reminded me that Bart Drummond considered keeping my real name quiet a favor, and he would expect to call on that someday too.

"Why would people put themselves in that position?" I asked. "He asks for horrible things in return."

"Not always. Sometimes the favors are as simple as deliverin' an envelope to Knoxville." He turned his head to face me. "Like you said, if they were all bad, no one would ask. There aren't enough people in town desperate enough to go to him, knowing they'll be asked to commit murder in exchange, but it's a lot like playin' Russian roulette. You just never know what you'll get."

"And no one's defied him?" I asked.

"I'm sure some have tried, but he retaliates by getting another person who owes him a favor to take care of them." He paused. "Or he got his right-hand man, Purdy, to do it."

Carson Purdy, who'd tried to kill me and Marco and Wyatt. Who'd supplied the tainted drugs that had killed Hank's daughter and been an accessory to his grandson's murder.

Exhaustion crept into Hank's voice. "Like you, I suspect Purdy wasn't acting on his own. Once I retired, Drummond saw Bingham as his biggest threat, and maybe he thought he could move into his market. Money's been tight for Drummond, and runnin' his land ain't cheap. His 'spa' in Ewing ain't bringin' in money, and neither is the Alpine Inn in town. It stands to reason that he'd try to find a new source of income, and he let Purdy be the face of it."

"Do you think he'd ask his new manager to pick up where Purdy left off?"

He turned to me in surprise. "Has he hired someone?"

I swallowed, my small hairs standing on end. "Jerry Nelson."

His eyes widened. "You're kiddin'."

A lump formed in my throat. "I wish I were."

He was silent for several seconds as he studied the bird feeder. "Jerry wouldn't hurt a fly."

"He killed Carson Purdy," I countered.

"That was different," Hank scoffed. "He was protectin' you and Marco."

"What if Bart convinces him he's protectin' someone?" Sure, Marco thought Jerry knew what he was doing—that he might even be playing Bart—but I couldn't see that man as anything but an innocent. I took a breath. "Maybe this makes me sound like a narcissist, but I can't help thinking Bart hired him because of me. He was hired at the tavern, of all places, and they kept giving him more and more responsibility. Drummond told him he was promoted to the overseer position as a reward, both for his hard work and for protecting Wyatt, but what if he did it because he wanted something else over me?" I leaned forward, resting my elbows on my knees. "I know I sound crazy, but Bart Drummond has made it clear there's a target on my back, so is it really that far-fetched?"

Hank petted the kitten in his lap, his gaze far-off. "Maybe not," he finally said. "Drummond's definitely playin' the long game here. He's gonna keep tethering you to him with hooks until he's ready to call in that favor. Maybe he thought he could use Wyatt to hold you, but when that fell through, he set his sights on Jerry."

"And you," I said, deciding to put all my cards on the table. "He's threatened to expose you." He'd made that threat back in November, and I'd kept it a secret, but I realized Bart had probably expected me to do just that. He'd isolated me by putting up barriers between me and the people I cared about, presuming I'd keep my silence to protect them. So far his plan had worked, but I was done playing by his rules. I was making my own, and the first step was to make Hank part of my team, not treat him like someone I needed to protect.

"Expose me?" he asked with a chuckle. "What exactly is he plannin' to expose? Everything's out there in the open."

"Then why aren't you in prison?"

"Because I had my own deals with the sheriff's department back in the day, and because there's no proof at this point, not to mention the statute of limitations."

"What if he has proof?"

He snorted. "Trust me, if Bart Drummond had evidence that could put me in prison, he would have used it by now, especially back in the nineties with Reagan's War on Drugs. He can't hurt me."

"What's the statute of limitations for selling drugs?"

Releasing a chuckle, he said, "The hard stuff? Fifteen years. I'm just about out of prosecuting range."

"But there's no statute of limitations for murder."

Hank's face lost all expression. "I did what needed to be done."

I was referring to the man Hank had killed last fall. One of his grandson's killers had broken into the house to murder me, and Hank had gotten to him first. It had been self-defense, but if Bart had somehow caught wind of it, he could find a way to construe it as cold-blooded murder. But Hank's choice of words implied there were more crimes that could be used against him. I suspected I wasn't the only person he'd protected in that way.

"What if Bart has evidence of a murder? Even if it's concocted?"

"He would have used it by now," he said. "Just like I would have used anything I had against him."

"Turned him in?" I asked with a short laugh. "Somehow I doubt it. Something tells me you'd handle things more like Bingham."

He was silent again. "I think it's fair to say I was a mix of the two. I could play the role of the gentleman, but I was ruthless when necessary."

I'd already come to that conclusion. His past had come up before, and the more I learned about how he'd conducted business, the more I learned that the man I currently knew was very different than the man he'd once been.

And some days I wasn't sure what to think about that.

Chapter Ten

Hank knew where Sandy lived, so finding her address was easy. She would have been able to direct me to Ashlynn, but I didn't necessarily want to ask. A lot depended on how our talk went. So instead I called Greta at Watson's Café, knowing she was on the morning shift on Wednesdays.

"I hope I'm not getting you into trouble calling you at work," I said.

"Not at all," she said in a cheerful tone. "We're past the morning rush. What's up?"

"I heard about Pam Crimshaw and I feel just terrible," I said, which was true. "I wanted to take her daughter Ashlynn a casserole, but I don't have her address. Do you have any idea who might?"

"I can help you there," she said. "Ashlynn was younger than me, but I dropped her off after school a few times."

"Thanks, but I need to know where she's livin' now."

"It's the same place," she said, then added, "well, kind of. She and Chuck live in a trailer on her parents' land."

"Oh." That was actually better. It gave me an excuse to see where Pam lived. I was about to thank Greta and hang up, but I couldn't help wondering what she knew about the whole situation. Even if it was just hearsay, I could sort out fact from fiction later.

"I just can't believe Pam would do such a thing," I said in a sympathetic tone. "She used to come into the tavern a lot, and she always seemed so quiet and meek around her friends. But then you probably knew her because of her daughter…"

"I didn't really know Pam," Greta said. "But the few times I saw her, she was with Ashlynn's dad, and he's not a very nice man, if you know what I mean."

"He's angry?" I prodded. "Short on patience?"

"That and more—rude, overbearing. I think he hit his wife and kids. It wasn't all that unusual for Ashlynn to show up to school with bruises."

"And no one reported it to child protective services?" I asked in disbelief. As a teacher, I'd been a mandated reporter of suspected abuse. Then again, I'd heard worse stories about Drum, including that Todd Bingham's little brother had disappeared, possibly murdered by his own father.

"If they did, nothing came of it."

"Do you have any idea why Pam would kill someone? I'm having trouble wrapping my head around it."

"She probably just snapped," Greta said matter-of-factly. "Everyone has their breaking point. Even nice people. *Especially* nice people. They stuff it all down until they can't anymore."

Maybe she was right. Maybe Pam had been beaten and berated one too many times, but if that was so, why hadn't she killed her husband?

Greta gave me directions on how to get to the Crimshaw property, then said, "You, me, and Lula should get together soon and have a girls' night out."

Her suggestion caught me by surprise, but then so did my elation. While I had Marco, I was lonely for female friends. I saw plenty of Ruth at work and Carnita at the library, but it wasn't the same as hanging out socially. "Yeah," I said eagerly. "I'd really like that." But I couldn't help wondering what a girls' night out in Drum would look like. The only things I could come up with were going out for drinks at Max's Tavern or hanging out at the Methodist church on quilting night, although it *was* rumored they drank wine while they sewed.

***

After spending an hour and a half in the kitchen, I was finally ready to go. I wrapped up Sandy's brownies on a paper plate, saving some to bring to work and two for me and Hank, then covered the casserole dish with tinfoil. I'd have to pick up another one at Target the next time I went to Greeneville. I didn't expect to get this one back.

The food went into a basket, and I went out the door.

"I left you a brownie on the kitchen table," I said to Hank, who still sat in his chair watching Letty. I'd already warned him I wouldn't back that night. His response had been to ask if I was sleeping with Marco or just teasing him. "And I put out fresh food and water for the kittens."

"That damn hellcat'll have to come inside to eat it."

I laughed. "Unless she eats a bird."

He shot me a dark look.

"I made a chicken and rice casserole for you too, and I portioned it out into containers for your meals."

"You're lettin' me have rice?" he grumbled.

"Don't get too excited. It's cauliflower rice mixed in with the real stuff, but be sure to check your blood sugar."

"I will."

I started down the steps, the basket slung over one arm and the bag with my work clothes and shoes over the other, but I found myself turning back to look at him. "Don't you get tired of hangin' out here every day?"

Surprise filled his eyes.

"I mean, I know you're retired and all, but did you used to spend all your time here before the surgery, or did you do other things?"

"I used to spend a lot of time at the hardware store," he said, his gaze turning to the bird feeder.

"The doctor said we could get an apparatus to help you drive. We should look into it."

He waved a hand as if swatting the idea. "Those things cost too damn much money."

"You could learn to drive with just your left foot. I'm sure it just takes practice." When he didn't respond, I decided to let it go for now. "Okay. Have a nice day, Hank."

"You too, girlie," he said affectionately.

I headed to Sandy's house first. It was a one-story bungalow on the way into town, close to where Marco lived. I got out and walked up to her porch to ring the bell, but the front door opened before I reached the steps.

"Carly, this is a surprise," Sandy said as she walked out onto the porch, closing the door behind her.

"I just feel awful about Pam," I said. "I know you must feel ten times worse and, well, my mother always seemed to think food helped heal all wounds, so I made a batch of brownies and brought some to you." I'd said the part about my mother as an excuse to show up at Sandy's front door uninvited, but it hit me that my mother really had believed that to be true. She'd made my favorite lunch for dinner on days I was sad—chicken salad— and my favorite dessert for celebrations. She'd done the same thing for my father...before it had all turned upside down.

"Is that why you work in food service?"

"What? No," I said truthfully. "Max offered me a job after my car broke down in Drum. By the time I could afford a new one, I liked the people I worked with far too much to leave."

"And you're livin' with Hank Chalmers?" she asked with narrowed eyes.

"That's right."

"No family or friends worried about you?"

"No," I said, wondering how this had gotten turned around so that she was the inquisitor. "I had a best friend—a fiancé—but he died." It was somewhat truthful. Jake might not be buried in the ground, but he was dead to me. "It was hard to get close to people after that. Especially since Atlanta's such a big city." I wondered if I was giving her too much information. Sure, I'd eventually shared as much with Max and Ruth, who'd started asking more questions about my past. They'd been sympathetic enough about my quote, unquote tragedy not to press, but Sandy seemed like a dog after a bone.

"You're from Michigan, right?"

"That's right."

"I've got relatives in Michigan."

"No kidding. Which part?" I asked.

"Detroit."

"I grew up near Traverse City."

"Mighty cold winters up there."

I gave her a grin. "Why do you think I moved to Atlanta?"

She studied me for a moment, then gestured to the two wicker chairs on her front porch, looking out over multiple flowerbeds. "Where are my manners? Have a seat."

Did that mean I'd passed a test? Or was she preparing for round two? "Thanks. I'd love to." I handed her the plate, then lowered into the chair farthest from the door.

Once she was settled in her own seat, I said, "I hope this isn't an imposition."

"No," she said, setting the plate on the table between us. "No one who comes calling with brownies could be an imposition."

"It's just that I'm still pretty shook up over Pam," I said quietly. "I realize I didn't know her that well, but I'm just... Well, it's all I can think about, and no one else seems to get it. So I thought I might come see you." I gave her an earnest look. "You always seem like you know exactly what to say and do. I guess I hoped you could help me make sense of it all."

"I would do that if I understood it myself," she said, shaking her head. "I have no idea what happened."

"People are saying that her husband beat her one too many times, so she lost it and went to Ewing just looking for someone to shoot."

"The *beatin' her one too many times* part might be accurate," Sandy said, "but Pam couldn't even put out traps for mice. She didn't want to kill them. I just can't fathom her killin' a human being."

I sat up and turned in my seat to face her. "Could they have arrested the wrong person?"

"Sadly, no. There's a surveillance video that shows her parkin' her car in the Palmer's Insurance parking lot and then leaving less than twenty seconds later, the gun still in her hand."

"And they're sure it was her?"

"I recognized the green shirt," Sandy said, her voice breaking. "It's her favorite."

We sat in silence for a moment. "It just seems so random," I finally said. "Was he even her insurance agent? One of the rumors goin' round is that Jim Palmer was her agent when her youngest son got a DUI."

"No, she's had Travis Keeling since Ashlynn started driving. Their insurance went up, and Travis got her a better deal."

"Could she have switched from Jim to Travis?"

"I don't think so," she said with a frown, "but I don't remember. We didn't make a habit of discussing our insurance."

So that theory was out.

If there was no direct connection between them, it suggested Bart had been involved, but a new angle occurred to me. What if Jim had represented the driver of the car Thad had hit? But Sandy looked like she was getting suspicious of all my questions, and I doubted she'd be able to clear up that particular issue.

I sat back in the chair, shaking my head again. "Sorry for the twenty questions. I just have this sick feeling in the pit of my stomach." I put my hand on my abdomen and pressed hard. "It's literally all I can think about."

Sandy's eyes narrowed. "I didn't know you were so close to Pam."

"I'm not," I admitted. "That's why I don't understand why I'm so upset."

She was quiet for a moment. "It's a tragic thing that Pam has done, and I think we all have questions. I'm just not sure we'll find the answers we're lookin' for. Pam has been dealing with depression. Maybe one of her meds made her do it."

"How long has she been depressed?"

She let out a defeated sigh. "I'd like to say ever since Thad's accident, but I think it goes back farther then that. That's just when she started taking medication." Reaching over, she patted my hand resting on the arm of the chair. "The best thing you can do is support her family."

"I was planning on taking a casserole to Ashlynn."

Sandy nodded. "That's a good idea. Ashlynn's not much of a cook, and those boys barely know how to turn on a microwave, but don't tell Diane that you're messing with her schedule."

Oh, crap. How had I forgotten? I gave her a wry look. "Then would *you* like a chicken and rice casserole for dinner? I don't want to upset Diane."

Sandy laughed. "I know for a fact that Diane penciled in Nora Burgess for today. She could burn boiled water. Trust me. Those kids'll thank you."

"Then that settles it," I said. "I'll drop it off after I leave here."

She gave me a warm smile, but I saw the worry in her eyes.

I leaned forward. "Do you know if Pam's family has enough money to pay for her legal fees?"

Her upper lip curled. "They don't have two pennies to rub together. She's using a public defender. Some guy just out of law school."

Which meant he was inexperienced and overworked.

"Should we try to raise some money to help her find a better one?" I asked.

"What's the point?" Sandy sank back into her chair and sounded defeated. "She confessed. She did it."

"A good attorney could mean the difference between getting twenty years or life in prison."

Sandy gave me a pointed look. "What difference does it make, Carly? Her life is over either way."

I swallowed a lump in my throat and blinked back tears. "Yeah, I guess."

Her expression softened. "You have a good heart, but Pam's a lost cause."

I didn't respond, because while I knew it was true, logically speaking, my heart wasn't willing to accept it. Sure, I was looking into the murder because I wanted ammunition to bring down

Bart, but I realized part of me was also hoping to find a way to get Pam out of this. Still, Marco was right: no matter what her reasoning, she'd killed a man. She'd stolen him from all the people who loved and cared about him. There was no fixing that. Maybe she deserved to spend the rest of her life in prison while his family lived in the prison she'd created.

Sandy patted my hand again. "When you live in Drum long enough, you'll realize it's the way of things."

"What's that mean?" I asked.

Withdrawing her hand, she shifted in her seat and seemed to think over her words. "Drum's like a whole other world, almost like we're stuck in time. Sure, some things change, but the sorrows of this place remain the same. It doesn't make it right, but we've become accustomed to it."

I wasn't accustomed to it, and I didn't want to be.

"If you hear of anything I can do to help in any way, be sure to let me know, okay?" I said.

A warm smile lit up her eyes. "I will. And thanks for the brownies."

I got in the car and took off.

The Crimshaws lived on a side road off the highway to Ewing, which meant it was on the way to the nursing home where Thelma lived. It also meant I had to drive through Drum. As I approached downtown, I decided to make a stop that was bound to make me uncomfortable. I'd spent the better part of the drive from Sandy's house thinking about Hank's definition of true love—that you would be willing to give up something of yourself to make the other person happy—and I realized he didn't just feel that way about romantic love.

I turned off into the Drummond Garage and pulled into a space in the front parking lot. One of the garage bay doors was open and an older pickup truck was parked inside, its hood up.

I headed toward the door to the waiting room, but Wyatt walked around the side of the truck toward me.

I stopped in the entrance to the garage, suddenly nervous, although I had no idea why. I knew he wouldn't refuse me. Maybe that was why I felt so on edge. In a way, I was using him.

"Carly, is everything okay?" he asked, squinting. The sun was at my back.

"Yeah," I said with a weak smile. I almost asked him if he could say the same. Something had driven him into the tavern to talk to Max, whether it was related to one of their father's favors or not, but I decided to hold that card for later. "I'm here about Hank."

He held his hand up to his forehead to shield his eyes. Still, I could see the concern blooming there. "Is *he* okay?"

"Yes and no."

Why was this so hard? Probably because I hated asking him for anything, even if it wasn't for myself. I gestured toward the garage beyond the pickup. "Do you want to go inside for this conversation?"

"Yeah." He stepped to the side to allow me to walk past him, and he followed several feet behind until we stood in front of the vehicle, out of view from people driving past. I glanced over at the other two bays, surprised to see them empty.

"Do you want to go into my office?" he asked, still looking worried.

"No," I said, my brow wrinkling. "Sorry, I think I'm making this into a bigger deal than it needs to be, so let me get to the point." I gave him a tight smile. "Obviously I didn't know Hank before his leg was amputated and Seth was killed, so I have no idea what his life used to be like. Did he leave the house much? Did he hang out with friends? He just sits at the house all day long, mostly by himself and…I'm just worried that he's lonely."

He leaned his hip against the side of the truck, the tension leaving his face. "He didn't leave much the last six months or so before the surgery. He was dealing with the sores on his foot and ankle, which made it hard to walk and drive. I'd been spending time with Seth and Hank since Barbara died, but I went out there more in those last few months."

My chest tightened. While I hadn't outright made Hank choose between me and Wyatt, he'd chosen anyway. "I took you from him."

"Hey," Wyatt said softly, pushing away from the truck and closing the distance between us. "You didn't do anything wrong."

"He chose me over you, and you were the one who'd been there for him for months."

"That's not it, Carly. He didn't approve of the way I was treating you. There's a difference." He grimaced. "He didn't just tell me to stop comin' round. We had a discussion about it. He knew I was keepin' things from you, and he told me to come clean. I told him I was protectin' you, but he insisted that you deserved the truth. It was after the Lula mess that it all came to a head. He said I was hurtin' you and that I needed to stop comin' round for a while."

Hank had given up part of himself to make me happy. While I loved him for it, I hated that I'd put him in that position.

I turned away, running a hand over my head.

"I think you remind him of Barb," he said softly. "How she was before she started using drugs. She had this sweet, generous spirit. Just like you."

I knew I should counter that statement somehow, especially since I wasn't feeling very sweet *or* generous. It felt like I kept hurting the people I cared about—Marco, Hank, and even Wyatt to some degree.

"But you're different than her," he said. "You're stronger. I think Hank wishes Barb had been more like you."

I spun around to face him. "You're sayin' I'm his substitute daughter."

"Yeah."

I suddenly felt sick to my stomach. Being a daughter had never worked out very well for me, and it made me feel Hank's affection for me wasn't for me, per se, but for the role I filled.

He studied me with a look of consternation. "That's a compliment, Carly."

It sure didn't feel like one, but I wasn't here to discuss me. This was about Hank and *his* happiness.

"I just want Hank to be happy," I said, "and I'm gone more often than I'm home, which means he spends hours and hours alone. My goal is to restore some of his independence. He should be able to take care of himself and become less dependent on me."

His body stiffened slightly. "Are you thinkin' about leaving Drum?"

I propped a hand on my hip. "What makes you ask that?"

"It just seems like you're paving the way to make your departure."

"By trying to give Hank his independence? It's more like I'm the Eugene to his Rapunzel."

He blinked hard. "*What?*"

"Obviously you haven't seen *Tangled* ten million times," I said, thinking back to my teaching years. "I'm not leaving Drum"—no, his father had seen to that—"but I think we should encourage him to drive and go places."

"We?"

"I don't have foggiest idea of how to make his car more accessible to him, and once it's properly equipped, he'll need to learn how to drive it with the new additions."

"You want me to teach Hank how to drive." The corners of his lips lifted a little. "Do you have any idea what kind of grief I'll get when I suggest such a thing?"

"Yeah, I know," I said with a sigh, "but I'm askin' you to do it anyway. I'll be happy to pay for whatever needs to be done to his car—"

He jolted, his back ramrod stiff. "I'm not takin' your money to help Hank," he said in disgust.

"I'm sure if the car needs to be altered—"

"I'm not takin' your money," he said, less angry this time. "But I will make a trade."

"What kind of trade?"

"You have dinner with me."

"*Excuse me?*" I stared at him in disbelief. "You're using your friend to try to win me back? If that's your goal, this is the absolute *worst* way to go about it."

"Then make it breakfast or lunch, and it's not so I can win you back. Hank's not going to yield unless he thinks you're comfortable having me around. If he knows we're spending time together, he'll welcome me back over and I can hang out with him in the evenings again." His mouth twisted to the side. "I miss the old fart."

Dammit. He had a point, although I couldn't help thinking he also hoped to wear down my defenses. Nearly three months ago, he'd told me he thought we belonged together, and that had been four months after our three-week-long relationship. I suspected he hadn't suddenly given up on me, especially since I still saw the wistful looks he shot in my direction at the tavern when he thought I wasn't looking. If I'd learned anything, it was that these Drummonds all played the long game.

"No dinner. I'll spend an hour with you, although I can't tell you when. I have to work until closing, and I'll probably be covering the lunch shift tomorrow since Max fired Molly." I glanced over at Junior's empty bay. "Where's Junior?"

"The baby's sick, and he's going to watch her while Ginger works the lunch shift."

I grimaced. "Seems like Junior makes more than Ginger."

"You'd be surprised; besides, we didn't have a car for him to work on this morning." He paused. "What about breakfast tomorrow?" he asked. "You can come to my place. I'll make pancakes and this time you can eat them."

His house was the *last* place I wanted to go. He was sure to get the wrong idea. I considered suggesting Watson's Café, but then *the town* would get the wrong idea. "Come over to Hank's. You say we're doing this for his benefit, so it makes more sense for him to see us together rather than hearing about it." Plus, he could chaperone.

"But I planned to cook for you, not the other way around."

"Then you can cook for the both of us," I said. "But you can't make real bacon. Hank really shouldn't have it."

He watched me for several seconds, and I was starting to squirm when he said, "Okay. I'll be over at seven-thirty. I'd make it later, but I'll need to be at the shop by nine."

"That's fine." I'd have to leave Marco's house early, but if Wyatt only stayed until nine, I'd have some time to work on the case before I had to be at the tavern. "When can you start looking at Hank's car?"

"How about I look at it tomorrow? In the meantime, I'll do some research on fitting cars for amputees."

"Thanks," I said, feeling unsettled, although I couldn't figure out why. Was it because Wyatt had made me begin to doubt whether Hank's feelings for me were genuine or meant for a ghost, or because Wyatt had gone to new lengths to try win me back?

Probably both.

Chapter Eleven

I left Wyatt and headed toward Ewing, glancing over the instructions Greta had given me. I wasn't surprised she still remembered where Ashlynn lived. It was only four miles down the road from her sister's mobile home, which looked even trashier than it had a few months ago now that Greta had moved out.

The Crimshaws lived in a one-story house set about thirty feet back from the road. An old, metal mobile home sat about fifty feet to the side of the house. A small rusted hatchback was parked in the driveway to the house, and a pickup truck sat in front of the trailer. The house needed to be painted, but it looked like Pam had tried to make it inviting. Or at least she'd tried at some point. There were beds of flowers on either side of the front door, but the yard was full of weeds.

I parked my car behind the hatchback, weighing my options. I'd planned to bring the casserole to Ashlynn, but that was before I knew she lived next door to her family. While I still wanted to talk to Ashlynn, now I also had an opportunity to talk to Pam's sons or possibly her husband.

I approached the house and had started to climb the concrete steps, taking note of the loose wrought iron handrail, when the front door opened and a teenage boy stepped out. A hard look filled his eyes.

"What do you want?"

Was this Ricky or Thad? Whoever he was, he was rude, but then again, his mother was semi-famous for murdering a man. I wouldn't be surprised if they'd had reporters knocking on their door. "Hi," I said with what I hoped was a friendly smile. "I'm Carly, and I work at Max's Tavern. I know your mother."

"She ain't here," he said, leaning against the doorframe. "She's in jail for offin' a guy."

I tried not to wince at his bluntness. "That's why I'm here. I thought maybe y'all could use a home-cooked meal."

"Diane send you?" he asked, lifting his gaze and taking in the road behind me as though she might be lurking out there.

"No, Sandy sent me. I know Diane made a schedule for people to bring you food, but Sandy said she was sure it would be okay."

"What is it?" the teen asked with a slight toss of his head.

"Chicken and rice casserole."

"Cream of chicken or cream of mushroom soup?" a male voice shouted from inside.

"Uh...cream of chicken," I called out.

"Tell her to bring it in," the voice shouted.

The kid stepped out of the way, letting me walk inside.

The living room was dark, but I could see another boy sitting on the worn brown microsuede sofa, his fingers furiously clicking on the controller in his hands as he played a video game on the TV screen. Dirty plates and open cans of pop littered the coffee and end tables, along with several open bags of chips.

"Put it on the table." He gave me a cursory glance and started to turn toward the screen again, but his gaze jerked back to me. "Hey, I've seen you before."

"She works at the bar in town," the first boy said.

"The tavern," I said. "It's actually different from a bar."

"No kidding," said the kid playing the video game. "How so?"

"A tavern serves food." I lifted my brow. "And lets underaged kids inside."

He laughed. "How do you know I'm underage?"

"*Please*," I said in a drawl as I carried the casserole dish into the kitchen. If the living room looked bad, the kitchen was worse. The limited counter space was covered in dirty dishes and pots.

He laughed again, returning his attention to the game. "You know my mom?"

"I know her from the tavern. She comes in with her friends for lunch."

"The old bitches' club," he said with a derisive laugh.

I tamped down my irritation. Neither one of them seemed concerned about their mother, but it wouldn't do me favors to say so. "Have you seen or talked to your mom since she was arrested?"

The kid on the couch made a face. "Nah. We can't see her."

"What about your dad?"

The kid who'd answered the door laughed. "He ain't gonna waste his time."

"Why not?" I asked, trying to hide my shock.

Disgust covered his face. "She's never gettin' out, so why would he bother?"

I stared at him in disbelief. "Because he loves her?"

The guy on the sofa slapped his thigh and barked, "That's a good one."

"Don't you guys care that your mother is in jail?" I hadn't intended to say it so bluntly, but it burst out of me.

The kid on the sofa looked up at me, and I saw momentary pain flicker over his face, but he quickly covered it up with a look of manufactured contempt. "I'm gonna be movin' to Knoxville in another year. So I wouldn't be seein' much of her then anyway."

So this was Ricky. It was obvious this was hurting him a lot more than he was letting on. "You planning to go to college at UT?"

He snort-laughed. "That's a good one."

I couldn't help myself from asking, "Do you have a career plan?"

"Now you sound like my teachers," he said with a sneer.

"Yeah, well…" Old habits died hard.

"Thanks for the casserole," Ricky said, returning to his video game. "We'll be sure to eat it later."

So I'd been dismissed. Not that I was surprised. "Yeah, sure." I headed to the door, feeling like I'd screwed up, not because I'd failed to get useful information, but because Pam's kid was hurting and he clearly didn't know how to express it. Or feel like he could.

I started to walk out the front door, but I couldn't bring myself to just leave like that. Turning around, I asked, "Hey, did you know Seth Chalmers?"

"What?" His gaze shot up to mine.

"Seth Chalmers. The boy who was killed last November. I think he was about your age."

His expression sobered. "Yeah, I knew him." His eyes widened. "Hey, you're the woman who saw him killed, ain't ya?"

"Yeah."

His forehead furrowed. "Why're you asking about him?"

"I don't know," I said truthfully, but to be honest, Seth was never far from my thoughts. I was sleeping in his bed. Living with his grandfather. I'd been the one to pack up his things. I'd held his hand while he died. The only people I knew who'd been close to Seth were Hank and Wyatt, but I suspected his friends had seen a different side. Still, I hadn't even thought to ask about him until I was leaving, thinking about Ricky's potentially wasted future. Maybe the reason I'd hesitated to leave Ricky like this was because I couldn't help Seth, but Ricky still had a chance to make something of himself. "Were you two friends?"

He didn't answer, but the boy I presumed to be his brother, Thad, said, "They were."

"What was he like?" I asked.

Ricky didn't answer at first, but then he swallowed audibly. His gaze was still on the TV screen, but I realized his avatar hadn't moved since I'd asked about Seth. "He was cool," he finally said.

"He was funny," Thad said. "At least until his mom died. Then he turned serious."

"I'm sure that was hard on him," I said.

Ricky shrugged, looking indifferent. "She was a meth head."

"But he loved her anyway," I said softly. "He died trying to find out who was responsible for her death."

He didn't answer.

"She screwed up," I said, "but he still loved her. We can't turn that off just because someone has disappointed us."

His head jerked up, his eyes locked on mine. "You think you're a psychologist or something? You're nothing but an old waitress at a dumpy bar."

His remark was meant to sting, and it did, but I saw the pain in his eyes. "No," I said, my voice tight. "I'm just a woman who has been disappointed by many of the people in my life, so

I get wanting to understand." I gave him a tight smile. "I'd love to know more about Seth. If you ever feel like talking about him, call me or drop by at the tavern."

He gave me a long look, then turned back to the TV and said in a flippant tone, "Whatever."

Thad glanced between me and his brother, then shrugged and headed into the kitchen.

There was nothing else to say, so I headed out the door, wondering if I'd just wasted my time and made Ricky feel worse. At least I'd given them a home-cooked meal.

I stopped next to my car, wondering if I should still try to talk to Ashlynn. For all I knew, she was at work. But then I saw one of the curtains in the front of the trailer flutter, as though someone had been watching me. Seconds later, the side door opened, and a young woman with long dark brown hair stepped out onto the wooden steps. Her maternity shirt was worn, and the pattern was something that had been popular over a decade ago.

"I ain't never seen you here before," she said with a wary look.

"I've never been here before." I smiled, hoping it would give me a non-threatening appearance. "I'm a waitress at Max's. Your mother came in every couple of weeks with her friends, and I got to know her pretty well. I heard about what happened and wanted to bring y'all some dinner."

"How'd you know I was her daughter?" she asked, her voice pinched.

"Sandy told me you lived in a trailer next to your mother's house. She said it would be okay if I brought y'all food."

"You ain't supposed to bring food today," she said. "Nora Burgess is on the schedule for today."

"Sandy suggested y'all might like havin' another option."

A slow smile spread across her face. "Nora can't cook worth shit."

I grinned at her. "So I heard."

She started down the steps, and as she turned, I noticed the rounded belly under her loose shirt. "You say you work at the tavern?" she asked in a much friendlier tone than moments before. "You're the new waitress. The one who found Seth."

"Yeah," I said in surprise, not because she'd heard of me, but because of the familiar way she said Seth's name. "Did you know Seth?"

"Sure did. He was Ricky's best friend."

I let that sink in for a couple of seconds as she closed the distance between us.

Did Hank know that? Had he lied to me when he'd said he didn't know much about Pam and her family?

A breeze kicked up, blowing stray hairs from my face. I reached up to brush them away. "I asked Ricky if he knew Seth, but he kind of blew me off."

"He didn't handle his death very good."

"Do you think he knew what Seth was up to?"

"Sure. He was trying to find out who gave his mother the bad drugs, and workin' with Todd Bingham to do it." She made a face. "Not many people know about that part, but Ricky did."

"It makes sense that he'd know, seeing how they were best friends. Did Ricky tell you anything about what Seth found out?"

She shrugged. "I don't know. He never talked about it. Even when Dad tried to beat it out of him."

I cringed. "Your dad doesn't approve of Bingham?"

She snorted. "Nope. Thinks he's white trash." She cocked a brow in challenge. "Don't you?"

I hesitated before answering, "Bingham is a customer at Max's."

She released a short laugh. "Good answer."

"He's a complex man."

"Even better answer," she said with a grin.

"I'm sorry about your mother. I couldn't believe it when I heard the news. It just seems so unlike her."

Tears welled in her eyes. "None of us saw this comin', that's for sure."

"Did she know him?"

"No," she said, wiping away a tear. "As far as I know, she'd never talked to the man before."

Something hardened in me, watching her grief for her mother. Bart had done this. I was more sure of that than ever.

"Does the sheriff have any idea why she might have done it?"

Bitterness filled her eyes. "They don't care. Case closed. And even if they did, they wouldn't tell us nothin'. They keep sayin' it's an ongoin' investigation."

Pushing out a sigh, I shifted my weight. "Been there, done that. I was a person of interest in Seth's murder, which is why they didn't tell me anything, but they didn't talk to Hank either."

"It ain't right," Ashlynn said, more tears tracking down her cheeks. "Our lives were turned upside down too."

"I know," I forced past the lump growing in my throat. "You want answers to make sense of it all. We wanted them too. I guess we still do."

She gave me a look of surprise. "I thought they knew what happened."

"We have multiple pieces, but it feels like some of the puzzle is missing. We know *why* he was there and what he was doing, but how did he get into that motel room? How did he know that's where the deal was supposed to go down?" I felt awful telling her a fib. The truth was we knew how he got there—Bingham. But there were still plenty of pieces missing, especially since the video footage he'd died to obtain was gone, erased by someone we still hadn't identified.

Being here, talking to these people who'd known him, I realized that I still wanted to know more about him. I'd just refrained from asking Hank because I knew it hurt him too much to talk about what he'd lost.

More tears fell down her face. "I just want to tell her I love her and that I forgive her."

"Have you tried to go see her?"

She shook her head. "My dad won't take me, and I don't have a car."

I tried to hide my surprise. "Do you want to go see her?" She hesitated, so I added, "I'd be happy to take you. I have to go to Ewing anyway."

For a moment she looked relieved, then she cast a fearful glance at the house. "My dad wouldn't like it. He said she's dead to us now."

"I take it your father has a strong sense of right and wrong."

She rolled her eyes. "You don't know the half of it." Tilting her head toward me, she said, "He's always in the front pew at the First Baptist Church in Ewing."

"Oh… Well, Jesus said to love the sinner and hate the crime."

An amused look washed over her face. "You don't go to church much, do you?"

"Is it that obvious?"

"Yeah. It's love the sinner, hate the sin," she said with a hint of disgust that made my stomach clench, but then she added, "But then you don't know my daddy. Do you go to church?"

"Um, no," I said. "Although Carnita, the librarian, has invited me to the Methodist service in Drum."

Her face brightened. "I know Carnita. She's always so nice when I drop by the library."

"What do you like to read?" I asked, starting to get excited. "I'm about to start a book club."

"Read?" she said with a sharp laugh. "I go for the DVDs. She's got a great collection."

I shouldn't have been surprised. Carnita had told me more than once that I was one of the only patrons who took any interest in the book collection.

Her eyes narrowed as she looked me up and down. "Why would you offer to take me to see my momma? What's in it for you?"

Now I felt like pond scum, because there *was* something in it for me, so I decided to be somewhat truthful. "Because I like your mother, and I can't help but think there are extenuating circumstances."

Her nose wrinkled. "What's that mean?"

"It means I want to try to help her. I don't know how to do that, but I *do* know she needs a good attorney, and I'm not sure the court-appointed one meets that description. So if you talk to her, maybe ask her what he's done to help her, and we can decide if she should get someone else."

"And who's gonna pay for that fancy lawyer?" she asked with a sneer. "My daddy's not payin' for him, that's for damn sure."

"Well, I don't know yet," I admitted. I figured I'd find out if a new attorney was needed before I picked at the problem of how we could afford one.

"Why would you care?" she asked suspiciously.

"Like I said, I like her and want to help."

"Nobody's *that* nice."

I understood her suspicion. Maybe I couldn't convince her to let me help, but I could at least try. "I have a tutoring club at the tavern. Two days a week, kids come in and I help them with homework. This summer I'm helping them either keep from falling behind or try to catch up. I don't get paid to do it, but I like kids and I like the feeling of helping them master something that was hard." I shrugged. "I don't have any answers for your mom, but she's always been nice to me, and I feel like I have to do something. Some people bring casseroles, others get their hands dirtier."

"And in your case, you do both," she said with less venom.

"Yeah," I conceded. "I guess I do."

"I want to see my momma, but I'm supposed to be at work at one."

I pulled my phone out of my pocket and checked the screen. It was a little after eleven. "Where do you work?"

"At the drugstore in Ewing."

"Well, if we go now, I can wait while you see her, then drop you off at work. Like I said, I'm going to Ewing anyway. I'm going to visit my friends at Greener Pastures, and then I'm having lunch with another friend. If you want, I can probably give you a ride home too." It might mean being late for work, but this wasn't just about getting information. I wanted to help her see her mother.

She twisted her mouth to the side, considering. "My friend offered to take me home, but I wasn't sure how I was going to get there. I've been trying to line something up for the last fifteen minutes. Mom's been taking me to work, but they impounded her car." She paused. "I still need to get ready."

"I'll wait."

She cast a glance at the house. "This will only take a few minutes, but you might want to come inside."

I was assuming her father wasn't home—otherwise she wouldn't risk coming with me—so maybe she was worried her

114

brothers would see me hanging around? Either way, I wouldn't mind getting a peek inside her trailer. "Okay."

I followed her inside, not surprised to see the cheap wood paneling on the walls or the avocado green counters in the old kitchen. She grabbed a cordless phone off its base on the counter. "I'll call Amber and tell her I found a ride. She said she'd try to figure something out for me if I couldn't."

"Mind if I get a glass of water?" I asked.

"Nope. Help yourself." She headed down the hall, disappearing into a room at the end and shutting the door.

I headed into the kitchen. The sink was full of dirty dishes that spilled out onto the counter, not surprising given there wasn't a dishwasher. I opened a few cabinets, searching for a glass, but also looking around the space, trying to find anything personal that would give me some insight into Ashlynn or her family. There wasn't anything. No pictures. Not even any artwork on the walls. The furniture consisted of what was likely yard sale finds, and the kitchenware looked like it had been pieced together with hand-me-downs and thrift store finds.

I finally found a plastic cup that was so worn and shaggy it looked like it had been scrubbed with sandpaper, but I didn't want to offend Ashlynn, so I filled it with water from the tap and carried it into the dining area at the front of the trailer. A bowed window with short curtains looked out over the driveway and the road behind my car.

A stack of papers lay on the small round table. I cast a glance over my shoulder to make sure the door was still shut, then set the cup down and quickly looked through the papers. There were plenty of bills, some in Ashlynn's name, including a bill from a doctor for five hundred dollars, but some of them were addressed to Chuck Holston, including a few credit card statements, a phone bill, and an electric bill—all to the same address, only a couple of numbers off from Pam's address.

I heard a noise behind me, so I picked up my cup and turned toward the hall.

"I'm almost done," Ashlynn said as she walked out of the room and through the door next to it. "I just have to put on a little makeup, then I'm ready."

I held up my water. "I'm fine. Just enjoying the view out your window."

"It ain't that excitin'," she said, leaving the door open.

I considered snooping in the living room, but there was nothing on the end tables or coffee table. I suspected it wasn't worth getting caught. But I noticed a photo on the side of the fridge, held up by a magnet bearing the name of Travis Keeling, the insurance agent Sandy had mentioned. I leaned closer, recognizing four of the five people—Pam, Ashlynn, Ricky, and Thad. The boys had on button-down shirts, and Ashlynn and Pam were wearing dresses. The man in the photo, whom I presumed was Pam's husband, was wearing a white dress shirt and black tie. He was the only person not smiling. The photo looked like it was a couple of years old, and from the background, I gathered they were at church. I mentally added the First Baptist Church to my list of places to check out.

"Oh, you found our family photo," Ashlynn said, catching me off guard.

I jumped, placing my free hand on my chest as water sloshed out of my cup and onto my other hand. "You scared the crap out of me."

She laughed. "I'm not sure how. I clomp around like an elephant these days."

I pointed to the man. "Is that your dad?"

A frown washed over her face. "Yeah. You ready?"

"Yep." I took a sip of the water, the rough plastic scraping my bottom lip. I dumped out the water in the sink and set the cup on the counter. "Sorry to add to your pile of dishes. Will your husband wash them when he gets home?"

She released a harsh laugh. "That's a good one. First of all, I ain't married, but even if Chuck washed dishes, he ran off with Becca Sloan a few weeks ago."

"Sorry," I said. "I heard you were married."

She snorted. "Momma liked to tell people that. She thought people were gonna judge me for having a baby without a marriage license, but Chuck would never pull the trigger. Guess now I know why."

"I'm sorry," I added softly.

She rested her hand on her belly. "My momma was supposed to help me raise him. We were gonna—" She stopped abruptly and sucked in a breath. "Now it's just me. I might be havin' this baby, but he ain't gonna get a job and pay the electric bill," she snapped, but I knew her anger wasn't directed at me. "Come on. Let's get this over with."

I hoped I was only getting started.

Chapter Twelve

We drove in silence for a few minutes. Ashlynn looked out the window, her body turned away from me. She reminded me a little of Lula back in December, when she was pregnant and thought she was alone. Unplanned pregnancies weren't all that uncommon here—not that I was judging—but all too often the women didn't receive much support. It was clear Ashlynn had lost her main supporter the moment Pam was locked up.

"When are you due?" I finally asked.

"The end of August," she said, still staring out the side window.

"And you're having a boy? You called your baby a him."

"Yeah." Her response was flat, making me wonder if she would have preferred a girl. Or maybe she was intimidated to now be facing this alone.

"Are you and your mother close?"

She didn't answer, and I glanced over to see her wiping a tear from her cheek. She caught me looking at her and shrugged. "Close enough."

"How long ago did you graduate high school?" I asked.

Her body jolted. "I graduated a year ago. This ain't no teen pregnancy." But then her cheeks flushed, making me think maybe she hadn't turned twenty yet.

"I'm not judging you, Ashlynn. You're about to have a baby and your mother's in jail, likely to go to prison. I'm just trying to figure out how to help you."

Her body tensed. "I don't need your help."

I inwardly groaned. While she probably *did* need my help, I needed to stop trying to force it on people. I was very much an outsider, and while many people in Drum had accepted me in a short period of time—likely because Max had given me his blessing, so to speak—not everyone appreciated my attempts at intervention. Max himself had bristled at my tendency to offer unsolicited advice. "I'm sorry," I said. "I didn't mean to insinuate..." I took a breath. "I just know how hard this will be without your mother. When I was in college, I had a friend who had a baby without the support of a significant other. Her mother had died years before, so she didn't have much support, and she was still in school. She didn't like to ask for help, so my friends and I kind of had to force it on her." Belatedly, I realized that Charlene "Carly" Moore had never gone to college, but I had to trust that Ashlynn likely wouldn't be repeating this conversation.

"You may be driving me to see my mother, but we ain't friends."

"You're right," I said, not taking offense and telling myself to let this go. "We're not friends, but if you ever need a friend, I'm here for you, okay? I can give you my home phone number before we part ways in Ewing, and you know I work at Max's Tavern. You can always reach me there."

Her eyes narrowed. "Why do you want to help me out so bad?" Then horror filled her eyes. "You ain't gettin' my baby."

"*What?*" I protested. "I don't want your baby! I don't even know if I want babies of my own!"

"Then why are you so interested in mine? Are you a trafficker?"

"Of babies?" I asked, incredulously. "No!" I pushed out a sigh. "Look, I'm not some evil person, I promise—I just like to help people. But I do admit to coming on strong sometimes." I took a breath, then tried to appear less crazy. "I'm sorry if I gave you the wrong impression."

"I ain't alone, you know. I've got my Aunt Selena."

I perked up at that. "Is she your mother's sister?"

"No, she's Momma's friend. But we call her aunt."

Selena? She never came to the ladies' luncheons. I wondered where she fit into Pam's life. "I take it she lives around here?"

"She lives in downtown Drum. By the Methodist Church."

She had an uncommon enough name that Ruth or Max probably knew her, especially if she lived downtown. I'd ask them later.

We sat in silence after that. Everything I thought of bringing up seemed too intrusive, and I didn't want to give her any more reasons to think I was a potential child trafficker. Instead, we listened to music on a used iPod Marco had gotten for me and preloaded with some of my favorite music.

Thinking about the day Marco had given it to me made me smile, but a wash of sadness quickly followed. For the first time since I'd arrived in Drum, I wondered if my priorities were off. Instead of trying to dig up evidence on Bart, maybe I should be putting all of this energy into figuring out a way to have a normal life. I could live as Carly Moore and maybe marry Marco. We wouldn't be safe in Drum, Tennessee, not with Bart Drummond holding threats over my head, but what if we went somewhere else? I could go as Carly Roland and keep dyeing my hair. Maybe my father would never find me.

That was a foolish pipe dream. My father wouldn't give up searching for me until the day I died.

So why was I spending all this time on Bart Drummond? Was it my way of burying my head in the sand and hiding from the real problem?

***

While I knew the location of the sheriff's department, I didn't know where to find the county jail. Strangely—or not—Ashlynn did.

"Do you want me to come in?" I asked as I pulled into the parking lot.

"I'm not a kid," she snapped. Obviously, she was still offended by my questions.

"I know, but it's your mom…"

She shot me a withering look, then got out of the car. "I'll be fine. Come back and get me in forty-five minutes." She shut the door with a little more force than was necessary.

As I watched her walk toward the entrance, I decided to run by the nursing home to see Thelma. It was five minutes away, which meant I had time for a quick visit before I needed to get back.

I bounded into the Greener Pastures Nursing Home, pausing only to wave to my two friends, Roberta and Gladys, who sat at their usual table in the main living area, working on a puzzle.

"Where are you goin' in such a hurry?" Roberta barked. She was notoriously grumpy and would likely hold this over my head for months. Especially when she discovered I hadn't brought her and Gladys a new puzzle or a bag of candies.

I just gave her another wave as I headed down the hallway toward Thelma's room. I was going to pay for that later.

When I reached her door, it was partially closed. I started to knock, but an orderly in the hall said, "She's in the garden. Her friend brought her some new plants last week, and she likes to dote on them."

I knew exactly who she meant. In fact, I was the one who'd first brought Emmaline Haskell to see Thelma. Thelma loved flowers, and Emmaline's property and small greenhouse were bursting with them. They'd hit it off, and Emmaline had made several more visits to see Thelma without me.

I let myself out the door to the courtyard, and sure enough, Thelma was leaning on a four-footed cane with one hand while she wielded a garden hose with the other, watering the plants. Emmaline had brought rose bushes on our first visit, but the space was now planted with multiple varieties of flowers.

"Carly," she exclaimed in surprise, leaning on her cane as she loosened her hold on the sprayer nozzle at the end of the hose. The flow turned to a trickle.

It was good to see her up and moving around. She had a bad knee and refused to have surgery, so she spent most of her time in her room. But the project of beautifying the courtyard had gotten her up and moving.

"You and Emmaline have been busy."

Her face beamed. "It's a real garden now."

"It is. It's absolutely beautiful."

"What brings you here today?" she asked, squeezing the handle and moving the stream of water to the next plant.

"I'd love to say it's just for a chat, but I don't have much time, so I need to be more direct."

Her smile faded some, but the cheerfulness didn't leave her voice. "I'm listening."

"Do you want to sit?" I asked, gesturing to a concrete bench.

"I'll keep watering, but you sit so I don't have to look up at you."

I took a seat on the bench even though she was only a couple of inches shorter than me. "Did you hear about the murder of the insurance agent a few days ago?"

She shook her head. "That's the beauty of a place like this. I don't have to hear about what's goin' on outside these walls."

"The woman who murdered him is one of my customers at the tavern. She's as sweet as they come. I would have thought her incapable of harming anyone."

"Do they have enough evidence to charge her?"

I grimaced. "There's no question she did it. She walked in and shot him in front of three witnesses. There's even security camera footage of her walking out of the office with the gun in her hand. Then she drove down the street and waited for the police to come arrest her."

Confusion filled her eyes. "Then what...*oh*."

"Yeah," I said quietly.

She laid the hose down in the flower bed and hobbled over to sit next to me. "You think Bart called in a favor."

I nodded.

Her shoulders drooped. "Tell me everything."

And I did, including the lack of an apparent connection between Pam and Jim, what I'd learned on my visit to her house, and how I'd just dropped Ashlynn off at the county jail.

"I remember the mess with her son a couple of years ago," she said with a faraway look. "I know the family of the man he hit. Karl Lister."

"Really? I didn't know his name," I said. "But I did hear there was a potential lawsuit. Do you think Bart might have had something to do with it?"

Her gaze turned to me. "I don't know all the details, but Karl struggled to walk after the accident. His legs were broken in multiple places and he had several surgeries. But I'm pretty sure the boy's insurance paid for most of it."

"So what was the lawsuit for? Pain and suffering?"

"And some medical bills," Thelma said. "I know he received a settlement of some kind, but I don't know how it came about or even how much he got."

"So if there was a lawsuit, I might be able to get the details from the courthouse."

"That's a good place to start. Tell Rosemarie that I sent you."

"You know just about everyone around here," I said with a grin. At least it felt that way.

"Not everyone, but enough of 'em."

We were silent for a moment before I asked, "What's your gut on this, Miss Thelma? Do you think Bart had any involvement in Jim Palmer's murder?"

"It's hard to say," she said. "You'll definitely need more evidence to prove it, but it's a new case. A fresh trail. If he was involved, you have a better chance of tracing it to him than any of the old cases. The question is: are you sure you want to pursue this?"

I wasn't surprised she'd asked. While she'd volunteered information in the past, I knew she was concerned about me getting too involved in Bart's business.

"Of course I want to pursue this. If we're right, he coerced—likely threatened—a woman to kill a man. A woman who can't even put out mouse traps because she doesn't like hurting living creatures. That kind of evil needs to be stopped."

Her lips pressed tightly together, she gave me a brisk nod. "Well, then. Do you know where to start?"

"I have a few leads," I said, reluctant to say more. While I trusted her, Marco was right: I could never be too sure about who might be listening.

She didn't look offended that I didn't elaborate. "When he's done this in the past, he's had help covering it up. You might see if the same deputies handled the previous cases."

"Good idea." The first place to start was my notebook full of cases—a few of the news articles had listed the investigators' names but others hadn't—and I might be able to get copies of the police reports for the rest. The Hensen County Sheriff's Department had earned a reputation for being corrupt, but not all of the deputies were cut from the same cloth. Some of them were good people who'd felt powerless to change things…but had hung on because they feared the situation would get worse if they left. Marco was a perfect example.

"I think I found something else worth mentioning," I said. "A family of five that died in a house explosion. It only happened about twelve years ago, so I think it's a different case than the one you told me about before."

Her face paled. "There seems to be a lot of gas explosions around these parts."

"So I noticed. There was another one too, five years ago, but thankfully the family wasn't home."

"Could have been a warnin'," she said.

I'd like to think Bart didn't kill *everyone* on his revenge list. "Do you know anything about a man named Ted Butcher?"

Her lips pursed. "The name sounds familiar."

"He crashed his car into a tree about a week after the explosion that killed the family."

"There are a lot of car crashes around here—winding roads and careless drivers."

"But Ted Butcher had two overdoses after that. The last one was two years ago."

"You think he killed that family and couldn't live with the guilt?" she asked.

"It's a theory."

She was silent for a moment, her eyes far off, then she shook her head. "I don't know him. I don't even know of any Butchers in the area."

"Honestly, there a good chance it's nothing." Hank and Bingham were proof enough that drug use was alive and well in the area. He could be an addict who'd crashed his car while he was high. Nevertheless, I wanted to talk to him. It was worth a try.

"Have you heard any more from Emily Drummond?" Thelma asked.

I gave her a tight smile and shook my head. "Not since our tea party in March." I grimaced. "What do you think will happen to her after Bart's gone?"

She chuckled. "I like your confidence."

"Someone has to stop him. It might as well be me. I can't let him do this to anyone else." I cocked my head. "Do you know anything about the Palmer family? I take it he owned Jim Palmer Insurance."

"Yes, but his father owned it. He was Jim, Sr."

"So the murdered man was a junior."

"Yes."

"Any idea what could have instigated Jim, Jr. to go to Bart for a favor in the first place?"

"It might not have been Jim, Jr. who went," she said with a knowing look. "It may have been his father."

"Or his wife?"

"Possibly," she said with a sigh.

I held up my hand as her previous statement sank in. "Wait. You're saying Bart holds the next generation responsible for the sins of their fathers?"

"And mothers too. A debt must be repaid regardless of who took it out."

"That's medieval."

"It's archaic." She grasped my hand. "It's time to end his reign. He's hurt far too many people, many of them innocent bystanders." She squeezed my hand tighter, and her eyes pleaded with me. "But you can't do this alone."

"I have Marco," I said. "Since he's in the sheriff's department, he can help me in ways other people can't."

"Still, he has his own job to do," she said evenly. "You need someone with you. Like when you were lookin' for Lula."

"There *is* no one else. And Marco only got involved with looking for Lula because he was bored out of his mind while he was on medical leave."

"I'm sure that's what you thought at the time," she said with a wink. She'd obviously been comparing notes with Gladys and Roberta.

I decided to ignore her insinuation. "I'll be careful, and if I feel like things are getting scary or out of control, I'll tell Marco."

"Good, because he won't let anything happen to you."

"I know," I said simply.

Her expression softened. "That boy loves you. When are you goin' to give him a chance?"

I groaned, but I couldn't help smiling. "Not you too, Miss Thelma."

"Even Greta's got a boyfriend. You've been single far too long."

I rolled my eyes. "There are other things in life besides having a boyfriend."

"Maybe so," she said with a wink. "But they sure do make life a lot more fun."

"Now I *know* you've been spending too much time with Gladys and Roberta."

"Seriously, though," she said, turning somber, "about this case—you need to do this quietly. You can't let Bart know what you're up to. Just keep playing it like you're a concerned friend. In fact, you might want to let this go for a few weeks, or even a few months, then pick it up after things die down."

"But then it will be too late to help Pam."

She shook her head, sadness filling her eyes. "Pam's a lost cause, Carly. There's no helpin' her now."

Chapter Thirteen

I pulled into the jail parking lot five minutes early. I didn't see Ashlynn waiting for me outside, so I parked in a spot that gave me full view of the exit. Then I waited for twenty minutes, getting more anxious as each one ticked by. I hadn't gotten her cell phone number—if she had one—and we hadn't made arrangements about where to meet. What if Ashlynn had come out early and left on her own? Or what if she was still ticked with me and had found her own ride to work?

I hadn't planned on going inside and calling attention to the fact I was this interested in Pam's case, but it didn't feel right to just leave without her. After another five minutes, I got out of the car and headed for the entrance. There was a metal detector six feet from the front door, not that I was surprised.

"Purpose of your visit?" a deputy asked in a bored tone.

I started to answer when I heard a man say, "Carly Moore?"

I turned in the direction of the voice and saw a deputy headed down the hall toward me. He looked familiar, but I couldn't place him. Then again, I'd met a lot of deputies after the Paul Conrad incident.

"Are you here to see Marco?" the deputy asked from the other side of the metal detector. He was close enough for me to read the name on his badge—Taggert. He was in his late thirties or early forties, with thinning light brown hair and medium brown eyes. I vaguely remembered meeting him during that mess, but it hadn't been memorable.

"Is he here?" I asked in surprise.

"Yeah. Just brought a suspect in. Do you want to wait for him?"

"Uh…" I wasn't sure whether to tell him the real reason for my visit, but it struck me that it would be a whole lot worse if I lied and Ashlynn came out looking for me. Besides, I wasn't doing anything wrong. "I'm actually picking up a friend. She's here visiting her mother."

"Inmate or an employee?"

"Inmate."

His gaze narrowed, but I didn't volunteer any more information. I could see judgment brewing in his eyes.

"Is there any way for me to check whether she already left?" I asked, trying to sound casual. "I was supposed to pick her up and take her to work."

"There's a desk where visitors log in and out," Deputy Taggert said, then motioned to the deputy next to me. "Let her through. I'm gonna take her back."

I placed my purse on the conveyor belt and walked through the scanner. Deputy Taggert watched as I walked through and then grabbed my purse from the x-ray machine.

"How have you been doing since the Deputy Conrad ordeal?" Deputy Taggert asked in a low tone as he led me down a hallway. There was a heavy metal door with a keycard reader on one side, and a counter against the wall next to it. A bored-looking man sat behind a plexiglass shield.

"I struggled," I admitted. I didn't think anyone could go through a hostage situation less than six months after having been hunted down by a killer and declare themselves to be just fine. "But I'm mostly good now." I gave him a smile. "Marco's helped me through it."

"He's a good deputy and an even better man," he said. "We're lucky to have him on the force."

I smiled again but didn't say anything. I didn't know if Marco considered Deputy Taggert a friend or foe, and if he was in the latter group, I didn't want to give him anything to use against Marco.

"Who's your friend visiting?" he said as we continued walking.

I hesitated, but there was no getting past this. "Pam Crimshaw."

Deputy Taggert stumbled to a stop and turned to me. "Say what?" His eyes narrowed. "How'd you get mixed up in the Pam Crimshaw mess?"

"I'm not," I said, hoping I sounded convincing. "I know Pam from the tavern where I work. Her friends set up a dinner schedule for her family and today was my day. When I dropped off my casserole, her daughter, Ashlynn, told me that her mother usually took her to work here in Ewing. I volunteered to bring her since I was coming to town anyway."

"You just dropped her off?"

"That's right, about an hour ago. She told me to be back in forty-five minutes. I visited a friend at the nursing home and cut my visit short to be back in time, but Ashlynn wasn't outside when I got here."

He gave me a long stare. "Did you know her daughter before this?"

"No." I gave him a wary look. "But she was trying to figure out a way to get to Ewing, and since I was headed here anyway…"

"You were just being neighborly," he said with a smile, but it looked stiff.

I shrugged, really wishing I'd just stayed in the car. "Yeah. Exactly."

"Just like you were bein' neighborly when you were tryin' to find out who killed Heather Stone?"

"That was different," I admitted. "I was helping a friend, and I freely admit that I was looking into who did it. Today I'm simply a chauffeur."

"And the friend you were helping was Wyatt Drummond." It was a statement, not a question.

"Yeah."

The look in his eyes suggested he didn't like my answer, but he didn't press the matter.

So much for staying under the radar. *Dammit.*

He continued the short distance to the plexiglass window and leaned his forearm on the counter. "Steve," he said to the man behind the desk, "can you look at the log and tell me if—" He turned to me with raised brows. "What's her name?"

"Ashlynn Crimshaw."

He turned back to the window. "If Ashlynn Crimshaw has already signed out after seeing her mother?"

The deputy looked surprised, but he glanced down at his sheet before looking back up at Deputy Taggert. "For Pam Crimshaw?"

"That's right," Deputy Taggert said.

"She ain't had no visitors today," the deputy said. "No one's been to see her other than her lawyer last night."

"Are you sure?" I asked in disbelief. "I dropped Ashlynn off about an hour ago."

"Positive," the deputy behind the glass said. "I ain't had no women visitors at all today."

I turned slightly, shocked at the realization that Ashlynn hadn't come in to see her mother. Why had she made such a show of coming? Why waste both of our time?

"Thank you for your help, Deputy Taggert," I said, glancing up at the man next to me. "Who knows how long I would have been waiting for her if you hadn't helped."

"I'm sure Marco could have found out for you. Have you told him you're here?"

"No," I said. "But then I didn't know he was here until you told me. I'm supposed to meet him for lunch later." I gave him a friendly smile. "Thanks again for your help."

"Don't think anything of it." He leaned over so our faces were even, his about a foot from mine. Lowering his voice, he said, "But a word of advice: You might be more careful with the company you keep."

A chill swept over my body. I hesitated, unsure how to handle this—was he speaking about Marco? Ashlynn?—but then the door at the end of the hall opened and Marco emerged.

His gaze swept over me, but it took a second for his brain to put things together. Worry washed over his face. "*Carly?*"

Deputy Taggert straightened and turned to face him. "There you are, Marco."

Confusion replaced Marco's worry. "You were lookin' for me?"

"She was lookin' for Pam Crimshaw's daughter," Deputy Taggert said in an even tone.

"When I dropped off her casserole, she mentioned she wanted to see her mother before she went to work, only she couldn't get a ride to Ewing for either purpose," I said, offering him a weak smile. "You know me. I'm always volunteering to help people."

Marco closed the distance between us and pulled me into his arms, kissing the top of my head. "I know. Your generous heart is one of the things I love most about you." He dropped one arm and turned to the side to face the deputy, but he kept the other around my back, his hand cupping my upper arm. His touch, so casual yet so familiar, unleashed something within me. He was doing this for show, because he wanted the other deputies to think we were involved, but I liked it. "Thanks for taking care of her, Tag. Sure do appreciate it."

"Anything I can do to be neighborly," Taggert said, his word choice intentional. "I'll let you two get to your lunch date." Then he headed down the hall toward the exit.

Marco watched him for a few seconds before turning his attention to me. "You okay?" he asked in a whisper.

I nodded. "You still have that meeting you need to attend?"

He tilted his head toward the door. "That was my appointment."

My eyes widened. "Your appointment was to arrest somebody?"

"Something like that. You want to head to lunch? There's a café you haven't tried yet. They have great fried pickles."

I cast a glance at the counter, where the deputy was watching us like we were his afternoon entertainment. "Yeah. I thought I needed to give someone a ride, but I guess not." I smiled up at Marco. "Let's get you your fried pickles."

"How about we get them to go?" he asked, sounding breezy, but I could feel the tension thrumming through his body. "We could have a picnic at Louis Park."

Which meant he wanted to talk about something he didn't want anyone else to overhear. Was it about why I was here, or something else? "I like that idea. It's a beautiful day."

"It is now that you're here." He placed a soft kiss on my cheek, then straightened. "I'm starving. Let's go."

I stared at him for a moment. Show or not, I couldn't ignore the butterflies in my stomach…or the urge to lift onto my toes and kiss him for real.

He dropped his arm and snagged my hand, lacing our fingers together as we headed out to the parking lot. His eagle gaze quickly zeroed in on my car. "I'd suggest we ride together, but I'm on duty and I don't want you to leave your car here. Follow me."

My stomach churned. I'd screwed up by coming here. "Okay."

He cupped my cheek and turned my face up so that I could see his warm eyes, which looked more blue than green today. "Everything's going to be okay."

I only hoped he was right.

Chapter Fourteen

I followed him about a mile to the café. I'd lost my appetite, but I knew Marco was probably hungry. His appetite had a mind of its own and seemed to be unaffected by pesky things like stress and worry. There were several empty spaces when we pulled into the café's parking lot, and Marco parked in a space, leaving me to pull in next to him.

He was already out of his deputy SUV and headed around the back of his vehicle by the time I opened door, but he held up a hand. "Stay put. I called in an order. It'll be ready in a few minutes. Let's sit in your car while we wait."

"Okay." I got back in and unlocked the passenger door so he could join me.

"What really happened at the courthouse?" he asked as he got in my car, his voice full of worry. "You weren't trying to see Pam Crimshaw, were you?"

"No," I assured him. "It was just like I said." I told him about how it had all gone down, then leaned my head back against the seat. "I should have never gone in there."

"It's okay," he said softly. "You didn't do anything wrong."

"Maybe not, but Deputy Taggert sure seemed suspicious of me." I swiveled my head to face him. "Do you trust him?"

"No," he said, then at my sharp intake of breath, he added, "But I don't have reason to distrust him either. He was friends with some of the old guard. But he always seemed a little distant from them, so he might have been friendly out of self-preservation."

"Can you talk to him and find out?"

He snorted. "He might not take it well if I ask him if he was as corrupt as his buddies."

"Okay, you have a point, but the state police are looking into the corruption within the department. You might be able to use that as a segue to find out where he stands."

"Maybe, but I'm not doing anything to bring more attention to what just happened or to you. For now, we presume he's the enemy until proven otherwise."

"An enemy who can now tie me to Pam."

"Your cover might still work," he said, "but he's going to keep an eye out."

"Which means he's a bad guy."

"Maybe not. Maybe he's trying to piece this all together and tie it back to Bart too."

"Do you think that's likely?"

"No."

We were silent for a moment, then I said, "The deputy at the desk said Ashlynn never checked in to see her mother."

"Really? What do you think happened to her?"

"I don't know," I said, shaking my head. "I confess that I pushed Ashlynn a bit to see her. I told her that her mother might need a better attorney than the public defender who was assigned to her." I ran my hand over my head. "But I was asking too many questions in the car, and it made her suspicious. Still, she seemed on board with the whole thing. She even told me how to get to the jail, and I saw her heading for the entrance. But I didn't see her go in."

"So the question is why she didn't go in."

"Yeah, I guess so," I said, feeling defeated. "I know she works at a drugstore and had to be at work at one. Maybe I should go find her after we finish our lunch. How many drugstores are there? I can think of at least two."

"I suspect there's three or four of them," he said as he checked his watch. "Speaking of lunch, I think our order's ready. I'll go in and get it, then we can head for the park."

"Okay."

He hopped out and strode across the parking lot, and I couldn't stop myself from watching him…and remembering that moment in the jail.

He came out a few minutes later and gave me a smile as he carried the bag to his SUV. When he pulled out of the lot, I followed him in my car, and we drove the short distance to the park.

With one set of swings and a single picnic table, Louis Park could barely be considered a park. But since it was so sparsely appointed, there usually wasn't anyone around. Today was no exception. We parked in the lot, then walked over to the concrete table together, sitting on opposite sides. Marco reached into the white bag and pulled out a paper-wrapped item, then handed it to me.

"I never told you what I wanted," I teased. "It was presumptuous of you to just order for me."

"Trust me," he said as he reached into the bag and handed me a bottle of water. "I had this last week, and instantly thought of you."

"Now I'm intrigued." I opened the wrapper to find a toasted sandwich cut into two triangles, stuffed with a creamy white mixture. "Chicken salad?"

"The best I've ever had. I would have told you last week if I hadn't been so busy. Then I decided to just surprise you."

My heart melted in a puddle of goo. For the past several months, I'd been complaining that I couldn't find a place that sold a decent chicken salad sandwich, let alone a good one. "You don't even like chicken salad very much."

He shrugged as he pulled out another wrapped sandwich. "I've been on the lookout."

My heart surged with an emotion that I recognized but didn't want to name. Even if I did, that didn't mean I was ready to take the plunge. And to tell Marco how I was feeling *before* I was ready would be unfair and unkind.

I took a bite and nearly wept in happiness. "Thank you," I said after I swallowed my bite. "It's *so* good."

"As good as your mother used to make?" he asked, unwrapping his own turkey sandwich.

I rested my hand on the table. "You remembered?"

Of course, I remembered too. One night we'd stayed up talking so late we were both half-asleep on the sofa watching TV. He'd told me about one of his good memories of his mother. She used to make him spaghetti with homemade meatballs, and one of the reasons he'd loved it so much was that she let him help make the meatballs, a thrill for an eight-year-old boy who loved to play with anything mushy. It was a simple memory, but given his complicated mess of emotions toward her after he found out about her affairs, it was special to him. And it had twisted something inside of me to hear him talk about it.

He'd asked what my mother used to make for me, and I'd found myself telling him about her chicken salad sandwiches. For some reason I had no trouble talking to Marco about my mother, something that didn't come easily with anyone else.

His gaze held mine intently. "I remember everything you tell me, Carly."

I stared down at the table, unsure what to do with this intense swirl of emotions.

We were silent for a moment before he asked, "What did you do while you were waiting for Ashlynn?"

Clearing the lump out of my throat, I picked up my sandwich again. "I managed to make my visit to Greener Pastures."

"Did Thelma have any helpful information?"

"Actually, she did. She knows the family of the man who Thad hit in the accident. His name is Karl Lister, and both of his legs were badly broken. He couldn't walk after his surgeries and had to go to rehab. She thinks they settled a lawsuit."

"I've pulled a report of the accident, but I haven't had time to look it over yet," he said.

I nodded. "Good idea. Thelma is worried about me looking into Pam's case. She thinks it's too soon. That Bart will figure out what we're up to and retaliate."

"I'd be lyin' if I didn't admit to worryin' about the same thing."

It wasn't an idle worry, so I didn't pretend otherwise. I just nodded and said, "I have some people not directly connected to Pam I can talk to. Ashlynn told me about a friend of her mother's. She and her brothers call her Aunt Selena. She lives in Drum, close to the Methodist church. What's strange is that she's supposedly best friends with this woman, but she never goes to the ladies' luncheons."

"That's because Selena is in her sixties," he said, then took a bite of his sandwich.

"What?"

"Yeah, Selena Martin. Might not be the same person, but I don't know of any other Selenas in Drum. And I know for a fact she lives about a block from the church."

"So she's a good twenty years older than Pam?"

"I guess so," he said. "I don't know anything about her connection to Pam, though. I know her from high school. She was my algebra teacher. She still might be teaching, as a matter of fact."

"Do you think Pam knew her the same way?"

"Maybe," he said, "but Pam's probably ten to fifteen years older than me."

I grabbed a small notebook out of my purse and uncapped a pen. "So I need to drop by and ask her what she knows about Pam. Do you think she'll be resistant?"

"I doubt it," he said. "She loves to talk. I'm sure she'll be worried about Pam. So as long as you let her know you're trying to help, I'm sure she'll talk."

"I could also tell her I'm worried about Ashlynn," I said. "Not a lie, because I am. Her boyfriend broke up with her a few weeks ago, and she's pregnant. She lives in a trailer next to her parents' house, but it looks like the utilities are all in his name. Then there's the way she took off from the jail."

"You think something happened to her?"

"I was already worried about her having a baby without her mother, even though she told me Selena would be helping her. Her father sounds like a classic controlling asshole, possible abuser. But yeah, after the way she took off, I'm *very* worried."

"Maybe talking to Selena will help put your mind at ease."

I took another bite of my sandwich, nearly moaning in pleasure, then took in the sandwiches, bags of chips, and bottles of water. "Where are your fried pickles?"

He laughed and patted his belly. "Decided I didn't need the grease."

More like he used it as a ploy to get me to try the café, not that he needed one.

"So Karl Lister," he said. "His address at the time of the accident is on the report. I'll try to find out if it's still his current address. I wish I could talk to him with you, but I need to stick to the behind-the-scenes stuff until we're ready to make some kind of move. *You* sniffing around will likely come across as nosy. *Me* sniffing around reeks of an official investigation."

Sadly, I agreed. He'd already helped me with two investigations, off the books, and with the state police sniffing around, we couldn't risk that he'd get away with a third. "Do you know anything about Karl Lister?"

"No, which means you should take someone with you. We need to be extra cautious."

I nodded. "Okay. I'll try to figure out who to bring."

"Maybe you can take Hank on a drive. And his shotgun."

I gave him a smile. "That actually sounds like a good idea." I paused, thinking, then added, "Hank seems to be getting stir crazy. Months ago he and I talked about getting his car set up so he can drive it, but this morning I decided to do something about it."

"Oh?" he asked. "Did you call his doctor's office?"

"No," I said quietly. "I dropped by Wyatt's garage."

If I hadn't known him so well, I wouldn't have noticed his reaction. But his breath hitched a little and his fingers curled in slightly. It bothered him. "That makes sense," he said, picking up a chip. "He likes Hank, so he'll give you a discount."

I grimaced. "He refuses to take Hank's money, but he insisted on coming by for breakfast tomorrow morning. Says Hank will only agree to accept his help if he thinks I'm okay with having him around."

He stared at me for a second. "Is this another desperate attempt on his part to win you back?"

"We both know it is, even if he won't admit it. Still, Hank spends so much time alone. I hate that he's stuck out there. And from what I've gathered, Wyatt used to spend a lot of time with Hank and Seth. It stands to reason that Hank misses him. I feel like I stole his friend from him."

A dark look rolled across his face, but I knew it wasn't for me. Wyatt had earned this one. "You did no such thing. Wyatt was the one who acted like an ass. Hank's a smart man, and he didn't approve of the way Wyatt treated you. And yeah, he partially sent Wyatt away for your sake, but consider this: Hank could have him come by when you're working evenings, and he never does."

"I suppose."

"Does Hank know you went to Wyatt?"

"Not yet."

He grinned. "You might want to let him know before Wyatt shows up for breakfast. That old coot is as stubborn as the day is long. He might not like it."

I made a face. "At least it's on home ground. Wyatt wanted me to have breakfast with him somewhere else, but I insisted on doing it at Hank's since he claims the purpose is for Hank to see us together."

"Good thinkin'," Marco said, then his smile faded. "You don't have to let him come. You can tell him you've found someone else to take care of it."

"But I haven't."

"But you *can*," he said. "I'll help you, and if it's a matter of money—"

"Marco. I'm not taking your money."

"If it's a matter of money," he repeated more firmly, "you have other options." He started to say something else, stopped, then shook his head. "We both know that Wyatt's manipulating you, but you're right. He gave Hank companionship. And if you have to leave Drum unexpectedly at some point, I'm sure you'll feel better knowing that someone's there for him."

He was right. I hated the idea of leaving Hank with no one. I knew Wyatt would step in, regardless of the state of their friendship, but Hank was a stubborn man. It would be better for him to work things out with Wyatt before I left.

"You think I'll be leaving Drum soon?" I asked quietly.

His gaze held mine. "I think we're about to embark on a dangerous task, and you need to be prepared to leave at a moment's notice. We can't afford for you to get hung up over your concern for Hank."

He was right about that, and it was part of the reason I'd gone to see Wyatt earlier. I knew it was possible. Still, the thought of leaving Hank put an ache deep in my chest.

Marco took a breath, then said, "You know that Wyatt will help Hank whether you have breakfast with him or not. You don't have to let him rope you into it."

"Yeah, probably, but he'd drag it out, making me think he won't help. And I don't know how much time I have to waste. If I have to leave, I need to know Hank'll be okay."

"I'll stand behind whatever you decide," Marco said. "You're a grown woman capable of makin' your own decisions. I'll never tell you what to do."

Yet I could see how badly he wanted me to tell Wyatt no. Nevertheless, he wouldn't ask, let alone demand or insist. He would always let me have complete control over my choices. It only made me appreciate him more.

So why didn't it silence that little voice in my head wondering when the other shoe would drop?

"One more thing," Marco said, his gaze dropping to his half-eaten sandwich. "I think you need to prep a go bag."

I narrowed my eyes in confusion. "What's a go bag?"

"A bag you have packed and ready so that you can leave at a moment's notice. There might not be time to say goodbye, Carly. You might just have to leave."

I swallowed. This was getting all too real. "Yeah, that's a good idea. I'll stop at the Dollar General and get a bag."

"It should probably be a duffel bag," he said, still not looking at me. "I've got one you can use. I'll help you figure out what you need to get. And let's not get the things here. Let's plan on going to Greeneville first chance we get. We don't want anyone watching you and getting suspicious." His face lifted. "How much cash do you have?"

"About a hundred dollars."

"And how much in the bank?"

"About seven hundred."

He stared at me in shock. "I know for a fact you make good money in tips, and you don't spend money frivolously. You don't pay rent or make a car payment, so where'd your money go?"

"Lots of places," I said, getting frustrated. "I've bought books and supplies for the Kids' Club. And then Hank's roof was leaking back in April so I paid a handyman to fix it, and the kitchen sink needed repairing too."

His gaze held mine. "You have to stop doin' that. You have to save your money, Carly. You're going to need it if you run."

I swallowed a lump of fear. I'd had nearly two thousand dollars when I'd gotten stranded in Drum, and it hadn't been enough to fix my car. If ran, I was going to need a lot more than the meager amount I currently had. "What was I supposed to do about Hank's roof? Or the sink?"

"Tell *me*," he said insistently. "I could have looked at the drain."

"But you couldn't have fixed the roof."

"No, but I might have been able to find someone to do it cheaper."

"You don't even know what I spent," I said in frustration. "And I'm not relying on someone else to fix my problems. I can stand on my own two feet."

"I know you can," he said, becoming frustrated himself. "But the roof and the sink weren't your problems. They were Hank's."

"Not true. I live there too, rent free as you pointed out. It's only right for me to contribute."

He started to say something again, then stopped, his hand tightening over mine. "Why do you think it's okay for you to help Hank with his problems, but it's a sign of weakness for you to accept help from me?"

"Because I counted on men before and look where it got me." The words tore out of me before I could stop them.

He didn't say anything, but I could feel the disappointment rolling off of him. I was disappointed too. What was it going to take to make me trust him completely? Would I ever be capable of it?

"So," I said, drawing out the word, ready to change the subject. "For now, I'll try to find Ashlynn and make sure she's okay, then I can talk to Selena before work. Do you have the police report for Thad's accident in your car? We can look it over together. Oh, and Thelma suggested I go to the courthouse and ask a friend of hers to pull the paperwork for the civil suit."

He pushed out a breath and sat up, likely disappointed that I'd changed the subject. "Let's hold off on that. Right now, the story is that you're being neighborly and you only showed up at the jail to pick up Ashlynn. If you go to Selena, you're still within the scope of that story. But if you start pulling documents for a civil suit for an accident several years ago, your behavior becomes a lot more suspicious. I'll look into it."

"What about talking to Karl Lister?" I asked.

"Hold off on approaching him. Maybe question Pam's friends more after you talk to Selena."

"Sandy's the most talkative of the bunch, and she didn't have much to say this morning. But I can try the others."

"I know you're careful, but I still feel the need to tell you to watch your back and pull back with the questions if you start making people anxious or suspicious."

"That's what I've been doin'," I said, my frustration getting the better of me, and I got to my feet.

"Why are you mad?" he asked, then grimaced. "I'm sorry if I insinuated that you don't know what you're doin'."

"But I *don't* know what I'm doing," I said. "I'm just a teacher turned waitress. I was never trained to do anything like this. What if I screw it all up? I don't want Bart to keep getting away with this!"

"You won't screw up," he said, still sitting on the bench. "You're a natural. But if things start to get tense, backtrack the conversation, and make a graceful exit. Try to leave the sources happy and open to talking to you again."

I nodded. "Okay." But anxiety was oozing out of my pores. I didn't feel qualified to do this. I'd already messed up with Ashlynn.

"Hey," he said softly, patting the concrete bench next to him. "Come here."

I walked around the table and sat next to him, resting my head on his chest when he wrapped an arm around my back.

After a few moments, he said, "You don't have to do this, Carly."

I lifted my head to look up at him.

"You don't have to do any of this. I'm not stuck in Drum. I can leave. We could go somewhere else. Start fresh."

"But what about the sheriff's department? You're working on becoming a detective."

"I only became a deputy sheriff to help out Max," he said. "My degree's in communications. I can change jobs."

I held his gaze. "You're not the running type, Marco Roland. You stare danger in the face and don't flinch."

"There are different kinds of danger, Carly. Starin' down a rogue deputy is different than starin' down a man who aims to hurt you usin' underhanded methods."

My mouth twisted into a wry smile. "Only with Paul Conrad, you got both." That man had been corrupt in every sense of the word.

"Bart Drummond's a lot sneakier than Conrad ever thought about bein'." He hesitated, then said, "I'd love to see Bart get his comeuppance, but I'm not sure it's worth riskin' your life over."

I turned to face him more. "What are you talking about? We both knew this was the plan. Hell, he's threatened to turn in information on Hank, and I wouldn't be surprised if it was real evidence and not concocted."

He cocked his head, his eyes boring into mine. "If it's real, what if Hank deserves to be in prison? What if he killed someone? Or multiple someones. You can't get as high as he did in the drug game and get away with squeaky clean hands."

I broke the stare. "Trust me, thinking about his past has kept me awake more than a night or two, but if he deserves to be in jail, let someone other than Bart put him there. Besides, the plan was to use Bart for practice. My father is the main goal."

"So let's forget Bart and go straight to the FBI."

I groaned. "We've discussed this already, Marco. Multiple times. My friend in Arkansas told me the FBI won't protect me. I don't have any evidence they can use to prosecute him. They'd just send me back to him, probably with a wire, hoping he'd share incriminating information. But he wouldn't. He's never trusted me, and he certainly isn't about to start after a year-long disappearance. He'd have me killed, and then he'd pay for someone to falsify evidence that I'd married Jake first. I'd rather live in hiding."

His eyes widened at my mention of Arkansas. Without my friends there, I never would have been able to come here. They'd had their own close brushes with my father's illegal organization, which was moving into their town like a cancer. They'd given me this second life as Carly Moore so I could stay on the run. Still, we'd hashed out the other options before I left. The FBI had been one of them. I'd only spoken to Marco about my time in Henryetta, Arkansas twice, so I understood his surprise that I was mentioning it now.

"If you have to run again," he said cautiously, "I want to go with you, but we need a plan."

He was talking about throwing his life away again. For me. I couldn't handle the guilt. What was I giving him in return? Myself? It didn't seem like enough, and I wasn't even sure I could bring myself to do that all the way.

"We can talk about a plan to run later," I said, getting to my feet again. "I have work to do."

Chapter Fifteen

I'd only eaten half of my lunch, but my appetite was gone. Still, I felt bad that I wasn't making the most of the surprise Marco had prepared for me. I mentioned it to him as I cleaned up my trash.

"Hey," he said. "Don't worry about it. We'll go back again sometime after this mess has been cleared up."

I grinned. "I like that enthusiasm. We'll plan on a celebratory lunch."

"It's a deal."

We threw our trash away and Marco walked me to my car.

"What about Ted Butcher?" I asked as we reached the driver's side door. "Have you had a chance to look into him?"

"No, I only had a chance to pull Thad's accident before I had to leave. I'll look into Butcher's arrest reports later this afternoon. Stick to Pam's friends and family for now."

"So you don't want to pick another old case to look at?" I asked. "We never settled on one this morning."

"No," he said with a worried look. "If people know you're asking about multiple cases, they might put together what you're doin'."

So basically we were hamstrung, and I'd only made the situation worse by showing up at the jail and asking for Pam Crimshaw's daughter. I never should have gone in.

"Do you still want to spend the night at my place?" he said. "We can go over the reports together. Then we can figure out what to do next."

I ran a hand over my head. "Yeah, okay. But I'll have to get up early and head over to Hank's for breakfast." I tilted my head to the side. "Wyatt says he's cooking."

A slow grin spread across his face. "Maybe you can show up a few minutes late."

I laughed. "I wondered when your testosterone would kick in."

"I'm trying my best, but I'm not a saint."

I turned serious. "I guess we're not mentioning the way you were touching me at the jail."

Worry filled his eyes. "That was for show. To let them know you're important to me."

"I figured."

We continued to look at each other, waiting for the other to say something, but silence hung in the air.

"Be careful, Carly," he finally said, his eyes pleading. "If you feel threatened at all, get the hell out of whatever situation you're in and call me. I'll get to you as fast as I can."

"I will." I gave him a soft smile. "You be careful too. I'll see you at the tavern?"

"I hope so." He grimaced. "I've got a mountain of paperwork to get through, but I'll stop by if I finish early enough. Otherwise, I'll meet you at the house."

"I know you saw Max last night, but I'm sure he'd like to see you anyway."

"Yeah, I've missed hanging out there." He reached for the handle and opened the door.

I got inside and he shut the door behind me, giving me a small wave.

I waved back, feeling a pinch of something inside of me.

We pulled out of the lot in the same direction, heading back toward town, but he took a turn toward the sheriff's station and I headed to Walgreens.

I didn't think Ashlynn worked at Walgreens. For one thing, she'd called her place of employment a drugstore and most people of the people who'd refer to a chain pharmacy by such an archaic term resided in Greener Pastures. But Marco was right about the go bag, and while I suspected he was also right about getting most of the items in Greeneville, I could easily explain getting personal hygiene products to put in it.

Grabbing a basket once I got inside, I headed for the shampoo aisle, grabbing my usual shampoo and conditioner, but I also picked up a box of dark brown hair dye. I preferred my hair long, and had let it grow out past my shoulders, but if I had to run again, I knew I'd have to drastically change it again. Which meant I'd have to go shorter than the shoulder-length bob I'd gotten last October. Much shorter. That or a wig. Sadly, I wasn't sure my vanity could handle something shorter than my chin.

I also picked up some ibuprofen and Tylenol, bandages, antibiotic ointment, a few skin care products I used, as well as some feminine hygiene items. Then, because I decided to be optimistic, I grabbed a puzzle I hadn't seen before and two bags of butterscotch candies for the ladies at the nursing home.

When I checked out at the counter, I gave the female cashier a big smile. "Is Ashlynn working today?"

She blinked in surprise. "Ashlynn? Ain't nobody who works here named Ashlynn."

I shook my head and laughed. "My grandmother must have gotten confused. She told me that her friend's daughter works at the drugstore. She thought it was Walgreens, but I guess there must be a few pharmacies in town."

"I've got a granny like that," the woman said as she scanned the items. "She gets everything turned around. She probably works at Jones' Pharmacy about a half mile down on Pine Street. Either that or the urgent care pharmacy."

"Thanks."

She picked up the box of hair dye and glanced at me. "You really shouldn't go darker. Have you considered going blonde? It would be a more natural fit for your coloring."

Didn't I know it.

I just smiled and said I'd take it under consideration and then handed my debit card over, resisting the urge to groan, over both her comment and the total. A few minutes later, I was on my way toward Jones' Pharmacy.

Jones' Pharmacy was old and had obviously been there for multiple decades. The parking lot was empty, and once I got inside, I found it small and surprisingly empty. The vinyl tile floors were yellowed and the edges of some of the sparsely stocked shelving looked rusted. I wondered how the place stayed in business, especially with Walgreens so close.

I really should have planned this out ahead of time, because I didn't want to just go in and ask for Ashlynn, which meant I had to make a purchase. I headed to the gift card endcap, figuring Ruth's birthday was coming up and she might appreciate a gift card to Target. Or maybe I'd give it to Jerry as a housewarming gift. My stomach dropped at the reminder that he was moving out to the Drummond property, playing into whatever plan Bart might have for him.

One problem at a time.

I took the gift card to the unmanned register at the front, but an older man waved me to the pharmacy counter in the back. "I'll check you out down here."

I walked up to the counter. He took the card and punched the numbers into the register instead of scanning it. I wondered how he'd activate it with his ancient machine.

"How much you want to put on it?" he asked, looking over the wire reading glasses perched on the end of his nose.

"Twenty?"

"Gotta be twenty-five or more," he said in a grumpy tone. I wasn't sure if he was irritated at me for getting a gift card or the company for setting the limits. Probably both.

"Then twenty-five." I glanced around before turning back to him. "Say, is Ashlynn workin' today?"

His forehead furrowed. "She was supposed to," he snapped, "but the dang fool hasn't show up yet."

I felt equal parts relief and concern. "Did you try to call her and see why she was late?"

He released a low growl as he punched in the numbers again and received an error beep. "It ain't my job to track her down! Your generation doesn't know the meaning of work. Why can't y'all just show up to work like you're supposed to?"

I almost told him that I was used to working six days a week, but I wasn't here to clear my character or stand up for "my generation." "Do you think her not showing up has something to do with her mother?"

His head jutted back. "Her mother? What about her mother?"

Did gossip not travel at the speed of light in Ewing like it did in Drum? Or maybe he felt he was above it all. In any case, I wasn't going to be the one to tell him. "Never mind."

He tried punching numbers into the machine again, which issued another loud beep. The man started cursing a blue streak. His cheeks were flushed an unhealthy red, and he looked like he might rocket out of his chair any moment and start beating the machine against the wall. Or me.

"I changed my mind about the gift card," I said, taking several steps backward. "I'll let you get back to…" I wasn't sure what he was getting back to. In fact, as empty as the place was, I wasn't sure how he could afford to employ Ashlynn.

"If you see her, tell her she's *fired*!" he shouted, spittle flying out of his mouth.

I really didn't want that responsibility, but I wasn't about to argue with him, so I continued backing up until I bumped into the front door and left.

I sat in my car, taking several deep breaths as I grasped the steering wheel. Why was he so angry? If that was his usual state, it was no wonder he didn't have any customers. How could Ashlynn stand to work there? And, more importantly, what had happened to her?

I cast a glance at the clock on the dashboard—1:45. I had to be at work at five, and since I couldn't go to the courthouse, I didn't have anything else to do in Ewing. Turning on the car, I decided to head back to Drum to pay a visit to Selena, but first I pulled out my phone and called Hank.

He answered after a couple of rings. "I'm watching my programs, so make it quick." Loud voices were arguing in the background.

I grinned. He didn't have caller ID, so he had no idea who was on the line. "Hank, it's me. Carly."

"Everything okay?" he asked, sounding concerned. I rarely called him, and he probably assumed I'd walked my way into another mess. He wouldn't be wrong. The volume of the voices lowered.

"Yeah, I'm fine. I'm working late so I wanted to warn you that Wyatt's coming over for breakfast tomorrow."

"Why?" he asked in a dry tone.

"He just felt like it," I said. "And he's cooking."

"Is he bringin' real bacon with him?"

"I don't know." It wasn't entirely a lie. While I'd told him not to bring bacon, I wouldn't put it past him to do it anyway. Then again, maybe not since he was trying to worm his way back into my life. "I didn't ask for the menu."

"Hrmph," he grunted.

"Third, he's going to be working on your car to make it drivable for you. That way you won't need to wait on me if you feel like heading into town." He didn't say anything. "That's a good thing, Hank. But if you don't want Wyatt do to it, we can find someone else." I cringed, then added, "Marco offered to help."

"That boy don't know shit about fixin' cars."

"He wouldn't do it himself," I said with a small laugh. "He offered to help me find someone else who could."

"Let Wyatt do it," he grumped. "He won't charge us much."

"Okay, then. Which means Wyatt's still comin' over to make us breakfast and look at your car."

"You don't need to be here for breakfast. I can let you know when he leaves."

Did I tell him that Wyatt's offer came with strings? I'd save that for now. He was willing to let Wyatt help, and I didn't want to screw that up. "I'll see you tomorrow, but you can always call me at the tavern after five if anything comes up."

"You be safe, girlie," he said gruffly. "And tomorrow morning, stay in bed with the man who deserves you instead of running to the man who turned his back on you." Then he hung up.

Looked like Wyatt had a lot of groveling in his future.

Before I headed back to Drum, I had somewhere else I wanted to see. Well, two places. I had no idea where Jim Palmer Insurance was located, but I *did* know how to get to Sonic. If the fast food restaurant was only a couple of blocks away, then the insurance office couldn't be hard to locate.

I drove past the Sonic, heading south. Sure enough, after I drove a block, I saw a crowd and some bright colors ahead. As I got closer, I realized the people were gathered around a makeshift memorial that consisted of flowers, stuffed animals, and homemade signs in a business parking lot.

I'd just found the insurance office.

I'd only intended to drive by, but I found myself pulling into the parking lot of an abandoned building next door. The lot was nearly full with at least ten cars, but I found a space at the end that was partially grass.

As I walked over, I took in the crowd, which consisted of at least thirty people of all ages. A group of women were hugging each other, and a couple of men stood to one side. There were several boys who looked like they were middle-school age.

I hung back, not sure why I felt drawn to stop, but allowing myself to take in the moment. There was an eight-by-ten photo of Jim in the center, and tears filled my eyes as I stared at it. It was easy to depersonalize this, to make it all about Pam, but the truth was a man's life had been snuffed out in an instant. Apparently he'd touched many people, and his loss would hurt for some time to come. Pam had done this. Pam had set this tragedy in motion.

No, Bart Drummond had instigated it. And while Pam might belong in a jail cell for her part, it was unfair that she alone should be punished.

I turned around and went back to my car, determined to make this right.

Chapter
Sixteen

While I knew the general area where Selena Martin lived, I didn't have an address. Since Drum was decades behind the rest of the world, the best place to look was the phone book, especially since Marco had made it sound like Selena had lived in Drum for ages. I could have stopped by the tavern to look through their phone book, but the library seemed like a better option. Fewer questions to answer.

Carnita was at her desk when I walked in, and all three computers were occupied.

"Carly, what a lovely surprise."

"I just need to borrow your phone book."

She laughed. "As often as you borrow it, you should see about getting one of your own. They don't have one at Hank's or the tavern?"

So much for not having to answer questions. "We do at both places, but it just seemed handier to stop here." I smiled at her. "I figured I could also check on the books you ordered. Two birds with one stone."

"They haven't arrived yet, but I'm expecting them any day."

"That's fine," I said. "Say, I meant to tell you the other day, I'm thinking of giving the kids a reading challenge. I'm going to give them prizes based on the number of books they read from the library."

I could hear Marco in my head, telling me that I needed to stop spending money on the kids and save it for my escape. But it wasn't that easy. I couldn't turn my back on those kids.

Which meant I just needed to make sure I didn't have to run.

"Oh, such a good idea! I used to have a summer reading program, years ago, but now my budget is too tight. Thank goodness for Dolly Parton's Imagination Library. I try to sign up every new baby I hear about to get their free book every month. But that doesn't mean the parents read to them."

"You're doing the best you can," I assured her. "And I'm picking up on the other end. Teamwork."

She smiled. "Teamwork." Then she reached under the desk and pulled out the phone book. "And here you go."

I took the phone book to the round table in the center of the book section and flipped the pages until I found the Martins. There were six of them, and while Selena's name wasn't in the book, S.G. Martin was, with an address on Parson's Street—the street behind the Methodist church.

I wrote the address in my notebook, then took the phone book back to Carnita.

"That didn't take long. Find what you were lookin' for?" she asked as she took it from me.

"I did. Thanks." It was obvious she was fishing for information, and while I would love to ask her if she knew Selena, I couldn't forget what Marco had told me. I needed to keep this quiet.

I headed outside and paused for a moment. My car was parked on the street, but it was such a nice day and Selena's house was only a few blocks away…I decided to walk instead.

The house was a cute light blue and white ranch style house with an older sedan in the driveway. The landscape beds were bursting with flowers, giving the home a cozy, inviting feeling.

I walked up to the front door and knocked, hoping the car in the driveway meant Selena was home.

A youthful-looking older woman with reddish-brown hair opened the door.

"Hi," I said, giving her a smile. "I'm Carly Moore. I know Pam from working at Max's Tavern, and I was wondering if I could talk to you about Ashlynn."

Her eyes widened in surprise. "Oh. I've heard of you. You're the one who found poor Seth Chalmers."

My chest tightened. This was the third time today someone had said that to me.

"Yes," I finally said. "I did."

"And you were with him when he died."

A lump filled my throat. "Yes."

She took a step backward. "Please, come in."

I walked through the door and took in her warm and cozy living room. The furniture was older, but it looked well-worn and loved.

"Would you like a glass of tea?" she asked as she shut the door. "It's warming up out there."

I nearly laughed at her idea of warming up. It had to be in the low eighties at the most. I was used to it being in the nineties in Dallas. "That would be lovely. Thank you."

She gestured for me to sit on the sofa as she walked into the kitchen. "I've been meaning to contact you," she said from the other room. "So you saved me the effort."

"About Seth?" I asked in surprise.

"Yes," she called out, and I heard the clink of ice cubes against glass. "And other things." A half minute later she walked out with two glasses of iced tea. She handed one to me and took a seat in the loveseat perpendicular to the sofa. "I hear you've started a tutoring club at the tavern."

"Oh, yes. Twice a week," I said, taking a sip of the tea, pleased that it wasn't sickly sweet. Iced tea in eastern Tennessee meant sweet iced tea, and some people overdid it to the point that it tasted like tea-flavored sugar water.

"How did that come about?" Her voice had a wary tone.

I could understand why she was leery. If someone who didn't know what they were doing started incorrectly teaching the kids, it could do more harm than good. "I used to work as a tutor in Atlanta," I said. "One of the kids who came into the tavern this spring with her parents was struggling with her math homework, so I offered to help. The mother of one of her classmates heard I knew how to do it, and they came in for dinner and asked me to help too."

"So you're doin' this to bring in more business to the tavern?" she asked in a firm tone. "I hear you aren't charging."

"I love helping kids, and three-thirty to five is our slow time. So it gives me something to do, and it's a way to give back to the community. Win/win."

"But you don't have a degree," she said. "You don't understand the state standards."

I took another sip of my drink, stalling. I *did* know the state standards. I'd looked them up, but a retail clerk likely wouldn't know. "I can assure you that I'm not harming their education in any way. I'm only bolstering them."

"I know you aren't harming them," she said, her tone still direct. "The mother of one of your students showed me what her child had been working on. It's obvious you know what you're doing."

"I only want to help."

"The elementary school is full of tenured teachers who don't give a crap about those kids. They want to finish out their thirty years and collect their pension."

"I don't know anything about that, ma'am." I said. "I only know that several children needed help, and it all just grew from there. I'm grateful that Max has agreed to host it."

Her gaze pinned mine long enough that I started to feel uncomfortable. She definitely had the teacher look down. I needed to change the topic.

"You knew Seth," I said. "Did you have him as a student?"

"For two years," she said. "That boy was smart as a whip. I had high hopes for him."

"I know he was a talented artist."

She nodded. "Once he set his mind to something, his determination helped see him through." Tilting her head, she said, "I hear you're living with his grandfather."

"I am."

"And how do you find that situation?"

I wasn't sure what to make of her question. "I find it just fine," I said with a tight smile. "I'm sure you're wondering why I want to talk about Ashlynn."

She sat back in her seat and took a sip of her tea. "It had occurred to me."

"Like I said, I know Pam Crimshaw from the tavern. She and her three friends used to come to lunch every other week or so, so I was beyond shocked when I heard what she did. I took the kids a chicken and rice casserole this morning, and Ashlynn said she needed a ride to Ewing for work."

She studied me for a moment. "That was certainly thoughtful of you."

"Ashlynn told me that her mother had stepped in to help after Chuck walked out on her a few weeks ago. When I told her that I was worried about her being alone, she mentioned her Aunt Selena would be there for her."

Her eyes narrowed. "And you thought you'd stop by and...?"

"Miss Selena," I said, scooting forward on the sofa and setting my glass on a coaster on the coffee table in front of me. "Ashlynn asked me to drop her off at the county jail so she could see her mother. She said her father had forbidden them all from visiting Pam, but Ashlynn wanted to go anyway. Since I was already headed to Ewing, I took her. I dropped her off at the jail, and she told me to be back in forty-five minutes. Only she didn't come out when she said she would. I waited nearly a half hour longer, and when I went in to check on her, they said she'd never signed in to visit Pam."

"Maybe she changed her mind and went to work."

"I was worried enough about her that I went by the pharmacy, and she didn't show up there either."

She frowned. "While I love Ashlynn, she's not always the most responsible person in the world."

"But why would she ask me to take her to the jail, then not go in?"

She shrugged. "Maybe she changed her mind. Her boyfriend was arrested for possession several months back. I'm fairly certain she went to see him while he was in jail. Maybe she remembered what it was like and changed her mind." She shrugged. "She's a flighty girl."

"So you're saying I have nothing to worry about? Because I would feel responsible if something happened to her."

She waved her hand in dismissal. "She's fine. She probably called a friend to give her a ride."

I nearly told her that I'd only brought Ashlynn because she'd struggled to find a ride, but I suspected she'd downplay that as well.

"Well, if you hear from her, tell her I'm worried," I said.

"You hardly know her. Why would you be worried?"

"Because, like I told you, I feel responsible for her after dropping her off. I worry that I should have stuck around to make sure she got in safely." Then I added in frustration, "She *is* pregnant, you know."

"Of course I know," she said, sounding irritated. "I was the one who took her to the doctor for her first prenatal checkup. I was also the one who took her to get birth control, fat lot of good that did her since she didn't take the pills." She released a sigh and some of her anger faded. "While I do question why you're so concerned, believe me when I say it's unfounded. This is typical for Ashlynn's behavior. Her parents were at wit's end with her, and I worry that her father will kick her out on her keister. Then again, maybe that's what she needs."

"She's counting on you for help."

"I'm sure she is, and while I plan on giving her plenty of tough love, I won't let her and her baby sleep out on the street." She grimaced. "Only don't tell her I said that."

While I was still worried, Selena knew her better than I did. "She won't hear it from me."

"Good." She took a sip of her tea. "I'm not surprised Ashlynn wanted to see her mother, but I *am* surprised she defied her father. No one does that. Maybe that's why she didn't go inside. She realized it wasn't worth risking his wrath."

"Maybe." The more I thought about it, the more likely that seemed. Her father might not be a good man, but she was probably dependent on him. Even more so now that she'd lost her job. Maybe she was flighty, like Selena had said, but I also suspected she was trying to protect her baby. Her mother was a lost cause. Her baby needed her more. "Ashlynn said her mother has a public defender, but I'm worried that he'll consider her case cut and dry and not try to get the best possible sentencing for her."

She shook her head. "I love Pam with my heart and soul. She's like the daughter I never had, but she killed that man in cold blood. All her apologies and excuses won't bring him back."

"Has she apologized?" Then a new thought hit me. "Have *you* seen her?"

"I went to see her yesterday, but it was like she was in a catatonic state. When I asked her why she did it, she got a glazed look in her eyes and started mumbling, 'I'm sorry.'" Selena shot me a look of disapproval. "Why are you insertin' yourself into this family's lives? Why are you so concerned about the children in Drum? Why are you livin' with the grandfather of the boy you saw murdered?" She leaned closer. "What are you up to?"

My mouth parted in surprise. "I just like to help people, and now that Drum's my home, I want to give back to my community."

"Nobody gives back to their community in Drum." She shook her head. "You're up to something, I just don't know what it is."

Not only had I not gotten answers, I'd just made this woman suspicious of me—which was exactly what I'd set out not to do. "I don't know what to tell you, Miss Selena. Hank needed someone to take care of him after Seth died, and I needed a place to stay. It worked out well for both of us. As for the children, I love kids. When I saw that little girl struggling, and I knew how to do the problem, it would have been wrong to stay silent. Helping made me feel like I was doing something good. Something important."

"Are you a saint?"

I forced a short laugh. "No, I'm definitely not. But I don't think caring about others is reserved for the religious. Otherwise, there wouldn't be nearly as many charities."

One of her eyebrows lifted. "And the Crimshaws?"

"It's just like I told you. I'm worried about Pam and her family. Maybe I didn't know Pam very well, but what she did shocked me to my core. If she could do something like this, then it feels like anyone could, you know?"

"So why get mixed up with her family?"

"Because if I'm shocked, they must feel like they're living in the Twilight Zone. I only want to help them and, if I can, figure out a way to somehow help Pam. Maybe she had a psychotic break. Maybe what she really needs is a psych evaluation, not life in prison."

Selena studied me for a long moment. "Pam's mentioned you, you know."

I jolted in surprise. "Oh?"

"She liked that you started tutoring kids. She said you were sweet. A lot sweeter than the other waitress. The loud one."

I laughed. "Ruth. She's not one to pussyfoot around." I tilted my head to the side. "But she sure knows how to handle the men on game nights."

Selena's shoulders seemed to relax. "I told Pam that I thought you were up to something. Nobody's that nice, but she insisted you were the real deal." Her eyes narrowed. "Tell me why you're really livin' with Hank."

It occurred to me what she was hinting at. "If you think I'm living with Hank to find his fortune, you're dead wrong. There's no fortune to be had. If he had money, it's long gone. I suspect he spent it all on his wife's medical care."

"Hank used to make money hand over fist back in the day. He had a whole enterprise goin' on. Hired almost as many people in this town as Bart Drummond did in his lumber business."

While Marco had said he was the largest marijuana distributer in eastern Tennessee, and I knew he'd had employees, I'd had no idea his operation had been so big.

"Surely you knew he was a drug dealer," she said in surprisingly kind tone.

"Yes, but he hasn't been for years. Or so I've been told."

"He turned away from it a good decade ago. Mary hated it all, and when she got ill, she asked him to give it up. Surprisingly, he did. For some reason, they've lived out in that rinky-dink house since they were first married, even when he was making big money. I asked Mary once why she didn't force him to move her somewhere nicer, and she said they had a tie to the land, but I always suspected Hank was just bein' tight-fisted." She gave me a smug look. "I wouldn't be surprised if there's a fortune buried on his land. Along with a few bodies."

I wasn't sure about the bodies, but I was about the fortune. "The man's roof was leaking so badly we had to put a bucket underneath the ceiling until we could get a repairman out, and even then we piecemealed it. Hank's flat broke, so if I were there for his money, I'd be wasting my time. And before you ask again, it's just like I said—I needed a place to stay and he needed help. He let me live there rent free in exchange for cooking his meals and taking care of him. Now we're friends, and I wouldn't move somewhere else even if I could afford to."

"Carnita says you've checked out diabetic cooking books."

"I'm not sure what you're getting at, Miss Selena."

"Just tryin' to figure out why you're living with a man twice your age."

Lots of people were curious, but few were bold enough to continue pressing the matter. "You're getting a little personal."

"And so are you with all your questions about Pan and her family."

She had a point. "I promise you that I'm only trying to help, but I understand and appreciate your concerns." I got to my feet. "I won't take any more of your time."

"Why are you really here?" she asked, turning to face me as I headed for the door.

"I already told you. I'm very concerned about Ashlynn. You know her better than I do, but I can't shake the worry that she might be missing. If there's a chance I was the last person to see her, I feel it's my duty to do something about that. And two, I'm worried about Pam. You're right, of course—nothing can justify what she did. Jim Palmer's never coming back. But I don't believe she'd just shoot a man in cold blood, not without a good reason. If Pam really did have some type of psychotic break, or if she knew Mr. Palmer and thought she was avenging some wrong, then it seems like that should be taken into consideration at her sentencing."

Her face softened. "You really *do* care about her. Why?"

"I've heard the justice system isn't always fair here, so if I can help Pam in any way, then I aim to do it."

She pursed her lips for a moment, then grimaced and motioned for me to sit back down. "I may regret this, but I guess you've fooled me too."

I stayed in place. "I'm not trying to fool *anyone*, Miss Selena."

"Okay, poor choice of words," she said. "I'm a math teacher, not an English professor. I deal with numbers and logic, not daydreams and fancy thinkin'."

I gave her a long look, then sat down. "Sometimes daydreams become reality. Do you know anything that could help Pam? Sandy said she was taking medication for depression."

"Not lately she wasn't. Rob insisted that taking an antidepressant was a sign of weakness. He told her it was all in her head."

I pulled my small notebook out of my purse and turned to the next available page. "When did she start taking them?" I asked, uncapping my pen.

"You're takin' notes?"

"We have to present a clear, accurate account. You bet I'm taking notes."

The suspicion had returned to her eyes, but she continued. "Around the time of Thad's accident. She'd been havin' a rough time leading up to it. He was givin' her and Rob fits with his bad behavior. Drinkin' and sassin'. Gettin' in trouble at school. Rob blamed her for it, of course. Said her coddlin' was part of the problem and she needed to let him handle it, but his way of handlin' it was with a belt and his hand. He beat that child badly enough that one of the teachers at the middle school turned them in to child protective services. The social worker made a home visit, but Rob convinced them he was exercising his parental rights and it didn't cross the line into child abuse. It scared Pam something fierce, knowing she'd nearly lost him and Ricky too, and Thad rebelled even more. Then he and his friend got drunk and stole Pam's minivan. They hit that poor man on Highway 25 out on the way to the overlook. If she was depressed before, she fell into a pit of grief after. Thad and his friend were hurt, but not as badly as that unlucky man in the other car. They were all in the same hospital in Greeneville, and Pam had to see the poor man's family and deal with their anger. She couldn't eat. Couldn't sleep. Her doctor put her on some type of medication, but she wouldn't tell me what. She hid it from Rob, and I didn't even know she was still takin' the pills until she told me about three months ago that Rob had found out and belittled her. She quit cold turkey and was nearly suicidal, but it all worked out. Or so I thought until I heard about that poor insurance agent."

We were both silent for a moment, the only sound was my pen on paper as I hurried to make notes.

"So it really might have been some kind of psychotic break," I said. "You can't just quit those kind of drugs. You have to be weaned."

"I tried to tell her that," Selena said. "But Rob insisted."

"If you don't mind me asking," I said, "why did she stay with him? It sounds like she wasn't happy."

"And where would she go?" Selena asked. "She used to run a home daycare, but to do that you need a house, and there was no way Rob would let her keep the house. He would have kicked her out, and he sure as hell wouldn't have let her take the boys. Those kids were her whole world. She stayed so she wouldn't lose them."

I pushed back my rising despair. There was so much poverty here, so many women trapped in dire situations without the money or the resources to escape. But then Emily Drummond had stayed with Bart for the same reason—for fear she would lose her children—so maybe it wasn't just limited to the impoverished.

"Did the other boy's family blame Pam and Rob for the accident?"

"Oh yes, and I think they considered suing, but they changed their tune. She only had to deal with a lawsuit from the guy in the other car."

"Do you know why the other family decided not to sue?"

"Not a clue, but Pam didn't seem all that surprised. I think she was numb by then."

Was this the smoking gun that Bart had given Pam a favor?

"Does the family live in Drum?" I asked.

"Out by White Rabbit Holler"

"No kidding," I said. "*I* live out in White Rabbit Holler. What's their last name? Maybe I know them."

"The Genslers. Their son is Spencer, and I taught both of his parents. Donald and Kay."

Pursing my lips, I shook my head. "Don't know them, but Hank might." I wrote down their names, then asked, "Do you know if Pam knew Jim Palmer?"

She shook her head. "No. She never mentioned him. Travis Keeling is her agent, and before that, she had an agent with State Farm. Jim Palmer's an independent agent." She grimaced. "Or I guess he *was*."

"Could she have known him from somewhere else? Maybe their kids were on the same sports teams?"

"The boys don't play any sports. Poor Ricky tried to play football, but he wasn't much good at it. Quit his sophomore year—mid-season." She shook her head. "Rob was fit to be tied over that."

"Did you know Jim Palmer? Did you have him as a student?"

She gave me a tight smile. "Yes. He was also my insurance agent, and his daughter, Laurie, was in my geometry class last year."

I'd just found my source of information about Pam's victim.

Chapter Seventeen

W hat about Jim's wife?" I asked, my pen poised over the notebook.

"No," she said with a frown. "Jim met Melinda at college and brought her back to Ewing."

"I heard Jim's father owned the agency before him."

"That's right. Jim, Sr. died from cancer about a decade ago. When the kids were small."

"And Jim had two children?" Marco had mentioned that fact, but it wouldn't hurt to verify it.

"A girl and a boy. Laurie was a freshman last year, and her brother Pete is in middle school."

"It sounds like Jim was well liked. I saw signs and flowers outside the office."

"Oh, yes," she said, still frowning. "One of the nicest people I've ever met. He coached his kids' sports teams and his business sponsored plenty of others. He was a strong presence in the Ewing Small Business Club. He even helped organize a food drive every year."

"Can you think of any reason why someone would hate him?"

"Jim?" she asked in surprise. "No. That's what's so shocking about Pam murdering him. Even if you can look past the fact that she was the one who pulled the trigger, Jim was the last person you'd expect to be murdered."

"So he didn't have any enemies?"

"Not that I knew of," she said. "Just a likeable guy."

"And his wife?"

She didn't answer, and I looked up to see her mouth shifted to one side. She gave me a hesitant smile. "I don't know anything for a fact."

"I'll take that into account."

"She never much cared for Ewing. It was no secret she wanted Jim to sell the business and move to Memphis—where she's originally from."

"Memphis to Ewing," I said. "That had to be quite the culture shock."

"I guess you would know," Selena said. "Since you dropped here from Atlanta."

"True," I said. "If they met in college, I wonder what she was studying."

"Oh, I know the answer to that one," Selena said. "She was studying to be a nurse, only she never finished. She was a year behind Jim, and she got pregnant toward the end of her junior year. Jim was planning on comin' back to run his daddy's business, so she dropped out and they got married and moved back here."

"So she gave up her dreams to become a wife and mother in a town with a population of eight thousand?"

"Pretty much."

"Do you know if she had a job?"

"She opened a home goods store in downtown Ewing, but it went under. After that, she worked for Jim some."

I paused and looked up at her. "How long ago was that?"

173

"I don't know…five years? Six? She made a go of it for two years, but then finally threw in the towel. They nearly lost the house after that."

If this was a Bart favor, maybe it wasn't Jim who'd asked for the favor. Maybe it was Melinda.

"So they're in financial trouble?"

"Not like they were a few years ago, but rumor has it their credit cards were maxed out."

"Melinda must have put a lot of money into her inventory."

"You don't know the half of it," Selena said. "She said she was trying to bring class and culture to eastern Tennessee, only her insinuations insulted half the town, and the other half wasn't about to buy her stuff anyway. Plus everything was overpriced for the area. I heard she started selling her inventory online, but by then it was too late."

"What about their kids?" I asked. "Have they been in any kind of trouble?"

Selena's eyes narrowed. "What do Jim's kids have to do with Pam shootin' him?"

How much should I tell her? She was a huge source of information, and the more invested she was, the more she might share. Still, I ran the risk of endangering myself. What if Selena couldn't be trusted? What if she picked up the phone after I left and called Bart himself?

"I'm just trying to understand the situation," I said. "Obviously, something made Pam snap. She has a controlling, abusive husband, and two of her three children have had issues—"

"Three," Selena said. "Ricky nearly flunked three classes this spring. Pam had to go to the school and ask the teachers to work with him so he'd bring them up to Ds."

Poor Pam, but I felt for her kids too. When children were unhappy, they acted out, and sometimes in big ways. "Unless

Pam just drove around randomly and stopped at Jim's office, he somehow fell onto her path. I'm trying to figure out the connection."

She nodded, her lips pursing as she contemplated what I'd said. "Laurie is a bright girl, but also pretty and sweet. She's not popular, but the other students like her well enough. Now that I think about it, she's a lot like her father."

"Is she in any sports or activities?"

She drew in a breath. "I don't know…" She sounded frustrated, but I didn't think her annoyance was with me. "I think she was on the yearbook staff." Getting to her feet, she walked over to a bookcase and grabbed a hardcover book off the shelf. "This is last year's yearbook. Laurie will be in there. You can see what she was involved in. Also, maybe check the newspaper. It lists all sorts of things from grade school game scores to dance recitals. I'm sure you'll find both kids in there. Plenty about Jim and Melinda too."

"Okay. I'll get it back to you soon."

She handed the book to me. "No hurry. I get them every year, then promptly place them on a shelf. I rarely have occasion to open them."

I placed the yearbook on my lap, covering it with my notebook, then looked over my notes. "Back to Pam," I said as Selena took her seat. "I know she had a daycare that she ended."

"Yes, after Thad's accident. It was only part time and the parents found other caretakers while she was dealing with his recovery."

"Did she get another job?"

"No, Rob preferred she stay home, but he let her volunteer at the church."

Rob sounded like a real prince. "And did she volunteer at the church?"

"Oh yes." She nodded. "She's in charge of the nursery, or I guess she *was*. She's always loved babies. After she got over the disappointment of Ashlynn's pregnancy, she started lookin' forward to his arrival. She planned on spendin' a lot of time with her grandbaby."

"Is there anyone who doesn't like her?"

She laughed. "Are you askin' if Pam has any enemies? Heavens, no. Everyone liked her, but people *did* take advantage of her."

That didn't surprise me. I'd seen her with Diane at the ladies' lunches. "Do you think Jim Palmer could be connected to anyone who upset her?"

Her lips pursed. "A revenge killing? Doesn't seem like Pam."

"But she went off her meds. I know anxiety is a side effect. I just don't know how long it lasts."

She shook her head. "I don't know. That was three months ago. Pam just isn't the vengeful type." She frowned. "Except…"

"Yes?"

"A couple of weeks ago, I saw her snap at the store clerk in Ewing. We were at a secondhand shop, and Pam found a crib she wanted to buy for Ashlynn. But we were going to lunch, so she asked the clerk to put it on hold. When we went back to the store, another clerk had already sold it, and Pam was furious. She yelled at the clerk and called her incompetent. I had to drag her out of the store before they called the police. Once I got her back into the car, she broke down, bawling. She was horrified at what she'd done. She apologized profusely and asked me to take her home even though we'd planned to go to another store."

"Was she under stress because of her husband?"

"I honestly don't know. I told her I thought Rob was being ridiculous about her medication, and she kind of clammed up after that."

"Is there anything else you can think of that might have upset her a couple of days ago?"

"And enraged her enough to kill a man?" She shook her head. "There's a big difference between chewing someone out and murdering them."

She was right, but I couldn't help wondering what had driven a normally meek and mild woman to snap, not once but twice.

I couldn't think of anything else, so I closed my notebook and put it back in my purse, along with the yearbook and my pen. "I need to head to work, but if you come up with anything you think would help, please let me know."

"I'm still not convinced this is goin' to help her."

"Maybe not," I said, "but at least we'll know we tried."

Selena walked me to the door, and I headed back toward Main Street, letting everything I'd learned roll around in my head. I'd learned a lot from Selena, but none of it had helped me reach any conclusions. Instead, I'd been left with more questions.

What I really needed was computer time, but there was no way that was happening at the library. I had to go to work soon anyway, and Max had no problem letting me use his computer as long as he wasn't working on the books. I didn't take him up on it too often—he and Ruth were far more curious than Carnita— but it might be worth the hassle tonight.

When I passed my car, still parked in front of the library, I thought about moving it but decided against it. It wouldn't be a long walk later, and if I felt uncomfortable, I'd ask Marco or Max to walk to my car with me.

Max looked surprised when I walked through the front door, so I headed to the bar to say hello.

"I was at the library and left my car down there," I said. "It seemed like a good day for a walk. Do you mind if I use the computer in your office?"

"Didn't you just use one at the library?" he asked with a laugh.

"They were all tied up."

Grinning, he shook his head. "Head on back and check your Nosy Book."

I snorted. "Facebook. And that's not all I do. I've been researching the town." I'd admitted as much to him and Ruth a while back, in case they ever came into the office at an inopportune moment. Part of me wanted to let Max in on what I was doing, but even if he hated his father, and I thought he did, I didn't know how he'd feel about me trying to bring him down.

"I think it's just a cover, so you don't look like you're killing your brain cells tweetering."

"Tweetering? You sound like a seventy-year-old man."

He laughed. "It's better than killing my brain cells." I started to head back, and he called after me, "Hey, you need the password."

I stopped and gave him a surprised look. "Password? You finally took my advice?" I'd been shocked to learn he left his office unlocked most of the time and didn't have a password on his computer.

He made a face and grabbed an order pad and pulled off a sheet, scribbling something on the back. "Yeah, well, I guess it makes sense." He handed the paper to me with a grin. "Guard it with your life."

"You know it," I said, taking the slip from him and heading to the back.

Ruth was sitting in a booth, reading a copy of *People Magazine*, a new one from the looks of it, and Tiny was scrubbing his grill. I waved hi to both of them on my way to the back. I wanted to ask Ruth about her friend—the one she was interested in hiring—but I'd ask later. I had more to research than I had time to type into the search engine.

Sure enough, when I woke up his computer, there was a password box. I entered the code—Max1$King—and laughed. He'd come up with that to irk Ruth every time she signed in to help with the books.

I did a search for Jim Palmer on the local paper's website, and it pulled up page after page about his community involvement. Too much to spend time on, so I searched for his kids next. Pete—Peter—had played T-ball and baseball, as well as soccer and basketball. He'd made the seventh grade B honor roll last year, and there was a photo of him at the high school homecoming parade. The float for his baseball team had been sponsored by Jim Palmer Insurance.

Laurie brought up more, but not by much. She'd been in dance recitals at Miss Nancy's Dance school since she was three. She'd also played sports when she was younger, but there was no mention of it once she hit middle school. She'd made the A honor roll all through middle school and her freshman year, and the single photo of her in the paper, from a high school student council, showed a fresh-faced girl who looked happy. Pete's photo had struck me the same way.

Next I looked up Melinda, realizing that I only had about ten minutes before I had to get out to work. Melinda's search brought up Jim's murder first, and I realized the kids' names had been left out of the news reports about Jim's death. I silently complimented the news editor who had made that decision. But after the stories about Jim's death—which had all the information I did, rehashed in multiple ways—were the articles about her store, Hometown Charm. There was a photo of Melinda standing next to the front window. With her short, wavy blond hair and her sweet, light-blue dress, she looked a bit like Reese Witherspoon. There were several other articles about the store, followed by some pieces about events she had attended with Jim. There were a few photos of the two together. Jim always had a big smile, his arm around his wife, but her smile looked fake in a couple of them.

Melinda didn't want to live in Ewing, Tennessee, but had she loved her husband? Was she the one who'd approached Bart Drummond and asked for a favor?

I glanced up at the time on the top corner of the computer and groaned. My time had run out.

Chapter Eighteen

We were busier than usual through the dinner rush, and then people showed up to watch the Braves' baseball game on Max's big screen TV.

Marco showed up after the dinner crowd left and headed toward the bar to hang out with Max. Ruth must have noticed, because she immediately sidled up to me.

"Why don't you take off early?" she said with a grin. "I'll close tonight."

"You've been here since noon," I protested. And because I didn't want to get into yet another conversation about Marco—just last week she'd accused me of giving him chronic blue balls—I changed the subject. "Hey, what's the word on your friend taking over Molly's position?"

"She's coming in tomorrow morning for an interview, so you don't need to come in until your tutoring club starts."

"Are you sure?" I was relieved that I'd have more time to investigate, but I didn't want to pile onto Ruth's workload.

"I'm going to be here anyway, and if it works out, I'll have her stay for her first shift." She pulled a face. "Besides, I can use the extra cash. Franklin's truck broke down, and some of the parts are expensive."

"Okay, if you're sure…"

"Good," she said. "That's settled. Now, you get on out of here. We're slow enough that Max and I have it covered."

It was only eight-thirty, but if she needed the money, I didn't feel inclined to say no. I'd prefer to talk to Marco sooner rather than later. "I guess I'll go check with Max."

"*Check?* Just tell him."

I hesitated, if only because Marco and Max looked deep in conversation, but they'd seen each other the night before, and I really, really wanted to know what Marco had learned. So I went over anyway.

"Hey," I said as I scooted up to Marco. "Ruth wants to close tonight. She said she needs the money for parts for Franklin's truck. In fact, she told me to take off now."

I expected Max to protest, but instead he nodded. "Sounds good." He shot a grin to Marco. "I suspect that means you'll be takin' off too?"

Marco looked guilty. "We can pick this conversation back up next time I come in."

"Don't worry about it," Max said with a laugh. "Just promise you won't stay away for over a week again."

"With things this busy at work, I can't promise it, but I'll try to at least stop in for lunch or dinner."

"Good enough for me." Max beamed as he offered Marco his hand over the counter.

Marco shook it with a matching grin. "Missed you, man."

"Missed you too." Max made a shooing motion. "You two crazy kids take off and do whatever it is you claim you don't do."

Marco followed me to the backroom so I could grab my purse, then we headed out the back door to the parking lot.

"Where's your car?" he asked, sounding concerned.

I groaned. "I left it in front of the library. I stopped there this afternoon to get Selena's address out of the phone book."

"Hop in," he said, gesturing to his Explorer, which was parked on the street next to the building. "I'll drop you off at your car. Did you have any problems today?"

"No, but I found out a few things."

"I did too, but let's wait until we get to my house before we start going through it."

"Okay."

We didn't talk on the short drive to my car, and I followed him out to his house. Lights glowed in the windows, and I felt some of my stress fade. I always felt like I was hiding from the world when I was with Marco at his house. Was that part of his appeal?

He took my overnight bag from me as I got out of the car, and we walked to the porch together. The smell of Italian spices hit me as I walked in the door.

"Oh!" I said as I set my purse on the kitchen table. "What did you have for dinner and is there any left?"

He laughed as he shut the front door and locked it, then he handed me the bag. "I saved some for you. Go take a shower if you want, and I'll make you a plate."

I offered him a warm smile. "Thanks."

Now that we'd gotten more comfortable together, he knew I liked to shower when I got off work, so if I was staying over, I usually showered right away.

Not only was I hungry, but I was eager to talk to Marco about our discoveries, so I emerged from the bathroom ten minutes later with damp hair, wearing pajama shorts and a T-shirt.

A plate of spaghetti and meatballs sat on the table, and Marco sat at the head of the table with his laptop open.

"Feel better?" he asked, looking up.

"Yeah. That looks delicious, but are you planning on sharing? That looks like it's enough for two people."

He laughed. "You know I always end up eating from your plate when you eat after me. I'm only planning ahead."

I grabbed my notebook out of my purse and sat down in front of the plate. "I had a good chat with Selena after I left you."

"And I found out more about Thad Crimshaw's case. And a bit about Ted Butcher too. Including the police report for the house fire in question."

I perked up. "Oh?"

"How about I start with Butcher?"

"Okay," I said as I picked up a fork and started to dig into the noodles.

"The car crash was Butcher's first run-in with the law. Not even any speeding tickets. His tox screen was negative, but his story changed about what happened—at first he said he lost control and hit the tree, and in a later statement he claimed to have fallen asleep. The officer who took the second statement said Butcher seemed despondent, but he attributed it to his injuries, which were extensive. Broken legs, a broken arm, internal injuries. The officer included in the report that Butcher was scheduled to go to a physical therapy rehab center and that he had no support system to care for him. He was divorced at the time of his accident, but I don't know for how long, and his parents were deceased. His next police report, two years later, was for a DUI arrest. He hit another car while high on Oxy. Thankfully, the occupants of the other car weren't injured, and neither was Butcher. He got off with probation. There are more reports, several overdoses, some breaking and entering charges. It's obvious he became a drug addict, likely after the accident."

I swallowed my mouthful of food. "Which goes along with my theory that he couldn't handle the guilt. He tried to kill himself, and when that didn't work, he tried to lose himself in drugs."

"Orrrr…" he said, drawing out the word. "He got hooked on painkillers after his accident. From what I can tell, he was just a normal guy, living his life. He had a job with a small metal fabricator in Ewing. It's not uncommon for people you wouldn't suspect of becoming drug addicts to get hooked on them after a major injury."

"So you don't think there's a connection?"

"I didn't say that," he said, tilting his head. "But it's not clear cut."

I swirled more spaghetti on my fork. "So we need to talk to him. Did you get an address?"

He hesitated. "Yeah. He's at the Northeast Correctional Complex in Mountain City."

I paused with my fork halfway to my mouth. "What's that? A drug rehab center?"

"No, it's prison."

"Oh," I said, then took a bite.

"His last arrest was for breaking into a house and stealing their electronics and jewelry to pay for his drug habit. At least he got sent to Northeast. They have a substance abuse counseling program."

"Maybe he'll get his life together."

"Yeah." But he didn't sound convinced.

"So talking to him is out."

"Not necessarily. We could make a request to meet with him, but he might refuse us, not to mention it will likely take a whole day to get up there, meet with him, and then get back. It could be a wasted effort. Plus, it's going to look suspicious as hell if word gets back to my department."

"Which means you can't go, Marco," I said insistently.

Disgust washed over his face. "I'm not letting you go alone, Carly." But then his face softened. "Honestly, I don't think either of us should go. It's likely a wasted trip, and his credibility is shot to hell. His word against Bart's?" He shook his head. "We'd be better served to turn our attention elsewhere."

"So what did you find out about Thad's accident?"

"Fifteen months ago, Thad and his friend Spencer Gensler were hanging out at the overlook, drinking. They took off toward town in Thad's mother's minivan and hit Karl Lister in his Subaru head on. The boys' tox screens were positive for marijuana and their blood alcohol levels were .16 and .10. Lister's tests were all negative. All three had significant injuries, but Lister's were the worst. He was life flighted to Greeneville."

"And the boys went to the same hospital."

"Yes. The friend—Spencer—was charged with underaged drinking, but Thad faced multiple charges. Felonies. And the prosecutor was considering trying him as an adult."

"Why didn't he?"

Marco shrugged. "He changed his mind? Thad was only thirteen, and it would have been a harder sell since no one died. I suspect the DA considered it because he was up for reelection, and there's a lot of public disgust for the booming drug trade in these parts, especially in Ewing. He might have thought it would make him look tougher on drugs. But while the boys had pot in their systems, the crash was due to Thad being drunk. As you've probably figured out from the large numbers of customers at the tavern, drinking is considered acceptable around here. And yeah, he was much too young to be drinking, but the good people of Hensen County are much more forgiving about DUIs."

"Except for Wyatt's DUI," I reminded him. "He was sent to prison."

"Well," he said with a sigh, "we both know that was different. Whether it was a judge bringing the Drummonds down a peg, or Bart convincing a judge to teach Wyatt a lesson, it was not the norm."

"So the DA dropped all the charges against Thad?"

"Oh, no. He still threw the book at him, but Thad was charged as a minor. Then, all of a sudden, everything got dropped except for a much lesser charge of reckless driving and the civil lawsuit. Thad only got twenty hours of community service."

"And his friend? What did he get?"

Marco rubbed his forehead. "I haven't found out yet, but I hope to tomorrow."

I nodded and then took another bite of food.

"Another thing…Pam's pleading guilty."

"What?"

"She entered an innocent plea at her arraignment, but I suspect it was only because her attorney was hoping for a bargain from the DA. Rumor has it she's planning to change her plea at her next hearing."

I set my fork back down on my plate.

"Look, Carly, I know you feel bad for her, but she pulled the trigger. Three times. She killed a man in cold blood."

"I know." I looked up at him. "I went to his office."

His face stilled. "What?"

"I planned to just drive by, but I saw all those people gathered at the memorial. So I stopped." When he looked panicked, I added, "I didn't talk to anyone. I don't know why I stopped. I guess I had to see it to make this all more real. She may have been used, but she's not innocent. I was only there for a few minutes, though. I looked like someone paying their respects. That's it."

Relief washed over his face.

"Selena gave me a lot of information about Jim and his family. She knew them."

"Really?"

I told him about Jim's involvement in the community and then floated my theory about his wife, Melinda, from the situation with her business to her reluctance to live in Ewing.

"If she ran into trouble with her business, she might have gone to Bart."

He didn't say anything, mulling it over.

"What I don't understand," I said, "is how a middle-class transplant to Ewing would find out about Bart."

"You'd be surprised," he said, shifting in his seat. "It's all based on rumors. It's possible."

"I started digging on the internet, but I ran out of time," I said. "I barely had a chance to look into Jim, Melinda, and their kids. I didn't even touch Pam and her family. And then there's Ashlynn's ex-boyfriend, Chuck Holston, the father of her baby. According to Selena, he was supposedly in jail several months ago for drug possession."

"Huh," he said, picking up my fork and stabbing a meatball.

"But from what I've heard about Pam's husband, Rob, I'm surprised he let Chuck live in a trailer on their land. Ashlynn said he beat his oldest son last year to get him to talk about Seth's involvement with Bingham."

"Seth Chalmers?" he asked in surprise.

"Yeah, Ashlynn told me Seth and her brother were best friends."

"Really?" His gaze turned worried. "How did you handle that? Was it weird?"

"Yeah. I usually only hear about Seth from Hank and Wyatt's perspective. I didn't find out much, but I told Ricky to reach out if he ever feels like talking about Seth."

"I hope he does."

"Me too." I took a deep breath. "I don't have to go to work until Tutoring Club. So tomorrow I'll spend some time doing research online. I'm already signed up for three hours at the library from several days back, before I even knew what I'd be searching for. I need to look into Rob Crimshaw. I don't know anything about him."

"I looked him up to see if he had any priors. He was arrested for some assault charges that were dropped, but those were a couple of decades ago. Bar fights."

"He beats his kids and likely his wife instead. Selena said that a teacher reported them to the state for suspected abuse, but Rob convinced them he was only disciplining."

"I hate assholes like that," he said, looking away.

"Yeah, me too. But I wouldn't be surprised if he went to Bart for something, then coerced Pam into fulfilling his task by threatening the kids."

"I don't want you talking to him directly. The man obviously has a temper."

"I won't," I said. "I'll see if I can find someone else to talk to about him." Then I thought of something else. "Did you get an address for Karl Lister?"

"Yeah, the most current address I have for him is out by where Lula used to live. I also have a phone number, so maybe it would be better to call rather than show up at his doorstep."

"Okay." But my mind was racing about how to find out more about Rob Crimshaw.

"You've hardly eaten anything," he said. "Did you eat dinner at work?"

"No. I'm just not very hungry anymore."

"Come on," he said, getting to his feet. "We've done enough for tonight, and I have a surprise for you."

"A surprise?" I said, perking up.

"Yeah, it's outside." He walked to the door and grabbed a jacket from a peg by the door and handed it to me.

I slipped it on, engulfed by the warmth and the smell of Marco, and slid my feet into a pair of flipflops I kept at his house. He shot me a smile I couldn't interpret, then led me outside and around the side of the house. A tripod was set up in the yard with a short tube attached on top.

"What's this?" I asked in excitement.

"I know how much you like lookin' at the stars on the porch, so I got a telescope."

"Really?" I threw myself at him, wrapping my arms around his neck and hugging him fiercely.

"I don't know how to use it very well, so don't get too worked up. I meant to get to the tavern earlier, but it was delivered today, and I wanted to get it set up before you came home. I figured we wouldn't want to fumble with it at midnight."

"It's okay." I squeezed him once more before releasing him and rushing over to the telescope. "What do we do?"

He turned it on, and we tried to line it up with some stars, laughing when we realized the "star" we'd found was a porch light of a house on a nearby mountain ridge. Using the flashlight on his phone, he read the manual and realized he could use his phone to help align the stars even though we didn't have internet or cell service. We spent the next hour scanning the sky, seeing the moon up close, finding Mars, and zooming in on stars, some of which proved to be multiple stars clustered together. I was giddy with each new discovery, squealing with excitement, all while Marco beamed. But it was seeing the Milky Way that had me hugging him again.

"I've always, always wanted to see the Milky Way."

"I know," he said, holding me close. I'd only told him that once, and it had been a couple of months ago.

I leaned back to look up into his shadowed face. "Why are you so nice to me? Why do you go out of your way to make me happy?"

"Because it makes me happy to see you so happy." He lifted his hand to my cheek. "But it's more than that. You're a smart woman, Carly. Do you want me to say it?" His thumb brushed my cheek, sending a sharp zap of electricity through my body. "I have no problem sayin' the words. I'm only holdin' back for you."

Tears filled my eyes. I wanted him to say the words, but I was scared to say them back.

He started to let me go, but I reached down and stopped his hand, holding it on my hip. "Hold me," I whispered.

He pulled me close, wrapping his arm around my back while he cradled my head to his chest.

I breathed him in, the scent that was so unmistakably Marco. I molded myself to the body I knew so well yet had never made love to. I clung to this man who loved me like I'd never been loved before, scared to take the leap of faith to give myself to him.

Why? What more could he do to prove himself to me?

I couldn't think of a single thing.

Pulling back slightly, I lifted my head to look up at him.

He searched my face as though looking for what I wanted, and I thought of all he'd given me. What had I given him? I wanted him to feel the joy I felt when he gave so selflessly to me, and then I remembered what Hank had said about love. When you truly loved someone, you willingly gave up part of yourself to make them happy, but it was okay, because they did the same for you.

I lifted my hand to his face and caressed his cheek. "I'll say them first." His eyes widened slightly, and I reached up to kiss him softly, a quick brushing of lips that sent more desire and emotion through me than any kiss I'd ever had. Then I smiled up at him and said, "I love you."

"Don't just say it because you think it's what I want to hear, Carly," he said, his voice rough.

"I'm not." A tear fell down my cheek. "I've loved you for months, I've just been too scared to tell you."

"I love you too," he said, his voice breaking. "Don't be scared. I'll do everything in my power to make you feel loved and safe so you never, ever have to doubt me." His face lowered and he kissed me, softly as though he was scared I'd change my mind, but I lifted both hands to his face and held him close.

The kiss deepened, and he lifted a hand to cradle the back of my head. His hands sank into my hair, grasping a handful of it, and I gasped into his mouth.

He pulled back, releasing my hair with a look of alarm.

Smiling, I shook my head. "I'm not fragile. I want you. All of you."

He kissed me again, with more passion than before, then lifted me clear off my feet and carried me to the front porch, only to bang my legs into the porch post as he climbed the steps.

"Oh God, Carly, I'm sorry."

I laughed and cupped his cheek. "I'm fine. Take me to bed, Marco."

He grinned. "I'll try not to maim you in the process." Then he carried me into his room, lowering my feet to the floor next to his bed.

"Are you sure?" he asked, worry filling his eyes.

"I've never been more certain of anything in my life."

He kissed me again, and we fumbled with each other's clothes, shedding pieces while we kissed and ran our hands over each other's bodies. His was every bit as beautiful as I'd known it would be. We lay down on the bed, and Marco grabbed a condom out of the nightstand drawer, then didn't waste any time putting it on.

He studied my face, seeming to hesitate again, so I rolled him onto his back and lowered myself onto him, leaning my head back and moaning at how good he felt.

"Jesus, Carly," he gritted through clenched teeth, grabbing my hips and holding me still.

I fell forward and kissed him, then bit his bottom lip.

He groaned, rolling me over onto my back, and grabbed my hips again. "I want to take it slow."

"Take it slow next time," I said, "I want to go fast."

He growled, then gave me what I wanted.

Afterward, he collapsed next to me, gathering me in his arms as though he worried I might regret what we'd done.

I looked up at him and smiled. "I'm not going anywhere. I won't change my mind."

"I love you." He stroked my cheek, staring at me with so much adoration I wondered why I'd wasted so much time.

"I love you too." For the first time ever, I felt like I was where I was supposed to be.

Chapter Nineteen

I overslept the next morning.

After Marco and I brought the telescope inside and put it away, we put on a movie but only made it a few minutes in before we started making love again. This time we took Marco's slow route, not that I complained. But I forgot to set my alarm, so I didn't wake up until Marco's alarm went off at seven-thirty.

"Shit," I said, scrambling to get out of bed. "I'm supposed to be at Hank's right now."

"You don't have to meet Wyatt, Carly," Marco said, sitting up in bed. The sheet fell down to his lap, exposing his broad, naked chest and drawing my attention to the erection the sheet was covering. "You don't owe him shit."

"I know," I said, hurrying into the bathroom to brush my teeth. "But I'm not doing it for him. I'm doing it for Hank."

I started brushing my teeth, catching a glimpse of myself in the mirror. My hair was wild, and I had the look of a woman who had been thoroughly satisfied.

Marco walked up behind me and pressed his naked body to my back. He lowered his lips to the curve of my neck as his hand pressed on my stomach.

"You're making this hard," I mumbled around my toothbrush.

"Good." He kissed his way up my neck to my ear, then bit my earlobe.

"You also realize this has got to be one of the most unsexy things I could be doing right now."

"See how much I love you?" he asked with a grin.

I leaned over and spat into the sink, then rinsed out my mouth. I stood and turned around to face him, resting my hand on his firm pec. Why was I leaving again? "You realize I'm an older woman," I teased. "Carly Moore just turned thirty, but Caroline Blakely is about to turn thirty-four."

"I guess that makes you a cougar," he said with a grin, his hand skimming over my shoulder and down my arm.

I sobered. "My biological clock—"

He leaned over and gave me a slow, sensuous kiss, then lifted his head, keeping our faces inches apart. "*You* are what I want, Carly. You. If we never have kids, I'm okay with that."

"How can you be so sure?" I asked with tears in my eyes. "*I'm* not okay with that."

"I would never want to bring our children into a world where they're not safe. We'll work it out, okay?"

I nodded, and he kissed me again. "Do you want me to call Hank and tell him you'll be late?"

"No. As crazy as it sounds, he'll be happy I'm late."

"Doesn't sound crazy to me. Just the other day he told me to quit takin' so long and make my move already."

I laughed. That sounded like Hank.

I quickly got dressed, wishing I'd taken another shower since I was sure I smelled like Marco. Not that I cared, but I didn't want an inquisition. Nor did I want this to be any more awkward than it already would be. Marco had left the room, and I found him in the kitchen, wearing a pair of gym shorts and pouring coffee into a travel mug. God bless the timer on his coffee maker.

"I can get coffee at Hank's," I said as I packed my notebook into my purse.

"I know, but I figured you could use the caffeine, especially since you're about to go deal with Wyatt's bullshit."

I walked over and kissed him, then stared up into his eyes. "You're the man I want, Marco."

He tucked a strand of hair behind my ear. "If you wanted to be with Wyatt, you could have gotten back together with him months ago. And I get why you're doin' this. You want to make sure Hank is taken care of."

"Thank you for understanding."

"I'm not goin' try to control you, Carly. Lovin' you doesn't mean puttin' you in a cage. I love the person you are, which means I respect the decisions you make."

Why had I ever questioned this man's intentions? I kissed him again, letting it linger for longer than I'd meant to

He groaned and pushed me back a few inches. "No doubt I'll regret this later, but you need to go now or I might keep you here for another half hour."

I grinned up at him. "Only a half hour?"

He swatted me on the butt. "Off with you." But he walked me out to my car and opened the door, giving me another kiss before I got in.

He handed me the coffee, then rested his arm on top of the car. "You get off at midnight?"

"Yeah," I said as I put the cup in the holder in the console.

"Do you need to stay with Hank tonight?"

"I don't know," I said, feeling torn. I hadn't seen Hank for nearly twenty-four hours, and now I was only dropping in for breakfast. Then again, he wouldn't be up when I got off work at midnight, which meant it would make no difference if I spent the night with Marco. "No." I grinned. "Do you have something in mind?"

"Obviously, I'm bein' too subtle." He kissed me again, so thoroughly that when he pulled away, I forgot why I was sitting in my car.

"I'll be here."

He only laughed for a moment before turning serious. "I'm coming to the tavern tonight, but call and check in with me at some point today, okay? Or multiple times."

"I'll check in when I can."

He hesitated, then reached in and cupped my cheek. "I love you." Worry filled his eyes, like he was still afraid to say it. Like I'd suddenly change my mind.

"I love you too," I said, still amazed that I was letting myself say it.

He shut my door, then watched from the porch as I backed out of the driveway and drove away. I indulged myself in a fantasy of coming home to Marco every night. He was the best man I'd ever known, and I knew that I could not only trust him, but he'd fill my life with happiness and fun. I wanted to give him that too.

If the chance wasn't stolen from us.

Wyatt's truck was in front of Hank's house when I pulled up a few minutes after eight. I was halfway surprised Hank hadn't convinced Wyatt to eat breakfast on the porch…and relieved that he hadn't. I hurried inside, hearing the murmuring of voices in the kitchen, and dropped my overnight bag and purse in my room. Before I left, I scooped up Letty, who'd been curled up on the comforter, and carried her with me.

The two men were sitting at the kitchen table, and it looked like they were halfway through with their breakfast. Wyatt had made pancakes, and while he hadn't cooked real bacon, he'd heated up some sausage links.

Hank glanced up at me and grinned from ear to ear, but Wyatt didn't look happy.

"Sorry I'm late," I said, standing in the kitchen doorway, rubbing the back of Letty's head. "I overslept."

Hank winked, then gestured to the empty chair on his right side, opposite Wyatt. "There's still some breakfast left and plenty of coffee."

Wyatt started to stand. "I'll get you a cup."

"I can get it," I said, putting Letty down and heading for the coffee maker.

"I wanted to wait, but Hank said he wasn't sure when you'd be here."

"Sorry," I said again, as I poured coffee into my cup. "I fully intended to be here, but like I said—"

"Don't you apologize for stayin' in bed," Hank said. "Make hay while the sun shines."

I glanced over my shoulder at him, trying to decide if he'd been become a pod person overnight. I'd never once heard him say something as quaint as "make hay while the sun shines." The glare on Wyatt's face suggested he'd never heard it either.

"Well," I said, plastering a smile on my face, "I'm here now, and the pancakes look delicious." I grabbed creamer out of the fridge and poured some into my cup, then sat down in the chair next to Hank.

Wyatt served me a couple of pancakes and handed the plate over the table as I sat down.

"Did Ruth hire a new waitress yet?" Wyatt asked, taking a sip of his coffee.

"No, not yet. Max is interviewing Ruth's friend today."

"Ruth's friend?" he asked in surprise. "Who?"

"She didn't tell me. I guess I'll find out when I show up to Tutoring Club." I spread butter over my pancake. "Because we all know the interview is a formality. If Ruth wants her working there, she'll get the job."

"Why's Max hirin' a new waitress?" Hank asked as he sawed on a sausage link.

I narrowed my eyes. "How many of those have you had?"

"Not enough," Hank barked. "Now answer *my* question."

"He finally fired Molly."

"'Bout damn time." Hank had heard plenty of Molly stories.

"How's the tutoring club goin'?" Wyatt asked. "Max says you're gettin' a good turnout."

"It's going well. A lot of times kids don't think learning can be fun, but I try to prove otherwise." I told him a few stories about the kids and my plan to start a reward system for kids who read books from the library.

"Is Max helpin' foot the bill for all of this stuff?" Wyatt asked.

"He's providing the space."

Wyatt frowned. "He needs to be makin' a donation. I'll have a talk with him."

"Don't do that," I said. "This is my project, not his."

"It's bringin' him business, and we both know it," Wyatt said. "Besides, it'll look good that he's supportin' the community."

The way he said it made me think about Jim Palmer and all he'd done to support his community. Had it been out of the goodness of his heart, like I'd assumed, or had he been driven by ulterior motives?

In between bites of breakfast, I steered the conversation to Hank's car, and Wyatt said he'd already ordered the parts and expected them to arrive in a few days. "The gas pedal gets shifted over to the left side to make it more comfortable for your left foot," he told Hank. "It'll just take some practice to get the hang of drivin' that way."

Hank scowled, looking skeptical.

"You need to learn how to drive again," Wyatt said. "Truth be told, I should have done this months ago."

"I ain't no invalid," Hank grumped.

"Which is exactly the point," Wyatt said. "There's no need for you to be stuck out here and dependent on Carly."

I finished my pancakes, then we all went outside so Wyatt could check out Hank's car, the kittens running out with us. Letty ran after the birds while Smoky sat on the porch, keeping her eye on Wyatt as though she didn't trust him.

Smart kitten.

When he finished checking the gas pedal, he pronounced it would be fairly easy to make the changes. As he spoke, his gaze swept over the house, stopping on the patched roof. "You had some work done on the roof?"

Neither Hank nor I said anything for a beat, then Hank grunted. "There was a leak."

"Who fixed it?"

"Corey Summers," Hank said. "Mark's boy."

"From the looks of the shitty patch job, I hope he didn't charge you much for it," Wyatt said, making a face. "I'll grab a ladder and take a look before I go."

Hank shot me a guilty look, and I shook my head. I knew what he was thinking. If he hadn't kept Wyatt away, he would have fixed it for free.

"I'm going to take a shower," I said, gesturing toward the front door, then headed inside without waiting for anyone to acknowledge my remark.

I took a long time in the bathroom, washing my hair and shaving, slightly embarrassed when I realized it had been several days since I'd last shaved.

When I got out, I took my time drying my hair and putting on makeup. I put on a robe and went into my room, pulling out one of the few dresses I owned, a pale blue sundress that brought out the blue in my eyes. I put on a pair of white sandals, then emptied my overnight bag and repacked it with work clothes and shorts and a shirt to wear back to Hank's in the morning.

When I went outside, Hank was in his chair with Smoky on his lap while Letty leapt at any bird that dared to land on the bird feeder.

"Your hellcat's at it again," he grumped.

"I'll grab her." I glanced over and realized Wyatt's truck was still to the side of the house. "Wyatt's still here?"

He pointed up. "He's on the roof. You look nice. You dressin' up for a certain man?"

I smiled. "If you're insinuating it's for the man on the roof, you've got another think coming."

"Marco?" he pressed. My face flushed and he beamed. "Wise choice, girlie. Wise choice."

"I know," I said with a smile. It felt good, knowing I'd be seeing Marco later. Knowing I no longer had to hide from him or myself.

I walked out into the yard and found Wyatt up on the roof, removing shingles. "What are you doing?"

"I'm fixing this the right way, then hunting down Corey Summers and makin' him reimburse Hank."

I pinched my mouth shut, because if Corey had done a crappy job, Wyatt was doing us a favor.

He shifted his weight as he lined up an asphalt shingle. "I need to get a few supplies."

"Okay," I said. "Can you make sure it won't leak if it rains tonight?"

"Yeah. I'll do a quick patch job and fix it tomorrow."

"Thanks."

I headed inside, because being outside felt like I was leading Wyatt on. I'd hoped he'd be gone by the time I finished, but I was grateful he was helping Hank. That was what I wanted, right? For Wyatt to be there for Hank when I couldn't be. The ultimate goal was to be free of my father, but I wasn't naïve enough to think that would come quickly. I had to assume I'd spend more time running.

The library didn't open until ten, so I decided to do some of the neglected housework. Since we hadn't cleaned up the breakfast mess, I put on an apron to keep my dress clean and filled the sink with soapy water. I'd finished washing and drying all the dishes and had started cooking a pot of black beans and rice for Hank's dinner when Wyatt walked into the kitchen, his hands covered in dirt. "I got it patched up, so it will be good to go for now."

"Thanks."

He started to head toward the bathroom before abruptly turning back. "You look really pretty. The dress makes your eyes bluer."

Oh crap. I was giving him the wrong impression, and I needed to nip this in the bud. "I didn't wear this for you, Wyatt," I said as kindly as I could.

Something flickered in his eyes. "I never presumed you did. I'm just makin' an observation."

"Well, thank you."

He disappeared down the hall and I got out a bag of carrots to roast while the beans and rice were cooking.

He came back a few minutes later, staying in the opening of the kitchen. "I didn't mean for you to have to clean up on your own. I intended to help."

"Don't worry about it," I said as I chopped up carrots at the counter. "I didn't mind one bit. I'm just grateful you're spending time with Hank again." I took a breath. "I never intended to get between you two."

"I know. That's not who you are." He gestured toward the stove. "Can I help?"

I started to tell him no, but I wanted to ask him a few things. Maybe I could work it into a conversation. "You can get out a cookie sheet and cover it with foil."

"I think I can handle that," he said as he opened the cabinet over the oven. "Hank said you were at Marco's."

Crap. "Yeah."

"Does he make you happy?" he asked quietly.

I looked up at him. "Yeah, Wyatt. He does, but more importantly, he's honest. We have no secrets."

He glanced down, then darted his gaze back up to meet my eyes, still holding the box of aluminum foil. "Marco's a good man, and you deserve to be happy."

His response caught me by surprise. "Thank you."

He nodded, but then he said, "But Marco's never going to leave Drum."

I stopped chopping. "What does *that* mean?"

"We both know you're not goin' to stay here forever, and if Marco's promised to leave with you, you can't count on that."

"Why not?" I asked before I could stop myself.

He set the box on the table next to the cookie sheet. "Because he and Max are tied at the hip. Hell, he went to college in Knoxville because Max went there, and before our mother fetched Max to run the tavern, the two of them were planning to open a bar in Nashville together. Sure enough, Marco came

runnin' back to Drum to be close to Max, goin' so far as to get a job with the sheriff's department to help protect him." He gave me a sad look. "He's never gonna leave Max, Carly, so don't delude yourself into thinking otherwise."

I stared at him in shock. "You think I don't know about his friendship with Max? The good *and* the bad? I suspect I know a whole hell of a lot more than you, because he *tells me things*, Wyatt." I left off the *unlike you.*

He grimaced. "Look, I just don't want you to get hurt."

Bullshit. He was hoping to drive a wedge between Marco and me while trying to paint himself as the good guy.

"God, you just don't learn, do you?" I asked, shaking my head. "Why are you really here right now? I thought you had to be at the garage."

"Junior's coverin', and I'm here because you asked me to come."

"Great way to twist things around," I said. "This was your condition for helping Hank with his car. I had to spend an hour with you." I waved my knife toward him. "I guess you're in here collecting your full hour, huh?"

"I came in here to help you with the dishes," he said.

"But for all Hank knows, we're in here having a nice chat, so I think we've both fulfilled our ends of the bargain, which means you're free to go."

He pushed out a heavy sigh and pulled off a sheet of foil. "Carly, this wasn't how things were supposed to go."

"No," I said, my voice cold. "I'm sure you had delusions about sweeping me off my feet and us getting back together, but that's never going to happen."

"Carly—"

This conversation was shot to hell, so I figured I might as well go for broke. "What were you doing at the tavern the other night?"

He froze. "What?"

"Two nights ago. You came in, you and Max went into the back for about ten minutes, and then you left. What was that about?"

"*Carly.*"

"Yeah. That's what I thought," I said in disgust. "You're so full of secrets you're buried in them."

"I was there to shoot the shit with my brother," he nearly shouted. "Do I need a reason to talk to my own brother?"

"You were talking to him, but it wasn't to shoot the shit."

His nostrils flared. "Then what was I doin' there?"

I nearly told him what I suspected, but I needed to keep my investigation under wraps for as long as I could, which meant I couldn't clue him in. I shouldn't have said anything at all.

"It's time for you to go, Wyatt," Hank said from the kitchen doorway.

Wyatt's face paled. "Hank, I realize we—"

"No," Hank said in a cold tone. "I told you to leave this girl alone unless you were ready to come clean, and here you are, pesterin' the shit out of her. You just can't stop beatin' a dead horse, can ya?" he sneered. "Just like the rest of you Drummonds. Now go."

"Do you still want me to work on your car and your roof?" Wyatt asked defensively.

"Yeah, but since you can't find the self-control to leave Carly alone, only when she's not here."

Wyatt gave me a pleading look, but I returned to chopping my carrots. The whack of the knife striking the board filled the room as I put a little more effort into it than necessary.

I heard rather than saw Wyatt walk away. Hank followed him out the front door, and the truck engine started then faded.

I was spreading the carrots on the cookie sheet Wyatt had covered with foil when Hank returned.

"I knew he'd pull some kind of bullshit," Hank said in disgust. "You should have stayed at Marco's."

"I promised, although I'm not sure I fully lived up to my end of the bargain."

"Then I'll pay him money, because you don't owe that man a damn thing." He heaved himself onto a chair and rested his crutch against the table. "I heard what he said about Marco." He waited until he had my attention. "While there's some truth to what he said about his friendship with Max, he's changed, Carly."

I gave him a reassuring smile. "I know he has, in more ways than one. I trust him, Hank. With my life and my heart." I released a small laugh. "I told him I love him."

Hank grinned from ear to ear. "About damn time."

I laughed again. "Yeah, he thought you'd have that reaction."

"Don't you let Wyatt give you doubts or make you feel guilty. I love that boy like a son, and I confess, at one time, I thought you'd be good for him, but I came to realize he wouldn't be good *for you*. He's got too much Drummond in him."

"What's that mean?"

"The Drummonds are born and bred to keep secrets. He can't help hidin' things, even things that don't need to be hidden. And while I believe he broke ties with his daddy, seems to me he's still up to something."

That didn't surprise me, but was it something that complemented my intentions or went against them? I had plenty of questions about Wyatt that he never seemed interested in answering. For all his pretty talk about the two of us, he'd never opened up to me.

"How do you feel about him workin' on the roof?" he asked.

I gave him a reassuring smile. "If he can do a better job, then I'm all for it."

"You don't have to pay to fix my house, girlie."

"I live here too, so it's only right."

"Did you make any progress on connectin' Bart to the murder?"

"Maybe?" I drizzled the carrots with olive oil, then sprinkled them with salt and pepper and put the tray in the oven. Hank might currently be cut off from the world, but he knew about Drum and the people in it. His opinion could prove invaluable.

I sat down at the end of the table. "So far, Selena Martin has been my best source."

Hank's face paled. "The high school math teacher?"

"Yeah. She said she had Seth for two classes."

He nodded. "The boy liked her."

"She liked him too." I hesitated, then said, "Pam Crimshaw's son Ricky was supposedly Seth's best friend."

He rubbed his chin. "Yeah, I suppose he was."

"But you didn't mention it when I was talking about the Crimshaws yesterday."

He was quiet for a moment. "Yeah, well, I guess it didn't seem important."

"I was trying to find out more about Pam, and you had information all along," I said, a hint of accusation leaking into my tone.

"I don't have much information on her. Nothing that will help you out."

"Why don't you let me be the judge of that?"

His gaze flicked to me, and I was fairly sure I saw a flash of pride. "I barely know the woman."

"What *do* you know about her?"

"She's a mousy thing. Scared of her own shadow but devoted to her kids. Seth didn't like goin' over to their house, but Ricky's daddy didn't approve of Ricky comin' over here. She let him come anyway, but she always seemed scared of me whenever she brought him over."

"Did you ever meet Rob, her husband?"

"No."

I studied him closely. He'd expanded on every other answer…why not this one? The first rule of lying is to never share more than necessary. Was Hank lying to me? If Seth and Ricky had been as close as everyone said, what was the likelihood his path had never crossed with Rob?

"What do you think of Ricky?"

His lips quivered with a smile. "He's a good kid. He was a good friend to Seth, especially after Barb died, but I hadn't seen him for at least a month or two before Seth's death."

"When Seth started plotting with Bingham?" I asked.

"Probably."

"Do you know anything about Ricky's brother's accident a little over a year ago?"

"Not much. Ricky's sister took care of him while his brother was in the hospital, but I don't know any details about the accident."

"You don't remember anything about the other driver?"

"I only know that Thad and his friend were in the hospital for several weeks."

"The friend's name is Spencer Gensler. Do you know anything about him?"

"Nothin'."

"What about his family? His parents are Donald and Kay Gensler."

He shook his head. "They're probably from Ewing."

I made a mental note to check. "Why'd you keep this from me, Hank?"

His eyes turned glassy. "It's hard to think about anything to do with Seth."

"Hank…" I reached out and took his hand. "I'm sorry."

He shook his head, then pulled his hand away. "Save your sympathy for someone who needs it. I should have told you, but like I said, I don't know much and I didn't want to dredge up old memories."

Was he telling the truth? I hated that I was questioning him, but the doubt wasn't so easily dismissed.

"Do you know much about the goings-on in Ewing?"

He shook his head. "Mary had some friends in Ewing, but I've lost track."

"Do you know anything about an insurance agent named Jim Palmer?"

His brow rose. "The man who was killed?"

"His father."

He got a pensive look, and he was quiet for so long I didn't think he was going to answer, but then he said, "I remember hearing something, but its only coming in bits and pieces. Something to do with his wife."

"You mean Jim, Jr.'s wife, Melinda?"

"No, his daddy's wife. Naomi."

"You don't remember anything else?"

He pursed his lips and shook his head. "No. But I remember Mary yappin' on…something to do with church, I think."

Well, crap. If it was flat-out gossip, I wouldn't find it in a paper or a police report. But Thelma might know something.

"That's good," I said. "It's something."

"But not very helpful." He looked frustrated.

"Hey," I said with a smile. "It's more than I had before, and I know someone who might know more details now that you've pointed me in a direction."

"You think Naomi's squabble at church had something to do with Bart?" He shook his head. "You're chasin' your tail on that one."

I'd chase anything at this point.

Chapter
Twenty

I had time to fold a load of towels that had been in the dryer for two days as well as sweep and mop the living room and kitchen before I portioned out the food I'd cooked into containers for several days' worth of meals. Even with the chores, I still pulled into a space in front of the library a few minutes before ten.

I sat in my car, looking through my notes to help prepare for my research. While I planned to do a search for Naomi Palmer, I intended to focus most of my attention on the Crimshaws, then the arresting officers for the cases I'd collected in the notebook. Good thing I'd started writing down the cases' web addresses in case I needed to go back later.

Carnita was walking down the sidewalk toward the library, so I closed my notebook, grabbed my purse, and got out of my car, meeting her at the front door.

"Oh," she exclaimed. "You're early today."

"I'm pretty sure I reserved a computer last week. Ten to one."

She beamed. "Well, let's get you started." She unlocked the door and flipped on the lights. "Go ahead and boot up a computer. Your pick."

I took the one at the end—fewer prying eyes, although I found most people who used the computers were more interested in their social media accounts than my research. After I turned it on, Carnita signed in, and I got started before the other two people who had reserved spots showed up.

As I'd expected, my search for Naomi Palmer didn't turn up much, but I did find an obituary that dated ten years back. The family had asked for donations to the American Heart Association in lieu of flowers, so I wrote down that she'd probably died of a heart condition. But it was an article in the Ewing paper that got me excited—a mention of her name at a coat drive run by the First Baptist Church of Ewing.

I told myself not to get too worked up. Sure, Jim, Jr.'s mother attended the same church as the Crimshaws, but that didn't mean the younger Palmers still did. They might not attend church at all, but given the fact they were fine, upstanding citizens, I suspected they did.

Leaning toward Carnita's desk, I asked, "Hey, Carnita. Do you happen to carry church directories?"

She made a face. "That's a new request. No, but it's probably a good idea for the people who are interested in genealogy. You'd be surprised how many there are these days." She cocked her head. "You trying to figure out a family tree?"

I couldn't confess what I was really up to. "Yeah, something like that."

"Which family? I might be able to help."

Crap. Who could I name without giving myself away? "The Binghams."

She chuckled. "Believe it or not, Todd and Lula have been doin' their own research into his family tree. Well, both of their

212

families now." She lowered her voice. "Lula's mother's gettin' out of prison next month, you know."

I couldn't hide my surprise. Last November, Lula had mentioned that her mother was likely getting out in the spring, but she'd never shown up and I'd assumed it had been a lie or her parole board had rejected her. "So Lula's researching her own family tree?"

"Seems like it," Carnita said.

That was news to pack away for another day. "Well, if Lula and Bingham have already started researching their family trees, I'll just talk to them about my questions."

"That'll save you some time," Carnita said. "The last time Lula was in, she told me they'd traced Todd's family back to 1827."

I wrinkled my nose in confusion. "I've never seen either one of them in here using the computers. When do they come in?"

"Todd has his own internet."

Likely satellite internet, not that I was surprised since he had a satellite phone. Marco had talked about getting satellite internet but had put it off up until now since it was well over a hundred dollars a month for super slow service.

Turning back to the computer, I searched for Jim Palmer, Sr. next. There was more about him than his wife. Jim, Jr. had apparently learned about civic engagement from his father. The older man had a friendly smile and looked a lot like his son. His obituary showed he'd died a year after his wife, also a heart attack based on the same donation request.

On a whim, I searched for the First Baptist Church of Ewing and found few hits other than their website and a Yelp review page with a 2.6 rating. I clicked through to the outdated website. There wasn't a list of church members, but there were some old photos of previous social events. On the page featuring an ice cream social from three years prior, I found a photo of several members of the younger Palmer family—Jim and his two kids, all three smiling and looking happy.

And there was my connection linking Pam to Jim.

Still, just because they attended the same church didn't mean they'd had any kind of relationship. If the church was large, they might not have even known each other, although I suspected it wasn't a mega church. Given the fact that Rob Crimshaw had earned a reputation for being an asshole, I doubted the two families were friends, but they probably knew of each other. It also put Pam and Jim within the same social circle, but I had a hard time seeing the younger insurance agent having an affair with the nearly decade older, unpolished Pam.

I turned to researching the Crimshaw family next, focusing on Rob. Not much pulled up on him, but there were several hits from twenty years prior. He'd been in multiple bar fights and acquired a few DUIs. His name often popped up in association with his father, Stewart Crimshaw. *He'd* been arrested multiple times for drug possession.

That would have been when Hank was in the thick of the drug game.

Stewart's last arrest had been for possession with intent to deal, and not a *sell to a few friends* amount. He'd been carrying a large quantity of OxyContin. Hank had sworn he hated the stuff, so did that mean Stewart Crimshaw had been working for Bingham? Only, it had happened decades ago, back when Bingham was probably just getting started. Whoever he was working for, he'd gotten a ten-year prison sentence. I couldn't find anything about him after that.

Had Hank lied to me about selling Oxy?

An unsettled feeling filled the pit of my stomach, but I reminded myself that he and Bingham had overlapped, with

Bingham selling the stuff that Hank wouldn't. The odds were greater that his supplier had been Bingham.

What had happened to Stewie? The last article was from eighteen years ago, so he should have been released by now. Had he come back to Drum?

I was about to do more research on Thad's accident when the computer suddenly shut down and the lights went off.

"What the hell?" the man on the far end shouted, banging the side of the monitor.

"Did you forget to pay the electric bill, Carnita?" the woman next to me asked with a chuckle.

Carnita didn't look so amused, almost like she was wondering the same thing. "It'll probably turn back on in just a moment."

But it didn't.

"How about I go out and see if anyone else's power went out?" I said as I closed my notebook and got to my feet.

Relief filled Carnita's eyes. "Good idea."

I headed out the front door, but since it was daytime, it wasn't so easy to determine at a glance. There seemed to be some commotion over at Watson's Café, so I headed over and realized right away that their power was out too.

"We're dealin' with this as best we can," Sheila, an older waitress, shouted over the excited voices in the dining room. Greta stood to the side, watching the uproar in dismay.

Sheila inserted her fingers between her lips and released a wolf whistle, and the room instantly quieted. She might be wearing a pink and white vintage style waitress outfit that made her look like a pushover, but she was tough as they come and wouldn't put up with crap from anyone. She could likely give Ruth a run for her money. "Now that I have everyone's attention," she said as though scolding a child. "The power is out and will be indefinitely. Watson found out the construction crew out at Drummond's new resort cut a power line and they have no idea when they'll get it fixed. Might be today, might be tomorrow."

There was another uproar, but Sheila whistled again, and the room quieted, although there was still some annoyed murmuring. "We'll be gettin' out as many orders as we can. The rest of you will be free to go, drinks on the house. We'll come around table to table to let you know where you stand."

I wondered what that meant for the tavern. I'd heard the power went out occasionally, but it hadn't happened since I'd shown up in town.

Greta saw me, and her face brightened as she hurried over. "Sorry we won't be able to serve you."

"I wasn't here to eat anyway," I said. "I'm working over at the library and thought I'd see who else lost power."

"The whole town from the sounds of it," she said. Her eyes lit up. "Looks like we both got the day off. Want to hang out this afternoon? I'll call Lula and see if she's in."

I knew I should say no, but part of me really wanted to have some girl fun. Besides, call me devious, but I was curious about Lula's mother. "I have a few errands to run. Maybe I can join you two at some point?"

"We'll probably just hang out at Lula's." When she saw my hesitation, she laughed. "Not her cabin. At Bingham's. You should see how she's fixed it up."

Her cabin, where she'd spent her entire life up until last December, was not only literally falling apart, but it didn't have electricity or running water. Still, I wondered if Bingham's house was much better. I'd never been inside, but I'd spent some time on his rundown front porch. Lula must have been a miracle worker to make his house hospitable in such a short period of time.

I pointed my thumb toward the exit. "I'll let Carnita know what's going on, then check in with Max."

"Great," she said, then gave me a hug. "I hope we see you later!"

I headed back to the library to give Carnita the news. The other two people at the computers had left, but Carnita said she'd stay open. The two front windows and glass door let in plenty of light, and she didn't need electricity to check out books and DVDs. She planned to write the checkout information down in a notebook until the system came back up.

I drove down to the tavern and used the key to let myself in the back door. It was close to eleven, but Max would be up and Tiny would be in soon to get ready for the lunch crowd. I could hear Max's voice coming from his office, and he didn't sound happy, so I stayed by the back door. I couldn't completely make out his side of the conversation, just a word or phrase here and there, including, "you better make this right." Then I heard the bang of the phone receiver slamming down on the cradle.

"Hey, Max?" I called out and was met with silence.

A few seconds later, he appeared in the hallway, his eyes wide. "Hey, Carly. I thought you weren't coming in until Tutoring Club."

"Yeah, I wasn't planning on it, but I was at the library and checked in at Watson's when the power went out. They found out the construction crew at Drummond's resort hit a power line and we might be out of power until tomorrow."

"Fuck," he said with a groan as he turned away. "I'll have Tiny and Pickle get the generators out of storage."

"You have generators?" I asked in surprise.

"Gotta plan for a rainy day," he said, but he seemed agitated.

"Is everything okay, Max?"

"It's fine...other than *this* headache." He made a face. "We'll probably be busier than usual tonight. Some people have generators, but most don't, so they'll be hungry and we'll be ready to help 'em out. I might need you to cancel Tutoring Club so you can do a supplies run to Ewing to buy us a bunch of hamburgers, buns, and potatoes. One generator can run the grill, fridge, and fryers, so Tiny and Pickle can fry up burgers and make fries pretty efficiently." He'd switched to business mode pretty quickly, but I was still wondering about that phone call.

Could it have been about Pam?

"I don't mind going to Ewing," I said, figuring I could visit Thelma to ask more questions. It was obvious my hangout with the girls wasn't going to happen anyway. "I can pay a visit to my friends at Greener Pastures, and maybe see if Marco has time to meet me for lunch. Just give me a shopping list, and I'll get what you need."

His gaze took in my dress, hair, and makeup, and a slow smile spread across his face. "Well, I'll be damned."

I cringed. "Don't make a big deal out of it."

His eyes flew wide. "So you two really weren't together before?"

My face flushed. "Max."

"What finally convinced you to take the leap?" he asked, leaning his shoulder against the wall, a sly grin lighting up his eyes. "It was me, wasn't it? All that pesterin' wore you down."

I snorted. "Hardly." Then because I didn't see a reason to keep it a secret, I added, "He got me a telescope."

He blinked. "Say what? *A telescope?*" He laughed. "Okay...maybe I'll have to try it sometime."

I nearly told him it wouldn't work, but I doubted he'd go to that much effort to bed a woman. Then again, although he'd apparently earned a reputation as a lady killer, I hadn't really seen him with many women. Occasionally, a young woman would come in late and stayed at the bar past closing, but I'd only seen a few of them.

His rakish smile turned friendly. "Let me call Tiny and we'll figure out what we need. Thanks for doin' this."

"Of course. No problem. Just tell me when you need it by."

"I suspect we have enough to tide over the lunch crowd. It's the dinner crowd that will bleed us dry. Let's say four so Tiny doesn't have a stroke worryin' about havin' enough food."

"Sounds good. I'll call a few people on the Tutoring Club list and have them spread the word that we're canceling today. No one will be surprised because of the electricity." Then I added, "Say, did you interview Ruth's friend? If she's starting, we should probably let her know she doesn't need to come in."

Blinking, he took a second to switch gears. Then he pointed a finger at me. "Ah! Good catch. She was supposed to come in at eleven and start the noon shift. I'll have Ruth let her know."

Max hurried off to his office, and I used the phone underneath the bar to call two of the mothers at the head of the phone tree we'd set up for Tutoring Club, and by the time I finished, Max had a short grocery list and some cash.

"You may have to go to a couple of places," he said, handing them to me. "In fact, I may head down to Dollar General and buy them out of hamburger."

"It's Thursday," I said, shaking my head. "They won't get a delivery of meat until Friday morning. If they have anything left, it won't be much."

He laughed. "Look at you. No one would ever guess you've lived here less than a year." Then he gave me a bear hug. "I couldn't be happier about you and Marco. Really." He released me and patted my cheek. "If I couldn't keep you in the family with Wyatt, at least I'll get you through my best friend. He's one lucky son-of-a-bitch."

"Thanks, Max." Tears stung my eyes. It was wonderful to feel so wanted.

"This is gettin' sappy," he said, stepping back and shuddering as though I had cooties. "Go visit your friends and be back by four."

***

As soon as I got cell service at the edge of Ewing, I put in a call to Marco, but it went through to his voicemail. "I'll be in Ewing for the next few hours, so if you get a chance, give me a call." Usually, I would have left it at that, but I'd finally let myself acknowledge that I loved him, and the floodgates had opened. "I can't wait to see you tonight. I can't wait to spend *many* nights with you, and not just for sex, although that was *amazing*." My face flushed. What was I doing? "*Anyway*, you just really make me happy, Marco, and I know I see you all the time, but I still can't wait to see you again." I knew how pathetic I sounded, but all these feelings were catching me off guard. While I'd loved men before, I'd never felt like *this*. I was like a stereotypical schoolgirl with a massive crush. "Okay, that sounded clingy, but if I haven't scared you off, call me. I love you." Then I hung up and tossed my phone on the passenger seat.

I'd be lucky if that message didn't send him running.

I'd planned on going straight to the nursing home, but curiosity drove me down a different path. I found myself cruising past Jim's insurance office. The memorial was bigger today, but there were fewer people standing in front of it. I parked in front of a laundromat across the street but stayed in my car and watched the people paying their respects. It was obvious people had really liked and respected Jim Palmer.

"Why did Pam kill you?" I said out loud.

Most of the circumstantial evidence pointed toward the possibility Bart might have guided her, but there was also the Baptist church connection to consider.

Behind the memorial, the front door of the insurance office opened, and a pretty blond woman walked out. She wore a mint green skirt and a short sleeve, button-up white shirt, both of which looked like they came from a Lilly Pulitzer store, along with a pair of black espadrilles. She looked remarkably put together for someone in Ewing. She walked toward a white, newer model sedan, and as she turned her face toward the street, I realized she was Melinda Palmer.

People walked over to her and several of them hugged her and patted her arm or her face. She started to cry and got into her car. It backed up, then she drove to the entrance of the parking lot and turned left.

Before I thought about what I was doing, I pulled out of my parking space and turned onto the street and started to follow her.

This was crazy. I had no idea where she was going, and I didn't really know what I hoped to accomplish, but I decided to do it anyway and hope I didn't get caught.

I didn't expect her to drive to the First Baptist Church.

She pulled into the parking lot, and I drove past it, turned around, and then drove by again in time to see her walk inside. But then I nearly ran off the road because about ten to twelve teens—boys and girls—were working in the flower beds, and one of them was Ricky Crimshaw.

I turned around again and pulled into the parking lot, making sure to park a couple of rows away from Melinda Palmer's car. Several of the teens watched me with wary expressions as I walked toward them. Ricky was on his knees, weeding around a bush. When he realized something had caught his friends' attention, he glanced up. His eyes widened, and he looked even more surprised when he realized I was walking toward *him*.

"Ricky?" I said as I got closer, standing about twenty feet away on the grass. "Can I talk to you for a moment?"

Several of the boys laughed, and one said, "Way to go, Crimshaw! Older women are where it's at!"

"What do you expect?" another boy said. "His mom went for a younger man too."

"Watch out," a girl called to me. "The Crimshaws are murderers."

"That's enough of that nonsense," I said in my strictest teacher voice. The look on her face told me it hadn't totally lost its effectiveness.

Ricky's face flushed, and he hurried to his feet and came over. The group got back to work, but they kept casting curious glances at us.

"What was that about?" I asked, lowering my voice so I didn't embarrass him any further.

He shrugged. "Some people are saying my mom was sleepin' with the guy she killed."

"Do you think she was?" I asked.

"No way," he said in disgust. "She was always around, so I don't know when she would have found time for anything like that."

People found ways, but it didn't seem prudent to tell him so. "Say, did Ashlynn come home last night?" I shot the group a glare as they continued to watch us.

"What? No."

"Do you know where she is? Because I dropped her off…" I stopped and started again. I doubted she'd want her family to know she'd almost visited her mother in jail. "I went by the pharmacy yesterday afternoon, and she never went in to work. Her boss told me to tell her she's fired."

He laughed, but it sounded forced. "That's Ashlynn. She works somewhere until she doesn't want to work there anymore, then she just stops goin'."

"But do you know where she was last night? Selena's worried," I fibbed.

He gave me a look of surprise. "You know Selena?"

"Yeah," I said, not wanting to admit I'd just met her the day before. "Small town."

"I guess…" he said, glancing back at his friends.

"So do you know where your sister might be?" I prodded. "Do you think she might have stayed with Chuck?"

Again, he looked surprised that I knew his sister's boyfriend's name. I supposed this was putting me in stalker territory. "Fuck no," he scoffed. "The night he left, I heard him tell her he'd shoot her with his shotgun if she tried to follow him."

"That must have been one hell of a fight," I said.

He gave me a *you had to be there* look. "You don't know the half of it."

"Do you think he'd really shoot her?" I asked, scared to hear the answer.

He gave it a moment's thought, then shrugged. "Maybe, but only if she hounded him. He's kind of got a temper."

"Do you think he could have hurt her yesterday?" I asked.

"Nah. I saw him last night. He was with Becca, and he looked pretty happy."

"Would he look upset if he'd hurt her?"

He gave that question an alarming amount of thought before he answered. "I don't know."

I squared my shoulders. "I'm gonna need Chuck's phone number and address."

"You're gonna go see him and ask him if he offed her?" he asked with a laugh.

"Yeah." I crossed my arms over my chest. "I need to know that she's okay."

"Why do *you* care? All you did was give her a ride to town yesterday, right?" He shrugged again. "And no, I haven't talked to her. I saw her get in your car. I know she was lookin' for a ride since I wouldn't drive her or give her the keys to my car."

"Why wouldn't you drive her?"

He chuckled. "That's a good one."

I didn't know why that was so funny, but I didn't press. He was volunteering information, and I didn't want to screw that up.

"If you *really* want to talk to him, you'll have better luck if you go by his work," Ricky said. "Once he gets off work, he's harder to pin down. Just ask Ashlynn. In fact, he's probably workin' right now."

"Where's he work?"

"At the feed store on the north end of town. Farmer's Feed and Tack." He gave me a puzzled look. "I still don't get why you're so worried. You hardly know her."

"I'm worried because she's pregnant and your mother's not here to help her and her boyfriend took off. I just want to make sure she's okay."

He shrugged. "Whatever."

I had a million more questions, but I worried I was pushing my luck, so I gestured toward the group. "What is this? Community service?"

"Hardly," he said in disgust. "The youth group is cleanin' up the church grounds for the funeral."

"Jim Palmer's funeral?"

Guilt filled his eyes and his chin dipped to his chest. "Yeah."

"Do you guys usually do that? Clean up for funerals?"

"Only if they're part-time youth leaders, I guess."

"Wait," I said with a shake of my head. "Jim Palmer was a youth group leader?"

"Yeah. Mostly just to help on trips. Not many of the weekly meetings."

"For how long?"

He shrugged. "I don't know. Ever since I've been in high school. Longer, I guess."

"Did your mom help with the youth group?"

"No." He made a face. "Gross. She watched the babies."

"I don't suppose the youth group does things with the babies?"

He snorted. "No."

"Where's Thad? Isn't he old enough to be in the youth group?"

"He refused to come, and boy, is he gonna be in trouble when Dad finds out." He sounded like he both admired his brother and thought he was a fool.

Melinda Palmer emerged from the door of the church and walked out to her car, and all the teens went silent as they watched her.

"We were sorry to hear about Mr. Jim," a girl called out.

Melinda looked up as though realizing for the first time that they were there. "Oh. Thank you." But she didn't say any more, just got into her car and took off.

"Jim was too good for her," the same girl said in a snide tone.

"Y'all don't like her?" I called out.

They looked at me like I'd grown horns.

"Nobody likes her," Ricky said. "She thinks she's too good for this place."

A man walked out of the church and scanned the group. "Seems to me there's a whole lot of chattin' goin' on, and not much weedin'."

"Sorry, Pastor Bill," they all called out in weak unison.

His attention turned my way, and a smile spread across his face. "Well, hello. I'm Pastor Bill Atkins. I don't believe I've seen your face around here."

Crap.

I walked over and extended my hand. "Hi, I'm a friend of Pam's. I saw Ricky working out here and decided to stop by and check on him."

His lips pressed into a thin line. "That poor family's been through the wringer with Thad and Ashlynn. And then this mess with Jim." He shook his head, his bottom lip pushed out. "They'll need lots of prayers."

"Pastor Bill," one of the girls called out while kneeling next to a bush. "Is this a weed?"

"Let me have a look," he said and started over. After taking a couple of steps, he turned back to me. "It was nice to meet you...?" His voice rose at the end, hinting that I should give him my name.

I waved back. "Nice to meet you too." Then I got in my car and pulled out of the parking lot.

It was time to talk to Chuck.

Chapter Twenty-One

The Farmer's Tack and Feed Store was busier than I'd expected, mostly because I didn't know of any farmers in these parts. There were horses and cows, and one of the families who came in to the diner a lot had a pond full of ducks, but no one was planting crops.

I parked in the lot and stared at the building, trying to figure out how best to find Chuck. There was a gardening section to the left of the building, and two employees were handling customers. A woman ran the cash register and a younger man was loading several bags of potting soil into the trunk of a car parked next to the curb. He loaded the last bag, then shut the trunk and gave it a couple of pats, and the car—driven by an older woman—drove away.

I supposed I could start there and work my way inside. I could grab a cart and pick up a couple of bags of cat litter.

Feeling more confident, I got out of the car and headed toward the garden section just as an older man came out of side entrance and called out, "Hey, Chuck! Move those bags of mulch to the front."

"Sure thing, Mr. Soto," Chuck responded, giving him a friendly wave, but as soon as the man went back inside, Chuck kept his hand up and lowered all of his fingers except the middle one.

I rolled my eyes. What a charmer.

The woman at the cash register must have thought the same thing because she shot him a disapproving glare.

While finding him had proven easier than expected, I didn't have high expectations for our conversation.

Chuck had walked to the back of the garden area and was hefting a large bag of mulch onto his shoulder. I could see why Ashlynn was interested in him despite his crappy personality. He had muscular arms and a pretty boy look. She was thinking with the brain of a teenager, not a woman. Then again, I knew plenty of women who'd fallen for a man's looks rather than his substance.

"Chuck?" I asked as I approached him.

As he walked toward me, his gaze swept up my legs, lingered on my breasts, and then took in my face. A smile lit up his blue eyes. "That's me. How can I help you, pretty lady?"

Pretty lady? I felt like I'd jumped in a pond full of slime, but I forced a smile. I could play this coy, or I could be blunt. I wasn't in the mood for games. "I wanted to ask you some questions about Ashlynn."

His eyes darkened, and he walked past me toward the front of the building. "No thanks."

"Did you see her yesterday?" I asked, hurrying behind him.

"Nope," he said, keeping his gaze straight ahead.

"I took her into town yesterday, but she never showed up at work and she didn't go home last night. I thought you might know where she is."

"I don't give a rat's ass where she is," he said, dumping the bag on the front sidewalk with loud thunk, then turning around and heading back to grab another.

"Don't you care about your baby?" I asked as he brushed past me.

He stopped and turned to face me, his eyes dark. "That's a good one."

That pissed me off. Maybe it was the fact my own father had turned his back on me, but the thought of him already blowing off his baby didn't sit right with me. "What's *that* supposed to mean?"

"Look," he said in frustration. He stopped walking and swept a hand in front of him. "I don't know what that bitch told you, but it ain't my baby."

"What are you talking about?"

His eyes widened, and he leaned forward as he enunciated each word. "That. Baby. Ain't. Mine."

"But—"

"She cheated on me. We went for the stupid ultrasound a few weeks ago, and they said she was six months pregnant, not five like she told me."

I shook my head, still not understanding what the problem was. "So?"

"I was in jail, lady, and I wasn't gettin' no conjugal visits."

"Oh, Crap."

"More like she fed me a crock of shit."

I hated asking this question, but it had to be done. "Do you know whose baby it is?"

"That slut's been sleepin' around with anybody with a dick, so there's just no tellin'."

"Take a guess."

"Probably Jonathon Whitmore's. Rumor has it she's been shacking up with him from time to time."

"Got any idea about how I can go about reaching him?"

He released a bitter laugh. "You're something else, ain't ya?"

"So I've been told."

He shook his head and then laughed again, only this time it sounded more genuine. "I like you, so sure, I'll tell you. He lives up toward Hogan's Pass. Blue house that looks like it's about to fall in." He clenched his jaw. "I hope it falls in around both of 'em."

"But what about the baby?" I asked in disbelief. I could understand his hateful feelings toward his ex, but an innocent baby?

He turned and spat on the concrete, barely missing a potted plant. "Ain't my kid. It'd be better off not coming into that sick as fuck family."

"Ashlynn's?" I asked.

"The tooth fairy's," he snarked. "Of course hers. They're as messed up as they come. Her mother murdered that insurance guy. Her brother nearly killed himself and two other people, and her father is a mean son-of-a-bitch." He paused, and I saw a momentary flicker of pain in his eyes, but rage burned it away. "And she's a fuckin' slut." He spun around and headed for the large pile of mulch bags in the back.

I considered following him, but I wasn't sure what else to ask him. His directions to Jonathon Whitmore's house sucked, but that was the best I was going to get out of him.

"Thank you," I called out, figuring I owed him that much.

Keeping his back to me, he lifted his right arm and flipped me off. If he flipped off the people he liked, I sure hated to see what he did to those he didn't.

I got back in my car and pulled out of the parking lot. Maybe Marco could get me an address for Ashlynn's other boyfriend. Or I could look it up in the phone book. I started toward the Ewing library, turning down a side street that would get me there faster. It was then realized I was on Bird Street, the street that matched the address I'd found for Jim Palmer.

Pulling to the side of the road in front of a bungalow with pretty flowers lining the sidewalk and the numbers 324 painted on the siding next to the door, I got out my notebook and searched through my notes. Sure enough, the Palmers lived at 758.

I pulled away from the curb and continued down the road for several blocks. When I was in the 700s, I saw a For Sale sign in a yard up ahead and gasped when I realized it was in front of 758.

Melinda had already put her house up for sale?

My phone rang, and my pulse picked up when I realized it was Marco.

"Hey," I said, hating that I sounded slightly breathless.

"I think sex with you is amazing too," he said in a low tone that set my body on fire. "But I'm relieved to know you feel the same way. Are you still in Ewing?"

"Yeah." Did he want to go to the Alpine Inn and rent a room? Was it wrong I kind of hoped he did?

"I'd love to meet you for lunch."

"How about a field trip?" I asked hopefully.

"I'm intrigued…"

"How about you get me an address, and we can drive by it together?"

He released a short laugh. "Way to get a man's hopes up, then dash them."

I grinned. "You're an officer of the law, Deputy Roland. Isn't sex in a parked car considered indecent exposure?"

"Public indecency, and it's only a problem if you get caught."

"You get me that address, and we'll see what happens. His name is Jonathon Whitmore. I'm guessing he's in his twenties, and he supposedly lives up near Hogan's Pass."

He laughed. "Challenge accepted. How about you pick up lunch, then swing by the station and get me?"

"You can get the address that soon?"

"You underestimate my desire to see you."

I flushed again. "What are you in the mood for?"

"You," he said, his voice deep. "As for lunch, surprise me. Get here as soon as you can." He hung up, and I realized I was smiling like a fool.

In front of a murdered man's house.

Guilt swept in like an arctic wind, but I told myself I hadn't known Jim Palmer. Sure, I was learning about him, but I hadn't *known* him. I wasn't expected to grieve. I was allowed a small sliver of happiness in my life.

Except...maybe the guilt I felt was deeper than Jim Palmer's death and Pam Crimshaw's ruin. It didn't feel right to be happy with Bart's threat hanging over Hank's head. With him carrying on with his violent chess game with the town and its people.

And when I looked really deep, I wondered how long it would take Marco to realize I was unlovable, something every man who'd come before him had discovered. How long would I have this happiness for before it was gone?

Now that I'd tasted happiness and love, how much would it hurt if I lost him?

Chapter Twenty-Two

I texted Marco after I picked up our lunch, letting him know I'd be there in less than five minutes.

When I got there, he was waiting outside the station in his uniform, the sunlight making his hair look blonder. A huge smile spread across his face as I pulled up to the curb. He got inside, then leaned over and gave me a lingering kiss.

"You look pretty today," he said as he settled back, his gaze dipping to take in my dress and my bare legs. When he met my eyes again, he looked dazed. "Your eyes are like the summer sky."

I grinned. "Now you sound like a poet."

"There are never enough words to describe how you make me feel, Carly."

We stared at each other for several long seconds, seriousness hanging on the edge of our playfulness.

"Did you get the address?" I asked, breaking the silence.

"I did." He reached for me again, then groaned. "Let's go to the park and eat, then we'll drive by your mystery address."

"It's not a mystery," I said as I put the car into drive. "I've learned a few things since I last saw you."

"I'm all ears."

As I drove toward the park, I told him about the electricity problem in town and Max's plan for the night.

He chuckled. "Max has always had a business head. I'm not surprised he pulled a plan out of his ass like that."

Then I told him about going by the memorial again and following Melinda Palmer to the church and seeing Ricky. "Not only are the Palmers members, but Jim was a part-time youth leader."

He sat up. "So Pam and Jim *did* know each other?"

"Ricky said no, but Pam was in charge of the nursery. Surely their paths crossed from time to time."

"You think something might have happened at the church to upset her?"

"I don't know," I admitted. "I know we're trying to prove this was Bart's doing, with the caveat that Pam might have had another motivation. And I found out something else." He turned to face me. "Chuck Holston says he's not the father of Ashlynn's baby."

"What?"

"He thought she was five months pregnant, but at her ultrasound a few weeks ago he found out that she was six months along." I turned to him briefly and lifted my eyebrows. "Which meant he was in jail when she got pregnant."

"Wow."

"That's why I had you get that address. Ashlynn didn't come home last night, and Chuck said she might be at Jonathon Whitmore's house. He insinuated Ashlynn slept around a lot, but Jonathon might be the father."

Marco was silent for a moment, and I pulled into the parking lot of the park.

"There's another possibility about who the father might be," he said when I turned off the car.

"Jim Palmer?" If I were honest, I'd considered it deep down.

"It wouldn't be the first time a youth leader took advantage of a young girl."

"But she graduated a year ago."

"How long had he been a youth leader?" he asked.

"Good question. I asked Ricky, but he wasn't sure. Sounded like he'd been a leader for as long as Ricky's been a member."

"And he's a senior?"

"Yeah."

"So Jim would have overlapped with Ashlynn for at least two years." He shrugged. "*If* she was a member."

"I'm pretty sure she would have been involved whether she wanted to be or not. Thad wasn't at the youth group landscaping project, and Ricky said their dad would be pissed if he found out. It sounds like Rob Crimshaw wants his children in the youth group." I remembered our lunch and reached for the bag in the back seat, then handed it to Marco. "The salad's mine."

"Thank God." He grinned as he opened it. "Whatever you got me smells delicious."

"I know you like Rockman's grilled ham and cheese."

He laughed. "I'll have to find time to work out later."

"Don't you worry. I'll give you a workout."

He turned to me with shock in his eyes, and truth be told, I was surprised too. I'd never been so flirty with a man before. I'd never felt safe enough to let down my guard.

He leaned over and cupped my face. "Don't take this as a complaint, but this is going to take some getting used to. You have no idea how much I've wanted to do this over the past few months. How many times I've had to restrain myself."

"A *few* months?"

He grinned. "Maybe longer. I'm trying not to scare you off."

"I'm here, Marco. I'm not going anywhere."

He kissed me, a feather-light press of his lips that left me hungry for more.

Still cupping my face, he pulled back. "This not getting arrested for public indecency thing might become an issue."

I laughed. "Then maybe we should get out and sit on opposite sides of the picnic table."

"I can't promise I won't lunge over the top."

"I can't promise I'll shove you away."

He grinned. "I guess we'll take our chances."

I grinned back. "I guess we will."

We got out and walked over to the table, but Marco snagged my hand and tugged me closer so we were walking side by side. His gaze roamed my body. "I'm not used to seein' you in a dress."

"I used to wear them all the time when I was a…"

He pulled me to a stop. "Do you want your old life back?" The worry in his voice nearly broke my heart.

I did, didn't I? But when I thought of my old life, it felt lonely and empty. I'd had comforts I didn't have now—a nice apartment, nice clothes, a nice job. But everything had felt strangely hollow. My life here, however imperfect, felt so much richer, mostly because of Marco.

"I want *you*, Marco. Wherever that brings us."

Emotion filled his eyes, and he pulled me to his chest, holding me for a long second before he kissed the top of my head and released me. I took his hand again, needing that connection to him, and we resumed our walk to the table.

"Jim Palmer's house is for sale," I said.

He jerked his head down to look at me. "Already?"

"Yeah. Apparently, his wife didn't waste any time."

We sat down on either side of the picnic bench, and he handed me the bag and pulled out his phone.

I reached into the bag and pulled out my salad container. "What are you doing?"

"Give me a second." He started tapping and scrolling while I set his Styrofoam container in front of him. He whipped his screen around to face me. "The house has been on the market for nineteen days."

My mouth fell open as I stared at the listing on a real estate website. "Right around the time Chuck found out he wasn't the father."

His body tensed. "Shit."

We sat in silence, until I finally said, "Selena told me that Pam lost it a few weeks ago. A sales clerk was supposed to hold a crib for her at a thrift store, but it got sold while they ate lunch. Pam was outraged and threw a fit. Totally unlike her. Then she insisted on leaving and sobbed in the car. Selena says she refused to tell her what was wrong."

"That fits with the timing too."

"Pam probably found out that Jim Palmer got her daughter pregnant, let it simmer a bit, then went off and shot him. He put his house on the market because he was trying to leave town."

"That's pure speculation, Carly," Marco said. "And it's a *lot* of speculatin'. The biggest part of that speculation is that Palmer is the father. All we have is circumstantial evidence, which is slim at that. For all we know, Chuck's lyin' to get out of supportin' his kid."

"So we find Ashlynn and ask her."

"That's presumin' she'll tell the truth."

Crap. He was right. About all of it.

"We'd need to corroborate this," he said as he opened his container. "We'd need to check with her friends to see if any of them noticed a connection between the two."

"Is there any point?" I said. "If Pam killed Jim Palmer because she *thought* he impregnated her daughter, nothing else matters. It means Bart didn't make her do it."

"We don't know that Pam made the connection," he said calmly. "We don't know that Ashlynn had a relationship with him at all."

I pushed out a sigh and opened my salad. "You're right."

Marco reached across the table and snagged my hand. "Do you want to let this go?"

Did I? Would I much rather revel in my newfound happiness with Marco? Absolutely. But happiness was fleeting, and my ability to hold on to it very much depended on Bart. I'd never be free until he and my father were off the streets.

"No. We'll keep going for now, but if it becomes obvious Pam didn't do it for a Bart favor, we'll let it go."

He squeezed my hand again before releasing it. "Okay. So we'll finish lunch, then drive by Jonathon Whitmore's place to see if Ashlynn's there."

"I found something else," I said, pouring dressing on my salad, then mixing it around with my plastic fork. "Before the power went out, I did some research at the library on Rob Crimshaw and his father, Stewie."

"I'm listening."

"Rob was arrested for some bar fights and few DUIs about twenty years ago, but his father was arrested multiple times for drug possession, the last time with intent to sell."

"How long ago?"

I pulled my notebook out of my bag, opened to the page, and told him about Stewart's case. He'd been given a ten-year sentence after being caught with a large quantity of Oxy over eighteen years ago.

"He was arrested during Hank's reign," Marco said.

"Yeah," I said quietly. "But Hank swears he didn't deal in that kind of stuff."

"You confronted him about this?"

"No. But I've asked him about this kind of thing before."

"I've heard that Bingham was hot on Hank's tail back then, picking up what Hank didn't cover. He likely worked with him."

I hesitated, then lifted my gaze to Marco's eyes. "When I asked Hank if he knew the Crimshaw family, he told me he knew Stewie. He said he had two sons and he was known for his temper."

Marco took a bite and swallowed before he said, "If Stewie was in the drug world, then it stands to reason Hank knew him."

"Because he was working for him?"

"Maybe because he was working for Bingham."

I nodded and stabbed several lettuce leaves, but for some reason I wasn't convinced. It bothered me that Hank hadn't told me about Seth and Ricky being so close. I understood that he found it too painful to talk about Seth—I'd witnessed it a dozen different ways—but it was hard to believe that he wouldn't realize the information was important to share.

Marco gave me a pensive look, like he was waiting for me to share what had made me so quiet, but I knew he wouldn't push me to tell. He'd wait until I was ready. Call me a coward, but I wasn't quite there yet. I didn't want to face the possibility Hank had lied to me.

"I'll see what I can pull up on Stewart and Rob Crimshaw," he said. "But if Stewart received a ten-year sentence, he would have gotten out almost a decade ago."

Thinking about Stewart Crimshaw getting out of prison put me in mind of Lula's mother.

"Carnita said that Lula's mother is getting out of prison soon."

Marco's brow rose.

"She also said Bingham and Lula are researching their family trees. Lula told her Bingham had tracked his back to the early 1800s." When he didn't respond, I said, "Don't you think that's odd?"

"Everyone's exploring their family history these days."

"Bingham doesn't seem to be the sentimental type."

"True…"

It was pointless to push the topic. It felt important somehow, but it wasn't pertinent to what we were investigating. "Greta invited me to a girl's afternoon with Lula."

"Oh?" he said, looking pleased. "Are you going to go?"

"I wanted to, but she was thinking we'd do it this afternoon. She didn't know Max would find a way to keep the tavern open."

"That's too bad," he said, taking another bite of his lunch. "I know you like hanging out with them."

I narrowed my eyes. I still found it hard to believe he encouraged me to hang out with Lula. Marco was a deputy sheriff, and Lula and Bingham had gotten married after their daughter was born. I'd told him so on several occasions, but he'd countered that to the best of his knowledge Lula wasn't up to anything illegal, and I crossed Bingham's path often enough that it wasn't a bad idea for me to stay on his wife's good side.

"I'd like to talk to the parents of Thad's friend, the one who was in the accident with him," I said, "but I don't know how to approach them."

"I wonder if they attend the same church," Marco said. "We could always attend a church service."

I gave him a wicked grin. "Such deviousness in church, Officer Roland?"

He lifted his shoulder into a shrug. "Wouldn't be the first time someone's done something devious, and it definitely won't be the last."

"I still haven't called Karl Lister, but there's no subtle way to go about that conversation either."

Marco pressed his lips together. "I put in a request for the paperwork on the civil lawsuit. I haven't gotten it yet, so maybe hold off until I do."

"What if someone finds out you're digging into it?" I asked.

"Don't worry. My source at the courthouse won't tell."

"Rosemarie?"

He looked surprised. "How'd you know?"

I raised my brow. "That's who Miss Thelma told me to go see about the case paperwork. Obviously, she comes highly recommended."

"I guess Thelma Tureen knows something about just about everyone."

"Unfortunately, not everyone."

We finished our lunch fairly quickly, then headed back to the car to drive by Jonathon Whitmore's house.

It was a twenty-minute drive up to Hogan's Pass. The road turned to gravel and became steeper, but my car's GPS finally steered me toward a pale blue house on the left side of the road.

"The guy lives here?" Marco asked, leaning forward and squinting as we drove closer. "It looks like it needs to be condemned."

"Chuck said it was about to fall down on them, and he said he hoped it did."

"Nice guy."

"He was upset and angry," I said, not quite sure why I was defending him. Chuck Holston might have been wronged by Ashlynn, assuming he'd told the truth, but he was still an asshole.

"I see a car next to the house. Let's see if anyone's home."

I shot a glance at him as I drove down the road at a crawl, letting my gaze drop to his chest for a second before looking back out the window.

A slow grin spread across his face. "Were you checkin' me out?"

My face flushed. That hadn't been my intention, but there was no denying I'd appreciated the view. "I was looking at your uniform. Do you think it's a good idea for you to come to the door?"

"In this case, yes. I'll make sure they know I'm there on unofficial business. You can just tell them we had lunch together and you decided to drop by to check on Ashlynn."

"Okay," I said, not totally convinced by his rationale. It didn't seem like a good idea for him to involve himself so openly, whether off the clock or not. For one thing, I doubted Jonathon and Ashlynn, if she was there, would talk to a uniformed officer, and for another, I didn't want him to risk his job, his life. But I wasn't about to tell him I didn't want him there. "That means I take the lead."

I drove into the mostly dirt driveway and parked behind the small rusted red pickup truck. Marco pulled a notebook out of his pocket and jotted down the license plate number from the truck. "Just in case," he said as he put it back in his pocket.

We got out of the car and headed toward the dilapidated porch. Marco wrapped an arm around my back, catching me off guard, and when I glanced up at him with a questioning look, he leaned down and gave me a quick kiss on the lips. "Like I said, I'm not here on official business. You're checking up on a friend, and I'm just with you because I'm on my lunch hour." He flashed a tight grin. "I say we sell the *this isn't official* angle hard."

"While also letting them know you're a deputy."

He tilted his head and grinned. "I knew you were smart."

We carefully made our way across the porch to the door, and I knocked. The door had so much wood rot I was worried it would fall apart from the jarring.

A few seconds later, a skinny guy who looked like he wasn't a day over twenty opened the door.

"Jonathon Whitmore?" I asked.

"Yeah." He had a panicked look when he saw Marco. "I wasn't no part of that mess, and you can't pin it on me."

Marco lifted his hands up. "I don't know what you're talkin' about, and I don't wanna know." He tilted his head toward me. "I'm just here with Carly."

The kid shifted his attention to me, his gaze dipping down to take in my dress before lifting back up to my face.

Marco took a step toward me to let the guy know we were together.

"Hi," I said in my sweetest voice. "I'm Carly Moore, and I know Ashlynn. I drove her into Ewing yesterday, and I know she didn't show up to work. I heard you might know where she is. I'm worried about her. With her momma in jail and her being pregnant…" I let my voice trail off and smiled.

The guy flashed a glance at Marco.

"I only here because we were eating lunch together, and she asked me to come with her. You know how dicey it can get for a woman alone in these parts."

That surprised me, but I filed it in my *questions to ask later* pile.

The guy nodded, seeming to find Marco's suggestion acceptable, then turned back to me. "You're the one who took her to the jail."

"Yes!" I said, getting excited. "That means you've talked to her."

He glanced over her shoulder into the house, and a few seconds later, Ashlynn appeared behind him.

I let out a genuine sigh of relief. "Thank goodness you're okay. I was so worried."

She scowled, but it looked forced. "I don't know why. I can take care of myself."

"I know, but I felt responsible. What happened? I went to pick you up, and you weren't there."

She shrugged. "Yeah, well, I changed my mind."

"That's okay," I said. "I went by the pharmacy to see if you'd shown up, but Mr. Jones said you were a no-show."

Her eyes narrowed. "I didn't tell you where I worked."

"I know, but I figured you didn't work at Walgreens, so I tried Jones."

Ashlynn didn't look impressed with my sleuthing skills.

"Are you okay?" I asked. "Do you need a ride home? Or maybe to Selena's place?"

"I'm fine," she said in a huff.

"Could we talk to you outside for a moment?" Marco said.

"Why?" she asked suspiciously.

"We want to ask you a question about your baby," I said.

No sooner had the question come out than I wanted to stuff it back in. Wow. I was handling this badly.

She eyed Marco, then asked me, "Did Chuck send you?"

"No," I said. "But I spoke to him."

Propping her hand on her hip, she shot me a glare. "And he told you that cockamamie nonsense that he's not the daddy?"

"Do you want to have this conversation here?" I asked. "Or would you rather come outside?"

"We don't have any secrets," Jonathon said, clamping a hand on her shoulder. "We're best friends. What are you talkin' about? Of course Chuck's her baby's daddy."

From the look on Ashlynn's face, she didn't want to have this discussion in front of him, but she also didn't want to tell him to go away.

"Ashlynn…?" I asked.

"Chuck's full of crap," she said.

"Why would he say he's not the dad?" Jonathon asked.

I really didn't want to bring this up in front of him, but Ashlynn wouldn't come outside, and she wasn't telling me to shut up.

"He says he found out you're a month further along than he thought." I hated myself as the words crossed my lips. "That he was in jail when you would have gotten pregnant."

Jonathon's mouth dropped open. "What?"

"It ain't yours," Ashlynn shot over her shoulder.

"But we screwed that one time while he was in jail!" he protested, his eyes wide. "When we got shit-faced on Fireball."

"It ain't yours!"

"Ashlynn," I said, figuring I might as well go for broke since I'd already blown it this much. "Did you know Jim Palmer?"

She stared at me for a moment, then said defensively, "Well, yeah. I knew him from church."

"He was your youth group leader, right?"

She rolled her eyes. "He wasn't the only one, and he was only part-time at that. There were two other couples who ran it."

"But his wife never helped much," Jonathon said. "The last year or two it was just him."

"What kinds of activities did you do?" I asked. "I saw Ricky pulling weeds. Did they have you do other kinds of work around the church?"

"Hell, yeah," Jonathan said. "We were like free labor. They called them service projects."

"Like what?" I pressed.

"Usually stuff outside."

"Like landscaping?" Marco asked.

"Yeah," Jonathon said. "And fixing up the playground."

"Did you do any other service projects?" Marco asked.

"Sometimes," Jonathon said. "We helped at the food bank. We also worked on older people's yards."

"Like mowing and weeding?" Marco asked.

"And raking leaves."

"Did you do anything fun?" I asked. I'd never spent any time in church so I wasn't sure what youth groups usually did.

"We went to Dollywood every year," he said. "That was fun. And we took a yearly trip to see the Grand Ole Opry Christmas display. We'd stay at the hotel and take gondola rides and stuff."

"Did Jim's wife go?" I asked.

Ashlynn shifted her weight and crossed her arms, looking uncomfortable, but Jonathon was oblivious. "No. He said she had to stay home with their kids, but the Johnsons have kids too, and both of them always went."

Sounded like a great opportunity for a man to get a young girl alone and take advantage of her. Especially if his wife wasn't around.

"Ashlynn, did your mom know Jim Palmer before she killed him?"

She'd denied it before, and she had no reason to tell me any different now. She had no reason to tell me anything. Her lower lip jutting out, she said, "They never had anything to do with each other. My mama ran the nursery and if she talked to a youth leader, it was either Fred Johnson or his wife Patricia. Like I said, Jim wasn't there all the time."

"Did you like Jim?" I asked.

"He was okay," Jonathon said. "But the Johnsons were funner."

"What about you, Ashlynn?" I asked.

Her gaze darted away. "He was all right."

Then, because we'd gotten this far, I decided to go for broke. "Did he ever do anything...inappropriate?"

Her eyes widened with a panicked look. "Why do you keep askin' all these questions? None of this is any of your business!"

Then she slammed the door in our faces.

Chapter Twenty-Three

Well, that went well," I said sarcastically after we got into the car.

"Actually, it went better than I expected," he said.

I backed the car out of the driveway, desperate to get as far away from this mess as possible.

"Carly when you're investigatin' a case, you have to ask uncomfortable questions. Sometimes makin' them uncomfortable is the best way to get an answer."

"Sure, that works if you're a sheriff deputy, but I'm a nosy waitress. We might have just alerted Bart that we're looking into this."

Even if it was starting to look like he might not have played a part in Jim's death. Because he would know why we were looking into it…and I didn't need him knowing I was taking an interest in his favors.

"I doubt he'll find out from Ashlynn. She'd rather keep this whole mess quiet."

I backed out onto the road, then headed down the mountain. "I thought you were going to stay out of it," I said in a snippy tone.

"I was, but I figured it was more of a conversation than an interrogation, so I might as well participate."

I shot him a look of challenge.

"Okay, so maybe it wasn't totally conversational, but it was close."

"Marco."

"I'm fine. It'll be fine."

I reached over and snagged his hand. "Please don't get yourself into trouble over me."

"Carly, I was in trouble the minute I saw you searchin' Lula's cabin last December."

He'd liked me for that long? But he was trying to distract me, and I couldn't let him do it. "You know that's not what I meant."

"I know," he said softly, squeezing my hand. "It'll be fine. I promise."

I shook my head. "You can't promise any such thing."

"Okay," he said. "You're right. But I truly think it will be all right. Trust me."

I pushed out a breath, my heart racing. I couldn't live with myself if anything happened to Marco because of me, and not just because of the guilt. I wanted him in my life. Always.

"What's goin' through that beautiful head of yours?" he asked, sounding worried.

I almost told him nothing, then reminded myself I was going to be honest about my feelings. "I'm scared for you."

"Carly. I'll be fine."

Tears filled my eyes, making my vision blurry. "We don't know that. Now that we're together, I wouldn't put it past Bart to kill you just to spite me."

"Pull over."

"What?"

"Just pull over." He pointed through the windshield. "There's a turnoff up ahead."

"You're gonna be late getting back to the station."

"I don't care. Pull over."

I nearly told him no, but the tears weren't going away, and I was smart enough to know that driving on this road was dangerous with obscured vision. I turned onto the small dirt road and put the car in park.

He leaned over the console and cupped my face, turning my head gently until I was looking at him.

"I'm scared for you, Marco. I never should have dragged you into my mess. I never should have let myself do this."

"Do what?"

"Love you."

A soft smile spread across his face. "Sweetheart, you've loved me for months. I don't think you could have stopped even if you'd wanted to."

I released a short laugh even as tears streamed down my cheeks. "Arrogant much?"

He grinned, his eyes lighting up. "Loving me and being with me are two different things. And we both know that Bart already knows we matter to each other. Whether we're together or not."

He was right. I knew it yet I was terrified for him.

"Carly." He said my name so tenderly, fresh tears stung my eyes. "We're gonna get through this, okay?"

I nodded, because what else could I do?

He wiped my tears with his thumb. "Do you want me to drive?"

"No. I think I've gotten ahold of myself."

"Let's take a couple of days off from the investigation. Let things settle down some." He gave me a soft smile. "You need rest."

"Yeah. Okay."

He leaned over and kissed me, his lips tender, and I lifted my hand to the back of his neck and sank my fingers through his hair.

Pulling back slightly, I said, "I love you, Marco. If anything happens to you because of—"

His lips cut off my words, as they became more insistent.

My whole body flushed. I wanted him naked, but we were on the side of the road, and he was going to be late for work.

He was the one to pull back, but the hunger in his eyes said it wasn't by choice. "Let's head back into town."

"Okay." But I didn't let go of his hair.

He grinned. "You're gonna make this hard on me, aren't you?"

I lifted a brow. "You want me to make it easy?"

"No," he said, giving me another kiss as he gently pulled my hand from his head. "I can't believe I'm sayin' this, but good things come to those who wait. Tonight. After you get off work. I hope you're not too tired, because I have plans for you."

I sucked in a breath at the thought.

"So let me get back to the station so I can finish my paperwork."

"Okay, but maybe we can get a few days off soon and go away."

"I really like that idea. We both know Max will give you time off if he knows we're going away for a romantic getaway."

I laughed, because it was true. "Okay." Happiness washed through me, but it scared me. I kept wondering when it would be snatched away.

I pulled back onto the road and continued on toward town while we discussed where we could go. Marco said he had someplace in mind in North Carolina that was secluded and cozy.

We were almost into town when I finally brought up Ashlynn again. "She acted pretty weird when Jonathon told us Jim's wife didn't go to the meetings."

"She acted weird about him in general," Marco said. "And she definitely didn't want Jonathon to think he was the baby's father."

"Do you think Jim Palmer's the father?" I asked.

Because we both knew what it meant, or what it probably meant, if he was.

"I don't know. We need more information." He gave me a pointed look. "But I meant what I said. Let's give it a rest for a few days, then maybe we can talk to some of the kids in the youth group. Or maybe you can talk to her brother again."

"Yeah."

"But not today and not tomorrow."

It felt like we were wasting time, but he was right. We'd been stirring hornet's nests, and we needed to let things settle for a day or two.

I turned into the sheriff department's lot and pulled up to the curb.

"I'll see you after I get off work," Marco said. "And try to talk Max into letting you go early."

"I don't think you'll have to do much convincing. He's all for us being together."

"Good." He gave me a kiss, then reached for the door handle. "Be safe, okay?"

"Of course."

It was him I was worried about.

I decided to skip seeing Miss Thelma and headed to the grocery store to get the hamburgers, buns, and potatoes. While I was shopping, Max called and asked me to get hot dogs and buns along with lettuce, tomatoes, onions, multiple bottles of ketchup, and at least three hundred paper plates.

"Are you feeding an army?" I asked with a laugh.

"Close enough. Can you also stop by the Dollar General and get some outdoor Christmas lights? White? And get back as soon as you can."

"Sure…" What in the world was he up to? I was about to ask, but he hung up before I could.

I had to go to both grocery stores in town to get all the food, then to Dollar General and the thrift store to find white outdoor Christmas lights. It was nearly four by the time I got back to Drum, and I was surprised to see the side street leading to the back parking lot blocked off with cones. I parked on the street in front of the tavern and walked around back to see if I could get help with the groceries. Max had moved his pickup truck down the street, and Ruth and Tiny's cars were down there too. The road was blocked off about thirty feet from the corner—between the vacant lot behind the tavern and the abandoned dry cleaner across from it—and a couple of wooden picnic tables were sitting on the side of the road, with another in the middle of the parking lot.

Max, Tiny, Ruth's boyfriend Franklin (whom everyone else called Tater), and a few of Franklin's friends were in the parking lot, pounding tall wooden posts into the strip of grass at the back edge.

"What's goin' on here?" I asked lightheartedly as I squinted up at Franklin, who stood on a ladder held by two of his friends, hammering in what had to be a twelve-foot post.

"Max got a wild hair up his ass."

"He decided to make a really tall clothesline?" I asked, shooting Max a grin.

"Aren't you the funny one?" Max said sarcastically, but his eyes were dancing. "And you were the inspiration for this, so you're welcome."

I shook my head in confusion. "What are you talking about?"

"You waltzed in this morning wearing that pretty sundress, lookin' like you were headed to a picnic or a summer festival, so I decided to take an unfortunate situation and turn it into an advantage. We're having a summer block party. I've got a few bands comin' and everything."

"What?"

He laughed. "We're gonna string the Christmas lights and plug 'em into the generator. And we'll have dancin', and Tater knows a guy who makes balloon animals for tips."

I propped my hands on my hips. "You're amazing, Max Drummond."

He grinned from ear to ear. "About damn time someone figured that out. Now where's the beef?"

I rolled my eyes. "It's in my car. I'm gonna need some help bringing it all in."

"On it." He called over several of Tater's friends, and they followed me to my car and unloaded as much as they could and carried it through the unlocked front door.

I took the lights around back and handed them to Max with an apologetic look. "I'm not sure I got enough."

"Ruth had a bunch and so did Ginger. With the boxes you got, I think we'll be fixed up. Not to mention the tiki torches we rounded up to put along the sides of the street."

"This is pure genius, Max."

He laughed. "I have my moments. Oh, and by the way, I don't want you or Ruth wearing your uniforms tonight. We're gonna serve food buffet style from six to eight, and customers will come up to a bar we're setting up. I dug some warming trays out of the storage area, so they can grab what they want and pay you and Ruth at the end of the line."

"Where's Ruth right now?"

"I sent her to Costco in Greeneville to get some cans of soft drinks and bottles of water. They'll be easier to sell. She'll be back in an hour or so."

"How will people know this is going on?" I asked.

He laughed again. "Just when I think you've acclimated to Drum, you up and say something like that. Gossip, my girl. Gossip. No one will want to miss it. We'll see people who haven't stepped foot in the tavern in years."

I couldn't help wondering who might show up, then I remembered someone who wouldn't.

"What's with the frown?" Max asked.

"I wish Hank could come."

"Don't you worry. We'll get him out here. Now, believe it or not," he said, "Tiny needs help in the kitchen makin' patties."

"I'll go help him, but I'm going to move my car down the street so the customers can park out front."

He nodded, and I walked around the side of the building, surprised that there were now folding tables and chairs being set up with the name of the Methodist church stamped on the backs.

My car had already been unloaded with surprising efficiency. I figured it was best if I left Main Street parking free, so I drove down Parson's Street, fairly close to Selena's house. After I got out of the car, I stared at her house across the street, debating whether I should go talk to her. Just as I started to walk away, she came out of her front door.

"Carly Moore! What's all the commotion about on Main Street?"

"A summer street party, ma'am," I called back as I walked across the street toward her. "Max has a generator, so he's serving hamburgers and hot dogs, and he has a band coming for dancing."

A wistful look filled her eyes. "It's been a while since Drum's had a party. It's not often we have cause to celebrate."

"You should come," I said. "It will be fun."

"I just might," she said, casting a glance down the street.

"Say, Miss Selena," I said before I could stop myself. "I saw Ashlynn today."

"You don't say? I told you she'd turn up."

"She was with Jonathon Whitmore out at his house, which looks like it would fall over with a strong wind."

"Aw, that's who she runs to when things get bad."

"She spent the night with him last night. She didn't go home."

"I'm not surprised. She and Rob never really got along."

"Chuck Holston told me he's not the father of Ashlynn's baby. That she's six months along, not five, and he was in jail when she conceived. Chuck suggested that Jonathon is the father, and Jonathon thinks he might be."

She shook her head. "That boy is a dumb as a stump. Let us hope not."

"I also found out that Jim Palmer is a part-time youth group leader at the Crimshaws' church."

She frowned. "I guess I forgot about that. Now that I think about it, I think Ashlynn mentioned him in passin'."

Which was peculiar, at the very least. Selena didn't seem like the kind of woman who was lax with details. "Ashlynn got very uncomfortable when I brought up him being a youth leader. Do you know why?"

She hesitated. "No. From what I remember, Ashlynn was very fond of going to youth group."

"Jonathon said they went on trips a couple of times a year. Do you know if she went on those?"

"Most definitely, but she got in trouble her senior year in high school. She wasn't in her room during a bed check. One of the youth leaders brought her home before the end of the trip."

"Do you remember which trip or which leader brought her home?"

She shook her head. "Oh, no. But I *do* know that Rob nearly beat that poor child to death."

I gritted my teeth, trying not to let my reaction show, but I hated men like Rob Crimshaw. "Do you know what happened to Rob's father, Stewart? I heard he went to prison, but I couldn't find any information about if or when he got out."

"Oh, he was murdered there."

"I didn't see an obituary," I said.

"There likely wasn't one. Rob had turned to the straight and narrow at that point and was focused on the church. He didn't want the mess of his father's life contaminating his new one. I'm not even sure he claimed his body."

"What about his brother?" Hank had told me there were two sons.

"Disappeared," she said. "Around the time his father was arrested the last time."

"No one ever heard from him again?"

"Nope, but he's probably dead somewhere. He was a drunkard. He probably drove his car down a ravine that no one's searched." Kind of like the ravine Bingham's men had rammed Wyatt's truck into when I first got to town. Only Wyatt wasn't a drunk.

"There seem to be a lot of car wrecks around here."

She tsked. "Drinking and driving on curves is never a good idea." She glanced down the street again. "What time does this shindig start?"

"Six, but the band starts around seven."

"Good," she said, looking at me with her sharp eyes. "I think I might just turn up." Then she turned around and went inside.

Chapter Twenty-Four

After we made a mountain of hamburger patties, Tiny decided he didn't want to be stuck inside, so Max borrowed multiple grills and fired them up by the back door, while poor Pickle would have to run in and out of the kitchen with the fries.

When I finished in the kitchen and headed back outside to help set up the serving tables, I saw that Wyatt had shown up and was helping Max set up the drink station. They'd gotten about ten coolers and had set up a keg of beer.

Ruth showed up around five. Tater and his friends moved some of the barricades so she could back her car up to the edge of the parking lot to make it easier to carry the cases to the drink station.

I was so shocked when Ruth got out of the car, I might have let out a small squeal. She was wearing a pretty white and yellow sundress and her hair was curled. She'd even put on makeup and looked a good five years younger. Her face broke into a huge smile when she saw the strings of unlit white lights strung from the building to the posts, covering the parking lot.

"This looks like something you'd see in a movie, Max," she said.

"We haven't tried 'em yet," he said, wrapping an arm around her back and snugging her up next to him. "I was waitin' for you."

"That's *my* woman, Max," Tater called out good-naturedly as he carried two cases of bottled water past them.

"Maybe so," Max teased, "but a man can keep tryin'."

Wyatt, who'd already started putting the cans and bottles in coolers, shot me a look before quickly returning to his task.

"Okay, Scout," Max called out to one of Tater's friends. "Flip the switch."

Scout picked up the surge protector strip and pressed the button, and all the lights burst to life. Ruth and I clapped and cheered, and Max beamed like he was Santa Claus bringing Christmas magic to Drum. The time of year wasn't right, but the analogy wasn't far off.

Families with young kids showed up at six. They went through the food line and then sat at picnic tables. A woman strummed a guitar and sang children's songs while Tater's friend made balloon animals.

More people trickled in, and by seven the lot and street were full of people. Tiny and Pickle were struggling to keep up with the food.

"How many people do you think are here?" I asked Ruth between tallying up orders. I'd already had to change out the cash box twice.

"I don't know. Over a hundred. Maybe one fifty?"

"I'm not sure we'll have enough food."

"Max's got a popcorn maker on the way for after we stop serving dinner. Maybe that will tide them over."

The man really had thought of everything.

At seven, the woman with the guitar was replaced by a bluegrass band of several older men. The kids danced around the tables and played in the grass strips on the side of the road, and a few older couples danced in the open part of the parking lot.

Soon after, Selena came through my line, looking pleased.

"This is lovely," she said. "It's exactly what this town needed."

I had to agree with her. I'd never seen so many happy people in Drum, and it struck me as odd that I hadn't noticed that they weren't happy before.

When Marco hadn't shown up by seven-thirty, I started to worry. I caught Max's attention and asked him if he'd heard from him.

His forehead creased. "No. But I'm sure he'll be here as soon as he can." He gave me a sly grin. "Wild horses couldn't keep the man away from you."

I smiled back, reveling in the fact that he was right. Then I turned back to my dwindling line, surprised when I realized I was face to face with Ricky and Thad Crimshaw.

"Hi, Ricky," I said. "Hi, Thad."

"You know my boys?" a man asked behind them, his tone accusatory.

Rob Crimshaw. His eyes were hard, and while I knew he was in his forties, the lines on his face made him look a good decade older.

"Hello, Mr. Crimshaw," I said with a smile that took plenty of effort. "I met your sons yesterday when I dropped off a casserole." I decided to leave anything to do with Ashlynn out of it.

"The chicken and rice?" he asked.

"That's the one."

He nodded, his face softening. "It was good. Thank you for your kindness."

"I was so shocked to hear about Pam. She was a customer here, and she was always so sweet. I'm sure there has to be a reason for what she did. I hope they find it to help with her sentencing."

His eyes turned to ice. "My wife is dead to us." Then he handed me thirty dollars and walked off before I could give him change.

Ruth shot me a look that suggested I was crazy, and she probably had a point. Marco and I had agreed to let this go, and here I was, poking another hornet's nest with a big fat stick.

The Crimshaws took a seat at a table in the street. The other families watched them but few spoke. The ladies luncheon group were there with their husbands, all sitting together, and while they shot sympathetic glances to the boys, Sandy looked like she wanted to get up and beat Rob with her hot dog bun.

"I can't believe they came," Ruth said, shaking her head. "They're gonna be the source of gossip all night."

Then Selena walked over and sat at their table, but Rob didn't look too happy about it.

There wasn't anyone else in my line, so I turned my gaze to resume my watch for Marco. Butterflies filled my stomach when I saw him crossing the lot, heading straight for me.

"Girl," Ruth drawled in a breathless tone. "Does the look on that man's face mean what I think it means?"

His gaze was on me, and happiness and a hint of wanting flashed in his eyes. He seemed like a man on a mission as he closed the distance between us.

"Max said you two were finally out in the open," she said when I didn't answer. "But I didn't believe it."

"It's true," I said, smiling at him like a fool.

"Sorry I'm late," he said when he reached me, stopping a couple of feet away. "I got tied up with paperwork, then I ran home to change."

I took in his short-sleeved, light blue button-down shirt and jeans that hugged his hips.

"Are you checkin' me out again?" he teased.

"Maybe I am," I said with a coquettish smile.

"Just kiss her already," Ruth said. "Otherwise y'all are just a big tease to the rest of us."

Marco lifted an eyebrow, and I decided to hell with propriety. I threw my arms around his neck and stretched up to kiss him. He wrapped an arm around my back and pulled me to his chest as he returned my kiss.

Ruth squealed, and people began to clap and whistle.

Marco lifted his head, radiating a happiness that I felt to the marrow of my being.

Ruth started touching the small of my back, and I realized she was untying my apron strings. "I swear to God, Marco Roland," she said, "if you don't dance with this woman, right now, I'll find a shotgun and shoot you myself."

Her threat was a little violent, but that was Ruth. Marco took it in stride and grinned. "Maybe I should clear it with her boss first."

"There you go again," she said in disgust, tugging my apron free, "pretending like Max is in charge. *Go.*"

Marco's brow lifted in question.

"You heard the woman," I said with a laugh. "I didn't just get you to let her shoot you. What if she hits some important bits?"

Releasing a full-throated laugh, he wrapped an arm around my back and swung me out into the dance area.

Several people cheered as Marco whirled me around, and I realized many of them were customers at the restaurant. We danced for several songs until the band stopped playing and announced a country band would be playing next.

"I had no idea Max knew so many bands," I said as we watched the band start to tear down.

He shrugged. "We planned to open a music venue in Nashville. He knew music and groups back then. It stands to reason he still knows some."

"Why doesn't he have them play at the tavern?" I rested a hand on his shoulder, still savoring that I could touch him like that.

"He doesn't think there would be much interest here. His customers are mostly men watchin' sportin' events at night. He figured it would flop."

"Maybe he needs to rethink that." I made a face. "Speaking of Max, I should probably check in with him and see if he needs me for anything." I let my hand slide down to rest on his pec, noticing the two top buttons of his shirt were undone. "Have you eaten?"

He grinned. "Is that some sort of come-on?"

I laughed and looked up into his dancing eyes. "It's a legitimate question." I gave him a sultry stare. "I'm worried about your stamina for later."

He laughed too, lifting me up, and I released an involuntary squeal as he swung me around in a circle. "Don't you be worryin' about my stamina."

"I'm gonna take that as a no about eating already," I said. "Let's go get you some dinner."

I led him over to the food table. Ruth had abandoned the serving table, but there were still a few foil-wrapped hot dogs and burgers in the warming dishes. I handed him a paper plate, and he grabbed a hamburger, then glanced over at me.

"Have *you* eaten yet?"

"No, but Max probably still needs me to work."

He grabbed another hamburger and put it on his plate.

I shook my head with a grin. "I'm going to go find Max. Find a place to sit, and I'll be over when I can."

He leaned over and kissed me. "I'll save you a seat."

Max was over at the bar, refilling beer cups by himself. Had Wyatt left while Marco and I were dancing?

"Sorry I abandoned my post," I said as I motioned to the dance area. "But Ruth pushed me out there."

"I'm not sorry," Max said, grinning from ear to ear. "That's the best thing I've seen all night. As far as I'm concerned, you're officially off the clock."

I made a face. "That doesn't seem right."

"Don't you worry, Ruth is too. I had her put the food table on the honor system. In fact, as soon as some of these rowdy teens take off, the bar will be too." He winked. "But for now, I've got to make sure those kids don't sneak some cups of beer." He gestured to a group of boys, which included Ricky Crimshaw.

I was surprised Rob had let him out of his watchful eye, but then I realized I didn't see Rob anywhere.

Max grabbed a cup and started to fill it. "As soon as I hand you these beers, I'm gonna need you to walk away. You and Marco were *on fire* out there, and I don't want anyone thinkin' you're hittin' on me. All the Marly lovers will have my hide."

"Excuse me?" I asked with a laugh.

"That's what they call you two," he said. "There were bets on when you'd finally go public. Pickle won, by the way, so you might make him buy you a drink later with his winnings."

I stared at him in shock, then laughed. "I'll do that."

He held out the full cup and reached for an empty one.

"Just a water for me. You might need me later."

"Come on, Carly," he said, filling it anyway. "You're off for the night, and even if you do help with something, one beer's not gonna make you drunk."

"Okay," I relented, because a beer did sound good. "But I want a bottle of water too."

He finished filling the cup, then handed me the water, which I tucked under my arm, and the beer. "Well, look who just showed up."

I turned around and caught a glimpse. "Bingham?"

"Him and Lula. It looks like they left the baby at home. Greta and her new boyfriend are with them." He gestured to a table in the farthest corner of the set-up, in the dark area on the street.

Bingham and Lula were sitting at one of the church-borrowed tables with plates of food, eating. Lula and Greta seemed deep in conversation while Bingham's gaze was slowly sweeping the area.

"Bingham hasn't been around all that much," Max said quietly.

Now that Marco mentioned it, he hadn't. I shrugged. "I think marrying Lula and having a baby changed him."

"Maybe so," Max said, but he didn't sound convinced.

I turned around to find Marco. He'd chosen a church table on the street too, although it was in the opposite corner from Bingham. Selena was sitting with him. As I approached, I could hear them discussing Marco's glory days in high school.

"Hello, Miss Selena," I said as I set down the beers and the water. "I'm so happy you came."

"Me too," she said. "Tonight is perfect."

I knew what she meant. The temperature was in the seventies, and the sun had set, so the light was a soft glow from the twinkling lights and tiki torches flickering along the edge of the street. It felt magical, especially when I sat next to Marco and he pressed his leg against mine.

"I saw the Crimshaws were here," I said as Marco handed me a hamburger that he'd doctored up.

"I was surprised to see Rob here," Selena said. "But he left when he saw the Genslers."

My mouth dropped open. Thad had been with the Gensler boy on the night of the accident. "They're here?"

She gestured across the parking lot. "The couple with the little girl. Spencer's over there with Thad."

I glanced around and saw a middle-aged couple sitting at a table with a girl who looked about ten. I continued scanning the lot and saw Thad hanging out with two boys his age.

"They still let their son spend time with him?" I asked in surprise.

"They're not friends like they used to be," she said, "but they *do* see each other. It's hard to prevent it in a school with so few students."

I resisted the urge to glance back at the couple. "Does their daughter go to school in Drum?"

"Yes, she's in the fourth grade."

I put my hamburger down on Marco's plate. "I'll be right back."

Marco snagged my hand and looked up into my eyes. "I thought we were going to just enjoy the evening." I knew he wanted to say more, but Selena was watching.

I leaned over and kissed him. "I only want to make sure they know about Tutoring Club."

He searched my eyes, and I found it disconcerting that I couldn't tell what he was thinking. Did he really not want me to take advantage of this situation? I'd been looking for a natural "in" with them, and it had been handed to me on an engraved silver platter.

Neither of us said anything for a solid two seconds, then he gave me a soft smile and nodded toward them. "Go give them the Tutoring Club pitch."

"Thank you," I mouthed and gave him a quick kiss.

Grabbing the bottle of water, I took a sip as I walked over to them, checking the crowd for other families with school-aged children who didn't attend the club. I stopped to talk to another family with two younger children, one of whom looked like he was in first or second grade, figuring it would look better if I was making rounds.

"Hi," I said as I took a seat opposite the family. I introduced myself and took a few minutes to tell them how Tutoring Club worked and assure them it was free. After I answered all of their questions, I made my way to the Genslers' table, my stomach in knots. I really didn't want to screw this up.

"Hi," I said, smiling brightly. "I'm Carly Moore, and I'm a waitress here at Max's."

Mr. Gensler extended his hand. "I'm Donnie, and this is my wife, Kay."

I shook hands with both of them. "And who is this?" I asked, gesturing to their daughter.

"Scarlett, say hello to Miss Carly," Kay said.

She gave me a shy smile. "Hi."

"This is so nice," Kay said, her gaze scanning the party. "I hope Max does this again."

"We've had a great turnout," I said. I wasn't sure how much money he'd made, but he'd definitely earned some loyalty. "I suspect he will." I glanced over at their daughter. "I didn't mean to interrupt, but I'm making sure families are aware that we have a tutoring program here twice a week from three-thirty to five. We call it Tutoring Club, and we try to make it fun with games and rewards. I don't know if Scarlett or any other children you might have need help, but I just wanted to let you know there's an available resource."

Donnie frowned. "How much do you charge?"

"Oh," I said, "I'm sorry. I should have mentioned that part first. It's totally free."

"Why would you offer free tutoring?" he asked suspiciously.

"Max loves Drum and feels compelled to give back to the community," I said. "Take tonight, for example; and Tutoring Club is a way for us to support Drum's most important resource—our children."

The couple exchanged a glance. "Do you tutor high schoolers?" Kay asked as she turned back to me. "Our son Spencer is in summer school, repeating English and social studies so he can start his freshman year in August."

An idea popped into my head. I felt guilty for even considering it, but I figured it would be a win for everyone. "I usually work with elementary and middle school students, but I'd be happy to meet with him and see if I can help."

"What experience do you have?" Donnie asked.

"I worked at a tutoring center in Atlanta before I moved to Drum last year. I confess, most of the kids in my group are significantly younger, but I'm willing to meet with your son one on one." I smiled. "The last thing he needs is to be coming in with the younger kids. I'm sure a tutoring session will be hard enough for him to accept."

"I don't know," his father said, his gaze sweeping over me. "Somehow I think he'll be okay with it."

I resisted the urge to cringe. I didn't want to encourage a fourteen-year-old boy to have a crush on me, but I could also put a stop to it fairly quickly. "I have time tomorrow if Spencer does."

"He doesn't have summer school tomorrow. Will late morning work?" Kay asked.

"Sure," I said. "I'm not sure if the electricity will be back on by then, but we can meet outside at one of the tables."

Kay made a face. "I was hoping you could come to our house. I realize that's an imposition, so we'd be happy to pay you twenty dollars an hour."

"Now, Kay, wait a cotton-pickin' minute," Donnie protested.

"He's failin' summer school, Donnie," she said, seething. "Neither one of us can help him. If she can…"

He pressed his lips together.

"If you don't mind me asking," I said, "when did Spencer start falling behind? I'll see how he's doing where he's at, but it might help to know how far back this goes."

They exchanged another look, then Kay said, "Spencer was in an accident a little over a year ago. He missed a month of school." She hesitated, her mouth twisting as though she struggled with how much to confess.

"He was arrested," Scarlett said knowingly. "He didn't go to jail or anything, but he was in *bad* trouble."

"Scarlett!" Kay hissed, giving her a feather-light smack.

The new band began playing an uptempo country song.

"It's okay," I said with a smile. "I really don't care about the reason. It's just helpful to know for context."

"I truly hope you can help him," Kay said with tears in her eyes.

"I'll do my best," I said truthfully. "And if I don't think I can, I'll be sure to let you know so we can hopefully find someone who can."

She reached across the table and clasped my hand. "Thank you. You're an answer to my prayers."

270

My guilt resurfaced. While I *did* intend to help him, I'd made the offer with ulterior motives. I glanced back at Marco's table, surprised to see he was approaching us. A quiet anger simmered in my chest. Didn't he trust me to handle this?

"Sorry to interrupt," Marco said as he reached the table, "but the band's playing our song." He held out his hand to me with an apologetic look.

"Of course," Kay said, grabbing her purse and pulling out a receipt.

"Marco," I said trying to swallow my anger in front of the Genslers. "This is Donnie and Kay Gensler and their daughter, Scarlett."

Marco tipped his head to them. "Pleased to meet you."

"Let me just jot down our address." Kay scribbled her address down, then pushed the receipt to me. "Will eleven o'clock work?"

"That works perfectly for me." I took the paper and tucked it into my pocket.

"Thank you. You're a godsend."

"I say that every day," Marco said, tugging me out of my seat and away from the couple, toward the dance area.

"What on earth was that about?" I asked, speaking as low as I could and still be heard above the band, barely restraining my anger. "You know this was a golden opportunity!"

"Carly—" Wrapping an arm around my back, he turned me to face him as we reached the edge of the dancing crowd. "—I know, but—"

"If you're going to be a controlling—"

He leaned down and kissed me. When he lifted his head, worry filled his eyes. "*Carly*," he said, starting again now that he had my attention. "Bart Drummond is here, and he's watching your every move."

My mouth fell open, and I realized I could practically feel his gaze burning a hole on my back. I turned my head to the side and caught a glimpse of him with his wife, Emily. They were waiting in Max's drink line, and both of them had their attention on us.

Chapter Twenty-Five

We began to move to the country song about a man and his truck and something about a cow. Despite my worries, I laughed. "*This* is our song?"

He laughed too. "You know I'm pretty fond of the Explorer."

I lifted my brow. "And the cow?" My eyes narrowed. "That better not be me."

"Never." He released my back and grabbed my hand, spinning me out and then reeling me in, catching me with my back to his chest. He placed a kiss at the base of my neck, and a shiver ran down my spine.

"If Bart hangs around much longer, I say we leave," he whispered in my ear.

"And if he leaves?" I asked breathlessly, torn between wanting to take Marco home and wanting to stay and enjoy a rare night of frivolity.

He wrapped an arm around my stomach and turned me around to face him. "I'm dying to get you home, but I also know that nights like this are rare. You deserve to have fun, Carly, to forget about everything for at least a few moments, and I'm determined to make sure you can."

"I love you," I said, losing myself in his blue-green eyes.

He smiled. "I love you too."

"Get a room," teased an older man I recognized as a customer as he danced near us with his wife.

"I would, Barry," Marco said. "But I heard you rented the last one at the Alpine Inn."

Barry and his wife laughed, and we laughed with them, and I let myself forget that Bart was watching me. He knew I was with Marco, so there was nothing I could do about that, but I could at least deny him the satisfaction of knowing his presence was bothering me. So I laughed and danced and occasionally caught a glimpse of him while Marco spun me around the lot. I wanted Bart to see my happiness, but I couldn't help feeling like I was poking more hornets' nests.

The song we were dancing to stopped and Jerry tapped Marco's shoulder. "Excuse me, but can I cut in?" He was wearing a clean pair of jeans and a button-down shirt that looked brand new. His hair was neatly combed, and he looked happier than I'd ever seen him.

"Just don't steal my girl," Marco teased.

"I know she's yours," he joked. A slow song came on, and Jerry held out his arms.

I put my hands on Jerry's thin shoulders, pleased that he smelled like aftershave and not the cheap soap Max stocked in the bathrooms at the Alpine Inn. Despite my worry, I was happy to see him doing so well.

His hands rested on my waist and we stood about a foot apart as we swayed to the music.

"I'm so glad you came," I said, my voice breaking. "I've missed you."

"I didn't move away," he said with a smile. "Just moved on to bigger and better things. I've got my own cabin on the Drummond property. With curtains and everything. The Drummond housekeeper even said she'd change my linens and towels."

"That all sounds wonderful, Jerry. I'm very happy for you."

"I know you think I'm foolish," he said, glancing down. "But it all seems on the up and up."

"Jerry." His gaze lifted to mine. "You are an amazing man, and Bart Drummond is damn lucky to have you. But if at any time you feel that's changed, you tell me, okay? Don't worry about where you'll stay or anything. You can always stay with us. Just tell me, and we'll sort it out. Together."

He made a wry face. "You think Hank Chalmers would let me stay with him?" He released a sharp laugh, then shrugged. "Maybe he's changed."

I stared at him in surprise. "You and Hank have bad blood, Jerry?"

"It was a misunderstanding," Jerry said, then waved his hand. "I'm sure he's plumb forgotten."

Did it have anything to do with Hank's daughter? It had only recently come to light that Jerry had witnessed a sheriff's deputy murder Barb's boyfriend. But Jerry, terrified for his life, had kept it to himself.

"I'm glad you're with Marco and not the other Drummond boy," Jerry said.

"Wyatt?"

He nodded. "He's up to something no good. I can feel it."

I frowned. "Like what?"

He shook his head. "I don't know. Got no proof. Just a feelin'. He's not gonna like it that you're with Marco, so you both better watch your backs."

I stared at him in disbelief. "You think he'd hurt one of us?"

"Nah," he said with a grimace. "But the Drummonds have plenty of other ways."

"If you don't trust the Drummonds, then why are you workin' for them?" I asked.

He grinned, but it seemed forced. "Now who said I don't trust all of 'em?"

Then the song changed, and he whirled me around with more energy than I would have expected. We laughed and danced, and when the song ended, he kissed me on the cheek. "Your man's waitin' for you. Thank you for sparin' a couple of dances for me."

"There's always room on my dance card for you, Jerry."

Marco swooped in as Jerry headed over to join a group of men. "Let's get a drink."

"Sounds good." I'd never drunk my beer, and I'd left my water at the Genslers' table.

Max was still working at the bar even though he didn't have any customers at the moment.

"I thought you were going to leave this to the honor system," I told him when we reached the table.

"Those boys are still circling like sharks and I don't want to lose my liquor license." He nodded his head toward Ricky's group of teens and then shot a wink at Marco.

"Where's Wyatt?" I asked.

"He's runnin' an errand. In fact, I'm surprised he's not back yet."

"You need a break," I said. "Let me take over so you can circulate and maybe even dance with a pretty girl." I waggled my eyebrows. "I've noticed a few eyeing you."

He hesitated instead of outright telling me no, so I gave Marco an apologetic smile, then walked around the table and gave Max a tiny shove. "Go. Have some fun. Reap the fruit of your labors."

"Fruit of your labors?" Max asked with a chuckle.

I rolled my eyes. "Just go with it."

"She's right," Marco said, walking around the other side. "Go have some fun. We'll run the table until Wyatt shows up."

Max looked uncertain, then he stood up straighter. "Okay. I think I will." And he poured himself a beer and headed out into the crowd.

"I hope this was okay," I said, "but Max deserves to have some fun too."

"It was a good call," he said. "I should have thought of it, but all I could think about was you."

I stretched up and gave him a kiss, then turned around to check out the cooler situation. "Let's organize the drinks while we're waiting for our next customer. I bet we can get rid of some of these."

"Good idea."

Five of them were nearly empty, so we moved the cans and bottles to the fuller containers, then Marco dragged the empty coolers to the back door to dump out in the kitchen sink.

He'd just gone inside when a man with a limp approached the table. He was wearing a T-shirt and jeans. His brown hair was short, and he had a trimmed beard. I would have guessed him to be in his thirties, but something in his eyes made him look older.

"What can I get you?" I asked cheerfully. I had to hand it to Max. Quite a few of the people who'd come to the event had never been to the tavern before, this man included. "We have draft beer, bottled water, and some soft drinks."

"Uh…a beer sounds good," he said, looking around like he was checking the place out.

"Did you just get here?" I asked as I grabbed a cup.

"About a half hour ago." He turned back to me. "I hear you're Carly."

The fact that he knew me made me a little nervous, but it wasn't all that uncommon since I'd started tutoring, not to mention I had some notoriety after Seth's murder. I held the cup under the tap and started filling it. "That's me."

"My name is Karl Lister."

My heart skipped a beat, but I tried to keep my cool. I did a quick scan of the crowd. No Bart, but that didn't mean much—there were plenty of people for him to skulk behind. "Hi, Karl."

"I'm sorry to just show up like this, but I heard you're asking a lot of questions about Pam Crimshaw."

So much for flying under the radar.

He leaned closer. "I'm here because of Thelma."

I pushed out a sigh of relief. "How do you know Thelma?" Because she'd claimed she didn't know him.

"My aunt is friends with Thelma's hairdresser."

I released a chuckle. "Six degrees of Thelma Tureen."

His nose wrinkled in confusion. "What?"

"Never mind."

"I told her I'd come by the tavern tonight, but then I saw it was closed."

"Yeah, the electricity's out." His gaze took in the lights overhead and I added, "Max has a couple of generators." I finished filling his cup but didn't hand it to him. "That'll be three dollars."

He dug into his back pocket and produced a wallet.

"I *have* been asking questions about Pam," I said. "I heard you were in an accident with her son Thad."

He inhaled sharply. "I was. Are you fixing to make her look like an angel or a devil?"

I looked him in the eye. "I only want the truth, Karl."

278

He pulled three ones out of his wallet. "Why?"

I hesitated, then said, "I think something else might have been going on."

"What does that mean?"

I took the money from his hand and handed him the beer. "Did you get a settlement from the lawsuit?"

"It settled out of court the morning of the trail." He paused, then shrugged. "I got one hundred grand. Not nearly enough, but my attorney encouraged me to take it anyway. They say it's pretty common," he added. "Settling out of court. I still wonder if I could have gotten more." Anger filled his eyes. "I lost my job. I lost my house. I walk with a permanent limp. My life was ruined, and all I got was a hundred grand, while that kid gets off scot free." He gestured toward Thad and his friends.

"I'm sorry."

"Not your fault, but his mother did anything and everything to get him out of it. All he got was community service."

I told myself to be careful and not get too excited. "Do you think the judge who sentenced Thad was corrupt?"

"What?" He squinted. "Maybe. I hadn't considered it before."

"Do think that Pam might have had outside help to get her son off?"

"You mean like an attorney?"

"No, like someone paying the judge to give Thad a lighter sentence?"

His face paled. "Son of a bitch."

I held up a hand. "I didn't say it happened. I only asked if you thought it was possible."

"Hell, yeah, I think it's possible."

The back door opened, and Marco emerged. He started toward me, but a couple of guys who were regulars at the tavern stopped him and pounded him on the back in presumed congratulations.

"Can we meet somewhere more private?" I asked. "What's your schedule like? I can meet you early afternoon tomorrow or anytime before five the next day."

"I have to work tomorrow, but Saturday morning sounds good." He pulled out his cell phone. "What's your number so we can connect?"

I gave him the tavern number. "That's the number here, which is the best way to reach me since I'm almost always at the tavern. If you call tomorrow night, we can set up a time and location."

He entered it into his phone and looked up at me, defeat filling his eyes. "Do you really think she bribed someone to get him off?"

"I don't know, Karl," I said sympathetically. "That's part of what I'm looking into."

"What does that have to do with her killing that insurance agent?"

"I'm trying to figure that out too."

He nodded, still not looking convinced, then limped away, the beer in his cup sloshing over the side.

Marco returned, casting a glance back at Karl. "Who was that?"

"Karl Lister." Even as I said his name, I looked for Bart, relieved that he was still nowhere to be seen.

Marco's eyes flew wide. "Why were you talking to him?"

"He came over to me. Besides, he bought a beer."

"Carly, if Bart—"

"*He* came over to *me*. He didn't dawdle long, and he just left. *Everyone's* getting drinks tonight. It's not *that* weird." But even I had a hard time believing that. At the same time, I wasn't sure what I could have done differently. Wouldn't it have looked more suspicious if I'd sent him away immediately? "He says he lost his job and his house, but they settled his case out of court the morning of his trial. All he got was one hundred thousand."

"Which means he only got about sixty or seventy thousand after his lawyer got his cut," Marco said. "Not much given what he lost."

"He said his attorney suggested he accept the offer. It wasn't much money, but what pissed Karl off the most was that Thad got off so easily."

"If his attorney pressed him to accept, he may have gotten a bribe, but the money probably came from the car insurance company. I highly doubt Bart had any influence over them, nor would they care. And sure, the Crimshaws' premiums probably went up a whole lot, but that would have happened anyway. I wonder if he got anything else."

"He wants to meet with me on Saturday morning to discuss it more. I can ask him then."

Marco pressed his lips together, then nodded. "Maybe I'll go with you. Jim Palmer's funeral is that afternoon."

I wasn't going to complain.

Movement on the street caught my eye, and I saw Hank hobbling toward the edge of the parking lot with his crutches. He was wearing a button-down checkered shirt and jeans, the right leg rolled up and pinned.

"Hank." I covered my face with my hands as tears sprang to my eyes.

Marco put his hand on my shoulder. "Go see him. I've got this covered."

I scooted around the edge of the table and hurried over to him. When he saw me, he gave me a big smile.

"You're here!" I exclaimed as I got closer.

"Wyatt came and got me."

Wyatt stood to the side, watching with his thumbs hooked under the waistband of his jeans.

"Thank you," I said to him as a tear slid down my cheek.

"No cryin'," Hank grumped. "I thought you'd be happy to see me."

"You have no idea," I said, throwing my arms around him and hugging him tight.

He patted my back. "There, there, girlie. You're gonna knock me over."

Laughing, I released him. "Are you hungry? Do you want to sit down? We can get you a chair. Do you want me to get you some water?"

"Slow down," he said with a grin. "I know I don't get out of the house much, but I'm not a shut-in. You're right. I need to get out more, and Wyatt's gonna get my car set up tomorrow so I can start driving myself around."

"I'm still going to your doctor appointments in Greeneville," I said in a stern voice.

"You're only sayin' that because you want your Church's Chicken."

"Maybe. But I also want to talk to your doctors and make sure you're not pullin' a fast one on me."

He laughed. "Deal. Now why are you standin' here talkin' to me? I want to see you dancin' with that man of yours."

"Marco's manning the drink table. Speaking of which, do you want me to get you a drink? Have you been good with your diet today? Maybe you can splurge and have a beer."

He cast a glance at Marco. "I'm fine with water. You go get it, and I'll find a place to park myself."

I went back over to Marco and walked behind the table to get a bottle of water.

"Did Wyatt go pick up Hank?" he asked.

I grimaced. "Yeah."

"That was nice of him. Honestly, I should have thought of it."

"I suppose Wyatt thought of it because he's fixing up Hank's car to make him more independent. I *did* mention earlier that I wished he could come, but we were too busy setting up for me to get him, and even if I had, he would have tired out quickly, staying here so long."

"See? This works out better. I'm glad Wyatt got him, Carly," he said earnestly. "I'm just sayin' I feel like a heel for not thinkin' of it myself. I could have gone and picked him up before *I* came."

"We're not used to the idea of him coming into town for things. We'll both think of it next time." I lifted the bottle of water. "I'm gonna take this to Hank."

"Okay. Have you seen Max? I don't see him anywhere, and we're going to need to change the keg soon."

"Maybe he went inside. I have to go to the bathroom, anyway, so I can look for him."

"Sounds good."

Wyatt had moved a chair to the parking lot, next to the grassy back edge, and Hank was sitting in it with his crutches lying on the ground next to him. He was watching the dancers with a wistfulness I'd never seen on his face.

I handed him the bottle, then squatted next to him. "Are you thinking of Mary right now?"

He released a soft laugh. "That woman loved to dance. The town used to put on monthly dances in the summer, and Mary always wanted to go. She would dance all night, leavin' me utterly exhausted, but she'd still be dancing through the front door when we got home. This makes me think of happier times."

I reached up and grabbed his hand, giving it a soft squeeze. "Did Bart come too? And Floyd Bingham?"

"Yep. The dance was considered neutral ground. No nonsense allowed." He cast a glance down at me. "It was for the town's sake. So people would feel safe, and they wouldn't worry about gettin' caught in any cross-fire."

"Literal?" I asked, wide-eyed.

He shrugged as though it was no big deal. "That too. There was a lot of divisiveness, and even though a good portion of the people in town had nothing to do with anything underhanded, they could still feel the tension. Drummond ran the town, so he started the dances and proposed they be Switzerland. Mary convinced me it was a good idea." He shot me a wink. "I teased her she wanted it to work for selfish reasons. I'll never forget the look in her eyes when she lifted her chin and said defiantly, 'Suppose I do. You know I'm not the only one.' And she was right, so I swallowed a lump of pride and accepted the terms, but the deal was he provided the moonshine and I provided the bands."

"And what did Floyd Bingham provide?"

Releasing a snort, he said, "Not a damn thing. He didn't come most of the time, but eventually his son did."

"Say, Hank," I said, feeling awkward about what I was about to ask. But I'd feel unsettled until I said something. "Is there bad blood between you and Jerry Nelson?"

His brow shot up. "What makes you ask?"

"I told Jerry to let me know if things turn sour out at the Drummonds'. I said I'd help him get resettled, and he told me that he doubted you'd want him stayin' with us for any length of time."

He snorted. "Two old men livin' with a young woman? Sounds like one of them sitcoms. That's what he probably meant."

Only I didn't think that was what he meant at all. Had Hank just lied to me, or had he forgotten some grievance that Jerry remembered? I was having too much fun to put a pall over it.

"So they used to have dances?" I said. "How many years did they go on?"

He pushed out a sigh. "I don't recall. Ten years? Maybe twelve? They stopped when the lumber mill went under. People didn't feel much like celebratin' when they'd just lost their jobs and the man hostin' the parties was the one who'd ruined 'em." He motioned to the dancers. "Max did a good thing. The town needed this."

"Speaking of Max…" I got to my feet. "I'm supposed to ask him about changing the keg. Save me a spot on your dance card, Hank. You're gonna dance with me."

He snorted again. "The hell I am."

I pointed a finger at him. "Just like your Mary, I know when to dig in my feet. I will get my way, and you know it, so you might as well accept it."

He shot me a dark glare. It might have scared someone else, but I just grinned and waited with a hand propped on my hip.

"Fine. Go." He made a shooing motion, and I laughed as I turned around and headed for the back door.

There was still no sign of Bart or Emily. I hoped that meant they'd gotten bored and left.

The back hall was illuminated with an overhead light. One of the generators was hooked up to the tavern to keep the refrigerators and freezer running, and Max had left the hall light on so people could see when they went in to use the bathroom. Since the tavern only had two restrooms with one toilet each, there'd been a line most of the night, so I was fortunate that there was only one person ahead of me. I got to the restroom quicker than I'd expected—the woman in front me had gone in to reapply some makeup—and when I got out, the hall was empty.

I walked around the table Max and Tiny had turned on its side to block the end of the hall and the entrance to the dining room, and headed to Max's office. It was locked.

Where was he?

I started to head back outside when I heard a loud thud on the ceiling above my head, coming from Max's apartment.

He'd seemed eager to enjoy the night, but maybe he'd gone up there for a break. Or to use his own bathroom. I considered finding Ruth and making an executive decision about the keg, but I decided Max would want some input. I headed up the dark stairwell and stood in front of the doorway, surprised to hear a couple of voices on the other side. They were too muffled for me to make out who they belonged to, but one of them was definitely female.

Well, crap. Had Max found a woman and brought her upstairs? I definitely didn't want to interrupt.

I turned around to go downstairs, but it was nearly pitch black, and I banged into the wall outside the door. Cringing, I was torn between bolting down the stairs and waiting to see if Max came to the door to check on the noise. Before I could decide, the door opened and Max appeared, his hand on the door. His apartment was dark except for a dim circle of light from a couple of candles on his coffee table.

"Max, I'm so sorry," I gushed. His face was swathed in shadows, and I couldn't see if he was pissed. "The keg's nearly empty, and I came up to ask which one to use as a replacement, but then I heard voices and started to leave so I wouldn't interrupt." I lowered my voice. "I didn't mean to bother you. You get back to whatever it was you were doing and we'll sort it out ourselves."

"Is that Carly I hear?" a familiar female voice called out.

Oh shit.

Max hesitated. "Yeah, Mom."

"Well, don't be rude, Max. Invite her in."

Max hesitated again, then backed up so I could enter the room.

"Well hello, Carly," she said from across the room. She was sitting on the edge of Max's sofa, but I didn't see Bart. "It's been too long since we chatted. I was hoping you'd come out to tea again."

I stopped a couple of feet into the room. "I've been busy."

"Yes, you have, haven't you? What with Tutoring Club and your community outreach to those in peril, I'm sure you don't have much spare time."

Was she talking about Pam? Had she caught wind of what I was up to?

Max gave me a wary look but didn't go over to join his mother.

"I didn't mean to interrupt," I said hastily. "I just needed to ask Max about the keg replacement, but then I heard voices and I wasn't sure if Max had invited a lady friend upstairs."

Emily laughed but it sounded forced. "Yes, one of my sons sleeps around while the other pines for you." Her mouth pinched. "Shame on the lot of you for lettin' me think you and Wyatt were together when you broke up months ago."

I didn't want to touch that subject. It hadn't been my lie. That one was squarely on the Drummond men. I backed up a step toward the door. "So, Max? The keg?"

"Yeah," he said, rubbing the back of his neck, looking thrown. "Just use your best judgment."

"Max, why don't you go take care of the keg so us girls can have a chat?" Emily said, but it wasn't a question.

"Oh, that's all right," I said, taking another step. "I'll just be on my way."

"Really, *Caroline*," she said in an icy tone. "I insist."

Chapter
Twenty-Six

Max's eyes widened. He started to say something, but when he saw I didn't correct her, he stopped.

Panic flooded my body, and I nearly ran down the stairs to escape, but I had to be smart about this. It shouldn't come as a surprise that she knew my secret. Even if Bart hadn't told her, no doubt the information was there at her house, available for the taking. Now, I had to find out what she wanted.

I turned to look at Max, not surprised by the confusion on his face. He thought Carly was a nickname for Charlene. "I think I'll stay and have a chat with your mother."

He still hesitated, as though he thought leaving us alone wasn't a good idea.

"Marco had almost run the keg dry about five minutes ago, so he needs an answer."

"Carly," he said, then cast a glance to his mother.

"*Really*, Max," Emily said in an amused tone. "Why are you acting so strangely?"

He opened the door, and I called out, "Would you refrain from telling Marco that I'm up here?" If he knew I was alone with Emily, I suspected he'd barge in.

"Uh..." He glanced back to his mother again.

"And also keep this from your father," Emily added. "Basically, this is all a big secret. Can you keep it?"

He shot her a dark glare. "Haven't I already?" Then he stormed out, slamming the door behind him.

"Don't mind Max," she said, making a dismissive wave with one hand. "He's a bit out of sorts after the conversation we were having before you appeared." A smile lifted her lips. "Which was quite fortuitous." Her brow lifted. "Or was it?"

"If you're implying that I was spying, you couldn't be more wrong. I thought Max had brought a date upstairs. I had no idea it was you."

"Well then, lucky me." She gestured to the chair next to the sofa. "Come have a seat. I'm straining my neck to look up at you."

I moved over to the chair and sat down. "Why did you call me Caroline?"

She laughed. "Please. Don't insult my intelligence. Bart's known your secret practically since you came to town. Of course I know it too. And I'm certain Wyatt does as well. Whenever I bring up questions about your past, he gets cagey and changes the topic. But Max..." She released a sigh. "He has a tendency to be short-sighted. I get the impression he knows you're not who you say you are, but he doesn't seem to care about the truth." She tilted her head as she studied me. "You should go back to being a blonde. It suits you better."

"Beauty tips aside, does any of this have a point?"

"I think perhaps we have a common quest, and it might be to our advantage to pool our resources."

My heart began to race. "I'm listening."

A slow smile lifted her lips, and the triumphant look in her eyes suggested she thought she'd already swayed me. "You've been asking questions about poor Pam Crimshaw, but perhaps you're looking in the wrong direction?" She lifted her voice at the end.

Did she know I was looking for information to tie Pam's case to one of Bart's favors? Was she looking to bring him down?

I hesitated. "I take it you have a suggestion?"

"Perhaps…"

"You're insinuating that you know what I'm up to," I said. "What is your interest in this?"

She laughed. "Carly, the last time we met, I told you I'd been looking for an exit strategy. Perhaps you and I can work together."

I considered her suggestion. Did she really want to put her husband away? Or was she using me to feed information back to her husband? "That would mean I'd have to trust you," I said.

She tilted her head. "Yes, but I would have to trust you as well."

"How do you figure?"

"What I'm about to tell you…only two people know. If Bart finds out that *you* know…let's just say it would be to my detriment."

"He wouldn't presume the other person had told me?"

"The other person doesn't like to discuss…business."

Who would she be talking about?

"Why would you trust *me*?" I countered.

She laughed. "Your true colors show through, my girl, which isn't necessarily to your advantage. But it is to *mine*." Pausing, she shifted her weight on the sofa. "I know my husband has threatened you to keep you in line. I also know you're not the kind of woman to take that lying down."

She watched me, waiting for a response, and when I didn't answer, she said, "Exposing my husband would benefit us both.

Bart would no longer have control over you, but he would also no longer have control over me. It's a win for both of us."

"Obviously you want me to do the dirty work," I said.

"Let's just say the other party doesn't care for me much, but I understand *you've* garnered favor with him. Perhaps he'll be more willing to accommodate you." Her lips lifted into a tight smile. "Taking care of Bart will benefit him as well."

"So why hasn't he done it himself already?"

"It can't come directly from him either, but I suspect he'd trust you to handle it."

Was she talking about Bingham? He would benefit from Bart's downfall and likely revel in it, but I couldn't imagine he would have failed to act if he had incriminating information on Bart.

"So I go to this person," I said, "and convince them to tell me what they know?" I shook my head. "I don't even know what this is about."

"I told you that you were looking in the wrong direction. You're looking at recent history, but you need to look deeper into the past."

I frowned. "I don't have any idea what Pam could have done in the past."

"Again," she said. "Wrong direction."

"Pam doesn't have anything to do with this?"

"She killed a man, didn't she?"

"But she was coerced?" I asked.

She smiled again. "But by whom?"

Was she insinuating that Pam hadn't asked for the favor? If not Pam, then who? Was her husband behind this after all?

"You need to look at Rob Crimshaw," she confirmed. "As well as his brother and his father."

"His brother disappeared, and his father died in prison."

She looked pleased. "And Rob Crimshaw is scot free. Do you know why his father was in prison?"

"Drug possession with intent to sell."

"You need to look at the source of those drugs," she said. "He has the answers."

Oh, God. Please don't let it be Hank. "And who would that be?"

"You're a smart girl. You tell me."

"Todd Bingham."

She nodded and my relief was palpable. "Tell him to give you what you need, and I'll give him what he wants in return."

"He'll know what I'm talking about?"

"He will. He'll be eager to talk."

"Why not approach him yourself? He's outside right now. It would be easy to arrange."

"He won't talk to me, plus it would be unseemly. I needed a go-between, and you're perfect."

"So you're using me?" I asked dryly.

"Don't pretend like you're getting nothing out of this," she scolded. "All three of us win."

I pushed out a breath. She was right, but I still didn't trust her.

"One more thing," she said. "You can't tell anyone about our deal. Not my sons and especially not Marco."

My back stiffened. "I don't keep secrets from Marco."

"Don't be deluded," she groused. "Everyone keeps secrets from the ones they love."

That pissed me off. "Not all of us have warped relationships like you do with your husband."

"There you go with your delusions of love." She gave me a sideways wave. "You may leave now but send Max back. He and I still have unfinished business."

I stared at her in disbelief. She thought she could just dismiss me? "Speaking of your husband, where is he?"

"He got called away to the construction site, which gave me more time to spend with Max." She gave me a shrewd look. "So no, he won't know that we talked."

I had other questions, but I didn't want risk Bart coming back and seeing me with his wife. He was already suspicious of me. I didn't need to give him any more fodder.

"You're certain this will bring him down?" I asked as I stood.

"I guess you'll need to see for yourself."

I certainly planned to.

Chapter
Twenty-Seven

Marco was helping Max change the keg when I went back outside. I was torn between telling him what had just happened, Emily be damned, and finding Bingham and pinning him down for a private conversation.

The worried look in Max's eyes sent me straight toward the two guys.

"Thanks for lookin' for those cups," he said as I approached. "I take it from the fact you're empty handed that you didn't find them?"

All of the plastic cups were outside, so I recognized we were talking around my visit with his mother rather than bringing it out in the open. "Yeah, sorry. You might want to go look yourself."

"We should be fine since people are bringin' their cups back up for refills," he said as he finished changing the keg. He stood and looked me in the eyes. "I hope you didn't go to too much trouble."

"Everything's just fine."

He held my gaze a moment longer. "If you ever get a request or order you don't want to fill, then let me know, okay? I'll find a way to get you out of it."

His sincerity and concern were overwhelming. I wrapped my arms around his neck and hugged him tight. "You too, okay?"

He hugged me back, and we stayed like that for a long second before he released me. "We should probably talk soon."

I nodded.

He went back inside, and I turned back to Marco, who was watching me with narrowed eyes.

"I'm reading a whole lot of hidden context there."

"I'll tell you about it later," I said. "In fact, we should probably leave soon to discuss it, but first I need to talk to Bingham. Have you seen him lately?"

"Why do you need to speak to Bingham?"

"That's what I need to tell you about later." I scanned the crowd. "I don't see him."

"I haven't seen him for a while, but I'll be honest—I haven't been lookin'. Come to think of it, I haven't seen Bart or Emily either."

"I have it on good authority that Bart got called away to the construction site."

"But not Emily?" he asked with a lifted brow.

I knew he was a smart man. "I'm going to make a pass around the lot to see if he's here."

"Should I come with you?"

I hesitated, but if it had been dangerous for him to accompany me to Jonathon Whitmore's house, it was much more so for him to be seen with me and Bingham. "No. It's probably better if you don't."

"Carly..."

I walked over and gave him a kiss. "It's okay. I promise."

"Okay."

As I made my way around the crowd, I didn't see him or Lula anywhere, but Greta and her boyfriend were dancing. The song ended, so I walked over and tapped her on the shoulder.

"Carly!" she said enthusiastically. "Sorry we missed you this afternoon, but I guess I see why."

"Max outdid himself," I said.

"I'm sure you had something to do with it."

"Less than you might think." I glanced to the side. "Say, have you seen Lula? I saw her earlier and wanted to say hi and ask about the baby, but I don't see her anywhere.'"

She laughed. "Todd took her home. She was nervous about leaving Beatrice so long."

"Oh," I said with a sigh.

The music picked back up and Greta shouted, "I think Todd had a special night planned for her." She winked. "I can't wait to hear about it tomorrow."

Which meant going to see him tonight was out of the question.

"See you later," she called out as her boyfriend spun her around.

My earlier joyfulness had faded, but I was eager to tell Marco what had just happened. On my way over to him, I saw Hank sitting to the side of the crowd, talking to a couple of older men. He saw me and smiled, then motioned for me to go on my way.

I was thrilled he was having fun, and I hoped this would inspire him to get out more. His accessibly fitted car would help.

When I reached Marco, I pressed myself to his side, wrapping my arms around his waist as I leaned into him.

His arm curled around my back and he pressed a kiss to the top of my head. "I could get used to this."

"Me too."

"I take it you couldn't find Bingham."

"No, and Greta said that he had a romantic night planned for Lula, so I don't think it's a good idea to interrupt that."

"It's close to ten. You really would have gone by Bingham's if not for their plans? Now I really want to know what happened inside."

I glanced up at him. "I'll tell you. I promise." Because the last person I was going to take relationship advice from was Emily Drummond.

He tugged me closer but released me as a customer approached.

We refilled more cups and handed out soft drinks and water. The cash box was overflowing, and I once again thought Max was more brilliant than he let on. We'd probably made a good deal more money than we would have on a regular night, and he'd provided a much-needed fun evening for the town.

But I was starting to worry about him. Max had a bad habit of getting blind drunk when he was upset, and his mother had been up there with him for a long time. It didn't bode well. A half hour later, he still hadn't come back, and I was desperate enough consider going up to press my ear to the door. Before I could decide, I saw Bart approaching our drink stand, wearing his smug grin.

"Marco. Carly," he said jovially. "I see that congratulations are in order."

Marco ignored his comment. "What can I get for you? The options are pretty limited."

"I'll take a beer," he said, reaching for his wallet.

"I hear construction's going well," Marco said, sounding like he was chatting with a friend as he started to fill an empty cup.

"It was until today," Bart said with a laugh. "But the power should be restored by late tomorrow morning." He looked up at the lights strung overhead. "Looks like Max has adapted."

"You know Max," Marco said with a hint of bite. "He's good at taking bitter lemons and making lemonade."

"You still won't let that go, will you?" Bart asked with a laugh. "Max's place was here."

I realized they were talking about Bart calling Max home after Wyatt quit running the bar.

"Max's place was anywhere but here until Wyatt threw it all away," Marco countered, his voice hard. "But then, we'll never agree on that topic. I was merely pointing out how adaptable your son is."

"Yes, he gets that from his mother," he said with a tight smile.

Marco handed him the cup.

Bart held out a twenty-dollar bill. "Keep the change." He turned his attention to me. "Cat got your tongue, Caroline? You're usually so chatty."

My blood ran cold as he turned to gauge Marco's reaction.

He smiled. "Ah...I'm not surprised Marco knows, but be careful, little one. The more people you tell, the more danger you're in." Then he turned around and walked away, walking up to a couple and enthusiastically shaking the husband's hand.

"That was a threat, Carly," Marco said under his breath.

"I know."

My stomach churned, but I didn't dare run away and let Bart know he'd affected me. Instead, I smiled and greeted a little girl who'd come up to get a Coke.

Five minutes later, Max finally emerged from the back door, looking more exhausted than I'd ever seen him. He came over to the table and plastered on a smile. "Thanks for covering for so long. You two are officially off duty."

"Yeah, I've already heard that a couple of times tonight," I said with a forced smile of my own. "Everything go okay with those cups?"

His eye twitched. "Yep." He walked behind the table. "Now go. Hank's here, and you've been stuck behind the table."

"I already checked on him. He's chatting with a couple of guys, and he shooed me away."

He laughed, but it sounded strained. "Sounds like him. Don't worry about taking him home. I'm sure Wyatt will do it."

"I haven't seen Wyatt since he showed up with Hank. I'm not sure he's still here."

"He'll be back."

Marco took my hand. "I'm going to dance with my girlfriend, and we'll sort out how Hank's going to get home later."

He tugged me around the table toward the dancers, then leaned into my ear. "I'd love nothing more than to leave, but Bart's here and watching. I don't want him to think he has that kind of power over you."

"I know. I agree. Let's stay for a bit before we go."

The band finished an upbeat song, then started a slow one. Marco tugged me to his chest and linked his hands at the small of my back and began to sway. I wrapped my arms around the back of his neck and stared up into his troubled eyes.

"How worried should I be?" he asked so quietly I was sure I was the only one who could hear.

"About which part?" I asked, tipping one corner of my mouth into a smile. "Bart or my chat with his wife?"

His eyes widened, then he cursed under his breath. "Where?"

"In Max's apartment. I was looking for him to ask him about the keg. His mother was inside, and she sent him out and insisted I stay."

He watched me intently.

"She knows my name, Marco."

His face paled. "Did Bart tell her?"

"I don't know," I said. "But she insinuated that he either doesn't keep secrets from her or isn't able to."

He lifted a hand to cup my cheek, and his voice shook. "It's time for you to go."

I stopped in place. "What?"

He turned to the side, pulling me with him so we were still dancing. "I never thought I'd say these words, but Bart's right. It's getting too dangerous for you here."

"I'm not ready to go yet."

He shook his head. "We'll figure out where to send you. I have money I can—"

I put my finger on his lips. "Marco. Stop. I need to talk to Bingham. She said he has what we need."

His eyes narrowed. "If he had something, trust me, he'd have already used it."

I couldn't help thinking he was right, but what was I to make of the barter situation she'd set up? Even if it was a bust, I needed to talk to Bingham, and I wanted to see his reaction when I told him about Emily's request. "We can't talk about it here. We need to wait until we get home."

He smiled softly, but his eyes looked sad. "You called my place home."

Despite my fear and my anxiety, I teased, "How do you know I wasn't talking about Hank's?"

"You meant my house. And I can't wait to take you *home*."

Chapter
Twenty-Eight

Hank wasn't ready to leave and insisted that Wyatt would be back to give him a ride. Then he told me that if he saw me before noon, he'd lock me out of the house. I laughed and reluctantly left him with his friends.

Marco wanted to drive me home in his Explorer, but I planned on going to Hank's first thing in the morning, and it would be easier if I had my own car.

We left the lights and music, and after Marco walked me to my car, I drove him to his Explorer. He followed me to his house. He got out of his car first and took my overnight bag as we walked inside.

I knew he wanted to take me to his room, but he was too worried about what had happened with Emily. So instead, he led me to the sofa and settled in next to me. "Tell me what happened. In detail."

I told him everything, including Emily warning me not to tell him.

"You told me anyway," he said carefully.

"Of course I did. I don't want there to be any secrets between us." I took a breath. "Since she mentioned Rob and his family, there's something else I need to tell you. Something I've been struggling with." I drew a shaky breath. "No secrets."

He grabbed my hand and squeezed.

"I'm worried Hank knows something he isn't saying about the Crimshaws. Seems like he would have known about Stewart's drug arrest, plus he didn't say anything about Ricky and Seth being so close. There's something he's not telling me. What if he was involved in something shady?"

He gave me a tight smile. "We already know he was involved in something shady."

"I mean *really* shady," I said, knowing it didn't make any sense. The fact was I didn't even know what I was afraid of, only that I sensed something off.

"What's your line, Carly?" Marco asked. "The line that Hank has to cross for you to turn your back on him?"

I swallowed a lump in my throat. "I don't know, Marco. I love him. He was there for me when no one else was. He's like the father I always wanted, and I know he would do anything for me." He killed a man to protect me back when he barely knew me. He'd offered to help me take on my father. I couldn't turn my back on him.

"I know, and I'm here to tell you that Hank's a different man than he was when I was growing up. He was hard back then. Ruthless. His hard edges have softened, but does that change what he did in the past? Does that mean he should be forgiven?"

Tears stung my eyes. "I don't know."

He pulled me into a hug. "I don't pretend to have any answers, and you don't have to make any decisions tonight…but you may have to decide it soon."

"I know."

He released me and leaned back. "So let's hypothesize why Emily wants you to talk to Bingham about Rob Crimshaw's father. Or even Rob himself. I suspect the elder Crimshaw was runnin' drugs for Bingham, but you need to be prepared for the possibility he might have been running for Hank."

"I know."

Marco made a face. "I agree that you should talk to Bingham, but don't get your hopes up too high. If we're to believe Emily's insinuation, Bingham has something to help bring down Bart, but he hasn't used it before because it wasn't worth his time?" He shook his head. "I struggle to believe that."

"Yeah, me too."

"Maybe you shouldn't chase this lead at all." When I glanced up at him in surprise, he said, "I meant what I said earlier. Maybe we cut our losses and figure out where you should go."

"Leave town," I said dryly.

"Carly, Emily knows your real name."

"Only my first name." It was a pipe dream to believe she didn't know my real identity. Especially after her statement about me being a blonde.

He cocked his head and gave me a look that said he knew I wasn't that dense. "We both know she found out who you are. And Bart was casually throwing your name around."

"Emily called me Caroline in front of Max."

Marco got to his feet, torment on his face. "Shit, Carly. How many people know now? Wyatt. Max. Me. Hank. Bart. Emily. That's four people too many."

"I know."

Agony filled his eyes. "You can't stay. I'll figure out a place for you to go."

He'd said it like that earlier too. He wasn't talking about going somewhere together. Had Wyatt been right? But Marco couldn't just run away. He was a sheriff's deputy, and if he went missing, people would go looking for him. Still, the thought of running again and leaving the people I cared about behind...I wasn't sure I could do it.

I got to my feet and walked in front of him, stopping his nervous pacing. "I'm not leaving you, Marco, and I'm not leaving Hank. Not like this."

"What if Bart's already told your father? What if they have someone watching you? We can't risk it."

"We're so close," I said, resting my hands on his firm chest. I suddenly itched to remove the cloth covering his muscles. "So freaking close to bringing Bart down. I can't stop now. I won't."

"I'm ninety-nine percent certain Pam didn't murder a man for Bart. And we both acknowledged Emily might be sendin' you on a wild goose chase." He looked tortured. "We're not close to bringin' him down *at all*. If anything, we've made him more dangerous."

"When I met Emily before, she made it apparent that she and her husband aren't partners. And she said she wants to bring him down. *That* is progress, Marco."

"Unless she's settin' you up." His hand swept over my cheek as he searched my face. "I don't want to lose you."

If he sent me away, he'd lose me anyway. Run and hide alone or take my chances here and then hopefully move on to deal with my father. If I left, I'd be starting from scratch with little money and no friends.

No. I'd stay and take my chances.

I gave him a soft smile, then moved my hand to the top fastened button of his shirt and worked it free.

"This isn't settled, Carly."

I undid a second button, revealing a good portion of his chest. "And it's not getting settled tonight unless you were planning on packing me a bag and sending me off before sunrise."

The look in his eyes suggested he'd been considering it.

"No more talk of running tonight," I said. "I'd rather see you naked."

"Just see me naked?" he asked with a teasing glint. "Nothing else?"

"The naked part comes first. The rest comes after. Which means you have to get naked to find out what happens next."

His gaze landed on my collarbone at the edge of my dress. He placed a kiss there as he pushed the top of my sleeve over my shoulder.

I quickly unfastened the rest of his buttons and tugged his shirt free from his jeans.

We didn't talk after that. He swept me into his room, and we made love with an intensity unmatched by our previous encounters. No man had ever made me feel a tenth of what I experienced with Marco.

Afterward, I lay in his arms, my leg draped over his as his hand trailed up my arm.

"I know you don't want to talk about this," he said softly, "but I care about you too much to ignore that you're in danger." His hand stilled. "Have you given any thought to where you might go?"

"You mean if I run away?"

He placed a finger under my chin and tilted my face up to look at him. "It might not be all bad. You ended up here…" He grinned. "It's gotta get better than Drum."

I didn't smile back. "I don't know if I can do it again. I don't want to be alone."

"I'll follow you, Carly. I'd just have to wrap up some things here."

I slowly shook my head as a tear slipped down my cheek. "And by that you mean you'd have to sell your house and resign from your job. If you did those things, Bart and anyone else would know you were coming to me. They'd follow you."

"Then I'll run with you. I'll leave it all behind."

"You can't, Marco. The state police would come looking for you. A deputy who's been helping root out corruption in his department? They'd suspect foul play, and your face would be all over the news. You'd be more recognizable than I am."

His arms tightened around me. "I won't lose you, Carly."

"Which means I'm staying," I said with a wavering smile. "Because I'm not losing you either."

It killed me to realize Wyatt hadn't totally gotten it wrong. Marco wanted to go with me...he just couldn't. I'd been deluded to think that he could. And as much as I'd insisted that I wouldn't run, when it came down to it, I'd go if left with no other choice. Marco and Hank would defend me, possibly to their deaths. I couldn't live with the guilt if that happened, which meant I needed to be prepared for the worst. I needed to figure out where and how to get a new identity.

If or when I did leave, I would be leaving everything and everyone behind.

Including Marco.

Chapter
Twenty-Nine

Marco didn't have to go into work until ten, so we had a lazy morning in bed. After we made love, he made me breakfast. I wore one of his T-shirts and my underwear and he kept sneaking glances at my bare legs as I leaned my back into the counter opposite him and watched.

"I have tomorrow off," he said as he scrambled some eggs. He was wearing a T-shirt and a pair of athletic shorts that showed off his butt, and my gaze kept straying there since his back was to me. "What time do you start work?"

"Five, but I guess it depends on whether Ruth's friend takes Molly's shift. If not, I might need to go in at noon."

He turned slightly to face me and grinned. "Are you checking out my ass?"

A sly smile lifted the corners of my lips. "Maybe."

His grin widened as he turned his attention back to the skillet. "Jim Palmer's funeral is tomorrow."

I frowned, momentarily forgetting about my view. "Do we care about that right now?"

"Yeah. We do," he said, shooting me a quick glance over his shoulder before he turned back to the eggs. "We don't know if you're going to get anything good from Bingham. For all we know, Emily's trying to throw you off. Maybe you're getting too close with Ashlynn or Thad, and she's protecting Bart."

He had a good point. "What time's the funeral?"

"One. So you could go before your shift."

"I didn't even know the man. Isn't it going to look weird?"

He shook his head. "There's gonna be so many people there no one will even notice."

"Do you really think we'll learn anything?"

"There's only one way to find out."

"Okay," I said wryly. "I'll be your date to the funeral."

He shot me a mischievous grin. "Look at me showin' you a good time."

I wasn't exactly feeling light-hearted, but I laughed anyway.

"How do you plan on approaching Bingham?" he asked.

"I guess I'll just drop by. It's worked for me before."

His mouth tugged down, but he didn't say anything, likely because Todd Bingham and I had an odd relationship, made even more so by the fact that he didn't usually tolerate people asking questions and I was known for being inquisitive. But I'd helped him find Lula when she'd gone missing, and I hadn't used up his limited allotment of gratitude.

He turned off the burner and started scooping eggs onto our plates next to the stove. "While I want to go with you, I think he'll be more likely to talk to you without me."

"I agree," I said. "I don't feel unsafe. I doubt he would hurt me and risk Lula's wrath. I am one of their baby's godmothers, after all."

He laughed, but it held a bit of bitterness. "Like that would matter."

"Strangely enough, I think it does."

We finished breakfast, talking about our schedules for the weekend. I would stay with Marco again tonight, then I'd go to Hank's on Saturday night and spend all day Sunday with him.

We started cleaning up the kitchen together, but I glanced at the clock and sent him for a quick shower and to get dressed so he wouldn't be late for work.

I'd finished by the time he emerged from his room in his uniform. Smiling softly, I walked to him and wrapped my arm around his neck, hating that we had to go back into the world.

"I really want to take time off like we were talking about. What do you say we plan on going away in two weeks?" he said. "We can both take off work on Friday and the weekend. If we head out on Thursday night, we'll have three full days together."

"Okay." But I wondered if it was a pipe dream. Would I be gone by then?

He gave me a deep, soulful kiss, and I suspected he was wondering the same thing.

"Call me today," he said. "Especially after you talk to Bingham and the Genslers."

"I'll see about heading to Ewing today. Maybe we can meet up."

He nodded. "You gonna stay here much longer?"

"I'm going to take advantage of your shower before I go," I said with a grin. "It's nicer than Hank's."

"Stay as long as you like," he said. "I like knowin' you're here, even when I'm not." He started to say something, then stopped. "I'll see you later."

"I love you, Marco." Maybe I'd been saying it too much, but it felt good to say it, and I didn't know how much longer I'd be able to tell him in person.

"Love you too." He gave me another kiss, and I walked him to the door and waved as he drove away. I headed to the bathroom and took a long shower, trying not to dwell on the uncertainty of our future.

I turned off the water and wrapped a towel around myself to dry off when I heard a noise in the front part of the house. Had Marco come back? But something told me it wasn't him.

My clothes were in the bedroom, but Marco kept his shotgun in the closet attached to the bathroom. I rushed into the closet and threw on one of his button-down shirts, my shaking fingers fumbling with three of the middle buttons. I pulled the gun down from his top shelf and quickly loaded it with three shells and dumped several more into my shirt pocket.

Tiptoeing back into the bathroom, I paused by the door and listened to the silence. Had I imagined it? No. I could smell cigarette smoke.

It definitely wasn't Marco.

I eased into the bedroom and paused again, the shotgun pointed toward the ceiling, when I heard a soft clang from the front of the house.

"Who's there?" I called out, wondering if that was wise, but Marco's only phone was in the kitchen and it would likely take a sheriff's deputy a lot longer to get here than I had time to deal with the intruder.

The person didn't answer, so I leveled the gun tip to point toward the living room and went out to confront them.

"Who's there?" I called again in a harsher tone.

"I'm not gonna hurt you," a man said with a short laugh. "You can come on out. I'm only here to give you a message."

His voice was coming from the kitchen and dining area, so I eased around the corner and saw a man I didn't recognize. He'd made himself at home, tapping his cigarette ashes onto one of Marco's plates while he sipped coffee from a mug. His hair was long and needed a trim, and his face was scruffy. He looked like he was in his forties, and most of those years had been a challenge.

"What do you want?" I asked pointing the gun at his chest.

"You know how to use that thing, little girl?" he asked as his eyes danced with amusement.

"Trust me, I do. Now what do you want?"

"I told you, I have a message." His gaze drifted down to my bare legs sticking out of Marco's shirt, which hit mid-thigh, as he took a drag from his cigarette. "Something sure smells good. You make your man some breakfast before he left? Want to whip some up for me?"

As if. "I'm going to ask you one more time, what do you want?"

His face turned hard. "You need to let this go, little girl."

"I'm afraid you need to be more specific."

He cocked his head and narrowed his eyes. "I think it's pretty clear."

"And if I don't?"

He stubbed the cigarette out on Marco's tabletop, then left it mashed on the wood. "You may have noticed there are a whole lot of accidents around these parts." He gave me a tight grin. "I'd hate to see something happen to someone you care about."

I swallowed my fear and thrust out my hip, hating that his lecherous gaze followed the movement. "You think you can scare me? You've just wasted your time, so go back to whatever lowlife sent you and tell them I'm my own woman and I'll do whatever I damn well please."

He rolled his shoulders in a lazy shrug as he set the mug down and scooted his chair back. "Your funeral." He started around the table toward the front door. "Naw, the funerals will be for the people you care about." He grinned. "I bet you look damn sexy in black. I might just off one of 'em myself to see those legs again."

Standing in place, I kept the gun tip on him as he reached for the door. "Who sent you?"

"That part's not important," he said. "The important part is that you listen." He tapped his temple with his fingertip, then opened the front door and strode down the steps toward an older black pickup truck parked on the street at the end of the long drive.

I stood on the porch with Marco's gun, watching as he got into his truck and drove away.

I tried to read the license plate, but the distance was too great and it was smeared with mud. Part of me wanted to grab my keys and follow him, but one, I wasn't wearing any underwear. Two, he had a head start on me. And three, if he realized I was following him, he might make me sorry I'd found him.

Instead, I went back inside and locked the door (which was pointless since I'd locked it before), set the gun on the table, and called Marco.

I wasn't surprised when I got his voicemail. I left him a message, trying to sound calm so I didn't freak him out.

"Marco. I'm still at your house, and I need you to call me as soon as you get this message. Just call me." Then I added, "Please, please, please be careful."

I hung up and immediately called Hank. It took him about ten rings to get to the phone, and he wasn't happy when he answered. "What?" he barked, sounding out of breath.

"Hank, it's me."

He must have heard the panic in my voice because his tone changed. "What's wrong? Is Marco okay?"

"Yeah, uh…" My adrenaline crashed and my body began to shake.

"Carly?"

"He's okay," I said, my voice breaking. I needed to get myself together. "I'm sorry. I'm okay. He's okay."

"Take a breath, girlie," he said, his tone softening further. "Are you in danger?"

"No, not at the moment. But a man showed up and threatened to kill the people I love. You have to be careful, Hank. Get your gun and keep it with you."

"First of all, who was he?"

"I don't know. I didn't recognize him. He said he was giving me a message. That I needed to let it go."

"Let what go?"

"I'm not sure." But I knew. If Emily had figured out what I was up to, then Bart had to know too.

"This must be connected to you lookin' into Pam's murder. Where's Marco?"

"He left for work. I took a shower, and when I got out, the guy was sitting at Marco's kitchen table, drinking his coffee and smoking a cigarette."

"He was in *the house*?" Hank sounded murderous.

"The door was locked, but he got in somehow."

"And he's gone now?"

"Yeah. But he might be coming after you. I told him I wasn't backing down, so he might try to hurt you to teach me a lesson."

He released a chuckle. "You think someone's comin' after me? Girlie, you need to worry about *you*. You've seen what I do to people who dare to threaten me or mine."

I couldn't help smiling a bit. "Be careful anyway, okay?"

"Of course."

The phone beeped with an incoming call. "Hank, I think Marco's calling me. I'll be home soon."

"You be safe too."

"I will." I hung up and answered. "Hello?"

"Carly," Marco said. "What's goin' on?"

"It's important for you to know I'm okay."

"Now I'm really worried. What happened?"

"Someone broke in after you left."

"Into the *house*? Where were you?" He sounded furious, but I knew he wasn't angry with me.

"In the shower."

He was quiet for a moment. "Oh my God, Carly. Did he...?"

"No," I said. "He didn't come into the bathroom, but he was waiting for me when I got out."

"*Carly.*"

"I'm okay. He didn't even come near me. After I got out of the shower, I heard a noise and knew it wasn't you, so I loaded your shotgun and went out to greet him. He was sitting at the kitchen table smoking a cigarette and drinking coffee."

"You should have crawled out the back window." He cursed under his breath. "I knew I should have put a phone line in the bedroom."

"I'm fine. He told me he had a message. That I needed to let it go, although he didn't say what *it* was or who sent him."

"It was Bart."

"That's my thought too."

"What was the threat?" Marco asked.

"He mentioned there are lots of accidents around here, and the people I love might be in danger."

"If you don't let it go?"

"Yes."

Marco was quiet for a moment. "Definitely Bart. I take it you didn't recognize the guy?"

"No, but he drove an older black truck and his license plate was covered in mud." I took a breath. "I don't know how he got in, Marco. I locked the front door. I don't see any broken windows."

"I'm getting an alarm system, but first I'm coming home."

"Unless you're coming home to take fingerprints or try to get DNA from the cigarette butt he stubbed out on your table, there's no point. I'm going home to get dressed, then I have to go to Spencer Gensler's tutoring appointment."

"Maybe you should cancel that."

"Not a chance. If I do, Bart wins." I couldn't let that happen, no matter how afraid I was for Hank and Marco. Because someone needed to take a stand against Bart, and we were close…we had to be if he was reacting like this. I stared at the burn mark on the table. "I'm sorry I let him burn your table. Maybe we can sand it out."

"I don't care about the damn table, Carly. I care about *you*," he said, sounding frustrated, but I recognized it for what it was. He was afraid for me.

"I'm okay."

"He was there while you were *in the shower*, Carly. He could have…"

"He didn't. I'm okay."

"You have to leave Drum," he said, his voice strangled. "It's not safe for you."

"It's not safe for *you* and Hank. I'm fine."

"For *now*." He was quiet for a moment. "I think I should come home."

"Are you going to file a police report?"

He hesitated. "No. I'm scared to draw any more attention to you."

"You can come home, but I'm going to the Genslers' place because whether I'm trying to wheedle information out of them or not, there's a boy who's flunking summer school and needs help."

"I'm scared," he said in frustration. "I'm a damn deputy sheriff, and I don't know how to protect you."

"I'm scared too, but for the record, I think not filing a report is a good decision. And to help put both of our minds at ease, I'll get my gun when I go home to change, okay?"

"Okay," he said. "Keep checking in with me, all right?"

"Yeah." Partly because I wanted regular assurance that *he* was okay. I had to find a way to protect him and Hank. Information was the best way to do that. As soon as I was done with Spencer, I was heading straight to Bingham.

Chapter Thirty

When I got home, Hank was sitting on his front porch with his shotgun propped against the house, Smoky lying in his lap. He assured me no one had shown up and that his concern was for me, not himself.

I kissed his cheek and told him that he didn't need to worry: I wouldn't be going anywhere without my handgun. I went inside and changed clothes, putting on another dress I'd gotten on my last visit to Target. Letty sat on the bed, watching me, so I scooped her up and took her with me into the bathroom while I put on some makeup. She batted at the toilet paper roll while I got ready, then raced off to places unknown. When I finished, I repacked my bag, bringing a change of clothes and my gun, and headed out the door.

I barely made it on time for my appointment with the Genslers, and I spent the next hour working with their son, splitting our time between English and social studies. It didn't take long for me to realize the boy was in serious trouble. I assured his parents I could help him, but one hour a week wasn't going to cut it, so I agreed to tutor him every Friday morning at their house for twenty dollars an hour, and for free an hour before Wednesday's Tutoring Club.

I left without getting a chance to ask about the accident, but it would have been awkward to shoehorn questions into our first lesson, and I genuinely wanted to help him. If I didn't get useful information from Bingham, then I'd try to quiz Spencer at our tutoring session next week.

As soon as I left, I headed back through town toward Bingham's, pleased to see the electricity had come back on.

When I reached his property, I pulled up to the house outside the fenced salvage yard. On my first visit last December, it had looked neglected and timeworn, but each time I came out, it was in better shape. It had a fresh paint job and was sparkling white with black shutters. There was even a nice wicker furniture set on the front porch.

I got out and walked up to the front door, smiling when I saw the ceiling of the porch had been painted haint blue.

Lula opened the door just before I could knock, her face beaming. "Carly! I'm so sorry I missed you yesterday afternoon. Greta and I painted each other's nails." She held up her hand to show me her bright pink manicure.

"I really wanted to come, but Max put me to work setting up the street party. I didn't get a chance to say hi to you and Todd last night."

She waggled her eyebrows. "You were too busy makin' googly eyes at Marco." She reached out and patted my arm. "Good for you, girl. Lots of women have tried to tie him down. I'm not surprised you were the one to do it."

"Why?" I asked, caught off guard.

"Because you're special, Carly Moore," she said with a laugh. "I knew it the first night I met you, when you drove me home. Greta's workin' today, but we can hang if you want."

I glanced toward the junkyard. "While I would love to take you up on that, I'm actually here to talk to Todd. Is he around?"

She made a face. "He had to run to Chattanooga. He won't be back until later tonight."

I tried to hide my disappointment. "I need to talk to him about something important. Can you tell him when he gets back? The sooner the better."

"You want to talk to him *tonight*?" she asked in surprise.

I would have waited until tomorrow, but this morning's intruder had made our need to have a discussion much more pressing. "Yeah. Tonight. Tell him it's about a common goal."

Her eyes narrowed. "Are you in trouble, Carly?"

"Nah," I said. "I'm fine, but it *is* important. Tell him I'm working at the tavern, so he can get ahold of me there to coordinate when and where we talk."

"Okay," she said, looking worried.

"I don't suppose my god-daughter's awake, is she?"

"I'm sorry. I just got her down for her nap about twenty minutes ago. I'd have kept her up if I'd known you were comin'."

"No worries," I said. "I'll try to come back next week."

Her eyes brightened. "Maybe we can meet for lunch at Watson's. I want to hear more about how you and Marco finally hooked up."

"And *I* want to hear more about you and Todd searchin' your family tree."

Her brow shot up. "You know about that?"

"Carnita told me. She said you'd traced Todd's family back to the 1800s."

She smiled. "Todd is more into it than I am. Maybe you should ask him when you talk to him."

"Yeah. Maybe I will." I lifted my hand. "I'll let you get back to your free time while Bea sleeps. I'm off next Wednesday if that works for you for lunch. I'll be free until my tutoring session at two-thirty."

A smile lit up her eyes. "Perfect! Meet you there at noon?"

"Deal."

I left and headed toward the highway. I didn't need to be at work until five, and I wasn't sure what to do next. I had plenty of housework at home to keep me occupied for the next few hours, but it wouldn't feel right to just go home. Something had been weighing on me since our visit to Jonathon Whitmore's house. I was worried about Ashlynn. I felt like I was part of the reason why she'd run off and lost her job, and I wanted to make sure she was okay.

I turned toward town and headed to the Crimshaw property. The beat-up pickup was there, but the car I'd seen before was gone. I parked in the driveway, then got out to walk over to the trailer.

"She ain't home," a voice called out from the house, and I saw Thad standing in the doorway.

"Ashlynn still hasn't come back?" I asked.

"Nope. She won't be comin' back either. Dad kicked her out."

Was that why she'd been at Jonathon's place?

I walked toward him. "I heard that she and Chuck broke up."

"Yep. He ran off with Becca Sloan after he found out the baby wasn't his." He slowly swung his head. "Man, was he pissed. Dad was pissed too. He called Ashlynn a slut and told her she had three weeks to get the hell out of the trailer. Mom was upset and tried to get him to let her stay, but he told her no and beat the shit out of her."

I couldn't hide my shock, and the small triumph in his eyes told me that he'd hoped to shock me. I decided to take advantage of that. "Did he beat her often?"

"Often enough," he said, crossing his arms as he leaned against the door frame.

"Does he beat you too?"

His brow lifted like he thought I was stupid to ask something so obvious.

"What did he do to Ashlynn when he found out?"

"He tried to beat her too, but Mom stopped him. She was scared he'd hurt the baby." Disgust washed over his face. "He should have done it and killed her baby. Then that poor bastard wouldn't have to live in misery like the rest of us."

I sucked in a breath. "Thad, I can get help for you."

He released a bitter laugh. "Yeah, I tried that a couple of times and it bit me in the ass every time."

"I know a teacher reported abuse…"

"I got an extra beatin' for that," he sneered. "Several, actually."

"And the other time?"

Disgust filled his eyes. "Jim Palmer ain't the saint everyone made him out to be."

"I've gathered," I bluffed, hoping to keep him talking.

"I bet you don't know everything," he said defiantly. "I bet you don't know why my mom killed him."

Oh God. Did *he* know? Had Jim Palmer impregnated Ashlynn like we suspected?

"No," I said. "I don't. Honestly, I've been trying to figure it out. I think she was pressured into it, and if the truth comes out, it might help her get a reduced sentence."

He released a sharp bark of a laugh. "My dad will never let you tell anyone."

"Why not?"

He started to say something, then stopped.

"Why won't your dad help your mom?" I pressed.

"Because." He glanced down at his feet and licked his bottom lip. Then he lifted his gaze to mine, his eyes shiny with tears. "Because my dad will never admit that his son is gay."

I wasn't sure what to say, but he looked at me expectantly, so I asked, "Are you gay, Thad?"

"Maybe?" He shrugged. "I don't know."

"There's no shame in being gay," I assured him. "I don't know if Jim told you it was a sin—"

Thad burst out laughing.

I stared at him in confusion. "I know he was a youth leader. So if you talked to him about—"

He started laughing harder, but then it turned to sobs.

I climbed up the porch stairs and wrapped my arm around his back, then led him down to sit on the top step. He rested his forearms on his thighs and leaned forward, his body shaking with sobs.

"It's my fault she's in jail," he wailed. "It's all my fault."

"No, Thad," I said, rubbing his back lightly. "Your mother is a grown woman. She did this on her own. It's not your fault."

He continued to cry. "I should have died in that wreck. We were *supposed* to die."

I gasped and leaned forward to study his face. Did he just tell me that he and Spencer had tried to kill themselves? "Thad, did you and Spencer…" I stopped and started again. Better to work our way up to it. "Is Spencer gay too?"

He hesitated, then nodded, breaking into a fresh round of wails.

"There's nothing wrong with being gay, Thad."

His tear-streaked face lifted, and he shot me a glare. "Do you know anyone else around here who is gay?"

Now that he mentioned it, I didn't. Not openly, anyway.

"Yeah," he said in disgust before I could respond. "That's because no one comes out around here. We're supposed to be men, and being a man means fuckin' women." His glare made me think that he was trying to shock me again.

"Maybe around here," I said. "But not in a large part of the country. When you're older, you can leave and be true to yourself." This wasn't coming out right. "Screw that. You can be true to yourself now."

"And be called fag and queer at school?" he scoffed. "No thanks."

"And what about at home? Does your dad know?"

He didn't answer.

"Your mom knows, doesn't she? You said she tried to protect you."

Tears welled in his eyes and he nodded.

"Did she protect you from your dad?"

"She tried."

"Why did she kill Jim Palmer?"

"She found out."

"That you were gay?"

Except...why would she kill him over that?

And then it hit me.

Jim hadn't taken advantage of Ashlynn. He'd taken advantage of Thad. We'd gotten nearly everything wrong, from the very beginning.

"Thad," I said slowly, "you said you and Spencer were supposed to die in your accident. Did you two intend to kill yourselves?"

He was quiet for a moment before nodding.

"Does anyone know?"

His chin quivered as more tears fell down his cheeks. "Mom. I told her in the hospital, but Spencer didn't tell anyone. Mom said we needed to keep it a secret. I tried to tell her I was gay, but she wouldn't let me finish. A few days later, she told me that Jim Palmer was going to talk to me. To help me work through *my issues*. But we had to keep it a secret. Especially from my dad." Disgust twisted his lips. "He doesn't believe in talkin' about our *feelin's*."

They'd kept it a secret, which likely explained why Selena didn't know. "What did your mom tell him?"

"Just that I'd tried to hurt myself. That was all. But after we started talking, he kept pressing me to tell him why I did it. I didn't want to tell him, but after a few sessions, he guessed." He swallowed. "He told me that he could help me make my feelings for men go away. That he could help them run their course."

My chest felt like it was splitting in two. "Oh, Thad," I choked out.

"I told Mom that I didn't want to see him anymore, but Jim told her I wasn't fixed yet. And I couldn't tell her what he was doin'. But then three weeks ago, instead of waiting for me out in the parking lot, she showed up early to one of our sessions." His face reddened. "She wasn't one hundred percent sure of what she saw, so she turned around and walked out, but she didn't make me go back the next week."

"She didn't talk about it?" I asked, swiping a tear from my cheek.

He shook his head and stared out at the road. "No. Not until the night before she shot him."

"You told her what happened?"

He nodded and more tears streamed down his face. "I didn't tell her much. Just enough so she knew it wasn't right. She promised me that I'd never have to see him again. She was weird the next day, but she kept hugging me, telling me she was goin' to make it all okay. She said she'd left a note for me under my pillow and that Jim was never going to hurt me again." He blinked, and fresh tears fell down his face. "I haven't seen her since."

I grabbed his hand and squeezed it, overwhelmed with what he'd told me. I wasn't sure what to do with this information. Jim was already dead, so there would be no justice if Thad went to the police, and if the story got out, it might do Thad more harm than good. Still, if Jim had done this to Thad, he might have done it to other boys. Not only had he been a youth leader, but he'd coached many youth sports teams.

"Thad, I want you to talk to a friend of mine."

He snatched his hand from mine, his eyes flashing with fear, then anger. "I ain't talkin' to no one. I'm not even sure why I told you."

"He did something awful to you," I said. "You can't just keep this to yourself for the rest of your life. It will eat you from the inside out."

"I ain't talkin' to no more counselors. I already done that, and look how it turned out."

"Jim Palmer wasn't a counselor," I said. "He was a pedophile wrapped up in a nice shiny package. And if he did this to you, he's probably done it to others."

His anger faded.

"My friend is a sheriff's deputy. Just tell him what you told me and let him decide what to do."

"What if he thinks I need to go public?"

I pushed out a breath. "I don't know, Thad. I can't promise anything, but this secret is tearing you up. I can't let you fester in it."

"I want to talk to my mom," he said, sounding like a lost little boy instead of the defiant teenager he was trying to portray.

"Do you want me to take you to the jail to see her?"

"I don't know if I can get in. My dad won't take me."

"Can I use your phone?" I asked. "I need to make a call, and maybe I can find out."

He hesitated, then nodded, and I hurried in before he changed his mind. I found the phone hanging on the wall, and called Marco's cell.

"Detective Roland."

"Marco, it's me. I need to know if a minor can see a parent in jail without the other parent's permission."

"Well...depends on how old. Does one of the Crimshaw boys want to see their mother?"

"Yes, and it's important. Can he see her?"

"Which one? The younger one is pushin' it..."

"Well, it's him."

He was silent. "It depends on who's on duty. He'll have a better shot if he goes with her attorney."

"This is important, Marco. Really important."

"You figured something out." He sounded hopeful.

"I found out the full truth, and it has nothing to do with Bart and everything to do with an abused child. He really needs to see her, and then I hope he'll be willing to talk to you."

"Where are you now?"

"The Crimshaw house."

"Meet me at the county jail in forty-five minutes. I'll get him in."

"Thank you, Marco."

"Are you okay?" he asked. "We were hopin' to pin this on Bart. This has to be disappointin'."

I hadn't stopped to let myself consider it. I supposed there was some disappointment, but mostly I felt sick that Thad had gone through so much trauma. "I found out the truth, and the truth is what's most important."

"So what was Emily orchestratin'? And why did that man come to my house?"

"I have no idea." But after I got Thad through this, I intended to find out.

Chapter
Thirty-One

Forty-three minutes later, Thad and I pulled into the parking lot of the county jail. He'd washed his face and voluntarily changed his clothes, now wearing a clean pair of jeans and a short-sleeved button-down shirt. He was jittery as we got out of the car and met Marco in the parking lot.

"Hi, Thad," Marco said. "I'm Deputy Roland, and I'm goin' to help you see your mom."

Marco held out his hand, and Thad reluctantly shook it.

"Your mother's attorney called and asked that you be allowed in to see her, which is circumventing typical procedure, but the deputy on duty is willing to permit it."

I wondered what strings Marco had needed to pull to make that happen.

"What does that mean?" Thad asked me.

I gave him a tight smile. "It means that your mother's lawyer said you need to see her. And Deputy Roland talked to the people in charge of visitation, and they agreed."

He leaned closer to me. "Is he comin' in?"

I shot a glance to Marco, and he shook his head. "No," I said, "he's not. But if you want to tell Deputy Roland what happened, it might help with your mother's case."

Thad linked his hands behind his neck and tilted his head forward as he released a heavy sigh.

"Thad," Marco said, and the boy looked up. "The only thing you need to worry about right now is talkin' to your mom. We'll sort everything else out later."

He paused then nodded, and glanced over at me. "Can I see her now?"

"Yeah," I said. "You can."

We followed Marco inside and through security, then headed down the hall. Marco took charge at the front desk, and after he got Thad logged in, he pulled us aside. "You can go in alone, Thad, or have someone go in with you. She'll be behind glass with a deputy in the corner, so you won't have total privacy, but you can likely have a private conversation."

"I want to go in alone."

Marco nodded, then shifted his gaze to me. "You wait here. I'll be back in a moment."

"Okay."

Thad glanced back at me, and my heart broke for him. The tough act had completely faded away, and he looked every bit a scared little boy. "Just talk to her," I said. "Tell her how you feel."

"Okay," he whispered, sounding close to tears.

I almost reached out to take his hand, but he'd been violated in the worst possible way, and I wouldn't touch him unless he initiated it.

Then he and Marco walked through the heavy metal door and disappeared from view.

I felt conspicuous in the hall next to the sign-in counter, so I moved down a few feet, surprised when I saw Deputy Taggert, the deputy I'd run into on my last visit.

"Well, Carly Moore," he said with a grin. "If I didn't know better, I'd guess that you're stalkin' your boyfriend."

I released a chuckle and hoped it didn't sound forced. "Actually, I brought a friend here."

"Pam Crimshaw's daughter?"

I lifted my shoulder into a noncommittal shrug. "You got big plans for the weekend?" I asked. "I hear there's a lake nearby with great fishing. Are you an angler?"

He studied me and then laughed. "I see what you did there. I like you, and Marco's happier than I've ever seen him. I hope you stick around." Then he gave me a two-finger salute and turned and walked away.

Marco came out of the back a couple of minutes later and reached out his arms as he walked toward me.

I closed the distance between us, and he held me close, one of his hands cradling the back of my head.

We stood like that for several long seconds before he kissed my forehead and leaned back. "You have no idea how happy I am to see you safe and sound."

"Me too, but I'm so worried about Thad." Fresh tears filled my eyes. "It's bad, Marco. So bad."

He stared into my face.

"I'm not sure that he wants to tell anyone else what happened," I whispered. "His father definitely won't want it to come out. The perpetrator is now dead"—Marco's eyes flew wide—"but I was mandated to report abuse."

"You're not a teacher anymore."

"So that absolves me? I feel a responsibility to help him, Marco. That didn't go away because I've changed my profession."

"Maybe his mother will convince him to tell someone in authority, and if he decides he wants to tell his story, I can take his statement or get Marta to do it. If he's been taken advantage of by a man, he might feel more comfortable with a woman."

I nodded.

We waited in the hall for another twenty minutes before Thad came out, his nose and eyes red.

"She wants to talk to you," Thad said as he approached us.

I touched my chest. "Me?"

"Yeah."

I glanced up at Marco, who looked just as surprised.

"Okay," Marco said, then helped me get through the red tape of arranging a visitation.

Once I was set to go in, he turned back to Thad. "Don't go anywhere, okay? I'm going to walk Carly back, and then I'm coming right back out."

He nodded, looking dejected.

Marco took me through the security door and down a hall, his hand at the small of my back. He stopped outside a door, where another deputy stood waiting.

"I'll be in the hall with Thad."

"If his dad—"

"I'll protect him."

I nodded, then turned to the deputy at the door. He opened it without comment and let me in.

Pam was sitting on one side of a short desk, behind a large sheet of plexiglass. The fluorescent lights gave her a deathly pallor.

I sat down in the chair opposite her and picked up the phone on the wall, and she picked up the receiver on her side.

"Thank you for meetin' with me," she said.

"Of course." I sucked in a breath, hoping I didn't break down. I couldn't imagine being a mother and finding out that someone I had trusted, someone I had actively encouraged to help my son, had betrayed him in the worst possible way. What would I be capable of?

"Thad said he told you."

I nodded and cleared my throat. "I don't think he meant to tell me. It just spilled out."

"He's been through so much. His daddy won't help him."

"I'm sorry. I'm sorry you're in here, but if Thad tells the sheriff's department what happened—"

Her eyes flew wide. "No. He can't tell anyone."

"But Pam," I protested. "Your sentence could be reduced."

She shook her head and took a breath. "No. It will ruin Thad. *Ruin* him. It won't matter that he's the victim. People will call him gay."

"But Pam," I said, lowering my voice. "He *is* gay."

She shook her head. "No. He's just confused, and that animal made it worse."

My heart broke a little more for him. Pam loved her son enough to kill for him but not enough to accept him for who he was. But it wasn't my place to convince her, nor did I think I could.

She lifted her chin and held my gaze. "Thad told me that you helped Ashlynn too."

"I was just so surprised by the news is all," I said. "I knew you wouldn't have hurt someone for no reason, and I wanted to find a way to help you."

"There's no helpin' me now," she said, wiping her face with a tissue. "But I need to make sure my kids are okay." She looked up at me. "Will you keep track of 'em? Rob kicked Ashy out, and if Thad gets it into his fool head to tell him he thinks he likes boys…" She inhaled sharply. "He might kick him out too. I don't know where he would go."

"He told me he and Spencer tried to kill themselves," I said. "Did he get help from anyone other than Jim Palmer?"

Her chin shook. "No."

"I'll talk to Selena and see if she'll arrange for him to see a counselor who won't take advantage of him."

"You must think I'm stupid," she said, starting to cry.

"No, I think you were a mother who put your trust in someone who was supposed to be trustworthy."

"It doesn't matter if I was stupid or not. He still hurt my son."

"I know."

"I realize I'm supposed to be sorry for killin' him, but I'd do it again. And again."

I wasn't surprised that she felt that way, but the fury in her eyes made her look feral.

"Thad said you walked in on them," I said carefully. "But you weren't sure of what you saw at first. I found out that Melinda put their house on the market around the same time. Did you talk to her?"

She shifted in her seat. "I called Jim that night to give him a chance to explain, but Melinda answered. I asked her if her husband typically fondled young boys when he was counseling them. She hung up on me, but I heard a couple of days later that their house was up for sale. *Cowards.*"

Which meant Melinda had known, and instead of turning her husband in, she'd chosen to run and let him molest other people's children. I felt like I was going to be sick.

"Are you sure you won't change your mind about Thad goin' to the sheriff?"

Anger filled her eyes. "You leave my son out of this. He's suffered enough."

"I know he has. I'm sorry."

She wiped more tears and snot from her face. "Just make sure they're okay. Make sure Selena helps them."

"I will."

She nodded and stared at me for a second. Then she hung up the phone and got up, heading for the door to leave the room.

Chapter Thirty-Two

Thad and Marco were waiting in the hall, and I looked at them both and thought, *what now?* What did I do for this troubled boy? I couldn't just drop him off at home like I'd taken him to the convenience store to buy a slushy.

"We've called Selena," Marco said. "She's on her way, and she and Thad are going meet with Pam's attorney."

"Oh," I said, clasping my hands in front of me. Thank God for Marco. We made a pretty good team. I searched Thad's face. "Are you good with this?"

He hesitated, then nodded. "Yeah."

She arrived a few minutes later, and we met her out at the curb. Thad got into the car, and Selena gave me and Marco a questioning look. "What's goin' on?"

"Thad just saw his mom," Marco said. "He has information to tell her attorney." He glanced at me. "It was his decision."

"Should I be scared?" Selena asked.

"He's going to need a lot of support," I said. "If he goes through with this, Pam thinks Rob will kick him out. I guess he kicked Ashlynn out of the trailer too."

"That man was always too hot-headed," she said in disgust. "It's too damn bad she married him in the first place." But for all her gruffness, she clearly loved Pam, and her kids. She got in her car and they drove off.

"Do you have time to take break?" I asked. "I need you for a bit after going through that."

He clasped my hand and squeezed. "You have me for as long as you need me."

We drove to the park, but we stayed in the car while I told him everything. We were silent for a long moment after I finished.

"I'm sorry," he finally said. "You've had a hell of a day."

I shook my head. "It's nothing compared to what poor Thad went through." I turned toward him. "Do you know anyone who is gay?"

"In Drum?" he asked in surprise.

"That and Ewing."

"I don't in Drum, but Thad is right. The town's about twenty years behind, so while I know there are gay people, I don't personally know of any."

"That's wrong," I said insistently, hating that Thad and Spencer felt they needed to hide. "If Thad decides to stay silent like his mother wants, Jim Palmer will keep his sterling image. But if he goes public, he's the one who'll suffer."

"Jim was probably countin' on that," Marco said.

"Yeah. You're probably right."

We stayed there for ten more minutes, while he held me awkwardly over the center console, but I soaked in his strength and support. I needed him more than I'd expected. I'd let him in more than anyone else before. Even Jake. And that scared the shit out of me.

"Why don't you take tonight off?" Marco said. "We can go to Greeneville for the night and get away."

"I'm sorely tempted, but I asked Lula to tell Bingham I'd be working and to contact me at the tavern."

"It's obvious whatever Emily is up to has nothing to do with Pam," he said. "In fact, I think you should ignore the whole thing. I don't trust her."

"Neither do I, but I'm not inclined to 'let it go' just because she's messing with me and Bart's sending men to threaten me. I'm not going to let him win."

"This isn't about winning or losing, Carly. This is choosing sanity over danger."

I pulled away from him. "Are you serious?"

"It can at least wait until tomorrow. You've been through hell. You're not expected to grin and bear it with *everything*."

"Don't tell me what to do, Marco."

"I don't get to have a say in what you do?" he asked in disbelief. "Does that mean I can do whatever the fuck I want, and to hell with what you think?"

No, that wasn't what it meant, but I couldn't ask him to follow a different set of rules. "Yeah, I guess it does."

He flinched as though I'd slapped him. "If I'm doing something dangerous, you don't think you should have a right to express your concern?"

"There's concern and then there's control," I snapped.

"You think I'm being controlling?" he asked, scooting back from me. "Are you fucking kiddin' me?"

That was the thing. I didn't think he was being controlling at all, but I was so scared of letting a man run roughshod over me, I found myself saying, "I don't know."

"Then I guess you don't really know me after all," he said, his voice strangled with pain.

I started to apologize, but his phone rang, and he pulled it out of his pocket and frowned as he answered. After he exchanged a couple of remarks that made no sense to me, he glanced over at me and mouthed, *I need to get back to my car.*

"Okay." I started the engine and headed back to the jail as he continued a conversation about warrants and judges.

"I'm about to head over there right now," he said as I pulled into the parking lot. He wrapped up the call and hung up as I parked next to his car.

He reached for the door handle, and I grabbed his arm. "I'm sorry, Marco. I didn't mean it."

He turned to me, his eyes full of anguish. "That's just it, Carly. You did." He leaned over and kissed me. "I have to go. We'll talk about it later, okay?"

"Yeah."

He got out and shut the door, and I watched him get in his sheriff vehicle and drive away.

I stayed in the parking spot and stared out at the road for several minutes.

I'd overreacted and Marco had every right to be hurt. What if I'd blown it? What if he thought I had too much baggage? I burst out laughing, which quickly turned to tears. Of course I had too much baggage. I'd been telling him as much for months. If he broke up with me, maybe that was my sign that it really was time to leave.

It was nearly three o'clock, so I decided to head back to Drum and go to work early. Ruth would pepper me with questions about Marco, but I'd soldier through, because I didn't want to be alone right now. Not when I saw solitude in my near future.

***

Max hadn't opened for lunch, and he and Ruth and the new waitress, Trixie, were cleaning up the parking lot and putting the dining room back together when I arrived. Trixie was outgoing and friendly, and I was immediately thrilled Max had hired her. Tiny and Pickle were taking the tables and chairs back to the Methodist church. The event had been such a success, Max had promised to have another block party in a few weeks for the Fourth of July. He was even talking about getting fireworks.

As I suspected, Ruth was full of questions, and to my surprise, so were Tiny and Pickle. I put my fight with Marco behind me and tried to sound happy as I answered. Last night's party—and probably Trixie's presence—had put everyone in a good mood, and it was contagious. I told myself that Marco understood my fears and hesitations, that he would forgive me.

We opened at five for dinner, and Max made sure we were prepared for the crowd for the Braves game, especially since Wyatt wouldn't be in to help. The customers were still talking about the night before, and we told everyone Max had plans for the Fourth. The dinner crowd cleared out, but some stuck around for the game, and more people poured in. We were busy enough that it kept my mind off of my fight with Marco, although I kept watching to see if he'd walk in the door like he usually did.

Bingham came in at around ten and took the booth closest to the door. Lula and his usual entourage weren't with him.

Ruth shot me a questioning look, as if she knew he was there to see me.

I walked over and slid into the seat opposite him.

"I don't like to be summoned," he said with a dark look.

"Don't be so dramatic," I said. "You could have used a phone."

He rested his hands on the table, linking his fingers. "I don't trust the phone."

Marco's phone or any phone? But I kept the question to myself. "I was approached by someone last night who has an interesting proposition for both of us, but this isn't the time or place to discuss it."

He glanced over at the bar. "Not interested."

That wasn't the reaction I'd expected. "You don't even know who made the proposition or what it's about."

"Still not interested," he said, not looking at me.

I stared at him. Months ago, he'd told me he was interested in anything that had to do with Bart Drummond, and he had to know whatever I'd brought to him pertained to Bart. "Even if someone's wife says she has something you want?"

He slowly turned to face me.

Did that mean he knew what this was about? Because I sure didn't. "As I mentioned, I can't discuss it here. But I'd like to make arrangements to discuss it soon."

"We'll discuss it tonight," he said unclasping his hands and sitting back in his seat. "In fifteen minutes in the back parking lot." He didn't even wait for an answer—just slid out of the booth and headed for the door.

Well, so much for controlling *that* situation, but maybe it didn't matter who was in control. I needed information; he had it.

Or did I? Whatever Bingham knew wouldn't help Pam. She hadn't killed Jim Palmer for Bart. She'd killed him for a mother's vengeance. Why was Emily using me as a go-between?

Marco was right. She'd been setting me up for something. Maybe Bart and Emily were both playing me.

A pain stabbed my chest. Marco.

I headed over to the bar and stopped in front of Max. "Has Marco called?"

His forehead wrinkled. "No, and I have to say I'm surprised he hasn't come in given the way he was glued to you last night."

I frowned. "We had a fight before I came in, and now I'm worried."

He studied me for a moment, then covered my hand with his. "Carly. That man loves you. One fight isn't going to make him break up with you. He didn't wait all this time to call it quits a couple of days in."

He was right, so now I was even more worried, because the man who had broken into Marco's house had been adamant that the people I cared about might have an accident if I didn't *let it go*. Bart hadn't been involved with Jim Palmer's murder, but he had to know why I was so interested in it. I hadn't thought bringing Thad to the jail was dangerous—by then, I knew the truth about the murder—but Bart may have considered it "interference."

"I need to use the phone?" I said, trying to tamp down my panic.

"Yeah." He motioned for me to come around the bar. "Use this one," he said as he lifted the phone out from under the counter.

I called Marco's home phone first and got his answering machine. "Marco. If you're home, please pick up, even if you're furious with me. *Please*." I waited a second, giving him a moment to answer. "Marco!" When he still didn't answer, I hung up and started to call his cell phone.

"Carly," Max said, his voice tight. "Why are you so freaked out?"

"Someone threatened me this morning," I said as I listened to his phone ring.

He leaned forward, getting in my face. "What do you mean someone threatened you?"

"They told me to leave something alone or someone I cared about would have an accident."

Marco's voicemail kicked in.

"Who threatened you?" Max demanded, sounding panicked. "Leave *what* alone?"

The message ended and the beep sounded.

"Marco. Call me," I said insistently. "Please!"

I hung up and looked at Max. "What's the number of the sheriff's department?"

"I don't know," he said in confusion. "Why would I know that?"

I turned and grabbed the phone book, then found the non-emergency number for the sheriff's department and dialed it. "May I speak to Deputy Roland, please?" I asked, trying to not sound hysterical.

"Let me check, ma'am," a woman said. "If you can hold, please."

I was about to respond, but she put me on hold before I got the chance.

She came back less than a minute later. "Deputy Roland has left for the evening. Can I take a message?"

I swallowed the lump of fear in my throat. "Do you know when he left?" Then, because I doubted they'd give that information to just anyone, I added, "This is his girlfriend, Carly."

"Oh, Carly!" the woman exclaimed. "I'm Anita, and I've heard so much about you. I hope I get to meet you soon."

How had she heard about me? Had Marco told her? Or had she heard about me after the shake-up in the department? It only mattered in that she was more likely to share information if Marco had spoken warmly of me.

"I'll have to come in and tell everyone hello," I said. "Do you know when Marco left?"

"Hold on. I'll find out." She was gone for about ten seconds, then said, "About an hour and a half ago."

"Do you know if he was going anywhere for a case?"

"No," she said, sounding worried. "Is he missin'?"

"I don't know. I expected him to show up by now, but he's probably fine." Please God, let him be fine.

"Should we send someone to look for him?" she asked.

Should they? If I said yes, she'd want an explanation, wouldn't she? I'd have to tell her about the intruder earlier, whose visit we had chosen not to report. It would lead to a cascade of questions that might shine a spotlight right on me. I hated that my issues were putting Marco's life in danger, but I knew what he'd want me to say. "No, that's okay. He's probably somewhere out of cell range, but if you keep an eye out for him, I'd appreciate it."

"No problem. Let us know when he turns up, and we'll do the same."

"Thank you." I hung up and glanced over at Max. "I have to find him."

"You can't go alone," he protested. "Where are you even goin'?"

"I'm going to see if someone ran him off the road coming home from Ewing," I said, tugging on the strings of my apron.

"Why would someone run him off the road?"

"Maybe you should ask your father," I snapped as I tossed the apron onto the counter.

"My father?"

I started for the back. "I have to go."

He grabbed my arm. "Let me come with you."

I turned back to face him and pulled out of his hold. "Wyatt's not working tonight. There's no one here to cover the bar."

"You can't go alone, Carly. Especially if my father's involved."

"And *you* can't leave the bar."

"Marco's my best friend. If you think something happened to him, I'm coming." He waved Ruth over and told her she was in charge.

"What's goin' on?" she asked. "Does this have something to do with Bingham comin' in?"

Oh crap. Bingham. He would be out back waiting for me in a few minutes. "No. I'll explain later." Or at least I'd come up with something to tell her.

I stopped in the storage room to grab my purse and quickly checked to make sure my gun was loaded.

"What the fuck's goin' on, Carly?" Max asked in a growl from the doorway.

I checked the safety on the gun, then dropped it back in my purse before looking up at him. "I'll explain what I can on the road. I'm driving."

He opened his mouth to protest, only to close it again without saying anything. My car was a lot smaller and newer than his truck. It would be better at handling the curvy mountain roads.

But Bingham was already waiting for me as we walked out the back door, leaning back against his SUV. He shot Max a dark glare. "I ain't talkin' to *him*. Just you or no deal."

"I can't talk at all," I said on my way to my car. "I have to go somewhere."

Bingham pushed away from his truck, his body tense with anger. "This is a one-shot opportunity," he said. "Talk to me now or not at all."

I stopped walking and gave him my full attention. It was going to take some fancy footwork to smooth his ego. "I'm really, really sorry, Bingham, but this is an emergency."

His jaw set and a hard look filled his eyes. "You are not my puppet master, Carly Moore. You do not get to say jump and expect me to do it. You've already irritated the shit out of me. You either talk to me now or not at all."

I held out my hand. "Bingham, I'm not trying to jerk you around. I swear."

He moved closer, until he was less than a foot away from me. Max took a step toward him, but I held up my hand to hold him off.

Bingham ignored him entirely. "Do you know how bad it'll look if I let you get away with this?"

"Who's going to know?" I pleaded. "I won't tell."

He gestured to Max and said in disgust, "Him."

Max lifted his hands. "I'm not any part of this. This is between the two of you."

But Bingham didn't look swayed.

"Look," I said, "I'll either call or come by your place tomorr—"

"No." His voice was menacing. He pointed to the ground. "Either now or not at all." When I didn't answer, he said, "I do not make concessions for people. They make concessions for me. I think you have overestimated my gratitude."

What was I doing? Marco was probably at home in the shower. I was throwing away the opportunity to find evidence to nail Bart to the wall, and it would probably take me five minutes, ten minutes at most. Even if Emily had had questionable motives for sending me to Bingham, he might have real, solid information. What difference would ten minutes make?

But images of Marco lying dead in a ditch flashed before my eyes. He might already be dead, but what if he wasn't? What if I got to him in the nick of time?

I wasn't going to waste a precious second.

I shook my head and started rushing to my car. "Sorry, Bingham."

"Don't you call me again, Carly Moore!" he shouted after me. "You may not like the welcome I give you!"

But his last words were muffled once I got in the car. I started the engine and shot out of the parking space, nearly taking out Bingham in the process.

I was going to pay for that one.

Whipping out of the parking lot, I turned right onto Main Street, my tires squealing in protest.

"Jesus Christ, Carly," Max shouted. *"What the fuck is goin' on?"*

I shot him a brief glance, then shifted my attention back out the windshield, driving well over the forty-five MPH speed limit. "Someone threatened me this morning. He said if I didn't stop, someone I cared about would have an accident."

"Who threatened you?"

"I don't know. I didn't recognize him, but he made himself very clear. And since he broke into Marco's house to tell me, it seems logical he'd go after him first."

"Was Marco there?"

"No. He'd already left for work."

"What did he want you to stop doing?"

I hesitated. I loved Max like a brother, but I didn't one hundred percent trust him, and neither did Marco. "I'm not at liberty to say, but"—I shot him another glance—"I think your mother knows."

"Is that what she talked to you about last night?"

"She was rather cryptic, but yeah."

"Carly, if this has something to do with my dad…"

I shook my head. "I can't think about that right now. I just need to find Marco. Where do most of the accidents happen on the highway from Ewing to Drum? Do you know?"

"There's a couple of places known for accidents," he said in a quiet voice.

"The guy this morning insinuated many of them aren't accidents."

He pushed out a long breath. "I would agree with that."

"Why doesn't anyone do anything about it?" I asked.

"What's there to do, Carly?" he asked in exasperation.

"You can take out an army one soldier at a time," I said as I gripped the steering wheel in a death lock. "Or you can take out the general."

"You're really tryin' to bring my father down?" he asked in disbelief. "Wyatt told me you were, but I didn't think you were so foolhardy."

I pressed my lips together. Damn Wyatt for telling his brother, not that I was surprised. I was more worried about who else he might have told.

"Was it one of my dad's men who showed up at Marco's?" He sounded panicked.

"I don't know. I'd never seen him before. Not even at the tavern. Don't most of his guys come in from time to time?"

"Not all of 'em," he grunted. "What did he look like?"

"Mid-forties. Lecherous. A smoker. He drove an old black pickup truck." I shot him a glance.

Relief filled his eyes. "Not anyone who sounds familiar. His guys are mostly younger now."

"Except for Jerry."

"Yeah." He looked troubled at the thought.

A light rain began to fall. We drove in silence for about five minutes, the steady rhythm of the windshield wipers the only sound along with rain drops hitting the windshield as the rain became heavier. I tried my best to keep images of Marco's mangled body from filling my mind. He had to be okay. *He had to.* I couldn't live with myself if he'd been hurt or killed because of me.

"There," Max said, leaning forward as far as his seat belt would let him. "I see something up ahead."

I rounded a curve and could see the flicker of light in the trees. My heart was beating so fast I was jittery with it.

"It looks like it's close to the road, so that's good," Max said, but his tone revealed his nerves. "That place up ahead is an accident site, but the cars usually go off the road and down the ravine. They often don't find the cars for days."

I turned another corner and saw Marco's Explorer up ahead. Relief washed through me when I realized it was parked on the side of the road and not crashed into a tree or a ditch. The headlights were on, casting beams through the rain, but the windshield wipers weren't moving.

"Do you see him inside?" I asked as we drove past. I'd slowed down enough to make a U-turn.

"No, but that doesn't mean he's not in there." He paused. "I didn't see any damage to his vehicle." He grimaced. "Or any apparent bullet holes."

The limited relief I'd felt was gone. I parked my car behind Marco's, threw it into park, and left it running as I grabbed my gun out of my purse. I jumped out and ran to the driver's door, raindrops pelting me.

Max was right behind me as I opened it.

"He's not here." I wasn't sure whether to be relieved or worried. "Where is he?" I asked, trying to stay calm. *Did someone take him?*

Max cupped his hands around his mouth and shouted, "Marco!"

We waited, and I thought I heard a faint sound.

"Marco!" I called out, desperation leaking into my voice.

"Carly!" Marco's voice was barely audible.

I turned to Max. He'd heard it too. "On the other side."

We looked both ways and then sprinted across the road. Marco wasn't within sight, so we both called out his name again.

"Down here!" Marco shouted.

I turned to the sound of his voice, which was coming from up ahead and down the hill.

"We're on our way!" I took off running down the side of the road, heading toward his voice.

"Call 911!" Marco shouted. "We need an ambulance!"

My heart skipped a beat, and I turned to Max, trying not to fall apart.

"Marco has a radio in his car," Max said, breathing heavily. "I'll go make the call, then come down to you guys."

I nodded, then took off running again, calling out Marco's name. I ran a good thirty to forty feet before I saw tracks in the dirt next to the shoulder, going down a sharp incline.

"Marco?"

"Down here!" He was definitely closer, but he sounded out of breath and upset. "Carly, go get help!"

"Max is calling," I said as I started to make my way down the slippery slope, not an easy task in the dark. The rain had slowed to a drizzle, but it still impacted visibility. "How badly are you hurt?"

"I'm not hurt. Go back and help Max!"

"If you're not hurt, *who is?*"

I continued down, and the silhouette of a truck came into view. "Whose truck is that, Marco?"

"Carly," he said, sounding much closer. "Go back up to Max."

His voice was shaking.

I could see him now. The passenger side had smashed into several trees. The driver's door was open, and Marco was in jeans and T-shirt, trying to find purchase on the muddy slope as he leaned inside. His body was moving up and down, and it took me a moment to realize he was administering CPR.

"Oh God."

He turned to me. My eyes had adjusted to the darkness enough to see the anguish on his face. His wet shirt was plastered to his arms and chest. He looked exhausted and his arms were shaking. Obviously, he'd been doing this for a while, and he needed a break.

"Who is that?" I asked, and when he didn't answer, I slid down toward him. It was then I saw the writing on the side of the truck.

Drummond Properties.

The air left my lungs and I stumbled. "*No.*"

Marco groaned. "Carly. Go watch for the ambulance so they can find us."

I ignored him, continuing down the hill. Although I didn't want to believe it, I knew who was in that truck. But I couldn't let myself dwell on the horror of what was happening. I had to focus on helping, and if we moved the driver out of the truck and onto the ground, CPR would be more effective.

I braced myself when I reached the open door, but nothing could have prepared me for Jerry's bloodied face. He eyes were closed, and he looked pale. Marco had adjusted his seat so he was in a semi-reclined position. I was milliseconds away from breaking down, but I could do that later. We had to save Jerry.

"I take you can't get him out?" I asked in my take-charge teacher voice.

He turned to me in surprise. "His legs are wedged under the dash."

I opened the back door and climbed inside.

"Carly, what are you doin'?"

"I'm about to take over and give you a break. How long have you been doing this?" I crawled over the back seat and across the console to the front passenger seat. I pushed his hands away and found my placing and began compressions.

I hadn't ever performed CPR on an actual person before, but I'd done it several times on a dummy for my teaching certification. While I didn't want to potentially hurt Jerry, I knew it was important to be aggressive…even if that meant breaking ribs. Plus, Marco was much stronger than me and had likely already done the worst.

Marco sank to the ground in exhaustion.

"How long, Marco?"

"I don't know. Twenty minutes? Forty-five? I kept hoping someone would stop, but I didn't dare stop CPR to go radio for help."

"Max is doing it now."

I stopped compressions, made sure Jerry's head was tilted correctly, then put my mouth on his, pushing air into his lungs.

"Did he have a pulse when you found him?" I asked as I started compressions again.

"He was conscious when I found him. I saw it happen. A black truck forced him off the road, then drove off. I stopped and ran down the hill to see if the passengers were okay. Then I realized it was Jerry." His voice broke, and he released a sob. "He was so relieved to see me. I should have run to radio for help, but he was scared, and I didn't want to leave him."

"You did the right thing," I said, continuing my compressions and refusing to believe it was too late. "He needed you there with him."

"He was worried Bart would be upset with him for wrecking his trunk." His voice broke again. "He said he was grateful to Bart for giving him a second chance and he didn't want to let him down." Marco wiped his face with the back of his arm. "I told him it wasn't his fault. That I'd seen someone force him off the road, and I'd make sure Bart knew it. And if

Bart still blamed him, I'd personally kick his ass." He looked up at me. "He laughed at that."

"So he was alive when you found him," I said more to myself than him. "That's good. He has a chance." But Jerry was so cold beneath my touch I was struggling to believe it.

"He's lost a lot of blood," Marco said. "He has a deep laceration on his inner right thigh. I used my belt as a tourniquet, but he bled quite a bit before I got it on." He took a breath and cleared his throat. "He was worried he'd lose the leg if we left it on too long. But I told him he and Hank could start a one-legged man club." He released a chuckle that turned into a partial sob.

Sirens wailed in the distance, and the sound seemed to invigorate Marco. He got to his feet as I gave Jerry another breath.

"I'll take over the breathing," he said. "You do compressions until you get tired, then I'll take over again."

I hoped to God an ambulance showed up before I got too tired, but I wasn't used to an upper-body workout, and I was already sore and fatigued.

Max called out Marco's name from the top of the hill, and Marco answered. I could see a flashlight beam bouncing around on the hill as he scrambled down to us. "An ambulance and some sheriff's deputies are on their way." Then he reached Marco and cursed before he wailed, "Jerry."

I looked up into Max's face, not surprised to see his anguish. He'd always had a soft spot for the older man. Max had made sure Jerry had a roof over his head and multiple meals a day for years.

The sirens grew closer.

"What happened?" Max demanded, sounding angry. "How did this happen?" He turned an accusatory glare at me.

"He was run off the road," Marco said, regaining his composure. "I ran down and found him like this."

The sirens were directly above us, and Marco turned to his friend.

"I set up a flare so they knew where to find us. No way was I leavin' Carly down here alone. We thought it was you."

Marco didn't respond.

We continued CPR for a couple minutes longer until the EMTs reached us. They took over and told us to go back up the hill to give our statements.

I didn't want to leave Jerry, but I knew we were in the way. Marco helped me out of the truck, then the three of us climbed back up the hill with the help of a rope the emergency personnel had wound around a tree. It reminded me of when Wyatt's truck had been run off the road after I'd first come to town, and I'd climbed down to help him.

That felt like it had been years ago now.

By the time we reached the road, my wet clothes were plastered to my body and I began to shiver. A sheriff deputy gave us blankets and offered to let us sit in the back of his car to warm up, but the three of us huddled together, watching the narrow clearing so we could see them bring Jerry up. We heard the sound of a saw, so presumably they'd managed to get him out. Then an EMT emerged from the clearing, glancing our direction before he got into the ambulance and grabbed a folded bag.

"No." Marco gasped.

"What?" I asked, grabbing a handful of his shirt.

He took two breaths before he said, "It's a body bag."

I broke into tears, which quickly turned into sobs. I cried so hard I hyperventilated. An EMT offered to look me over, but Marco led me to his Explorer. Max chose to stay with the ambulance, but he gave me a worried look before we crossed the highway.

Marco's car was already running, so it was warm when we both sat in the back seat. He wrapped an arm around me and assured me it was okay.

"It's *not* okay," I said emphatically. "This is my fault. He's dead because of me!"

"You did *not* run him off the road, Carly," Marco said in a stern voice. "And you have no idea what you did to provoke this. Jim Palmer's murder had nothing to do with Bart."

"But they knew I was looking into it because I thought it was one of his favors. Maybe something else we discovered was more on the mark. Or...I contacted Bingham. Maybe they found out? But Bingham didn't come to the tavern until around ten."

"After Jerry was run off the road."

I started crying again. Poor sweet, kind Jerry was dead, and it was all my fault.

Marco pulled me onto his lap and held me close as he tried to comfort me. But it all felt hollow.

Jerry was dead, and I might as well have been the one to run him off the road.

Bart Drummond was going to pay.

Chapter
Thirty-Three

Less than a dozen people attended Jerry's graveside service. His supervisor at the construction site, a couple of other construction workers, plus Max, Wyatt, Ruth and Franklin, and Marco and me. Marco and I clung to each other during the short service, both of us devastated, and Max looked no less miserable. I wasn't sure who he thought had run off Jerry off the road, but if he believed it was his father was responsible, he didn't let on.

I'd half expected Bart to show up—he'd paid for the funeral since Jerry had died while on the job—but thank goodness, he'd stayed away.

Max had closed the tavern for the weekend, but he opened it after the service to hold a wake to celebrate Jerry's life. At his encouragement, the guests took turns sharing stories about Jerry. They lifted their glasses and spoke about how kind he had been. How much he'd adored his wife. He'd lost everything in his efforts to save her...only he hadn't succeeded.

Marco stood next to me and squeezed me tighter, staring down at me with so much love and adoration, it took my breath away.

"I would go to the ends of the earth to protect you," he whispered.

"And I you."

He leaned over and kissed me, and when he lifted his head, I realized Wyatt was watching us with an uncomfortable interest.

The sheriff deputies hadn't found the truck or the person who had run Jerry off the road. For all they knew, it had been a case of road rage.

But I knew different, and I was still struggling to deal with my guilt.

Thad had chosen not to give a statement to Marco or Detective White, but two other victims—a now twenty-year-old man from a rec basketball team Jim had coached a decade before, and an older teen from the same youth group—had come forward, and the sheriff's department planned on questioning Jim's wife to see how much she knew about her husband's activities. Marco and I had decided Ashlynn must have acted so strangely at the mention of Jim's name because she'd discovered her brother's secret and kept the information quiet to protect him. Selena had confirmed it. Ashlynn was living with her now, and she still refused to name the father of her baby.

It was too early for Pam to have worked out a plea bargain, but Marco said it wasn't looking good for her. Her crime seemed random and motiveless, which suggested she was a risk to society. He didn't expect the DA to go easy on her.

Since I hadn't needed to work over the weekend, Marco and I had holed up in his house, trying to pretend the rest of the world didn't exist—a pretense that might have worked better if he hadn't kept trying to discuss my escape plan. Hank had assured me he could take care of himself, that I only needed to consider my own safety, and Marco had said the same. They'd

About the Author

*N*ew York Times, Wall Street Journal, *and* USA Today bestselling author Denise Grover Swank was born in Kansas City, Missouri and lived in the area until she was nineteen. Then she became nomadic, living in five cities, four states and ten houses over the course of ten years before she moved back to her roots. She speaks English and smattering of Spanish and Chinese which she learned through an intensive Nick Jr. immersion period. Her hobbies include witty Facebook comments (in her own mind) and dancing in her kitchen with her children. (Quite badly if you believe her offspring.) Hidden talents include the gift of justification and the ability to drink massive amounts of caffeine and still fall asleep within two minutes. Her lack of the sense of smell allows her to perform many unspeakable tasks. She has six children and hasn't lost her sanity. Or so she leads you to believe.

You can find out more about Denise and her other books at www.denisegroverswank.com

Made in the USA
Thornton, CO
06/21/23 13:30:36

85e15832-d727-4bba-be12-c9bb46ceaf3eR01

both insisted I could afford to let my psyche rest and heal before I did anything.

But now that we were back at the tavern, facing the world again, I felt equal parts anger and terror.

Who else would pay with their life because of me?

Was I selfish to stay?

If I'd hoped to find out what Bingham knew, that option was gone, but I had no regrets.

The tavern dining room felt too hot and too tight, and I suddenly needed fresh air.

"I'm going to go out front for a moment," I told Marco.

Surprise filled his eyes. "I'll go with you."

I shook my head. "Just give me a few minutes, okay?"

He hesitated, and I saw a war raging on his face. "Five minutes, then I'm checking on you."

I gave him a tight smile. "Deal."

I headed out the front door and paced the sidewalk, sucking in deep breaths. I sneaked a glance over at the motel, and fresh tears sprung to my eyes. Would I ever be able to think about Jerry without crying?

"That's where you found him, huh?" a male voice said from behind me.

I spun to face him, shocked to see it was Ricky. "What?"

He gestured to the motel parking lot. "You found him over there."

He was talking about Seth.

My throat burned, and the pain of Seth's murder resurged with a vengeance, compounding the grief and guilt I already felt for Jerry. I nodded. "Yeah."

"Was he alive?" His voice broke.

I nodded again. "He was worried about his grandfather."

"Was he in a lot of pain?"

I took a breath. "No. I don't think so. I held his hand, so he wasn't alone."

Ricky was quiet for a few seconds, his gaze lingering on the parking lot.

"You said you'd like to know more about him." He glanced down at the sidewalk and toed a crack with the tip of his sneakered foot. "Nobody wants to talk about him. They think it's weird." He glanced up. "Do you still want to know about him?"

My chin quivered as I fought tears. I worried I'd scare him off. What teenage boy wanted to deal with a weeping woman? But there were tears in his eyes too.

"Yeah," I choked out.

He sat down on a bench in front of the tavern, then gave me a questioning look. "What do you want to know?"

I walked over and sat down next to him. "Tell me everything."